Best of British Science Fiction 2022

Best of British Science Fiction 2022

Edited by Donna Scott

NewCon Press
England

Table of Contents

Introduction

Donna Scott

This is the seventh Best of British Science Fiction, and for the previous six I have included in my introduction a bit of a snapshot of what I'm up to, and a little of my impressions of what is going on in the world of short science-fiction stories: the sorts of things people are writing about. The zeitgeist if you will.

This year it was good to see a wide variety of publications to choose from, including many I'd not received stories from previously. The short fiction market appears to be a healthy one.

Each year I do this, I try to see if I can detect any common themes among my submissions. There still seem to be a few pandemic-inspired stories in the mix, but they have tailed off considerably. Sifting through the rest of the stories it became clear that there were two simmering societal concerns feeding into the creative psyche: colonisation and the disruption of AI.

AI in particular has been of growing concern to creatives of all kinds, and it concerns me too. AI content scrapers that produce convincing images in any bespoke style following just a few prompts, or Language Learning Models that can churn out any type of prose or poetry in seconds have grown from the laughable crudeness seen by early adopters to more and more sophisticated and convincing outputs as the months have passed. 2022 saw an outcry as first a theatre company advertising a ballet, then a major publisher revealing a cover for a popular author were discovered to have used AI art instead of employing a human artist.

Remember the government poster from a few years ago of a ballerina tying up her shoes saying, "Fatima's next job could be in cyber"? Well, Fatima had probably best stick to dancing, as it turns out the LLMs are getting better and better at coding too.

It would be a very strong-willed person indeed who hasn't experimented a little with these 'toys.' I myself was curious enough to try Craiyon – just for making some throwaway visual jokes to share in an online chat, and I had a go at prompting ChatGPT, just to see what it could do. The results weren't terribly good, but they were delivered speedily, and that was the scary thing to me. Writing copy was not bringing in the big bucks for friends, but they have already seen their work opportunities diminish as a result of AI. There is a certain tone to AI writing that can't really be flattened out using the provided filters and parameters, but it seems the corporations who just want some copy aren't that discerning.

It's enough to make you wonder what will happen with story writing. *Clarkesworld* editor Neil Clarke announced in February that the magazine would be closed to submissions temporarily due to being flooded with an unmanageable quantity of AI-generated stories. Other editors have shared similar tales of an uptick in spammy submissions. And yes, AI stories are nothing but spam. If you can't write the story yourself, why bother? I would urge any writers who are tired of rejection to just keep writing and improving, and one day it will happen. Not every story is good. Not every good story is published. Not every good, published story gets picked up for anthologies like this one. Take it from me, rejection is character building... and world building... and prose tightening. You will get there. Please don't use AI.

When it comes to writing ourselves out of the singularity, I noticed several stories in the submissions pile had the robots falling in love with *us*. Perhaps one day, we will be living together in a sort of electric dream, but for now at least I'm confident that ChatGPT and its like could not write with the skill and nuance of the writers we have, and we can cut a clear channel between true art and the cheaters' prose.

Many stories were about making deep explorations in space, terraforming and colonisation. In many ways this theme is harking back to the 'Golden Age' as it is often termed. Now, though, following many billionaire-funded rocket launches over the past couple of years, it's not difficult to see what could be possible, eventually. And there are tinges of future-past anxiety in some of the stories that engage the reader on a deeper philosophical level. We could, but should we? Why would we even go? Perhaps, here too, is a buried dread of venturing further out than our home in a much more down to earth sense: the end of the

Global Pandemic; general feelings of reluctance at the idea of leaving the place where we feel safest.

All of these stories are ones that really made me feel something – that's the kind of story I like, be it hard or soft SF, space opera, technological, parallel dimensions, alternative history, quirky, satirical, militaristic, or funny.

I really can't conclude this introduction though without saying something about one of the contributors, who has sadly left us very recently.

Eric Brown was one of my favourite writers. Both as a solo writer and along with Keith Brooke, he wrote some excellent stories that have appeared in previous books in this anthology series. Eric passed away on 21 March 2023. He was a prolific and award-winning author of more than seventy books and was also known as a respected critic and reviewer for the *Guardian* and other publications.

Eric's fiction was known for its humanistic and compassionate exploration of alien cultures, such as in *Kéthani* – a book I loved so much, I got him to sign it twice.

Eric leaves behind a rich legacy of stories. I would compare his prose to whales: gentle and vast, greatly intelligent, and there should be more of them.

Here are the stories that featured in Best of British Science Fiction books that Eric either authored or co-authored.

"Me Two" – Keith Brooke and Eric Brown, *BoBSF 2021*
"Panspermia High" – Eric Brown, *BoBSF 2020*
"Targets" – Eric Brown, *BoBSF 2017*
"Beyond the Heliopause" – Keith Brooke and Eric Brown, *BoBSF 2016*

And not forgetting "Assets" in this anthology. Keith sent me two co-authored stories this year to consider and it was hard to pick between them, so if you can get hold of it, I suggest you also read the excellent "Farewell, Pavonis," which was published in *ParSec* magazine.

Eric will be greatly missed by so many people in the SF community. I would urge you to seek out the many amazing stories he gave to us.

Donna Scott,
Northampton
May 2023

Assets

Keith Brooke and Eric Brown

I squirt myself over to my asset in Rome. I awaken, the resuscitation software pumping life into the body. In a minute I feel human again. I quit the tank, dress, and leave the clinic, revelling in that rush of novel sensations. New country. New city. New *body*.

I walk the Via del Corso, aware of lustful male glances. It's good to be in possession of a female somaform again. I swipe away a dozen requests for dates then tell my implant to take no more. I'm here on business, not pleasure.

The pavements scintillate with noon heat, hot as a griddle. The air flashes with corporate logos and brand symbols. Once, pigeons were the nuisance in Rome. Now virtual signifiers are the menace. I can hardly make out the architecture for polychromatic decals and ads.

Take the next left, my implant says in my head, and an augmented reality arrow appears in my field of view to indicate the turning.

– How long do I have, Imp?

It's twelve-twenty-three. We're due at one.

I'm nervous. Sweating. Imp kicks in with sedatives and response masks. It wouldn't do to let the guy know I'm nervous. It isn't every day I negotiate to buy an illegal somaform.

"Spare a euro, lady?"

I blank the beggar. He persists, drawn to my élan, my high-end couture. I wonder if he knows I'm a soma. The occipital implants are subcranial these days, no longer visible. But style and wealth are always identifiable, and the money and somas go together.

I subvoc my imp to handle the beggar, and a couple of seconds later a cop strides up and tasers him to the ground. I scan the crowd as he goes down, twitching and drooling. Twenty-eighty in approval/disapproval of the cop's actions. I guess the approving twenty per cent are somas, just like me.

Time was when we were a privileged minority, an elite. A decade ago there were perhaps a thousand of us, worldwide. The super-rich who counted our worth not in monetary wealth but in bodily assets. Now we're more common.

Over the years I've steadily added to my soma stable, first acquiring assets in every continent and shuttling myself between them on a regular basis. Then, dissatisfied and wanting more, I extended my collection. Bought assets in all the major cities of the world – and branched out. No longer content with just men or women, I bought children – and even babes in arms just to thrill again at the sense of pure helplessness. Some territories prohibit this, but laws are made for people like me to bend, and break.

I've been content for a year, experiencing everything there is to experience. But now I want more. That's only natural. No one is ever satisfied, and if anyone claims that they are, they're lying.

Which is why I'm in Rome, to meet with someone who could give me more. At a price.

I come to the cafe on Via Bellini and sit under a sunshade. I order a Campari with plenty of ice, sit back and cross my long legs. I've never used this soma before. Imp bought her, sight unseen, a week ago.

I take time to appreciate her beauty, her perfection. The athletic power of her body. She's young, African, stunning.

I ask Imp for her details.

Eli Dakane, 18, Somalian.

– Buyout? I subvoc.

Total.

– What, no release option?

Since when did matters of morality stay your hand, K? Imp asks.

Touché. Since the most recent firmware upgrade, Imp has become more like that. Characterful. Sassy. I kind of like it.

Truth to tell, Imp knows me inside out: I get a kick from the fact that I have the power to buy an entire human being out. That Eli Dakane had been one of the have-nots, like two billion others around the world who'd never asked to be born, is no concern of mine. Planet Earth is a market, and I'm a buyer.

– Tell me more.

Her parents fell into debt. Same old story. War, famine, or plague, what the hell? They needed funds and we supplied. And after all they'd lost, their prime remaining asset was a beautiful daughter.

I have sufficient empathy to wonder at their dilemma. Or is it schadenfreude, as I dwell on the fact that to save themselves, they'd sold their daughter – killing her, in effect.

Hell, it's great to be alive.

I can tell I'm going to enjoy myself with poor Eli.

I take a sip from my drink. Every sensation feels so much richer in a body that has only recently become mine.

"Excuse me..." a young guy says in Somali, my imp translating instantly.

I hadn't seen him come up to me, blindside. A tall, wiry African with an elongated face and hooked nose.

"Eli...?" he says. "My God, it is!"

I keep my expression neutral, considering my options.

Imp scans the guy, tells me: *Michael Jamal, 24, knew Eli in school, 2050 to 2055. Known as Mikey. Eli was friendly with his sister, Karmen.*

– But he's not our man? I subvoc.

He's not. You have twenty minutes before he arrives, and I suspect our man will be somewhat better dressed. Imp's tone dripped disdain.

Mikey is wearing jeans, a grubby t-shirt and trainers that are falling apart.

I lean forward, smiling. "Mikey," I say in English. "Please, join me. A drink? How's Karmen these days?"

"She's doing fine." He hesitates, perhaps wondering at the price of drinks in a place like this. He sits down, nervous.

He palms the table for a menu, but I cancel it immediately.

"Water," he says.

I wave, cancelling the order too. "A Campari for my friend." The table flashes acknowledgement.

He stares at me. "Eli, the last I heard... You'd disappeared. Your parents–"

"Yes?"

He shrugs his bony shoulders. His drink arrives. He stares at it, then sips, pulls a distasteful face.

"They said you'd found a job in Tokyo. Said you were sending them money. But Karmen... she couldn't contact you. She was worried. Why'd you cut her like that?"

I sip my drink, watch him. He takes another sip, mirroring. He's nervous. Does he suspect? Has he heard rumours, and is now wondering just what it is that sits across from him, in the body of his old friend? I speculate: have we ever been lovers, Mikey and Eli? How delicious a thought.

I ignore his question and say, "What brings you to Rome, Mikey?"

He shrugs again, smiles shyly at me. No, he suspects nothing. His discomfort is wholly the result of feeling inferior to this new, well-dressed, sophisticated Eli Dakane, who insists on speaking in English rather than their native tongue.

"Looking for work. My folks back in Merca... Well, my father fell ill, and my mother – you know how bad she's been. We need money."

I look him over, take in his sinewy frame, his handsome face.

"You found work?"

"Some. A little. Not enough. Sent back a couple of hundred euros last month, but that won't help much." His gaze falls away, regarding the pavement. Maybe he realises it sounds almost as if he's begging me to help – I clearly have money. I recall the beggar I'd had tasered only a short time before.

I subvoc, – Imp, run a health scan.

A second later: *Within the parameters. No major concerns. Potential lymphoma, but treatable.*

– Estimate the cost.

VR transfer?

– We could make that offer, yes.

A split second later, Imp says, *Going rate, half a million euros.*

I stare across at the young man, imagining myself looking out through his eyes, in control of his sleek, powerful body. I like the idea of *having* him like that.

Uneasy, he says, "So, Eli... what you doing in Rome? Didn't you like Tokyo?"

"I found work with a VR site, tour-scanning. Did California last week. San Francisco, LA, Yosemite. This week it's Europe. I get the travel; they get a copy of my impressions. Back in Japan, the rich want to see the world vicariously from the comfort of home."

"Pays well?"

I watch his shock when I say, "Half a million Somali dollars a month."

He swears, laughing, shaking his head. "Wait till I tell Karmen." He takes another sip of his drink, then says, "Hey, you should contact your folks."

I wave. "All in good time, Mikey." I stop, think about it, then say, "Look, about work... I might be able to help you there. But not now. I have a meeting in five. How about we hook up for dinner tonight, say seven? My treat."

His eyes are wide, now, visibly excited at the prospect of work. Or at least a free meal.

"Seven's fine. Where?"

"The Trevi? I know a little place nearby."

He nods, finishes his drink, says he'll see me there at seven.

I watch him go, smiling to myself.

I finish my Campari and order another, testing my Italian on the waiter when he brings the drink. I feel good, confident. No longer nervous. The meeting will go well. I know it. Soon, I'll have what I want.

When I was six, my father blessed me with what he called Life's Lessons. He stood me on a tabletop, held out his hands, and said, "Jump." I jumped. He backed off and I hit concrete. He smiled down at me, said, "Lesson number one. Trust no one." The following day he placed two éclairs before me, one large and one small. "Take one," he said. I looked from him to the cakes, trying to work out the correct response. I took the small one. His backhander stunned me. "Lesson number two. Always take what you want." He picked me up from the floor. "Life's a jungle," he said. "It's dog eat dog out there."

K, Imp says. *He's coming.*

I look up from my drink.

A white guy in his fifties, well-dressed, slim but carrying a paunch, greying hair and sunglasses. He'd identified himself only as LM over the Cloud.

He sees me, smiles, crosses the street.

– Soma? I subvoc.

Imp scans. *Soma, but that's all I get. He's shielded.*

15

– Hiding something?

Other than 'his' true identity? It's impossible to tell. I'll run a deep probe.

– Do that.

LM approaches, beaming. He holds out a hand. "Ms Dakane? *Enchanted...*" He speaks French. He's smooth, I'll give him that.

"LM?" I say without standing up.

"Call me Laurent," he says.

He sits down in the seat Mikey had vacated and taps the table to order a beer.

"So good to meet you at last, in the flesh, Ms Dakane."

"Likewise."

"I do hope that we can do business."

"That," I say, staring at him, "depends entirely on you... and what you can offer."

"I can offer everything that money can buy." He smiles. "The limitation is not what I can supply, but what you can afford."

I don't like him, but that's fine. I don't like many people. And I tell myself that I shouldn't be taken in by what is, after all, no more than a somaform. A flesh puppet.

Imp says, *I've cracked 'his' firewall... He's legit. Operator called Sylvia Mastrani, 64, from Palermo. She runs a dozen somaforms globally. Made her money from trading health futures. That's a front, now, to shield her illicit activities.*

"We can trust her?"

We can, for what we want.

"If I might ask," LM says, "what the limitations of your budget might be?"

"I'm thinking a million."

"Euros or dollars?"

"Euros."

He nods, trying not to appear impressed.

I say, "And for that I can get?"

His beer arrives and he takes a sip. He appears cultured, suave. I wonder who the body had belonged to before the buyout, and what the original identity is doing now. If anything.

Imp reads my thoughts and a second later supplies: *The soma was Giorgio Tardelli, a big cheese in the Sicilian mafia. And one of Sylvia Mastrani's main rivals. Injured in a police stake out in 2057. Hospitalised for a year in a persistent vegetative coma, before Sylvia Mastrani bought the soma from his widow, who was only too happy to sell. Now 'Tardelli' does Mastrani's legwork.*

The more I learn of Sylvia Mastrani, the more I like her.

LM subvocs a command, and his imp projects a series of images above the table. A slide-show for my eyes only.

The first moving image shows a lion, pacing. The second a tiger, followed by a jaguar, a panther, and finally a cougar.

I take in their feline beauty, their stealth and grace. My pulse quickens at the thought of taking possession of one of these magnificent animals, of *inhabiting* it.

"But the lion and tiger," I say. "Aren't they protected species?"

He smiles, gestures. "Quite rightly so. Which means that only those of us who can afford to do so can supply a beast."

I sit forward, my pulse soaring. "The lion!" I say, staring at the animal as it pads back and forth, stops, opens its vast mouth in a silent roar.

"One point two million," he says, staring at me.

"Does that include the cost of the operation, the gelware?"

"That would be two hundred thousand euros extra, Ms Dakane. Our technicians are the best."

"One point four million..." I say.

I had lied about my budget, of course. I would readily go up to three million to get what I want.

He says, "I wonder if I might ask, Ms Dakane? Why are you interested in...?" He gestures to the slide-show still playing in the air.

I can't tell him, just yet. In truth, I don't know quite how far I want to take this myself. I will keep the truth from LM until such time that I might need to bribe him – or, rather, bribe Sylvia Mastrani – to turn a blind eye.

I shrug. "To experience, from the inside, the wild, raw power of such an animal, to see the world from a different perspective."

I sip my drink, smiling at him. He seems happy with my spoilt, rich ingénue act. Or to accept it, at least. "So... do we have a deal?"

He waits a fraction of a second, no doubt receiving instructions from his operator.

"I can have an animal ready by midday tomorrow at my villa in the Alban hills."

"And the transfer process would be ready... when?"

He gestures. "I'll get my clinicians working on it right away," he says. "I think we can safely say we could pair you with your new soma tomorrow evening."

I nod. I'll meet him tomorrow, have my imp assess the situation, the danger.

"And payment?" I ask.

He smiles. "Let's take care of that tomorrow," he says. He finishes his beer, smiles his farewell, and leaves the cafe.

– Thoughts? I ask Imp as I watch LM disappear into the crowds.

We have no reason to suspect that Mastrani is anything but legitimate, and trustworthy.

I swallow. I am aware of my heartbeat. I've dreamed of this for a year, more, and now it is almost within reach.

I explore the city for a while, enjoying doing the tourist thing. Then I check into my hotel, shower and change, and make my way to the Trevi Fountain. I choose an al fresco bar across the piazza and order an ice-cold beer, waiting for Mikey to show.

A handful of passing men, and a couple of women, squirt me compliments and requests. I've had a good day, business-wise, so I subvoc Imp to run instant background checks before swiping to accept three men of Imp's choosing.

– One European, one African, and an Asian. You know my preferences. They can take me to dinner tonight. Then fight over me.

Or then again, I might fuck all three. I'm looking forward to putting this soma through its paces.

I sip my beer and watch the passing crowds.

Mikey arrives at seven on the dot, dressed as he had been this afternoon in jeans and discoloured t-shirt. He crosses the piazza, bobbing nervously, and takes a seat across the table from me.

"A beer?" I ask.

"Please."

I order, and we sit in silence for a while, enjoying our drinks. At least, I enjoy mine. Mikey, he's antsy.

He says at last, "You've done well for yourself, Eli."

You don't know how well, I think.

I shrug dismissively.

I catch the glances from passers-by, wondering why someone like me is drinking with this scum.

"So…" he says. "You said you might be able to help me, Eli?"

"Karmen and I always said we'd look out for each other, didn't we? That extends to family." I'm making this up, of course. I have little idea what Eli and Karmen talked about, and even fewer shits to give.

To his credit, Mikey says nothing about how Eli had abandoned that principle when, in his eyes, she'd gone to Tokyo and cut off all her old friends and family.

"What kind of work do you do, Mikey?"

He looks down at the ground. "Whatever I can," he tells me.

I can guess the kind of work a young illegal in the Eurozone would end up doing. Not that I care. It's a free economy and his health scans have come up clean.

I consider pressing, just to ram home the difference between us. Then I relent. There's something strangely appealing about this kid and his gauche awkwardness around me.

"You ever worked with animals, Mikey?"

He's a city boy. Of course he hasn't.

"You count my brother in that?" His face splits with a wide grin, not even trying to hide the fact he's avoiding the question.

"Big cats, specifically. A lion."

The grin melts. The eyes widen. He doesn't even ask if I'm serious because he can see that I am.

"Let's order." I flash a hand across the table and menus hang in the air between us so that Mikey is, all of a sudden, ghostlike, seen through floating text and images.

Risotto agli asparagi for me. *Linguine ai gamberi* for Mikey.

"A lion?" he says when the menus have faded away. He's scared, but also excited and intrigued. I like that combination.

"It's perfectly safe," I tell him. "Tomorrow, I come into possession of a lion, for a client in Kyoto. The people I am dealing with… I feel a little out of my depth. I could do with someone to accompany me. Moral support." I stop short of fluttering my eyelashes, playing the weak girl. I don't need to.

Mikey is laughing, shaking his head. "Really, Eli," he says. "Karmen always said you were unpredictable. A lion? In Rome? Hell, yes, I'll help you."

"You'll be paid, of course. My client is wealthy. And we'll get you cleaned up, buy you some new clothes."

For a moment he looks shamefaced, embarrassed that I have not only noticed but stated it out loud. Then that grin breaks his face again and he laughs.

Mikey has scrubbed up well. He sits beside me as the hire car drives us up into the Alban hills, to the southeast of Rome. Freshly shaved, in a simple white short-sleeved shirt and new black jeans, set off by Santoni bit loafers, he looks the part as my companion.

And it had been fun getting him scrubbed up like this. Last night I ditched those three swipes Imp had found me and settled on getting to know Mikey a little better.

"You okay?" I ask him. I'm not concerned. Just making sure he's not going to embarrass me in front of LM and his people.

Mikey nods, but I can tell he's nervous. Perhaps having second thoughts about what he's getting himself into.

Truth to tell, I'm a little conflicted by my responses this morning. Maybe it's nerves. Maybe there's a physical chemistry with Mikey that pre-dates my purchase of Eli.

Whatever. I'm not used to complications.

Next time he smiles across at me, I ignore him.

LM's villa is a simple, if expansive, whitewashed square building high up in the hills above the Lago di Nemi, with sweeping views across the lake and its surrounding caldera. The hire car enters through wide gates that swing open and then shut behind us, and it is clear that the villa's grounds extend across much of this hillside.

Secluded and discreet is perfect for me.

"Ms Dakane!" LM clasps my hands in his and kisses my cheeks in turn. "And...?" He shakes Mikey's hand, even as he asks the question.

"Michael," I say. "An old friend, and now business partner." Mikey does well to show no surprise at his sudden promotion.

During the greetings, I let my gaze sweep across the villa, and then to the formal gardens all around.

Surveillance principally by fixed cameras and a swarm of microdrones, Imp tells me. *The cameras are armed with microcalibre weaponry, all legal and registered. There are also three armed guards observing from the villa.*

No more than I would have expected.

"Would you care for lunch on the terrace?" LM asks. "Or refreshments, at least?"

"Forgive me, Laurent," I say, "but I'd rather see my cat." Then I add, "And I have deliberately remained hungry for the occasion."

This is the first time I have seen LM's expression falter in any way. "Hungry?" he says.

I say nothing. Let him fill in the gaps.

As we follow LM up the steps to the villa, I take Mikey's hand. I like his strength. I like that it reminds me of last night. And I like that it makes me think of what is to come.

A short time later, the three of us stand on a high timber gallery overlooking a compound. It brings to mind the amphitheatres of the ancient city to the north. Of gladiators, and Christians, and…

In the compound a lion paces. A magnificent beast, in prime condition. Imp tells me he stands easily one metre thirty at the shoulder and he weighs just shy of two hundred kilos. His mane is thick, of a golden gingery hue. His eyes are penetrating, an intense amber.

I watch the easy roll of his shoulders as he walks. I can almost taste the power of that body.

I glance across at Mikey. He is in awe of the great beast, too, but also confused. I have told him his role here is for show, so that I do not – quite literally – enter the lion's den alone. Perhaps it all seems too easy to him now we are here.

"One point four million," I say to LM.

He nods. "Half now, half when you return to us."

Imp tells me LM has squirted his bank details across – an account at the bank of the Vatican, no less – and I approve the first transfer.

LM nods, the transaction complete.

"Forgive me," he says, "but you said something about wishing to be hungry for this experience?"

I smile. "I do hope you haven't fed my cat," I tell him. "Because I want to do that. I want to hunt. I want to kill. Can that be arranged?"

Laurent smiles, gestures. "This way, Ms Dakane." And he leads me to the room where the technicians are waiting.

I want to kill.

It sounds so crude when you put it that way.

I want to feel the power of that big cat body. The athleticism and speed.

I want to know what it is to sense the world in the way a predator does. The impression of the world compiled from sight, sound, scent, touch.

I want the excitement of the chase.

I want to read the *fear* of my prey.

And that moment... The moment when I strike, when my great paws, my claws, come down on the back of my prey, shredding through flesh, hooking into bone. Ripping and opening up.

I want to taste blood still hot from the body. To eat meat still alive.

I want to kill.

It sounds so much better when you spell it out.

Across the room, the head clinician nods to Laurent and makes the transfer...

And I am no longer in Eli Dakane's body.

When my senses coalesce again after the transfer to my new somaform, these are my thoughts. My desires.

I want to kill.

I have never done this before. Become something... *else*. Not human. Animal.

Has anyone? There are stories. Urban myths. But even in the realms of approved scientific research there are no accounts, no published papers. It is a step too far.

My senses coalesce...

I sense that power. That athleticism.

I marvel at how my world is a mosaic-like compilation of the senses: sight, sound, scent, touch. How that compilation makes the world almost palpable around me, so that the call of a bird, the movement of a cricket... they leap into my awareness, are read, measured, dismissed as of no interest. No threat, and of no appeal.

I am after bigger prey.

The compound that had appeared so large from the gallery, feels cramped to me now. This soma is accustomed to a far greater range: the plains of Africa.

Boulders occupy one end of the arena, but they provide only scant cover for my prey. I sense movement, taste fear on the air. Although I cannot see the fallow deer buck where it cowers behind the rocks, my senses pinpoint it precisely.

All this time, I have not ceased in my pacing. Following small circles in the open space below the gallery, where people look on. LM is there, and Mikey, and three men who I assume are the villa's security unit.

With each lap of the open area my circling grows wider, until I come close to the rocks where the sense-impression of fear becomes a veritable stench.

I feel a rumble deep in my chest that is somewhere between growl and feline purr.

I start to run, finding a gap between the boulders.

The deer erupts from the rocks in a clatter of hooves and flying pebbles, a ribbon of silver drool swinging from its foaming mouth. It is so close I could leap now and bring it down with the swipe of one great paw.

I relent. Let it find a path through the rocks and out into the open area where previously I had paced.

Now, though, it does not know where to run. Round in circles, or cower in the most distant corner?

I break into a full run. I remember sitting by the Via Bellini and savouring the athleticism of Eli's fresh soma, but this is so much more intense and rich! I have never felt stronger, or faster.

The deer reaches a corner and swerves, legs flying at all angles.

Instinctively, I cut the corner and leap, all in a single instinctive motion.

The deer crumples beneath me. A terrified squeal erupts from it as bones snap. I close my jaws around its neck and bite hard. More bones crunch as metallic heat bursts into my mouth.

The creature goes limp, and the spark of life goes out.

I have never known anything like it.

Each time I think I have experienced life to the full, I find something richer and deeper.

I pull my head back, feel the power of the muscles in my neck and jaw, feel the fallow buck's head ripping from its shoulders.

I am such a lucky person.

Later… much later, I come to my senses again.

LM's technician helps me sit up in the gel tank, her gaze discreetly averted from my nakedness, even though I sense she likes what she sees. Briefly, I debate inviting her to join Mikey and me later, but I doubt LM would allow it.

Instead, I ask her, "Have you seen Mikey, my partner?"

I find him in the garden, standing by an immaculately trimmed laurel hedge, a fountain before him breaking the night's silence.

"Mikey?"

I don't need a lion's heightened senses – or the lingering sense of them – to read that he is perturbed.

"Mikey?"

I stop beside him, put a hand to his arm and he flinches, backs away.

"I saw it," he says. "I watched from the gallery."

I know. I was aware of everything in and around that arena. So very aware.

"I saw what you did."

"And didn't you feel at least a hint of excitement?"

His hesitation tells me he had. His eyes tell me just how bad he felt that he had experienced such a response.

"You're not her, are you? You're not Eli. You're just riding her body, like you rode the body of that lion."

"When I rode that lion," I tell him, "I *was* that lion, every bit as much as I was me. I saw the world as the lion does. I sensed it. I responded as the lion."

"But Eli…"

"I am Eli, too. I see the world as Eli. I respond as she does." I reach for his hand, draw it towards me, place it on my cheek, then drag it down to my breast. "Tell me I'm not Eli, go on. I'm her. She's here, with me. And together we are so much more."

24

All lies, of course, but hey. They work, those lies. I see it in his look. In his need to believe me.

I take a small step towards him, so that his hand presses harder against me.

"Help me, Mikey. Be with me. When I was that lion, I... I need more." Chasing down that poor deer in the confines of the arena – looking back, it was so artificial. Nearly one and a half million euros for an experience that was, at best, incomplete.

"I want so much more, Mikey, and you can help me find it."

I pace, my stride steady, easy. I feel the power of the big cat's body. The athleticism and speed. I read the world in sight, sound, scent, touch.

I sense that my prey is nearby, and...

I want to kill.

I want to taste blood still hot from the body, to tear apart flesh still alive.

We are on the estate Imp found for me in Tuscany. Fifty hectares of walled woodland, high in the hills. Secluded and remote.

I pace, frustrated as only a top predator can be that I am confined within a wooden stockade, my prey safe on the other side of a high gate.

My initial deal with LM had been for a one-off experience, but we had both known that the option was there for a complete buyout, at a price. Now the lion is mine, with LM's cute young somaform technician thrown in as a deal-sweetener. All in all, three million well spent.

I approach the gate.

I had been careful not to let on to LM, and Sylvia Mastrani pulling his puppet strings, my real motivation for securing the lion. My true desire. My need to take every new experience to its ultimate conclusion.

And in this case, that conclusion could only be top predator meeting top prey.

I smell my prey so strongly now. I hear his every movement, his every breath.

Mikey has been good for me. That chemistry had surprised me, and I don't easily surprise these days.

But all things must pass.

And now… not only prey, but prey laced with history. The chemistry of prey, but also the chemistry of lover, of history that reaches back to before I ever met him. So many layers!

Mikey…

The gate swings open, away from me. The estate lies beyond. So many hiding places, so many obstacles to the hunt.

I sense that this will be a peak, an experience to top all others I have ever had, or will have. I feel like an artist, or a great composer.

But…

The gate opens and Mikey steps through. He just stands there. Not running. Not even scared. If anything, his expression is pitying.

For the first time I can remember, I am at a loss.

Then Mikey's glance shifts beyond me, he gives a gesture, the dismissive wave of a hand, as if to cancel an order from a café's table menu, and I feel…

Falling… Spiralling darkness. Dizziness.

Gone.

When I come to, I look back upon myself.

Or, rather, I look back upon the creature I had been.

I look back at the great lion, his amber eyes locked on mine.

I glance up at the balcony overlooking this stockade, and there I see the security guards, the soma technician… and Mikey. He lies on a lounger; for some reason he is unconscious.

I stare at the lion. I look into those great amber eyes, and now I understand, and I know exactly where Mikey is.

I glance down, and see that I am back in the somaform of Eli Dakane.

I look up to the balcony again, see a nod of acknowledgement from the onlookers.

– Imp? Do something, Imp.

You wanted experience, Imp tells me. *Now you have it.*

– Imp, help me!

You're beyond help now, K.

Imp? I think back to that last firmware upgrade, the subtle changes in Imp's persona that had ensued. The chain of events that had led to this place: buying Eli, encountering LM in the Cloud, coming to Rome to take my experiences to new heights… All of it a set-up: my bank accounts emptied by now, my life dismantled, and now the final weighing of the scales against me.

– You're not Imp, are you? Not *my* Imp…

Does it really matter? You have that one final experience. Enjoy it.

The lion gives a slight sound then, coming from deep within. A low growl that might easily have been a purr.

It takes a single step towards me and pauses, and in that instant, I turn and start to run.

I don't know how long I have, whether the great beast will toy with me or kill me in a single leap.

In that instant, I experience the world in a tumultuous rush, in ways I never have before.

And I tell myself I must try to enjoy it, because it's all I have left.

The Marshalls of Mars

Tim Major

When the host returned her attention to the camera, Rich remembered to reinstate his broad smile. He glanced at Meryl: hers was genuine.

"Thank you both once again," the host said. "Now. Do we have time for one or two questions from the audience?"

Excuses ran through Rich's mind. Maintenance. Scheduled provisions check. Fatigue, which was closer to the truth.

Before he could settle on one in particular, Meryl said, "Absolutely."

Rich stifled a groan. He tapped out a message on his sketchpad: *oh god kill me now*. Meryl read it and squeezed his knee.

The image on the screen changed to show the audience. Around forty of the two hundred or so children had their hands in the air. They raised themselves up on their crossed legs, straining to reach higher than their neighbours, directing silent appeals off-camera.

One child leapt to her feet, responding to an unheard invitation. She stared wide-eyed for several seconds before managing to say, quietly, "Will you do experiments?"

"Will you do experiments?" the host repeated.

"Oh sure, a few," Rich replied.

When he didn't elaborate, Meryl said, "Conducting experiments isn't our main objective, but it would be a missed opportunity if we didn't do as many as we could. We don't have a lab or any specialised equipment, but we do have complex organic mechanisms that we can observe during the journey – our own bodies. Most of our experiments will be simple observations about how our bodies respond to prolonged space flight. How does microgravity affect growth? How does the stress of lengthy periods of space travel affect the immune system? How does it affect circadian rhythm, the unconscious understanding we all have about what time of day it is? Poor old Rich is already getting muddled. He was up at four o'clock this morning."

That had been nothing to do with circadian rhythms. How Meryl could sleep so soundly in the capsule, braced against the wall like a mountain climber against a sheer rock surface, Rich would never understand.

"Okay. Next?" the host said.

A boy stood up. He was younger than the first child. Printed on his red T-shirt were three cartoon rockets, their flames making parallel diagonal streaks. His hair was an untidy mop.

"I don't have a question," he said. "But I named my turtle after you."

"How lovely!" Meryl bent closer to the screen. "Just one turtle, then? Whose name did you use?"

"Meryl, of course," the boy replied indignantly. "Her full name is Meryl Marshall of Mars. She can do loop-the-loops underwater."

Rich beamed, this time for real. It rang true that the public would focus on Meryl. *Meryl Marshall of Mars*: it suited her. Rich was only along for the ride.

Meryl chuckled, then said to the boy, "And what's your name?"

"David."

Rich turned from the screen to look at his wife. She had stiffened, but nobody watching would have noticed.

"Thank you, David," she said, her voice no less pleasant. "I'm honoured and I feel very proud. Give Meryl the turtle our best wishes, would you, please?"

"I love you!" David blurted, before he was shushed by somebody off-camera.

Rich felt for Meryl's hand. Her fingers danced on his upturned palm, but then she pushed him away gently.

"I think we'd better wrap things up there," the host's voice said.

But a red-haired teenaged girl in the audience had already clambered to her feet. She appeared sullen and a little surprised, as if her outstretched arm had lifted her against her will.

"You guys are married," she said bluntly. "So have you had sex up there in your rocket?"

Snorts of laughter rippled through the audience. Several of the children glanced to one side, presumably at a teacher attempting to regain control.

"That's all the time we—" the host said.

Meryl interrupted her. "It's okay. That seems a fair question, in the circumstances."

Rich's cheeks began to burn. It really was hot in here.

Meryl turned to face him, stuck out her tongue, then returned her attention to the screen. Rich's stomach tightened. He could not love her more than he did at this moment.

"The answer is yes," she said. "But it isn't easy, let me tell you. Rich, how about you fetch one of the suits?"

Rich's eyes widened. He shook his head. "Lucia already said our time was up."

Meryl smirked. "Quite right." Rich imagined she was relishing his red cheeks and the knowledge of his acute embarrassment. She had always enjoyed pushing him beyond his comfort zone. To the girl onscreen, she said, "I can describe them to you perfectly well. We have two special flight suits, each with a special front flap that unzips. Inside there are lots of little straps — harnesses, I suppose you'd call them — which can be fastened to one of the benches or a wall. There are enough harnesses that some of them can be used to fix one person to another."

Slowly, Rich pushed himself away from the terminal. In the miniature screen within a screen, he saw himself edge out of shot.

Meryl reached out and pulled him gently back into position.

"So that just means that we don't go whizzing about all over the place every time we're in the mood — that's Newton's Third Law at work." She beamed. "And, you know, it's sort of sexy."

"Thank you, Meryl," the host said, stern as a headteacher. Her voice sounded more nasal now, with pitch-flattening artefacts. "And thank you, Richard. We—"

The communication cut.

"You'll get us in trouble, talking like that," Rich said. "The parents of those kids won't take kindly to it."

Meryl grinned. "What are they going to do? Come up here and scold us?" She double-tapped the screen to turn it off. "Anyway. All that talk about space sex…"

She propelled herself from the wall with both feet, lunging at him, and he caught her instinctively. Their hug sent them spinning head over heels across the length of the capsule and bumping gently against storage units and bunks.

It had been Meryl's idea, of course. Rich had seen the initial appeal on social media, and the idea had fascinated him, but it was in his nature to assume that such adventures occurred to other people. *One married couple required to perform a return trip to Mars.* When Meryl had joked about it, he had joined in with the game happily enough. When she later revealed that she really had submitted the application, and that they were not only viable candidates but their names were on a shortlist of only twenty-four couples, it had seemed less funny. But Meryl's confidence and calmness had always been infectious. And Rich would follow her anywhere in the world or, in this case, beyond.

Rich frowned at the blank page displayed on his sketchpad. Outside the box room he could hear Meryl and David playing. There was a high-pitched roar, then a crash. On his second birthday Colleen had presented David with a set of blocks she had sculpted herself. Now every day he played the same game: he built the highest tower he could, then tiptoed around it, trying not to disturb the teetering structure, his hands curled into claws and his teeth bared. Neither Meryl nor Rich could determine whether their son was playacting at being a careful monster or an angry construction worker.

His fingers hovered over the screen of the sketchpad. Perhaps he might write about them, Meryl and David.

"Rich?" Meryl called; her voice muffled by the door. "I think we might head out for a bit."

"Okay. Where?"

"Dunno. Colleen's just rolled up. She's cleaned the car and it looks spanking new. David could do with a change of scene. You know, show him the world a bit."

Rich looked up, but there was no window in the box room. "How does the sky look?"

"Hold on," Meryl called. "Kind of dark."

"Could be a storm coming. Don't go too far? And—"

"Roger that, Rich. We'll wrap up warm."

Comms were down until late the next day. Rich darted over to the screen the moment it powered up.

"Control?" he barked. "Darmstadt? Are you receiving? You had us worried. Thought you'd abandoned us."

But it wasn't a live link, only the arrival of a digital package. Hurriedly, Rich downloaded and uncompressed the files. Some official correspondence, some personal, a handful of html transcripts. The usual selection.

"Anything interesting?" Meryl said, slipping her arms around his waist and peering over his shoulder. She pointed at one of the list items. "Oh! Flip that one over to my pad, would you?"

Rich scrolled through the ESA documentation on the main screen as Meryl tapped at her sketchpad. By the looks of it, the comms outage had been expected – or at least, not *un*expected. He exhaled with relief.

"Meryl Robinson, you skinny bitch!" said a recorded voice from Meryl's sketchpad. Colleen's Australian-Irish hybrid accent was unmistakeable, and she and Meryl had known each other their whole life; Colleen had never made the transition to using Meryl's married name. "Those flunkies told me I wouldn't be able to call till next month, but you know what I said?"

"Fuck you," Rich said.

"Fuck you!" Colleen echoed. "So they said I could record a message instead. Course, it isn't the same, but then nothing's the same as having you in the flesh anyway, is it? I'll just pretend I'm talking to you, okay?" A pause. "Good. Then how the hell are you?"

"She's ridiculous," Rich said.

Meryl flashed him a smile. "And I wouldn't change a thing about her."

"Very glad to hear it," Colleen said, almost seamlessly. Then, after another pause, "Yeah, I'm not bad, thanks for asking. But you know that guy I told you about? Turns out he wasn't a famous concert musician. Turns out I misheard his mate who was just referring to him as – get this – a well-known *penis*. Penis, not pianist, you see? Fuck me."

Colleen's face crumpled. She exhaled a ragged sigh and rubbed the back of her hand across her mouth. "I miss you, Meryl. Sorry, Rich – you too, but you know what I'm saying. There's an empty fucking house at the end of my street and I keep finding myself veering onto the driveway every time I take Bigly for a walk. Tell me you're both coming back?"

Rich and Meryl exchanged looks. Meryl's eyes were wet.

"I'm waiting," Colleen said. "I'm waiting for you to say something reassuring. I don't want to lose my best friend, or even her uptight husband, come to that. Tell me you'll be coming back."

Meryl was still looking at Rich. He cleared his throat. "We're coming back."

When Colleen didn't respond, it took Rich a moment to remember that this wasn't really a conversation.

"We're eighty-two days in," he said, to fill the silence. "So, uh, four hundred and nineteen days to go."

He cleared his throat again; it had become very dry. The capsule was so hot. Meryl put his arm around him and leant her head on his shoulders.

"Okay. That'll have to do," Colleen said. "Thanks for trying. I love you more than Earth and Mars put together."

Rich found himself checking their stores every morning after coffee. It was galling to continue amending the manifest and only ever see the values decrease. He reassured himself with the numbers that remained unchanged: bandages, antiseptic creams, hypodermic needles, blood-thinning pills, as well as blandly-named items such as multi-purpose filters, outer binding agents, patch packs. If they ever had need of these things, he would have to trust that the ESA, or the capsule itself, would advise them about their use.

Meryl often huddled before one of the portholes, the sketchpad balanced on her knees but her attention on the starscape outside. She complained of the heat, and claimed that the coolest area changed location every day.

She was becoming quieter, Rich noticed. They made love, sometimes using the flight suits and sometimes not. He loved her no less, and she was as tender towards him as ever. But he wondered whether they had done the wrong thing, coming here.

One day he said, "He'd have been very proud of you, you know."

Meryl turned from the porthole. Outside, the stars looked like a frozen whirlpool. She didn't respond.

"Did you hear me?" Rich said.

"I'm too warm," Meryl said. "Budge out of the way. I'm on the prowl for the nice chilly bit."

"I said David would have been proud."

She shook her head. "Please, love. I don't want to talk about him."

The temperature in the cabin increased a little each day. Rich checked and rechecked the manifests and tapped on the terminal screen, trying but failing to access thermostat controls.

They hadn't heard a word from Darmstadt in more than a hundred days. The data packages kept coming for a time, but contained only bland updates about their trajectory and a few video notes from friends. None of the ESA memos acknowledged their inability to converse.

"Something's wrong," he murmured. "We should be just about to turn back for the return journey. Why haven't we seen Mars?"

"There's nothing wrong," Meryl said in a soothing voice. "Anybody would feel nervous."

Her cheeks were flushed with the heat.

"I'm scared," Rich said.

Two hundred and eighty-two days.

"There," Meryl said. She pointed; her fingertip flattened against the surface of the window.

"What? Can you see Mars?" Rich listened, trying to determine whether the engines had kicked in, whether they were finally turning around.

"I don't know what it is. But no. Not Mars."

Meryl shuffled aside but kept peering out, so that their heads were touching. Rich had a compulsion to kiss her, to ignore whatever was outside the capsule for as long as possible.

But he looked, all the same. He saw nothing but black ink and white grains of salt. Then a grey shape gradually became visible, darkness clinging to its surface. It was ovoid and plain.

"A ship?" he breathed.

"We should say hi," Meryl said. "Do we have a way to do that?"

Rich smiled. How like her, for her first instinct to be a cheerful hello. He shook his head. "I'm pretty sure the only comms line is to Darmstadt. If they'd only answer."

"What do we do, then?"

He stared out at the craft. It wasn't fear he felt, either. Since they had passed the hypothetical halfway point of the journey – in terms of calculated flight time, at any rate – he had experienced a strange sense that it wasn't only their route that was predetermined, but also their fate.

"Our course is locked, love. There's nothing we can do to change it." Then, "Wait."

Meryl gazed up at him, her cheeks pink.

"You don't feel that?" Rich said. He put his palm against the wall of the capsule to feel the vibration.

Meryl's expression was a complicated one: it expressed exhilaration, anxiety, nervous anticipation. Rich thought of their wedding day, and the moments after Meryl had made her slow procession into the registry office to stand beside him. They had turned to look at each other, and then their seriousness and the audience's expectant silence had made them both start giggling at exactly the same moment, and then they couldn't stop.

Now Meryl's mouth twitched and she began to laugh. Rich's hands clenched, but then he laughed too, at first because he wanted that to be their mutual reaction, and then because it was only right that they should be laughing, two hundred and eighty-two days and who knew how many miles from Earth, facing the unknown together. Meryl took him by the hand and spun him into an embrace.

Her skin was hot all over.

When the capsule docked it barely produced a jolt. Rich and Meryl had dressed in the same smart blue boiler suits they had worn during the launch, and stood waiting as the door slid open. Meryl wiggled her fingers in Rich's grasp and he realised he had been gripping her hand far too tightly.

"*There* it is," Meryl breathed. Cool air rushed into the capsule from the long, dark corridor ahead. "Now I'm positively glad that we don't have stuffy spacesuits. Come on – let's see if they have air-con, or a fridge."

"Are you serious?" Rich asked.

Beads of sweat dotted Meryl's forehead. "Danger be damned, Rich. What I need is a cold shower. And a cool beer – imagine that!"

Rich peered into the darkness. "This can't be protocol. None of this seems right at all. Shouldn't there be an airlock? Something between us and the inside of whatever this place is?"

She shrugged. "Let's go and ask at the front desk."

He allowed his wife to drag him over the threshold.

Meryl had insisted that she would be the one to carry him over the threshold.

"Honey, we're home!" she called out, only very slightly breathless beneath Rich's not inconsiderable weight.

The doorway of the cottage was narrow, and Rich's head struck against the frame upon entering. But he didn't say anything.

When she had reached the centre of the sitting room, he said, "You can put me down now, love."

She pulled him close for a long kiss, and then in a fluid motion she swung him around and set him on his feet. He looked around. The familiar surroundings had been made alien because of their changed circumstances. It seemed a lifetime ago that he had last seen the framed pictures taken on their travels in California, France and Spain, the rudimentary portraits they had painted of one another one Christmas when they had been too hard up to afford real presents, the sofa with one of its cushions torn after having been worn away by the bottoms of innumerable guests.

"I'll fix us drinks," Meryl said, "and you'd better welcome the lodger."

Rich snorted softly and turned. Framed by the doorway, he saw David outside, a little way from the house, bent double at the waist to poke a stick into a strange knothole in the ground.

Rich woke with a start. He was at a table, sitting opposite Meryl. The only illumination came from six candles.

"What?" he said. His tongue was furry and he could taste red wine.

"I was just going to say the same thing," Meryl said, rubbing her eyes. "How did we get here?"

"What do you remember last?"

She looked around. The room in which they sat appeared vast, though the candlelight made everything beyond the table indistinct, and Rich noticed that their voices didn't echo.

"We came aboard," she said. "That's all I know. Did we look around already?"

"Of course," he said uncertainly. "That's the first thing we'd do, isn't it?"

She raised an eyebrow. "You don't remember."

He looked down at the empty plate before him, upon which were a few uneaten carrots and peas, and traces of a dark sauce. His stomach told him he had eaten his fill.

"So how about let's explore all over again," Meryl said, "to refresh our memories."

Rich reached for his glass and took a gulp of red wine.

Rich laughed until his sides ached. Then he stopped.

"Hoi, what's so funny?" Meryl asked. She was sitting directly opposite him again, but this time her stockinged legs were tucked up beneath her as if she had been folded carefully into the wing-backed armchair. Her hair was loose, and seemed longer and lighter than usual. Her cheeks glowed with good health.

Rich looked down at a chessboard on a low, square table halfway between their armchairs. Between the thumb and index finger of his right hand he held chess piece, a bishop.

"Oh fuck," he said. "I don't know, Meryl. I don't know why I was laughing. I don't even know how we got here."

They stared at one another.

"What was that?" Rich murmured. He rolled onto his back and listened, staring upwards into the dark.

He heard it again. A cry.

"Meryl. Meryl," he hissed. He reached for the light switch, but found only a blank expanse of wall. "Meryl. Are you there?"

He reached out blindly, patting the covers of the bed. The sheets had been thrown back.

He heard the cry again.

He stumbled out of the bedroom and along the wide corridor. Its ceiling was so far above him that it might as well be the night sky. He passed doorway after doorway, tracking the sound. Eventually he saw a glow of light spilling into the corridor.

At first, he only saw Meryl. She was bending with her back to him, wearing her favourite David Bowie T-shirt in lieu of pyjamas.

"I heard—" he said, but he stopped as she turned around.

She was holding a child in her arms, nestled up against the Ziggy Stardust on her bosom.

"He's okay now," she said quietly.

Rich could only stare at her. Finally, he turned his attention to the room. On the walls were pictures of octopuses and sailing boats. A mobile with a dozen felt fish on strings hung from a cord above a white wooden cot.

"Put him down," he said. Then, more forcefully, "Put him down, Meryl. We don't know what that is."

She gave a lopsided smile. "I'd say we do. Come closer. He's awfully cute. He has your frown."

Rich shook his head, and he was still shaking it when he stood with his shoulder touching hers, gazing down at the baby, whose eyes were scrunched tight and whose right hand clawed ineffectually at Meryl's chest.

He found himself reaching out with an index finger. The tiny hand grasped it.

"Do you remember?" he said.

"Not as such."

"Meaning what?"

"Meaning that memories aren't everything."

He turned to face her. "Yes, they are. They absolutely are, Meryl. If we don't remember how we got here, or where this even *is*, or how we came to have a *child*, for God's sake… how on Earth can we…"

Meryl shook her head. She held up the child.

Rich continued gawping at it.

"Here, hold him," she said.

"No. It's not safe."

"It's safe."

"No."

But he raised his arms and allowed her to slide the tiny body to him. The baby's thin arms lifted briefly, like an ape reaching for a branch. Rich froze, terrified that the head would slide away from the crook of his elbow. Then, gradually, the posture began to seem less foreign. He turned at the torso, back and forth.

"He's really ours, isn't he?" he whispered. It occurred to him only now that the child wasn't a newborn, but perhaps two or three months old.

Meryl said, "I think we should call him David."

They moved the cot to their own bedroom. They played with David and they cooked, and in the hour-long periods when David slept, they talked or played chess or read. The ship contained plentiful supplies of food, facilities and activities. Its corridors were not labyrinthine, but the vastness of each room resulted in doors and entire areas being missed during their explorations. Eventually, Meryl discovered a small swimming pool and took to bathing there every morning. Rich discovered a library filled with books he had always intended to read.

David grew quickly. Following one of the blackouts, which were becoming less frequent, Rich found himself calling out frantically to Meryl, hurrying her to come and see their son smile for the first time.

They returned often to their capsule, at first only to fetch their clothes and sketchpads, then making trips to check on the communications console, which remained inert.

One day, they found the door to the capsule closed and could find no means of opening it again. Upon its surface was a glistening web.

The only window was in the area they had dubbed the conservatory, an enormous warehouse space filled with foliage. One wall was entirely transparent from floor to ceiling.

Meryl looked up as the internal lights changed again, this time to a vivid green, then back to red.

"Perhaps the lights are the only means of conveying information," Rich said thoughtfully. "Like some kind of an alert."

David tottered from plant to plant, which grew directly out of the soil covering the floor. He was becoming increasingly steady on his feet.

Suddenly, Rich felt as though he were falling – upwards – and his arms rose as though he were performing a star jump. He saw Meryl and even David perform the same odd motion. His feet left the ground, but then they returned, and everything was normal.

"It's definitely trying to tell us something," Meryl said.

She stood directly before the window and placed both her hands flat on its surface. The silhouette of her body was haloed with stars.

"What's wrong?" she said, addressing the ship in a quiet voice. "It's okay. We're here."

Then she said, "Oh."

"What?"

She pointed along the flank of the ship.

Rich joined her at the window, pressing his cheek against the pane to look. "Is that–"

"Yup. Whatever it is, it was us that brought it."

It was the first time since leaving Earth that Rich has seen the outside of their capsule – though it was barely recognisable now. The silvery webs had spread over the entirety of its surface, distorting its shape, giving it the appearance of a puffball ready to burst. The cobwebs stretched beyond the capsule, all the way to the back of the ship.

Meryl addressed the ship. "Is that what you were trying to show us?"

The lights flicked from red to a warm blue.

"Does it… hurt?"

The lights dimmed entirely, then pulsed orange.

"Are you afraid?"

Rich felt himself rising from the ground again. He turned to David, saying, "It's okay. It's okay," but David only chuckled as he began a slow somersault.

The refraction of the helmet visor made Meryl's face appear bulbous.

"Now I feel like the real McCoy," she said. Disconcertingly, her voice was now transmitted from a speaker on the wall of the ship, the real sound muffled by the suit. "All these months in space and it's only now that I get to be a real astronaut."

The suits were mint green, with no identification markings. Rich and Meryl had found two of them laid out on the floor when they had approached the rear of the ship.

Meryl bunny-hopped towards him, startling him with her sheer bulk. "Give us a kiss, then," she said.

Obediently, Rich placed his lips on the curved surface of her visor. "I don't want you to go."

"I'll just take a quick look, then I'll be right back."

She bent to lift up David. His little hands pawed at her helmet, and he grinned and stuck out his tongue.

"Stay cute, buster," she said.

She plodded into the next chamber and closed the door behind her. Rich watched through the circular window as she approached the hatch on the outer wall.

He gripped the door frame as gravity lessened again. It was different this time: on and off, rapidly, making his guts churn.

Meryl turned and marched back to the doorway.

"Sorry, Rich," she said once it had opened. She pointed at the second suit lying on the floor. "Looks like you'll need to come too."

"No," Rich said immediately.

"I know you can be brave."

"It's not about bravery. What about David?"

"Go down the corridor, first left, look on the table."

Rich did as he was told. He returned several minutes later with the hibernation pod under his arm. It was far shorter than the others.

"This behaviour isn't going to win us any parent-of-the-year contests," Rich said.

Meryl shrugged. "We have a responsibility to show him the world. The universe, even. Anyway, this is just what we have to do, isn't it?"

It was only when the gravity flicked off and then on again that Rich realised that the question hadn't been addressed to him.

David didn't complain as Rich lifted him into the seed-shaped pod, and he was still chuntering happily as the curved door closed. Meryl entertained him by pulling faces and playacting moonwalks as Rich struggled to pull on his suit.

"All right then," he said as he pulled on his helmet. "But I want you to know I still think this is suicide."

Meryl grinned. "Well, if it is, you'll have the satisfaction of knowing you were right."

They passed into the next chamber, and waited before the hatch, each holding one of the handles of David's hibernation pod.

Rich looked up and groaned. "It's not just this one – look. All three, totally covered."

Each of the thrusters was the size of a roundabout in a children's playground. At first, he had been wary of approaching them, but Meryl had insisted the ship wouldn't fire up its engines while they were outside – though on this occasion her uncertainty was more evident than usual.

"Don't fret," Meryl said. "Here, I'll need a hand with this one."

Before he bent to wind his fat fingers into the knot of white cobwebs, Rich turned to look at David's pod. They had discovered that its base was magnetised, like the soles of their boots, and so it stuck immediately to any flat part of the ship's surface – but, even so, Rich had been reluctant to stray more than a few metres away.

"He's okay," Meryl said softly. "Aren't you, Davey?"

David continued making soft popping noises with his lips.

"One… two… three," Meryl said, and together they tugged the cords of the web free.

They worked methodically, and took it in turns to plod back to David and make faces through the curved glass.

Despite it being the furthest from their capsule, the webs that covered the third thruster were the densest and the most tangled. Each strand required both of their strength in order to snap it, and even then it was no small matter to disentangle each thread and cast it aside.

"Almost there, and then I'm having a steaming cuppa," Meryl said. "Maybe a bath when David's down. You'll hop in too, won't you, Rich?"

Rich almost burst into tears at the suggestion. He was exhausted, and his lower back ached terribly. He nodded his heavy head, his throat clogged.

Meryl placed her gloved hand on his arm. "Not long now. I'll just tug you off one more time." She laughed at her own dirty joke. "Heave ho!"

Rich just wanted it to be over. He pulled sharply at the final strand of web without first checking the placement of his feet. Instantly, he understood that he had made a mistake. He made a gulping sound as his body jerked away from the surface.

He flailed around, uncertain which way he was moving.

This is it, he thought as he spun away from his wife. Nothing more profound than that.

But then his hand struck something, and he realised that his pace had lessened. Panting, he swung his feet towards the ship, using the object he had caught to balance him. It was at precisely the same moment that the soles of his feet clicked safely into place that he recognised that the object that had halted his trajectory was itself now moving, and that it was the hibernation pod containing his son.

He glimpsed Meryl, propelling herself away from the ship, a giant leap for mankind.

The pod spun above him, already out of arm's reach and receding as though bobbing on an outgoing tide.

Meryl arced gracefully to meet it, both her arms outstretched so that when she reached the seed-shaped structure, she caught it in an embrace that seemed natural and calm.

"Meryl!" Rich cried.

The only response was her panting breaths.

He looked around. They had spooled the cobweb threads around projecting parts of the ship to avoid them floating free. He stumbled over to one of the spikes and, with fumbling fingers, pulled at the strands.

This isn't how space works, he thought as he gathered the strands and swung them in a clumsy lasso.

So maybe it was something other than physics that ensured that the silver thread reached his family and allowed him to pull them slowly back to safety.

The ship landed on the planet without so much as a sigh. It hadn't spoken to them since they had resolved the issue with the thrusters.

The journey had lasted another month, and they had experienced no more blackouts.

When they approached the hatch, they discovered that the suits were no longer there.

"I think we have to trust it," Meryl said.

"Easy for you to say," Rich scoffed.

"Why's that?"

"Because you're a trusting sort of a person."

She put her arms around his waist. "No more than you, love."

Rich lifted David and together they watched as the hatch opened.

The air tasted sweet.

They walked for an hour. Rich realised the ship was out of sight over the green hills. Perhaps they might follow the river to return to it, but something told him they wouldn't. They climbed over a wooden stile and continued on.

It was another hour before the first building came into view, at a point where the track became a narrow, tarmacked road. A sign above the door read *The Open Arms*. They stood at the roadside for several minutes, debating whether to enter. But David needed a change, and they were hungry.

The landlord greeted them warmly, and served them two halves of bitter and two packets of crisps.

Afterwards, they walked slowly through the village, hand in hand, David trotting before them.

"A lot of this seems familiar," Rich said.

Meryl squeezed his hand. "It's hard to put your finger on, isn't it?"

Rich reached out to the drystone wall before the nearest low house, and pulled away a hunk of moss. He rubbed the soft substance between his fingers.

Soon, people began to emerge from the houses. They didn't make a song and dance about Rich's and Meryl's arrival, but it was clear that they were pleased to see them. Most said hello, and children watched them pass or raced around excitedly in circles. One elderly man sitting on a plastic chair outside his front door applauded.

When they reached their little cottage, they found a post-it note stuck to the front door. It read: *You were out but I'll be back soon. Gone to stock up the fridge. Welcome home, Marshalls.* Beneath, Colleen's name was written in her unmistakeable scrawl.

Meryl wept, right there on the pathway of their house. Rich knelt, hugging David in one arm and his other encircled around his wife.

Meryl recovered quickly, and then she insisted that she would be the one to carry him over the threshold.

"Honey, we're home!" she called out, only very slightly breathless beneath Rich's not inconsiderable weight.

The doorway of the cottage was narrow, and Rich's head struck against the frame upon entering. But he didn't say anything.

When she had reached the centre of the sitting room, he said, "You can put me down now, love."

She pulled him close for a long kiss, and then in a fluid motion she swung him around and set him on his feet. He looked around. The familiar surroundings had been made alien because of their changed circumstances. It seemed a lifetime ago that he had last seen the framed pictures taken on their travels in California, France and Spain, the rudimentary portraits they had painted of one another one Christmas when they had been too hard up to afford real presents, the sofa with one of its cushions torn after having been worn away by the bottoms of innumerable guests.

"I'll fix us drinks," Meryl said, "and you'd better welcome the lodger."

Rich snorted softly and turned. Framed by the doorway, he saw David outside, a little way from the house, bent double at the waist to poke a stick into a strange knothole in the ground.

The Memory Spider

Fiona Moore

Carrie didn't notice the cat-sized spider at first, perhaps because she was too busy packing Nancy's photographs, award certificates, prizes and miscellanea into storage boxes and loading them on to the back of the walkbot. Perhaps because, sensing an alien presence in the room, it was hiding. When it finally emerged, tip tapping upside down along the ceiling by the lighting fixture, she jumped in surprise.

"Oh," she said, realising what it was. Motionless now, it held its front legs raised and moving slightly. She remembered Zeynab, the postdoc with the arachnid research project, explaining how that was part of how they sensed their environment. It was brightly coloured, like a tarantula done over in neon... or no, maybe it was a peacock spider, all teals and crimsons. But it was the wrong shape. Maybe it was a jumping spider? Didn't they come in bright colours?

"Can I look at you?" Carrie held out her hand, beckoning the spider closer. It obeyed, cautiously, tipping down the wall and trotting across the floor.

The cleaningbots at the university where Carrie was assistant research director (her PhD in psychology had taught her that she was good at research but took rather more pleasure in talking government agencies into giving the university money) were the usual institutional kind. Designed to stand out as little as possible as they ran over the floors, walls and ceilings like speedy horseshoe crabs, the only customisation the university logo watermarked discreetly onto their shells (and with a few alarm-and-security features intended to put off the inevitable attempts at sabotage or hacking by students who were convinced they were the first ones ever to think of doing this). The cleaningbot in Carrie's own apartment was an ancient model that the landlord refused to upgrade, and Carrie refused to spend her own money to improve, so it mostly just sat in its charging hutch in the cupboard while Carrie did the cleaning the old-fashioned way.

She'd seen ones with customised exteriors before. People with kids, especially, would go for fluffy big-eyed shells that made them look like anime characters, and she'd dated a man with an arts degree who had one that looked like a moving sculpture, a shifting array of cubes and spars flashing rhythmically as it moved. Never anything like this, though.

Still, it made sense. Nancy liked beautiful things, and eccentric things. She'd had quite a lot of time on her hands after her forced retirement from performance, modern joint-replacement technology finally unable to keep up with the punishment she inflicted on her knees. And Nancy had liked spiders: there was a wall full of close-up photos of them in her studio (the idea that this might scare some people seemed to be a feature rather than, so to speak, a bug), and critics still talked about the spider-themed version of Tchaikovsky's *Sleeping Beauty* she'd choreographed fifteen years back. And, Carrie thought unkindly, female spiders often ate their mates. And sometimes their young.

"Show me your ident," Carrie said. The spider obligingly flipped over and opened a port on its abdomen, so Carrie could read the details. "I suppose I'd better call the company and let them know to collect."

Presumably, they'd take off the custom shell. It was a shame to lose something that beautiful. Still, it wasn't Carrie's, and it hadn't really been Nancy's.

"OK, you can go back to work," Carrie stood up, clapped her hands at the spider. Amazingly, it gave a little bow before scuttling off to inspect the corners for dust.

She, Carrie thought. Zeynab had said the ones with the big abdomens were female. Part of her thought, *that's ridiculous, robots don't have genders.* Another part thought, *well, if Nancy designed it that way, then it's a female.*

"Back to work for me, too," Carrie returned to her task of taking things off the shelves in the living room.

People said that the way to get to know somebody was to look at their photographs, the ones they'd kept, the ones on display, the ones they'd hidden. But after half a day of looking at Nancy's photographs, Carrie didn't feel like she knew her any better.

Aside from the framed spider collection, there were pictures of Nancy at dinners and events with people who were evidently important enough for Nancy to print out and put on the wall, but Carrie didn't know and couldn't be bothered to find out. Professionally-done publicity shots. A scrolling digital frame of Nancy in performance, an array of leotards, shoes, and makeup, some that Carrie recognised and others she didn't. One man she'd evidently cared enough about to press in a book; Carrie lingered over this one, a casual shot of him in a garden, smiling awkwardly but endearingly next to a camellia bush. The photo was old, the colours fading.

It wasn't her father.

Carrie's father, a gentle soul who had worked as marketing manager for an arts charity, had, in Carrie's sixth year, reached the limit of his ability to support and nurture the career of a top-level artist. Carrie remembered the day he'd sat down with her and asked who she'd rather live with during the week: him or Nancy.

Carrie hadn't had to think about it much.

Theoretically Nancy had weekend custody, but in practice she was away so much on tours and the like that Carrie didn't see a lot of her. When she did, it was often wonderful: premieres, and events, and exhibitions, where she'd be called *Carmen* instead of *Carrie*, she'd get to wear pretty dresses – and, when she got older, get her nails and makeup done – and be told by a lot of people how beautiful she was, and how grown-up, and how much she looked like Nancy.

When she was thirteen, she finally realised how completely creepy that was.

Back in real life, her father met a graphic designer with short dreads and a broad smile and big yellow glasses, and before long Carrie was calling her *Mom* and Nancy *Nancy*, and before much longer than that was actually thinking of her as *Mom* and Nancy as *Nancy*. Nancy became a fairy godmother of sorts, a glamorous, maybe a little bit dangerous, creature who could transform your life. If you let her.

There weren't any photos of Carrie either.

Carrie put another load on the walkbot – this one mostly books – and sent it down the stairs. She'd borrowed the walkbot from work, knowing that the low-rise Nancy lived in didn't have an elevator. It was an old model but serviceable; it bore the university logo across both sides, and a stylised honeybee. Because, Carrie remembered, it had originally been bought for a long-term project looking into memory in bees; something to do with the way they embodied routes through dancing.

She followed the walkbot down, carrying a smaller box herself, loaded the boxes into the back of the storage facility's van, went back up the stairs, hearing the slight squeak and hiss of the six-legged, jerky machine behind her.

She didn't know what she'd expected from this clear-out. She didn't need to have done it herself; she could afford to have a moving company do it, and her father had offered to chip in on one, just to help. But she'd refused his offer, refused to spend the money.

She told herself to stop being disingenuous. She knew perfectly well what she'd been after.

Closure.

It was a cliché. *I never knew my mother, but, looking through her things, I now feel like I understand her.* Poor little Child of Divorce. Or Child of Celebrity Parent.

Nancy – well, she was all public persona. It seemed unkind to say it; all those letters from people saying how they'd looked up to her, especially little Black girls dreaming of being dancers, and women who'd once been little Black girls dreaming of being dancers.

But it was the images they loved; mirrors they saw themselves in.

It wasn't only the photos. The books were exactly what you'd expect: coffee-table books based on her dance companies or tours in the living room, textbooks and histories in the studio. A swathe of assorted novels gave Carrie pause for a moment, until she realised they were all ones which had been adapted for stage performance.

So, Carrie thought as she sealed up another box of prizes, small abstract sculptures on fake wood bases, just a narcissistic woman obsessed with herself and her career.

The phone company had unlocked Nancy's phone to her, as next-of-kin; Nancy had barely used any of the smart features. The diary was functional. The television box was well stocked, but again nothing you wouldn't expect: dance performances, especially her own, with an assortment of popular dramas and nature documentaries, mostly dating from the last few years of Nancy's life. Carrie scrolled through, stopped briefly on a how-to-dance video.

She switched it on. Nancy, in her sixties, still graceful and poised, smiling to the camera, talking the viewer easily and kindly through the steps. She'd always been a good teacher, Carrie thought. She'd had countless messages, emails, even physical cards and letters, forwarded from the funeral service, all from students of hers, talking about what a difference she'd made in their lives. It was one of the things that had made Carrie regret not getting to know her better, had prompted this misguided attempt to find nostalgia.

On the screen, Nancy moved through a simple exercise. Now Carrie did suddenly feel a surge of actual nostalgia. A memory, long-lost, of Nancy teaching Carrie the same exercise, her clumsy, fat child feet trying to mimic the graceful moves.

Smiling at herself, Carrie stood and moved through the exercise. *There you go,* she thought to the screen-Nancy. *Still no good at it, but I can do it.*

She froze, a flicker of movement in the mirror over the bookshelves catching her eye.

She turned, expecting maybe one of the moving company's reps or someone from a utility company, come to switch something off or collect something.

But it wasn't.

It was the spider.

The spider was dancing. Peacock spiders did, Carrie remembered, belatedly. But that was the males, not the females.

And she wasn't dancing like a spider.

She was moving her feet through a complicated, eight-legged version of that basic exercise.

And as Carrie watched, standing still now, she went on. Ran through other basic exercises; ran through more complicated ones.

Finally she began to do a short dance, clearly moving to a music Carrie couldn't hear. Then she shifted her rhythm, did another. And another. Finally, she sank, forelimbs extended and abdomen curved upwards, into a kind of arachnid curtsey.

There was a moment of silence.

"Well," Carrie said.

Nancy had tried several times to encourage Carrie to dance. Teaching her those little exercises when she was small. Enrolling her in classes as soon as she could walk, which five-year-old Carrie had abandoned with an overwhelming sense of relief once she and her dad had left, signing up for soccer lessons instead. Nancy had continued trying, and, for a while, Carrie had obeyed, just to please her and hopefully find some common ground, but eventually Nancy decided that whatever natural talent and drive she had, it hadn't passed to her daughter, and she gave up. Carrie, meanwhile, urged on by an adolescent sense of rebellion, had gone on from soccer to Australian-rules football and rugby, eventually playing left wing on the university team.

The coach said she could have been world class. Maybe she could have been, but she really didn't want to put in the hours, break her body for the sake of a game. Nonetheless, she'd enjoyed the physicality, the coordination, the strategy, the fun of talking over the match with her friends afterwards. She'd been the one responsible for starting a staff soccer club at work, which was still going strong, and gaining members, five years later.

And it seemed Nancy had found someone she could teach to dance.

Carrie called the spider to her again, ran her hands over her, examined her. Nothing you wouldn't expect on a cleaningbot.

"Did she teach you?" she asked. "Or did you copy her? Or was it both? She saw you copying her, decided to teach you some moves?"

The spider looked at her with, Carrie fancied, an expression of innocence.

Then she began to dance again.

*

This time, it was different. More complicated. Carrie recognised some of the steps; others were new. Some were humanlike; some more arachnid.

"That spider movement," she said, realising. "She taught you that, didn't you? How to move like a spider, not like a cleaningbot."

The spider kept dancing.

Carrie watched, holding her breath. Seeing Nancy's movements, seeing Nancy's creativity. Something no one would know, or see – since almost no one came to her apartment, and if they did, they wouldn't be looking for a dancing cleaningbot.

The movements slowed. The spider made one final flourish with her middle legs held high in the air, then settled back.

There was a silence.

"Damn," Carrie said. "They're going to wipe your memory."

Carrie was reading over the terms of the bot lease when a call came through, with eerie coincidence, from the company.

"Oh, yes. It's about the cleaningbot, isn't it?" Carrie held her phone, looked at the neatly groomed man on the other end; white, be-suited, and looking so much like Kyle McLachlan that she wondered if he might perhaps be a bot himself.

"Yes. We were wondering if tomorrow morning would be a good time to pick it up?"

Carrie felt her insides twist. "I suppose so," she said. With painful timing, she saw the spider begin to move gently on the ceiling, making the gestures she now recognised as the precursor for its dances.

The man smiled sympathetically. "I'm very sorry for your loss," he said. "It's hard, losing a parent, isn't it?"

Well, it's complicated, Carrie thought. Aloud, she said, "What do you do to the bots, when you get them back?" Clarifying, she added, "You wipe their memories, right?"

"Running memory, yes," the man said. "They go on to new assignments, and it wouldn't do to have it cleaning someone else's place in the same way that the last person liked. They have to learn new systems."

"Is there another kind of memory?" Carrie asked, facetiously.

"Sort of," the man said, to her surprise. "The deeper memories. What you might analogise to the personality. They're part of what they are; not only can't we get rid of them, it would be a bad idea if we did."

"Thanks," Carrie said. She ended the call, watched the spider finishing another dance. They kept getting more complicated, more involved.

"You'll forget how to dance," she said.

The spider flourished her limbs, uncaring.

Carrie kept on packing well into the evening, pausing to order a delivery from the Japanese place whose card was tacked to the kitchen wall (Nancy hadn't been interested in cooking. Of course). Started taking apart the bookshelves, wrapping the furniture – there would be a moving team in the morning that would take those, but it didn't hurt to get a head start.

Every so often the spider would dance, and when she did, Carrie would stop what she was doing and watch it.

Sometimes the dances were familiar; sometimes less so. Carrie realised that Nancy had been creating, experimenting. Developing something just for herself; a secret art, something she could enjoy. Not for the public, not for the people for whom she'd taken the pictures, collected the books, made the videos. Just something for herself to enjoy.

And now, for Carrie.

She started recording it, on her phone. Every time she did, she locked the video from wider access, encrypted the password. There was no way she was showing this to anyone, not even the people at work who might like to see a giant spider dance.

"I found it," she said aloud. "I found it."

"Thank you for letting me see it." Even if she hadn't deliberately intended it, her mother had left her something of herself.

The spider settled down, tapping its feet gently. Carrie went to the kitchenette, started sorting the empty bottles. Basketball-style, she hurled one across the room at the wastebasket, scoring a direct hit.

There was a grating noise from the ceiling. She turned to see that the spider had rushed into a corner, was cowering.

Oh.

"It's okay," she said to it. "She could be scary sometimes. I know."

Not that Carrie had much conscious memory of it. Just sometimes, impressions of fear, of anxiety. Like the time she'd had an unusually volatile Head of Department and realised that the way she'd avoided him had been the same way she'd avoided Nancy during one of her moods, just afraid of becoming a random target.

And there were more subtle things. The way Carrie could never see her perfectly-healthy, well-muscled body as *right*, that her default idea was that a body should be thin, all ribs and legs and no breasts. Not her mother's fault, just some kind of ducklike imprinting, something that not even all the years being parented by her dad and her mom could undo.

Maybe it wasn't a bad thing that the spider's memories would be lost.

Still. She couldn't leave it feeling that way.

She stood up and, again, began to dance herself, clumsily. The spider, after a few minutes, responded, coming out and mimicking her movements, upside down.

"That's the way!" she said, the fear and guilt receding.

She laughed as she realised the spider was imitating her perfectly, clumsiness and all. Not mocking, not judging, just doing exactly as she did.

And then, she shifted. Went into footwork exercises from her soccer days; aerobics, dodging drills, kicking drills. Using an old therapeutic squeeze-ball, the blue foam emblazoned with the name of a fashionable private physiotherapy clinic, to show the spider how to juggle the ball, on her knees, chest, head. She wasn't top-notch at the best of times, and she was rusty with lack of practice, but it was amazing how it all came back.

The spider incorporated it into the dance, shifting its legs and body to juggle invisible balls, moving side to side, kicking out and in.

"Okay," she said as the dance ended. "I guess I did have something to teach you."

All too soon, the night was over. The boxes were packed, the furniture labelled, either for the recyclers or for storage, for Carrie and her father and anyone else to argue over and use and eventually give away, most likely, but at least the effort was made.

The walkbot trotted back up the stairs, its back unladen.

Carrie spared a glance at the spider as she went into the kitchenette to make some coffee. She'd managed a few hours' restless sleep on her mother's bed, and, although she felt she'd come to terms with it, she was sad to leave the spider.

She told herself not to be sentimental.

She wrapped her fingers around a mug bearing the logo of some world-famous ballet company or other, trying a mindfulness exercise of focusing entirely on the moment. Listen to your heartbeat, the rush of blood in your ears. Listen to the sounds of the house, the hums, creaks, and rustles.

Rhythmic tapping.

Loud rhythmic tapping.

Carrie hurried out to the living area, and there she saw it.

The spider, dancing on the ceiling, as usual. If a bit slower, more exaggerated

And the walkbot, on the floor. Imitating her steps, in a six-legged gait.

She watched as the spider repeated sequences for it, slowly, then speeding up until the walkbot was able to do the steps quickly. For one dance. Then moving on to another dance. Then, amazingly, starting in on Carrie's own soccer moves, turned into a graceful ballet.

She felt her face break into a smile.

She wondered if the walkbot would teach the others. Or teach the cleaningbots at work. And if it did, they would teach the others. And the others, and the others. Which was even assuming that the dancing was part of the surface memories – maybe, just maybe, it was part of the deep memories, and, in its new form, with its new owners, maybe the cleaningbot would go on teaching her mother's dances to new learners, over and over, developing new eight-legged ways of moving, ballets of unseen cleaningbots moving in simultaneous rhythm all around the world, over and over.

And even if it didn't –

Whatever happened to the spider, the dance would go on.

Junk Hounds

Lavie Tidhar

The walls were beige and you could see where the rust took hold. A tiny dead robot floated past Amir, feelers drooping. It was the same colour as the walls and shaped like a grasshopper. Amir made a grab for it but a hidden maintenance duct sucked it up and it vanished with a soft, almost hungry *pop*. Other tiny robots crawled along the wall, attempting to repair a recent fracture.

The Heavenly Palace, a hundred years on from its grand opening. Once it was glorious. Now it was just another piece of floating junk.

Amir loved it. He loved the worn grooves in the floor and the faded carpets in the Stargazer's Lounge. The whistle of the ivory balls in the old centrifugal roulette wheels and the way the bartender still mixed a martini like he was serving it to Neil and Buzz at the Oasis Hotel in Maspalomas after *Apollo 11* came back from the moon. The Heavenly Palace was a junk hound's Mecca, and if one day the owners would decide to stop boosting it and doom it at last to the inevitability of orbital decay, you could bet Amir and every other junk hound in Low Earth Orbit would be swarming over the spoils like locusts.

He wondered uneasily if Aya would be there. He hadn't seen her since before the start of his bad luck streak.

"What do you want to do?" Woof said. Woof was a dog. She trotted next to Amir in her little magnetic boots: head too big for her body, thin pipes trailing from her skull to her second brain, buried under muscle, skin and fur. She stopped and scratched herself half-heartedly.

"We still have time before they finish setting up," Woof said.

"I want to *see* what everyone else's got," Amir said.

"We don't even have a table, Amir," Woof said.

They had a meagre haul, it was true. Amir hated to admit it. Low Earth Orbit was too crowded, there were too many amateurs getting into haulage and salvage, there were more junk storms recently, there was…

Bad luck, that's all it was. You got a run of it and it could wipe you out clean. He and Woof were down on their luck and dangerously low on funds. The *Domestic Entropy* was docked against the Heavenly Palace and it was badly in need of maintenance. They needed to sell the few rarities they had at the Rummage – that, or one or both of them would have to get an honest job.

Amir shuddered. He'd done odd jobs before to pay the bills. He was a croupier at the Floating Dragon Casino once for over a year. A year stuck without the freedom to move at will through space. A year with the monotony of the same landmarks passing under you at the same time, sixteen sunrises and sunsets a day, the same bland buffet food day in and day out, rude gamblers and mean shift supervisors, the same canned music playing everywhere you went. He never wanted to hear a muzak version of "Space Odyssey" or "Life on Mars" *ever* again.

After a year he'd saved enough to get the *Entropy* out of hock and pay for the repairs. But he swore he'd never go back after that.

"I need a pee," Woof announced.

"You want me to take you out for a walk?" Amir said.

"You're a funny guy," Woof said. She tottered to the bathroom (canines), a modesty screen hiding the suction cups. Amir headed to the Rummage. The Grand Ballroom of the Heavenly Palace hosted free-fall dances and (so rumour had it) more than one zero-g orgy in its time. Now it had the same faded feel as the rest of the giant habitat. Tables have been bolted down to the floor and lethargic staff were setting up for the exhibitors. Magnetised holders provided purchase for the (currently empty) displays.

Amir scanned the room, searching for familiar faces. His heart sank when he spotted a group of scruffily-dressed scavengers at one end. Too late – their boss spotted him, grimaced and gestured him over. Amir went reluctantly.

"Helmut," he said.

"Amir. Didn't think you'd show up."

Helmut Blobel of Helmut's Haulage was tall, stooped and smelled faintly of disinfectant.

"We have two tables," he said.

"Yeah?" Amir said.

"You find anything recently, Amir?"

The other scavengers smirked.

"I have a few things," Amir said.

"Yeah? Like what? An original Long March satellite? Laika's collar?" The other scavengers laughed.

"Very funny, yes," Amir said.

"Speaking of Laika, where's your partner?" Helmut said.

"She's around somewhere," Amir said. "So what have you got, Helmut?"

Not like he needed to ask. Everyone's heard of Helmut's latest haul. How he got to know about it or how he even made it there nobody really knew. Somewhere in Mid Earth Orbit and smack in the middle of the Van Allen Belt with all the radiation that entailed – only a desperate salvager or a crazy one went in there for too long without proper shielding.

It was worth it, though. A nearly-intact, centuries old LOE pleasure cruiser – the sort they carried the early tourists around in to take in the views. How it survived, or how it drifted that high up, was a mystery. The story Amir heard was that it got an indirect boost from some old explosion, but that was just a theory. Now Helmut had it – intact internal fixings and all.

"This and that," Helmut said, falsely modest.

"Nice score," Amir said, hating to hand over the compliment.

"Got a buyer already," Helmut said, bragging now. "Wants to re-equip it and put it back into use, you know, take sightseers on a vintage cruise like in the olden days and all that. Sit in the exact same seat some historical figure sat in. That sort of thing."

"All they're gonna see is junk," Amir said.

Just then he spotted Woof coming in and so he left Helmut and his haulers with some relief. They had a right to brag, he thought. They made a score and it was good. But when would be his time again? He felt restless suddenly. Why did he even come to the Rummage this time? It was not like he had anything good to sell. He should be out *there*, in orbit, where more and more junk accumulated every day and fortunes could be made.

"They give you a hard time?" Woof said.

"A little," Amir admitted.

"Don't let them get to you." Woof wagged her stump of a tail. "Our next score is just around the corner, I can feel it."

"You've been saying that for months," Amir said, feeling defeated. This wasn't like him, he thought. A junk hound was naturally optimistic. You had to be, in this line of work. It wasn't a job; it was a *calling*. He still remembered the first time he saw a piece of real space junk. Still a kid, still on Earth, with its impossible rain that just fell from the skies, its profusion of flowers and streetside hawkers selling every manner of food, its myriad of smells – cumin-spiced lamb turning on a grill, frangipani, rose water and clove cigarettes. Busy crammed streets, bicycle bells ringing, hawkers shouting, a thousand pieces of colourful cloth and batiks moving in the wind, monks chanting, mosques calling, church bells ringing, the buzz of low-flying drones and the whisper of cleaner robots scuttling underfoot.

He didn't miss Earth, only sometimes he dreamed of it still. He hadn't been back down the gravity well in twenty years.

Back then, running through the market, he came across a hidden shop buried in the shadows of an indoor mall and stopped, astounded. Cheap trinkets adorned the walls, flags for vanished empires: USSR, CCP, USA – stars and stripes, and sickles and hammers, yellows and reds, blues and whites. The shop was dim and a cheap plastic globe on the floor projected moving images of planets on the walls. Behind glass shelves lay mysterious objects whose purpose Amir could not even begin to guess.

An elderly figure behind the counter sorted metal tokens into plastic boxes.

"What are these?" Amir said.

"Coins," the owner said. He looked up irritably. His thin wispy hair was white, his colourful shirt decorated in Dragon modules and NASA mission patches. A name badge said he was called Mr Ng. "Old coins. People used to buy stuff with them."

"How?" Amir said. He knew nothing back then.

"You just handed them over," Mr Ng said. "See this one? It's Roman."

He handed it to Amir. The coin felt heavy. It was little more than a metal slug, with just the hint of a human profile still visible on one side.

"Trajan, maybe," Mr Ng said, answering an unspoken question. "It's hard to tell for sure." He put his hand out for Amir to give him back the coin. "He was one of the Five Good Emperors."

"Is it expensive?" Amir said. He was reluctant to give back the coin. Tried to imagine an old woman rummaging in a purse to pay for a loaf of bread in some age so long ago that they still used physical money.

"This one is," Mr Ng said, and he firmly took back the coin and put it away, "but not because it's old. The Romans minted a lot of coins for a very long time, you know."

Amir didn't know, of course.

"So why is it expensive?" he said.

Mr Ng said, "Because it was flown."

There was something reverent in the way he said the last word. Amir didn't understand it, but the magic of it was there. The dim light and the moving planets on the wall, the smell of rust, the cough of an ineffectual fan struggling to move the still air around, all combined in some way to make him forget where he was...

"Flown where?" Amir said.

"It means it was in space," Mr Ng said. "Someone took it up in the old days on a rocket, and then brought it back down with them again. Flown objects are expensive. Well, they were once, anyway. Now everyone can go up to space."

"I've never been to space," Amir said.

"If you had a car, you could just point it up at the sky and be in orbit in half an hour driving," Mr Ng said. "It's only just up there. So close you can almost touch it... The place where the world ends and the universe begins." He sounded wistful.

"I've never been, either," he said.

"All this stuff?" Amir said. "It's from space?"

"Almost all, yes," Mr Ng said. "I have some replicas, of course. Mission patches and so on. Plus meteorites. Just rocks from space. Oh, and gold. Did you know all our gold came from space? Every ring, every bracelet, the gold in the circuit boards of old machines... All of extra-terrestrial origin. Are you going to buy anything, kid?"

"I don't have any money," Amir said.

"Well, come back when you do," Mr Ng said.

Lavie Tidhar

Amir shook off the memory. Woof was growling at some unseen insectoid repair robot. Woof was ex-military. She'd been a sniffer dog in another life. There weren't that many augmented dogs around and even fewer in space.

"Stop barking," Amir said.

"I can't help it," Woof said. "I'm a dog."

She looked up innocently at Amir.

"What were you thinking about?" she said.

"My first real score," Amir said.

He'd gone back to Mr Ng's shop after that first visit. Finally he bought something – a golf ball from the Shepard Golf Course (eighteen holes) in the lunar highlands. It was named after Alan Shepard, the first person who played golf on the moon. Now the golf course regularly sold branded balls to Earth collectors. Amir had put everything he had into buying that single item.

Then he turned it around and sold it to a collector in Djibouti at almost double the price. After that he never looked back.

"Shepard, right," Woof said. "You told me that story a thousand times already."

"It's a good story," Amir said.

"I don't care much for golf," Woof said. "Come on, let's get a drink."

Amir followed Woof to the Stargazer's Lounge. The bartender mixed drinks. Amir ordered a martini and a beer for Woof. Woof liked beer. They could hardly afford the prices round here but it was worth it for the view. Windows opened on all sides of the room. Earth passed below, blue and white, enormous, like an eye that stared right into your soul. Beyond it was space itself – an endless ocean of dark silence speckled with an infinity of stars.

Then there was the moon, hanging in the sky in monochrome like in an old photograph, and the bright flashes of rocket stages as they climbed up the gravity well. It all looked so beautiful, and there were no junk storms just then. They had their own beauty, Amir thought. But other people didn't see it that way.

Woof barked.

"What?" Amir said. He sucked on the martini he couldn't afford. It was served in a suction bulb. You could brew alcohol anywhere, even

62

in space. And the olives came from the garden belt satellites that circled the Earth replete with solar-powered hydroponics.

Woof barked again.

"Aya at three o'clock," she said.

"Aya? What's *Aya* doing here?" Amir said.

"Hello, Amir."

She perched with her elbows on the bar next to him. Short-cropped hair the colour of rust, eyes that looked at him like at a chart of moving objects in orbit.

"Aya," Amir said. "You're here for the Rummage?"

"I figured I'd find you here," Aya said.

"You were looking for me?"

She smiled – just a tiny bit.

"Heard you'd had a bad run," she said.

"Well, you know how it is," Amir said.

"I do."

He saw something in her eyes. The smile – Aya didn't smile often. He felt excitement stir inside him.

"You have something," he said.

"I could smell it!' Woof said. She fastened her jaws on her beer bowl's spout and drank. "This is good," she said.

"I might have something," Aya said. "How is the *Domestic Entropy*?"

"Flight-ready," Amir said. "You *do* have something!'

"Maybe," Aya said. "Talk after the Rummage? I still have to buy a few things for the Institute."

Amir nodded. Aya touched his shoulder briefly.

"It's good to see you," she said. Then she was gone.

"She still likes you," Woof said. "It's a shame you…" She didn't finish the thought.

'Junk hounds don't mix with junk hounds," Amir said.

"She's not a junk hound," Woof said.

'Oh, on that one you're wrong, Woof," Amir said.

And they left it at that.

Junk hounds come from anywhere. Attracted by history and its financial remuneration, they scavenge and pilfer with no care for the strata and context of their finds.

That was what Aya always used to tell him. Aya was an archaeologist. A pretty good one, too, he had to admit. She worked for the North Australian Alice Gorman Institute of Advanced Space Archaeology. He first met her at a Rummage when she was just a newbie fresh off-Earth.

Most archaeologists saw junk hounds as a necessary evil at best. Low Earth Orbit was too crowded. Frequent collisions abandoned orbitals and decaying satellites created a field of debris only a junk hound would be stupid enough to willingly go into.

Aya was different. Amir saw it the first time they met. Not the way she looked at the displays, which was professional, detached, evaluating items with a quiet expertise. But the way she looked at the junks.

He'd taken her to the port side of the Heavenly Palace. Observation windows set into the walls showed the docked ships. The junks, so-called less for the historical connection with sailing ships than for their overall appearance. Junk hound ships were a lot like junk hounds themselves: rusted, beat-up and constantly patched together with whatever was to hand.

Amir saw the way Aya looked at them. That dreamy look that meant a junk hound could look at another and recognise them instantly.

She wanted to be out *there*, he knew.

She wanted to be looking for *treasure*.

They'd had a short, on-off relationship. This was before his run of bad luck, before the gig at the floating casino. He hadn't seen her in a long time. Now it was like she'd always been there.

"Come on, Amir," Woof said. "You're thinking about her again."

"What? No, I was just thinking."

"Aha. Let's go rummage."

He followed Woof back to the ballroom. The tables were all set up and people were milling around, some already haggling over items. Amir felt like a child again. He rummaged through the displays and chatted to people he knew. He saw a capsule of ashes that was sent into orbit – this used to be common but the habit died down and now the capsules were rare collectibles. He saw an old camera, lost by some long-ago astronaut on one of the early space stations. Someone was selling a spatula and claiming it was the one Piers Sellers lost during a spacewalk on a *Discovery* mission. Another claimed to sell waste bags from an *Apollo* landing site. There were a lot of fakes or items with dubious provenance on the market. It was amazing how much junk there was in space. People sold bits of broken satellites and solar panels, old circuitry, ancient manuals supposedly flown, and everything in between.

One stall sold replicas: Golden Records and commemorative Soviet pins for *Vostok 6*, early NASA mission patches, miniature Dragon modules and copies of artist Paul Van Hoeydonck's sculpture "Fallen Astronaut" that was put on the moon by *Apollo 15*.

He looked for Woof in the crowd. She was growling at Helmut Blobel. Amir rushed over.

"Get that wild animal off me!' Blobel said.

"Who are you calling a wild animal!' Woof said, outraged. She lunged at Blobel. He fell back, his magnetic shoes detached from the floor, and he floated upwards with a look of affronted surprise on his face. Woof growled. Amir started to laugh.

"Well, pull me down, you idiots!' Blobel said. He was ungainly in zero-g. Woof leaped up, turned smoothly in the air in a somersault and grasped Blobel's arm with her teeth. She floated serenely back to the ground with Blobel in tow.

"What did he say to you, anyway?" Amir said when he got Woof away.

"Said you were bad luck," Woof said. "That I should ditch you and come work for him."

"Let's just go back to the ship," Amir said. His good humour evaporated. "I'm sick of this place."

Maybe Blobel was right, he thought. Maybe he really *was* bad luck. He followed Woof down the corridors to the row of airlocks.

Aya was leaning casually against the wall. Woof barked once. Aya knelt down and scratched Woof behind the ear.

Woof whined and wagged her stumpy tail.

"Missed me?" Aya said.

'Not in a million years," Woof said. But she didn't stop wagging.

"What do you want, Aya?" Amir said. "We were just leaving."

"I figured you wouldn't stick around," Aya said. "So come on. Let's go."

"Go where?" Amir said.

"To the *Entropy*," Aya said. "Well?"

She hit the code for Airlock Number Six. Amir didn't ask how she got the code. The airlock opened. Aya floated through.

Woof barked. She jumped up and floated after Aya. Amir stared at them both, not moving.

"What have you got?" he said at last. Quietly.

"Coordinates for an object," Aya said. A little smugly, even, Amir thought.

"What object?" he said. But that feeling inside surged, that feeling that set you out as a junk hound. It doesn't *matter*, the feeling whispered, sending seductive tendrils through the fog in his mind. There's *something* out there, something precious, something only you can find.

A *score*.

He knew it as soon as he saw Aya at the bar, even as he tried not to, even as he remembered all the hopes that were forever dashed. The unlucky streak. But none of it mattered now.

"I'm coming, I'm coming," he said, not even waiting for her answer, and he floated after her into the airlock and shut it from inside. Aya smiled. The cabin pressurised and the second lock opened onto the *Domestic Entropy*.

Woof floated in and Amir followed. The junk was tiny, and they spent half their time in suits – in space, space was a premium, as the saying went. Aya had been on board before, though. She floated in after them and secured herself with easy familiarity, and the glint in her eyes told Amir this was it. Aya was a junk hound, he always knew she was, and no advanced degree or talk about strata could change that. He initiated the disengagement routine and the junk detached slowly from the corpse of the Heavenly Palace and floated free.

Unshackled at last from the burden of walls and regular orbit, Amir was back in a more natural state of being. The Earth below was covered in a film of black moving objects: satellites with mirrored solar panels, rockets climbing up, debris. If Saturn had its ice rings, then Earth had its trash. And both, Amir thought, were beautiful. The *Domestic Entropy* moved away from the gravitational pull of the Heavenly Palace and dropped altitude as it cruised above the planet.

"It's old Blobel's vault," Aya said.

Woof said, "Come on, Aya. That's just a story."

Amir didn't say anything.

He stared at the Earth moving down below.

Space was full of spooky stories. Dead astronauts still floating in their tin cans. Laika's ghost manifesting itself in passenger capsules sitting on top of rockets as they left the atmosphere. They said *Voyager* came back from the stars and was trapped in orbit with its priceless obsolete tech and a genuine Golden Record still on board. And there were always aliens. Loebians thought every 'Oumuamua that came drifting into the solar system was an alien spacecraft.

Amir wasn't a Loebian. He didn't believe in little green men.

But he believed in old Blobel's vault.

The Blobels had been in orbit for a long time. They were an old family. The first Blobel got off-Earth in a hurry (or so the story went). You looked down the Blobel family tree far enough and you hit some pretty nasty roots.

In orbit the Blobels quickly multiplied. And they got into the junk business when it was just starting out. First it was just disposal and haulage. Then old Johann Blobel discovered the collectors' market back on Earth, and ever since then the Blobels have hunted treasure.

'One person's junk is another person's treasure," Amir said. Quoting the Blobels' old motto. By the time Otto Blobel came along the family (so the story went) had an entire orbital filled with space's most valuable treasures.

The first seeds grown in space. Roddenberry's ashes. Buzz Aldrin's watch. The frozen corpse of one of the first five mice (either Fe, Fi, Fo, Fum, or Phooey) who orbited the moon.

It was an Aladdin's cave hidden somewhere in a cloud of debris, like a diamond buried in a field of coal.

The story went that only Otto Blobel knew the coordinates. Then he had a heart attack and died while vacationing on the Sea of Tranquillity playing golf.

Old Blobel's Vault had been lost ever since.

"It isn't real," Woof said.

"It's real," Aya said. "It's in a disposal orbit, ready to drop into the South Pacific."

"It's going to fall into Point Nemo?" Amir said.

"Yup," Aya said.

AKA the South Pacific Ocean Uninhabited Area.

AKA The Spacecraft Cemetery.

The biggest junk yard of them all.

Mir. Six of the *Salyut* stations. The ATV *Jules Verne.* SpaceX rockets and ESA cargo ships and Russian *Progress* resupply ships. The *ISS.*

Hundreds of satellites.

All lying four kilometres deep under the surface at 48°25.6' South latitude and 123°23.6' West longitude, in the biggest scrapyard and treasure hoard of them all.

"SpaceX marks the spot," Woof said, and barked a laugh.

"We can get the Blobel vault before it hits the atmosphere," Aya said. "We can save it. Everything the Blobels collected over decades."

"It would make Helmut's haul look like a whole lot of nothing," Woof said.

Amir stared out into space.

"How did you get the coordinates?" he said.

Aya shrugged.

"Got lucky," she said. "Its beacon came back online and tried to ping an obsolete satellite network. I monitor for that kind of thing."

"You do?" Wolf said.

"The Institute has a few trackers in different orbits," Aya said. "You never know, so… One of the trackers just happened to be close enough at the right time to pick up the signal."

"So no one else knows?"

'No."

"Is the beacon still online?"

'No. It died again straight after."

"Could be a ghost signal," Woof said.

"Could be, would be," Amir said. Focused now. Everything else, the Rummage and bad luck and Helmut's jibes, none of it mattered any more.

This was a chance, at least. This was a *promise.*

"Get into your suits," he said. He was already putting his on. "You worked out the trajectory I assume, Aya?"

"As much as I could from the data."

Amir sat at the controls. Aya sat beside him. She fed the numbers into the computer. The *Domestic Entropy* hummed with a thrust of power.

"Changing course," Amir said.

The little junk floated like a tiny ice particle around the Earth. Amir let the planet pull it in its orbit, conserving energy, only firing out for course corrections. It was going low, so gravity did most of the work. The return climb would require most of the fuel.

Continents, seas, clouds and people went past below. Amir couldn't see the people but he knew they were there, in their billions. He was one of them once. Now he was up here where he truly belonged.

He just hoped the vault was still there.

Round the Earth and dropping lower, and in the viewport window he could see a swarm of debris floating over Europe. A junk storm forming, made up of broken fragments of satellites and ships.

"We can't go in there," Woof said.

"What if we go under it?" Amir said.

"It's low," Woof said. "Too low. If the Earth catches us…"

Amir stared. The vault was somewhere in that field, masked by all that useless junk. He fed instructions to the computer. The *Entropy* dropped, adjusted course, began to trace a path that would take it under the storm and close to the envelope of atmosphere.

The Earth grew huge. The first astronauts on the moon were the first to see Earth as a tiny marble in the sky, lost in the vastness of a universe. But from orbit Earth dominated, it was the beating heart of the cosmos. Amir couldn't imagine being parted from it. But they were close, too close –

"There!' Woof said. Aya said nothing. The screen, tracking the movement of thousands of particles, showed the outline of a large satellite, seemingly intact, almost touching the mesosphere.

"It's too close, too late–' Amir said. The realisation hit him; the hope he had felt earlier faded away. He would try, he thought, not willing to let it go, this promise hanging in the skies above the world –

He took manual control, the *Entropy* dove, a film of black fragments roared like bees in front of it and Woof barked but Amir took her down, down, the Blobel vault growing larger on the screen, larger…

and yet, and still –

The Earth pulled, *pulled* at the junk, Amir gritted his teeth, the Blobel vault right *there*, so close he could almost touch it…

He eased the *Entropy* back. He fed it power and felt it strain against the planet's pull.

They rose again at last, moving away from the junk storm.

Amir watched as the vault slowly vanished from sight.

Dragged by the gravity of the Earth it was summoned back, called at last to its watery grave and taking all its treasures with it.

They sat in the Stargazers' Lounge on the Heavenly Palace and sipped martinis from gently-floating bulbs (Woof had a beer).

Aya paid.

"Well, it was worth a shot," she said philosophically.

"What do you think was in it?" Amir said. He didn't feel so bad. He thought he would be crushed by yet another loss. But somehow he felt better.

"A *Kitty Hawk* bible," Woof said.

"The *Juno* Lego set," Aya said and smiled.

"The Andy Warhol sketch for the *Moon Museum*," Amir said.

They started to laugh.

Amir felt a great ease wash over him. They had not found the treasure, but they came close enough, and there would be other opportunities, there always were. He had forgotten that, but Aya had reminded him.

He looked out of the window and for a moment he thought he saw a red convertible car float past, with the mannequin of an astronaut still sitting in the driver's seat. He laughed again.

Woof wagged her tail.

Aya said, "I got you something."

"What?"

She reached in her pocket and brought out a small round object.

Amir didn't need to examine it to know it was a lunar golf ball, and for a moment he felt like a child on Earth again, looking up at the skies, and dreaming.

"Until our next score," Aya said, and she took his hand in hers.

Amir nodded, smiling. They finished their drinks and walked back to the junk, and Woof watched them go and sucked on her beer.

"I give them six months," she said complacently. Then she jumped into the air and floated after them, her stump of a tail still wagging.

A Moment of Zugzwang

Neil Williamson

The localised weather information Stina pulled from the bees on Wehlstrasse suggested this spring morning would be mild, but it didn't take into account the chill coming off the river. Crossing the Lennard Lohmann Bridge, she blinked the app away in her IntaFace lenses and snugged her collar around her neck, silently cursing the decision to leave her cardigan draped over her chair back at the Inspectorate. She'd agonised over that because, though she hated to be cold, she hated even more to be overwarm – it was the interviewees that were supposed to sweat, not the detectives. Data did not yet completely describe the world, she thought testily. However much certain people would like to believe that it did.

Descending the staircase from the bridge, she found Wehlstrasse itself more sheltered and paused to smooth down her collar and fix her hair. Then she took a moment longer to arrange her bulleted case notes, focusing on the job at hand. There would be no point in coming all the way out here if she was going to allow herself to be distracted. No point at all.

Wehlstrasse was a quiet street. Seldom frequented stores and cafés lined one side. Along the other, trees evenly ranked like soldiers guarded the low balustrade above the rolling, grey river. They'd proved poor guardsmen, at least as far as Albert Vogel was concerned. Stina had watched the bee footage a thousand times. The old man visible at the edge of the frame making his way down that side of the street, coming and going behind the trees as he approached the bridge. The distinctive bushy beard jutting before him. The slow but steady gait suddenly faltering, the hand going to the jaw is if he'd forgotten something as the induced heart failure had kicked in. The stumble, the lurch. The plummet into the waters below. No witnesses, either in person or online, so no one had come to his aid and his body hadn't been found until a couple of days later among the Hundred Island reed beds six miles downstream. Bloated, the skin of his extremities wrinkled and nibbled at by hungry critters.

Completing the impression of inept soldiery, the trees though dressed in winter's drab sported splashes of vivid green among the upper branches like gaudy braiding. Between their trunks clustered dusty velos like mooching dogs, as well as tables and chairs belonging to the cafés. Most of these were empty so early in the day but further along, where the street followed the river's gentle curve, Stina could see a few hunched, seated forms.

The chess players.

She knew which café to go to, knew what to order, even though she oughtn't to. The woman she was going to meet wasn't a suspect. Not officially. Officially, she'd been a person of passing interest, no more than that. The AI that evaluated whether to allow a person's private data to be opened up to investigation had not done so in her case. Nor in anyone else's. Although Albert Vogel had most definitely been murdered by administration of a drug that had exacerbated an already serious heart condition, not one person in the city had a probability score anywhere close to the required sixty-five percent threshold. The AI had analysed thousands of potential contacts. Zeroing in first on the people he'd had passed on that final walk, the luncheoners, the *kaffe und kuchen* brigade, the chess players. Then scraping the vast WatchNet archives for interactions in the months leading up to the man's death that might contain signs of threat. Scouring personal records – financial, medical, business, social – for hints of motive. Looking, above all, for changes of behaviour. That had always been true of crimes of this nature. People changed their behaviour before, during and after. But according to the AI, no one had. And now the net was being widened, the current hypothesis favoured among the investigating team being a professional hit for reasons unknown. So the AI was working full time on tracing arrivals and departures for several weeks either side of the day of the murder. Trains, buses, taxis and car hires. Officially, the investigation had moved on.

Unofficially, Stina had a hunch. This woman – this Dimitra Klimala, a foreigner although she had lived in the city for so long it was doubtful anyone knew that – may have been discounted as a potential suspect after scoring a mere thirty-eight percent, but that thirty-eight percent was significantly higher than anyone else Vogel had been acquainted with. The blind spots of the trees notwithstanding, she'd been the last person who was known for sure to have spoken to Albert, a mere ten minutes before he was struck down. In her interview, she'd claimed that they'd simply played chess, which footage from a different bee to the one that had recorded his demise had corroborated. Stina had watched it on a loop. It had been a cold day, flecks of snow in the air. Vogel bought the coffees and sat down. They'd each kept strictly to their own side of the board. No touching, no tampering. Not even a handshake when, thirty-two minutes later, the game was over. After Albert left, Klimala got herself another coffee, reset the board and had already begun a new match by the time Vogel's body drifted past unnoticed.

The chess games were a regular thing between the pair and that day's had played out exactly the same as the others for which there had been available footage. Nothing out of the ordinary. But still Stina had a feeling in her gut. She'd argued with the Super and been told flatly, in front of the whole team, to forget it. Things didn't work that way any more. The other officers, the younger ones, so full of confidence, had schooled their inattention but she knew they'd been laughing at her. She had come slowly to the realisation that she was considered out of touch these days. Her professional ratings, her proticks, were the lowest they'd ever been. Her perticks, the aggregated social media ones, were little better, and small wonder. If any friend or neighbour ever bothered to drop in on a bee in the house she shared with Tomasz, her son, they'd despair at the stilted bewilderment that went on between them. His contributions to the household were prompt and adequate but she didn't know what he did to make his money, only that he did it from the privacy of his bedroom and the maddening politeness that everyone practiced now made it impossible to have it out with him. And that just seemed to be the way things were. Well, fine, so she was a dinosaur. But intuition had been recognised as an invaluable asset in a detective once, and she had finely honed hers over the span of her career. No way was she going to let that old man's death go unsolved just because a computer was supposed to know better these days.

She went about it the old-fashioned way. Rode the bees around the Wehlstrasse area for hours, observing Dimitra Klimala until she knew

Neil Williamson

about as much as she could legally manage about her quarry. Which in the end was astonishingly little. The woman was a black hole of publicly available information. She had no social media accounts, wasn't registered with a doctor, had no history of employment either here or elsewhere. Stina found it alarmingly suspicious but without a direct link to Vogel's death there was nothing she could do about it. Knowing that Klimala liked her coffee two-shot strong and bolstered with a slug of hazelnut liqueur was an in at least. And that, she fervently hoped, would be all she'd need.

As she left the café and crossed the street, the cups she carried rattled in their saucers. Nervous? She'd interviewed a thousand suspects in her time. Yes, in the last decade she'd had the advantage of knowing that they were all almost certainly guilty but she wasn't *that* out of practice. She calmed herself and approached Klimala's table. It was square and had a blue checked paper cover clipped to it, the tails of which riffled in the breeze. In the centre sat an old scholastic chess set, the board softened and mildewed. The simple wooden pieces, waiting patiently in their ranks, bore the scars of years of battle.

The occupant of the table, bundled up in a bulky, brown coat and a woollen hat, was staring distractedly out over the river. Stina didn't think Klimala was even aware of her arrival until she put the coffee cups down beside the board. The old woman turned. Looked at the cups first, then at Stina. Her face was weathered but her grey eyes were sharp.

"Polizei, huh?" Klimala's lips crinkled into a maybe smile.

Stina hovered, thrown off by her directness. "Is it that obvious, Frau Klimala?"

The old woman shrugged. "The suit? The haircut? The presumption? Who else could it be?"

"Fair enough," Stina said. "Can I sit down?"

Klimala's eyes narrowed, then she gestured at the board. "Do you play?"

"I've just a few questions…"

"Do. You. Play?"

"…and it'll only take ten minutes of your time, I promise."

"Detective whatever-your-name-is. People come here for chess, not chit chat. If you sit, you play. If you don't play, you can fuck off."

Stina sighed, reminding herself that she'd chosen this theatre of engagement. So be it. Her Oma had divulged the principles of chess when Stina was very small and they'd often played on rainy afternoons during summer visits. It had been a long time but she was fairly sure she remembered them. "Fine." She sat down. "And it's Detective Wolter."

"Good." Klimala didn't bother to suppress her supercilious smile. "White goes first."

"I *know*." Stina instantly regretted the snap in her reply. She had to stay professional.

Klimala laughed like a goose, her teeth bared in glee at so easily needling her opponent. Without looking, Stina pinched the round head of a pawn between thumb and finger – she didn't even register which pawn, one of the middle ones, it didn't matter – and clipped it down on the next square up. Her eyes were locked with Klimala's.

"As I said, I have questions."

Klimala held up her hands. Her fingers were knobbed with arthritis and trembling. "Oh, go on then, ask your questions." The words wheezed like air from a burst balloon, as if what little reserves of defiance she'd possessed were already spent.

Stina realised how wary she'd been of this confrontation, but now doubt sidled in. If she was wrong about this, all she might really be doing was harassing a frail old woman. Was her hunch really that strong? She looked away. To the dowdy sparrow pecking for crumbs under an adjacent table. To the WatchNet bee drowsing above the balustrade, one of millions supposedly making life safer for people now. The security of mass public surveillance. Anyone could be watching through its eyes right at that moment. Maybe even her colleagues back at the Inspectorate. All gathered round and having a good chuckle.

Stina cleared her throat and returned her attention to the woman across the table. "Albert Vogel," she said. "My questions are about him."

Klimala was scowling at the board. Then with a tiny shake of the head she made her own opening move. "What about him?" she said. "What do I know? I know he's dead. That's what I told the last of your lot who came around asking questions."

"You don't sound very sorry," Stina said. "You played chess against him most days. Wasn't he your friend?"

"No, he wasn't my friend." Klimala lifted her cup, took a slurp and winced. Too hot? Too sweet? Had Stina got the coffee wrong? "He was merely my opponent."

"You didn't like him, then?"

"We played chess." Klimala indicated the tables around them, the boards set out. When Stina had arrived one had been occupied by a dapper gentleman, collared and tied and sporting studious round glasses. Now he'd been joined by a scruffy student type. With barely a few words exchanged they were shaking hands, ready to begin a game. "People don't come here to make friends. They come just to play." Klimala nodded at their own board. "It's your go again."

"And how long did your rivalry with Herr Vogel last?" Stina moved the pawn another square, eliciting a tut from her opponent. "The café owner said you pair were at it when her mother was a girl."

Klimala scowled in the direction of the open café door. "Janssen said that? I wouldn't pay too much attention. She's just in a bad mood because of the grilling you lot gave her."

Stina shrugged. "Albert had a drug in his system that caused his heart to fail. We had to be sure he didn't ingest it in his coffee."

"Of course he didn't," Klimala growled. "Anyway, yes, Vogel and I played a lot."

"I ask again, how long…?"

"I don't know an exact date," Klimala said, but then she clamped her lips together and stared at the board meaningfully until Stina made another move. A different pawn this time. Then Klimala nodded and continued. "But I do know how many matches we played."

"Really?" Stina was surprised. "How many?"

"Seven thousand and fourteen."

It was all Stina could do not to gape. In her notes she'd estimated the rivalry to have gone back perhaps a decade but they were potentially talking at least double that. Way before WatchNet and the comprehensive datasphere had been established: the very foundation of the criminal evidence chain these days. The AI couldn't look that far back. "That's quite a legacy," she said.

"So, now you see?" Klimala said. "That's how chess is. It's a conversation, a rapport you build with every game. It's not merely a way to pass the time while you get chummy. It's a thing of value in itself."

"And yet, it must be impossible not to learn things about your opponent. You're really saying you knew nothing about Albert Vogel?"

"I know how he played chess." In a single, swift movement, Klimala's black knight replaced Stina's advanced pawn and the captured piece was dropped into a pocket of the voluminous coat. Despite the encumbrance of arthritis, it was done with the deftness of a conjuror. "Which is all I needed or wanted to know about him."

Stina found the insistence of ignorance hard to swallow, but she moved on. "And who, would you say, won the majority of your games?"

Klimala snorted at that. There was a spark in her eyes. "Albert Vogel didn't win a single match against me. Not fairly at least."

Stina had been about to nudge out another pawn. She paused; her hand poised in mid-air. "Are you saying he cheated?"

Klimala's shrug was a lumpen movement inside her layers. Then she sniffed and pointed at the board. "This is going to be a short conversation if you make that move."

Stina retracted her hand, thinking about what she'd just heard. It had sounded like Klimala was hinting that she *wanted* the conversation to go on for longer. For the first time in the game she gave serious thought to her next move, settling eventually on bringing out a knight.

"So, you do this every day?" she said casually and then took a sip of her coffee. She'd let it sit for too long, but even piping hot it wouldn't have been great. She understood why Klimala had grimaced earlier. The woman who ran the café really had a grudge against the police.

Klimala nodded but didn't speak. Just moved a pawn.

Stina mirrored the move. "Must be nice to have the time to come out and enjoy a leisurely day playing chess."

"It's called retirement," Klimala grunted. "Aren't you supposed to focus on the things you enjoy when you retire?"

Stina could have delved deeper there, asked what else the old woman had been doing with her retirement, but she already knew the answer to that. No friends, no late blooming romances. Just here, the food store and occasional trips to the park or the local repertory cinema. A picture was building. "And what did you do before you retired?"

Those deft fingers brought a bishop into play. Stina didn't think she was going to get an answer to her question, but then she did, and it was carefully worded. "I worked in the diplomatic service."

Stina nodded, pretended to consider her pieces. "In whose diplomatic service?" she asked quietly.

When Klimala looked up, the grey eyes were shining with cold humour. An imperceptible shake of the head. Stina advanced her own bishop.

"Is Dimitra Klimala even your real name?"

No answer to that either.

The moves came thick and fast while Stina tried to sift her thoughts into some sort of order. A person's data should tell you everything about them, and that Dimitra Klimala had impossibly little of it was no accident. She wasn't some doddery oldster with no clue how the world worked. And she knew full well that she didn't have to divulge anything unless they charged her. Even then, how little might there be? This woman had gone to great lengths to avoid connections to the world. But everyone needed some kind of connection, didn't they? The coffees, the chess. It wasn't a cover. Those were really all she had.

Stina moved a knight and rather pleasingly put Klimala in a fork. "I'll bet some of those chess games with Albert were close," she said.

"Of course." Klimala saved her knight, sacrificing her bishop. "He was a good player."

Stina took it. "And then?" Her short-lived satisfaction crumbled as Klimala's next move with the knight forked her back, threatening queen and rook.

"And then he didn't come for a while." Klimala said.

"Well, he *was* convalescing from a heart attack." Stina saved her queen, watched her rook vanish, and then tried to build again on the other side of the board. "That must have been upsetting."

"I was… disappointed." Klimala said it quietly, but Stina heard something in the word. A glittering glimpse of truth. While Klimala took another of Stina's pawns off the board, Stina pulled up the feed of the bee on the balustrade in her lenses. Saw the old woman's fingers fretting nervously with the wooden piece before dropping it into her pocket.

And that was when Stina knew how it could have been done. A piece could have been set up on the board at the beginning of the game coated with contact poison. It would have to be a piece that might not be touched until near the end of the match. The king, logically. And after it had been taken, how easy for someone with quick fingers to swap it for an untainted one hidden in that deep pocket, and dispose of it later so that when the pieces were tested no trace would be found. It was like something from an old spy film, but it was possible. Especially for someone who might once have been an old spy.

But why? What was the motive for it?

Then she saw it. *Seven thousand* games.

"When he came back from his time away, that was when he cheated?" Stina said. "That must have been galling. To have sullied the legacy you'd built between you. All those close matches. His valiant attempts to best you. Your ongoing run against a worthy opponent."

She looked across the board and saw that Klimala was shivering. No, not that, laughing. Silently, mirthlessly. So hard that tears were welling in the corners of her eyes. The old woman composed herself. "How perceptive. Yes, that's when he cheated. He moved a rook while I was ordering coffee. He realised almost immediately that he'd moved it into trouble and pulled it back a square. He thought I hadn't seen, but I see everything."

"He must have wanted to beat you very badly. After his brush with mortality perhaps he doubted there would be many more opportunities."

"Ah, you picture Vogel nobly striving for a win in a longstanding friendly rivalry," Klimala said, and again Stina caught the glitter of truth in her tone. It was sharp and steely. "Well it was that, once. Our matches were... *close*. But Albert was not an honourable man. He ruined what we had the *first* time he cheated. He'd been trying to redeem himself ever since."

Stina stared at her opponent, then she said, very quietly, "And you weren't going to let that happen. You beat him over seven thousand times to teach him a lesson, and turned that lesson into a — what was your phrase? – a *thing of value*. But only to one of you, it turned out. That must have been *very* galling indeed."

Klimala's eyes twinkled but she made no confession, and Stina realised that she could see no way of ever getting one. She studied the board. Most of her pieces were gone now, her options for keeping the game going limited. Out of desperation, she castled.

"Can I ask," she said, "why you agreed to talk to me?"

"That's a good question." Klimala's hand hovered for a moment then shifted the black queen one square, and it was like a conjuror making her final reveal. Devastatingly impressive. Stina scanned her options but quickly saw that every possible move she made would lead her into mate in the next move or the one after.

"Why? Because as soon as you turned up here today, I could tell you were like me. You're in *zugzwang*."

"Zugz...?" Stina frowned. "What is that?"

"Zugzwang is when you have to move but can't do so without making your position worse."

Stina's breath caught as she saw the sudden, glaring truth of it. In the game, in this conversation, in her life. For all her efforts today, what had she really expected to gain from this? To prove to herself that her instincts were still good? Fine, but it had resulted in a lot of conjecture and no evidence. She had nothing to take back to the Super that would justify her seeking override powers on the AI. Nothing but the intuition that screamed that Dimitra Klimala had killed Albert Vogel.

Worse, what she'd done here today just made her look more old-fashioned and desperate. If she even tried to make a case, she'd end up side-lined, farmed out until the next round of headcount cuts allowed them to get rid of her. If she said nothing, she'd keep her tattered reputation a while longer, but it'd only be a matter of time. Either way, a murder would go unexplained. It was an awful, despairing feeling. Stina would probably never know the hidden details of Dimitra's life but how precarious must her position have been to balance on its edge, making no move at all, for *decades*?

And yet, she seemed happy in her limited existence. How was that possible?

"So..." She gently laid her king on the board.

"So." Her opponent had already begun setting the pieces up again. "You don't play badly, you know, but you'd improve if you cut out the chit-chat."

"I suppose," said Stina. "I'm sorry."

"You'll do better next time," Dimitra said.

Stina laughed at the presumption of the offer, but appreciated how skilfully it had been crafted. Despite everything, she liked this old woman. And besides, what else was she going to do with her time?

"Same time tomorrow, then?" she said. She could come over on her lunch hour, and if anyone happened to be watching on the bees, they would see an old woman and a middle-aged one, out of step and off the grid, playing one of the oldest games in the world. But what would really be happening was something else entirely.

Long Live the Strawberries of Finsbury Park

Stephen Oram

I'm late. The early morning heat and the faint hiss of the autobus driving itself down the through-transit have woken me from the most wonderful dream of swimming in deep, ice-cold water.

This is not good. I quickly tear clumps of grass out of the ground, spit on them, and wait for the saliva to do its job on the bioengineered turf. While I'm waiting, a rabbit–penguin hobbles past awkwardly. Not every experiment we try is successful, but Finsbury Park welcomes one and all. Even the strange hybrid creatures can make their home here safely.

After a few minutes, the grass becomes a green-brown mush, which I rub into my arms and face. As my dad used to say, 'Solar protection is life protection,' which I'm sure he'd seen on some tacky old advert. Sally-Luke is asleep and looks pale and gorgeous, and vulnerable. At least the precious bio-enhanced strawberries that I'll get for a day's work will help keep the love of my life's tumour at bay. That's presuming I'm successful in my tasks. I turn my blanket into a bag and quietly slip it on my back, making sure the greatest possible area is exposed to the sun so it can recharge while I'm at the shoreline. A shoreline that gets closer to the park every year.

It could be a long day, competing with other areas of London to convince one of the refugees that cling to the side of the city ships to join us. And I have to do it quickly enough to be home in time to greet the day visitors from the same city ship to fulfil one of our centuries-old founding principles: *to alleviate the conditions of the poor.* It's not always convenient, but I am glad our bylaws give these day visitors every right to come and sit on the soil, commune with mother earth, and restore the richness of good mental health that we all desire. The stress of living on a city ship is too much for their mental wellbeing, making them the poorest of the poor despite their wealth.

There's no time to waste. With a whistle and a click of my fingers, the Mydrone drifts down from the tree and settles a few inches above my head. I reach up, grab it, clip it on my harness, and let it lift me to the treetops.

It still has plenty of charge, but I'll need it later, so I shift it to my belt and use the slackline instead. Running, flipping, running, and flipping, I cross from one tree to another with the bounce of a newborn tree hare. City ships don't dock that frequently or predictably, so I have to get there first and make the most of this opportunity. I must entice an inventive mind to become a Finsbury Parker to keep us ahead of the tech race – and I can't believe I overslept on such a crucial day.

The hydro farm has left a punnet of juicy, ripe-red strawberries on the shelf near the top of the park's outer wall. I pop the punnet into my bag. I feel guilty for being late and a small knot of acid settles in my throat at the thought of not getting paid, and what that'll mean for Sally-Luke's sickness.

With a deep breath of determination, I focus my lenses on the nearby half-completed skyscraper that's covered in all manner of homemade attire, and grab the Mydrone, which carries me across. Like one of the human transients that populate the hostile areas, the building is draped in plastic dragged up from the east-end shoreline of Canning Town and stands unique in this beautiful hotchpotch of a city.

Hurrying along the rickety walkways between the tall unfinished buildings with their makeshift additions and plastic repairs that shimmer in the sunrise, I cross the cityscape. I stay within the confines of public airspace, carefully avoiding any hostiles my spydrone has alerted me to and paying any compulsory tolls in strawberries.

From Walthamstow, I make my way down the flooded marshes towards Canning Town with the Mydrone skimming me across the water and lifting me over the dry gaps. I'm now fractionally behind a Victoria Parker, the only other barterer heading for the city ship that my spydrone has found.

When I arrive, the Mydrone lifts me up to the layer of semi-transparent, crustacean-like spheres clinging to the side of the city ship.

The refugees sit patiently looking out through the gaps they've torn in the sides of their pods. They know how highly their survival skills are valued by those of us bartering for their residency, so they sit and smile, and wait. The Victoria Parker is hovering in front of an old woman wearing the t-shirt of the International Guild of Bioengineers. She could be the sort of person we need, and although there is always a risk of choosing a dud, the wisdom that comes with age and the t-shirt that would have disintegrated if she wasn't genuine make me feel optimistic that she could be an asset.

The Victoria Parker holds out a peach, and I do the same with a strawberry. The refugee accepts both into cupped hands, and after taking small bites of the peach and then my strawberry, she smiles a red-juice smile and closes her eyes.

We wait while she decides.

Finally, she holds her hand out to me, we shake, and as our palms touch the data from her health app transfers to mine. The mental health biomarkers are good, which isn't the case for everyone who travels across the world stuck to the side of a city ship in a crinkly bubble. She's especially strong on cognitive control and emotional valence; she'll fit in nicely, so I beckon her to follow. She's now a Finsbury Parker with the solid promise of our superior food supply. She grabs her Mydrone from the back of the pod, and we set off on the journey to Finsbury Park.

"Krapy Rubsnif," mutters the Victoria Parker as we pass.

Side by side, we bob up and down along the marshes. She grimaces every time I check in with the spydrone to see how far away the autobus and its day visitor passengers are. I'm sure she knows I'm late and might not make it home in time to look after the wealthy residents of the city ship on their rejuvenating visit. I push the Mydrone harder, and it screeches with every alarm it has. We're catching up, but not fast enough. There's an almighty screech and the Mydrone slows down. It's exhausted. I'm screwed.

The refugee taps me on the shoulder, points at the autobus, and utters a complicated whistle. There's a low boom from her Mydrone and the autobus slows to a crawl. I knew she'd have more advanced tech than us. She hooks our Mydrones together and we pass overhead, leaving the autobus behind.

As we touch down on the wall surrounding the park, I carefully place the few remaining strawberries in the box waiting for me, making sure I take my own payment first. We sit quietly, waiting for the autobus. I thank the earth that I'm here in time to host the wealthy-poor and that I have a few of our precious strawberries for Sally-Luke.

"I'm Lotte," says the refugee and holds out her hand for me to shake. "I saw them do some incredible stuff," she says. "Good and bad." She points towards the autobus as it comes into view.

"Good? Bad?" I ask.

"You know, successful and not so successful," she says. "Although, the experiments on people were more likely to work than those on the animals; they're more cautious with the humans. There are some really old people on board that ship."

"You saw them?"

"They came to see me and we swapped knowledge. They know about extending life, about fixing damaged cells, and I know about biotech in hostile climates."

"Did you come here out of desperation?" I ask.

She chuckles. "No, not at all. I've travelled the world on the side of that ship, in demand wherever I went."

"So why here?"

"To put down roots. To belong rather than be a bioengineer for hire. And I happen to love strawberries."

We chat about the park and Sally-Luke until the autobus arrives. "Could the city ship heal her?" I ask.

"Who knows? They'll certainly try. They love experimenting – on others."

A group of ten well-dressed city ship dwellers disembark, chattering noisily to each other, seemingly uninterested in their surroundings. Another, much older woman glides out from the autobus. A large plastic cage attached to her ankle is being carried behind her by a set of four mini-drones. She must have brought some failed experiments. 'Are you our guide?' she asks.

"Yes, I am."

"They don't have much time," she says, glancing towards the others.

"And you?" I ask.

"I have no need of your tiny plot of land. I'm a top-decker. I have an estate in New Zealand. I've regularly spent time on terra firma there since my childhood."

The party of ten each grab a drone to travel to the rejuvenation area. We move quickly across the park a few feet above the ground. The gate recognises me and swings open on its hinges with a gentle but fake creak, giving the impression of an ancient and magical place inviting us to explore. The drones set us down in a circle, and all the day visitors except the top-decker quickly unhook themselves. Their chatter declines as they waste no time in communing with the soil, the grass, the plants, and the trees. Sally-Luke shuffles over from our camp, twitching with spasms and looking drastically pale. The strawberries seem insignificant in comparison with the sickness, but I hand them over with a hopeful smile. "Thanks," she rasps and proceeds to gorge on the fruit.

I lick the juice trickling down that gorgeous chin and plant a huge kiss on those strawberry-red lips. I'm happy. Sally-Luke has eaten, Lotte the refugee is fitting in nicely, and I can turn my attention to helping the city ship dwellers rejuvenate. It's a good day.

The top-decker clicks her fingers. The drones release the cage and return to hover above her shoulder.

"This is for the park," she says.

The cage door opens, and a creature with the head of a monkey and the body of a cat stumbles out. It releases a high-pitched scream, launches itself at the nearest tree, bangs its head against the trunk, and falls to a heap on the ground.

"All yours,' she says. "You take the failures, don't you?"

The cat-monkey scratches at the dusty ground making unearthly groaning noises and then, on its back legs, awkwardly approaches the top-decker. Dropping to all fours, it scratches at her and utters its unnerving meow-howl of pain. She ignores it, but it paces beside her, meowing and howling and nuzzling her legs. She presses her hand to the back of its head, and it shudders.

"Even if it's only fit for food," she says.

It slumps to the ground and thick blood oozes from its mouth, turning the dust into a paste. Sally-Luke turns away. The drones lower themselves, hook the corpse, and drop it by the gate.

The day visitors are oblivious to the drama playing out right next to them. Most of them lie on the ground inhaling deeply, eyes closed, palms flat against the earth. A couple have stripped off all but their flimsiest of underclothes, and another is entirely naked, revealing her scaly skin. A youngish man is eating the dirty soil, his mouth oozing a brown sludge as he chomps away with abandonment. It seems the tales of adapted worm-like humans able to extract nutrients directly from the soil are true. The naked woman is rolling around, rubbing her scales on nettles that were planted by day visitors a few months ago. She has enhanced skin, so her immune system will be stimulated by their sting.

A man sits on the nearby bench, listening to it replay recordings of past visitors. He adds his own memories. I'm so pleased we can provide what they need.

The sun has reached its height, and Sally-Luke has already settled under the shade of a tree for a siesta. I snuggle alongside and drift off into a wonderful sleep.

When I wake, she is no longer there. I stretch my limbs and stand up slowly, basking in the final warmth of the day.

"I think Sally-Luke may have just left with that woman," says Lotte.

I look around the enclosure. The top-decker has gone and there's no sign of my love. I scan the park using my flydrone and find them heading towards the autobus. Lotte immediately understands my despair and my dilemma, caught between the obligation to the day visitors and my concern for Sally-Luke.

"I'll go," she says.

"Please. Can you find out what's happening?"

In a flash, she's clipped on her Mydrone and is soaring across the park. All I can do is wait. The rabbit-penguin and a tree hare look on, almost hidden by the undergrowth. I can see their eyes and smell their faint odours on the breeze. I'm proud to be a Finsbury Parker, but it's possible that Sally-Luke would be better off on the city ship – and might even be healed. In truth, what do I really offer in the way of a decent future? The hand-to-mouth existence of a daily dose of strawberries? Am I only delaying the inevitable? In my wildest optimism, I imagine we will discover a cure. In my deepest darkness, I expect to wake up and find my love dead beside me.

There's a scraping noise coming from the cage, and a child's hand covered in lumpy blisters pokes through the bars as it pushes the door open. A boy creeps out and lies on the ground in the same way as the day visitors, except his eyes are wide open, staring up at the trees. As I get close, he curls up into a ball. His whole body is covered in uniform, rectangular lumps as if he's littered with implants beneath the surface of his skin. I reach out to touch him and he recoils, snarling through clenched teeth. I wish Sally-Luke was here to comfort him. The flydrone reports that Lotte is catching up with them. That's a relief. I hesitate near the boy for a few moments then decide I'd better check on the day visitors. Maybe they'll know what to do.

Having satiated themselves, they've made their way to the Museum of Artefacts, where row upon row of weather-worn compartments line the wall – a testament to the park of the past. Most of the printed descriptions beneath the artefacts have faded, but we know about plastic plates, bottles, and bags because of the stories passed down by the residents of the plastic-covered tower blocks. A glass bottle has captured their attention – a crack pipe, whatever that is. They stare and point and discuss it with amusement. It's sad for them and sad for us that they can't see its true value as a precious piece of the history of our park and my home.

"There's a child over there," I say. They ignore me and I repeat, "There's a child over there – and he's in a bad way."

One of the men mumbles something along the lines of *this lot couldn't run a splicing lab, let alone a park,* and proceeds to tell me he believes he has a solution to the financial burden this amenity places on our park. A problem he says is evident from the decaying museum. "Go on," I say, more out of politeness than curiosity, all the while keeping my eye on the flydrone feed and worrying about the boy.

"I want to make you an offer," he says. "It'll be generous."

I'm stunned. Genuine stop-Mydrone-in-its-tracks stunned. "Why do you think it's for sale?"

"I want to preserve it for the future. It's an important part of our heritage, and I can make sure it's not lost." He scratches his nose and tilts his head. "Life on the city ship is good," he says. "We have it all, and I want to share my good fortune with others. I want to buy this tiny corner of the park and preserve it properly."

"No," I say. I click my fingers and the Mydrone drifts down. I clip it on, synchronise it with the flydrone, and it lifts me up. I call down. "Help the boy then find your own way back to the autobus."

Lotte has caught up with Sally-Luke, and the flydrone is sending me a live feed of their conversation. Sally-Luke is speaking, and I catch the end of what she's saying. "...but what about my love? I'm not sure I should leave."

"Like I said earlier, I'm sure we can fix you," says the top-decker.

"And I can come back today? After one treatment?"

"You don't have to rely on a few strawberries every day just to stay alive. That's ridiculous. Come back to the ship. We'll have you back here in no time, one hundred per cent fit and healthy."

Sally-Luke says nothing. It's Lotte who replies. "You can't guarantee anything."

"We have more knowledge than you'll ever have," says the top-decker.

"That I doubt," says Lotte. She turns to Sally-Luke. "I can't make any promises, but I think I can do something with the bioengineered plants you already have, and I have a few more tricks up my sleeve. Will you come with me?"

The flydrone warns me that the autobus is close, so I press the Mydrone as hard as I can and hope with all my heart that Lotte has done a good job of mending it. The added boost thrusts me forward, and the flydrone confirms I'll reach them before the autobus arrives.

The Mydrone lowers me to the ground close to Sally-Luke, who stands behind me and wraps those precious, loving arms around my trembling body. The sun is setting and the glowing embers of a day well-lived colour everything with the burnt tinge of its decline. The world begins to cool.

Close by, but out of sight, the top-decker continues. "I guarantee we can repair you."

Sally-Luke whispers in my ear and draws me in even tighter. "I want to be well. I want to be cured."

"I know," I say. "Lotte?"

Lotte stands in front of us. The setting sun frames her face and creates a shimmering halo. "Can you guarantee you can heal Sally-Luke?"

"No, I can't," she says quietly. "But neither can she," she says, pointing at the top-decker.

"Sally-Luke?" I ask, turning around.

Lotte's haloed image is reflected in the tear-filmed eyes that stare desperately back at me.

"Say it's alright," says Sally-Luke.

"Stay with us," I reply.

"I trust them. Please."

The pleading in those sad, scared eyes is too much to bear, too much to deny. I nod and wipe a sun-red tear from the soft cheek that I've spent so many moments kissing and stroking in the cold of night and the warmth of day.

"Come back soon," I say.

Sally-Luke puts a hand on the back of my neck and pulls me to those familiar lips. We share a lingering, bittersweet kiss, and then we disentangle. The top-decker is next to us. She holds Sally-Luke's elbow with a firm grip, and they walk towards the autobus. My knees give way and I crumple to the ground as the two of them disappear inside.

Lotte squats next to me and lays her hand on my back. "I can follow and keep an eye on them if you'd like me to," she says.

"No. No, you don't need to," I say. "I have to let this become whatever it becomes."

I shiver; it's cold, and I'm scared.

"They will heal Sally-Luke, and you will live a life of luxury together with the earth beneath you and the stars above," says Lotte as she takes hold of my hand, enfolds my fist in the wonderful security of a squeeze, and forces the constant everyday feeling of life's fragility to flee.

"Thank you," I say, and close my eyes to soak up the peace of the park. "Thank you."

The FenZone

Ian Whates

I hate them with a passion.

I remember when it was called the Great Fen – an ambitious project to restore a large swathe of land to its 'natural' state, linking together a couple of shrunken remnants of surviving fenland such as Holme and Woodwalton, turning back the clock to recreate the sort of habitat that used to dominate East Anglia before it was all drained for farmland. Those aspirations seem ironic now, given what it actually became.

"Do you fancy going out for lunch?" Tab asked.

"If you like," I said. "Where do you have in mind?"

"I thought maybe the Pike and Eel."

Of course she did. It was always the Pike and Eel.

"Okay." I was proud of how steady my voice sounded.

Tab and I didn't connect online, we met in a bar; you know, the old-fashioned way – human to human rather than browser to profile or finger to swipe. This didn't make us unique, but we were a dying breed. I was pants at the whole dating game. I kept getting 'friendzoned.' Every time I built my hopes up, daring to believe that this time I'd made a real connection with someone, the little green heart would appear – never the red one – beating away with its Banner of Doom: 'I like you and I value you, but as a friend.'

I was rich in friends, me, the richest man I knew.

My best mate, Doug, reckoned I was my own worst enemy. "You're being too honest," he'd said to me more than once. "Your avatar looks exactly like you. Your profile always *sounds* like you."

"That's because I *am* me! What's the point in pretending to be someone else? They'll only be disappointed when they meet me in the flesh."

"Don't be so naïve. You have to play the game. Nobody's *that* honest. Everybody… exaggerates a bit."

"Lies, you mean."

"Exaggerates," he repeated. "When you meet someone online, when you bring up their profile, you know that fifty per cent of what's in there is bullshit, embellishments designed to make them seem more attractive, more interesting. That's how it works. When someone comes across a profile as dull as yours and then adjusts downwards for the bullshit factor, what's left sinks way below the level of boring. It's as if you're trying to push romance away, not invite it in to sit down and say hello."

He didn't get it. "I don't want to meet someone like that. I can't be the only person in the world who's after a relationship based on honesty rather than…" I was trying not to say 'lies' again.

"Embellishments," he supplied.

"Exactly."

"Look, all I'm saying is… jazz it up a bit. Insert a few nuggets here and there that are obviously blowing smoke and not meant to be taken seriously. Make 'em humorous and people will love you for it. That way, you won't be misleading anyone but you'll still be showing a bit of personality, rather than just parading a list of drab facts guaranteed to get them flicking to the next profile. I can help you with the wording if you like."

My lack of enthusiasm must have shown. "At least promise me you'll think about it."

"Okay, I will."

We both knew I wouldn't.

Our ability to adapt as a species never ceases to amaze me. In defiance of every portent we wreck the world's climate and move on; in the space of a few years we accommodate the impact of Covid and move on; in the space of a few decades we leap from the pedestrian awkwardness of first-generation analogue phones to sixth generation instant connectivity and hardly miss a beat.

We build a wall around a supposed nature reserve after declaring it a deadly no-go area and nothing changes, even for those of us who live in its shadow. Oh there's been consternation, questions, speculation, a brief outburst of fear and outrage, but essentially, we shrug our shoulders and get on with our lives. Most of us do, at any rate.

I first met Tab at a bar in St. Ives – not the picturesque Cornish resort that's always in the newsfeeds, tugging at the heartstrings as it wages a losing battle against rising sea levels. No, I live in the market town near Cambridge which is forever associated with Oliver Cromwell. Here there used to be a cluster of pubs and bars where Broadway splits to become Crown Street and Merryland: Floods Tavern, the Lounge, the Royal Oak… all gone now, swept away by the Covid pandemic, victims of humankind's retreat into the digital. The Nelsons Head still survives, though, and that's where I ended up on this particular rainy evening, seeking refuge from both sodden skies and the prospect of another night spent home alone with a ready meal.

The bar was practically empty. The only patrons were a couple occupying a table near the fireplace at the back, a young woman perched on one of the plush padded barstools, and me.

I chose to sit at the bar, four empty stools separating me from the woman, and tried not to study her too overtly. She intrigued me. What was she doing here alone? Not waiting for a friend – there had been no glances towards the door since I arrived, not even when I came in – so perhaps she was taking refuge from something, or someone.

A glass of pale golden wine, which I imagined to be Pinot, sat on the bar in front of her, barely touched, and her posture – hunched slightly forward – meant that most of her face was obscured by long dark hair that hung straight down like a veil.

Realising she was never going to glance up long enough to make eye contact, and despairing of her ever finishing that wine, I took the plunge, standing up before courage deserted me to stride over and claim the stool next to hers.

Doug was shocked when I told him about this the following day. "You did what? *Are you mad?* Going up to a complete stranger like that…?"

I shrugged. "It felt like the right thing to do."

She didn't seem phased in the least by this man plonking himself down uninvited beside her and trying to strike up a conversation. Okay, so she didn't seem especially thrilled by my approach, either, but I'll settle for polite any day.

Her name was Tabitha, Tab for short. I can't pretend there were fireworks or that she gave any indication of fancying me, but conversation happened and at the end of the evening we arranged to meet again. Looking back, I suspect that's the whole reason she was there: to connect with someone like me.

That was two years ago. We moved in together six months later, or rather Tab moved into my place. She's a couple of years younger than me, and there's a hint of Asian or perhaps eastern European heritage in her features which I've always found attractive, though she told me she was born here in the UK. She doesn't like to talk about her childhood, which I gather wasn't a happy one.

"The weather's looking good today," she said as I drove us towards the Pike and Eel.

She always said that; we only ever came here when the weather was good. "We can sit outside, if you like," I suggested – my pat response.

"That'll be nice," she said, completing the ritual.

We were happy, in our own fashion. For two years we had pointedly ignored each other's eccentricities and played at being normal, which is ridiculous because I've never been that, and I'm pretty sure Tab was as far away from normal as you could get.

For me it was the sense of being out of sync, a feeling that I had somehow been left behind as the world raced forward into a connected future. It was probably why I felt such an affinity with the Great Fen project and its dogged determination to turn back the clock – Canute standing against the tide. I've always felt out of step with the rhythms of modern day living: an analogue spirit in a digital age, a 1G person stranded in 6G reality. Initially, I thought that in Tab I'd stumbled upon a kindred spirit, but the longer we were together the more apparent the differences became; now I think the opposite was true, that the world had yet to catch up with her. Maybe it was a case of opposites attracting, or maybe I was just convenient.

A traditional country pub, the Pike boasts six – always six – wooden tables with attendant benches, arranged haphazardly on a long lawn that runs down to the river. There were two other couples outside when we arrived, one with young kids running around, but Tab was able to claim our 'usual' table while I went in to fetch drinks – a pint for me and a large glass of Pinot for her – I'd been right about that much on our first meeting, at any rate.

I came back to find her staring across the river. At the wall.

"You look lovely today," I said as I put the glasses down and sat opposite her. She did, too.

She glanced at me, smiled and said, "Thank you," before turning her gaze back to the wall.

That was what she always said, whenever I complimented her appearance, her cooking, her anything. Never, "It's a new top, I'm glad you approve," or "I found the recipe online and thought you'd like it," or even "You look pretty good yourself." Just: "Thank you."

I studied her face in profile, and wondered again who she really was. I'd never been introduced to any of her family: "We're not close," and only knew the sketchiest details of her past. She on the other hand had heard all about me, had met my mother (my father having passed away years ago), who professed to love Tab; mind you, I think she would have loved anyone who was willing to put up with me, and she'd briefly met my sister, who declared herself thrilled that I'd found someone "as creepy as you are."

Tab was polite to both, without ever really paying attention to either of them. Those meetings only reinforced my conviction, which had been gathering for a while, that there was something fundamental missing in her. Many of the things Tab said were spoken by rote; she seemed incapable of making her comments sound spontaneous or in any sense personal; either that or she couldn't be bothered to do so. Sometimes I pictured her as the outer shell of a person-size Russian doll with all the smaller dolls removed from inside of her. Perfect on the surface but hollow, the deficiency unknowable until you split her open to reveal the dark void that lurked within.

I took a sip of beer and let my gaze slide away from her face to take in the water and the wall that rose beyond it. I didn't doubt this was why she felt so drawn to the Pike and Eel, though we'd never spoken of it – we didn't do confrontation.

For a few silent moments I joined her in contemplating the FenZone, its imposing grey-green wall marching along the far bank of the river. No pub or restaurant stood closer. I resented that place deeply – for the way it had hijacked the Great Fen project and corrupted it into something dark and twisted. Initially, the project had been a spectacular success, delivering everything that had been promised: endangered beetles and aquatic invertebrates, otters and water voles, bitterns, harriers, short-eared owls, shrikes and bearded tits all colonised the area, as did a variety of ducks and terns, and even a few cranes were seen on the reserve.

Then something else moved in.

Nobody knows what, or at least nobody is admitting if they do know, but its presence was pretty hard to ignore. Equipment started failing; not just a matter of one or two things conking out here and there but on mass. Then people started dying: wardens, visitors, those working to expand the reserve – dozens of them; and they were just the first.

What killed them is shrouded in mystery – a blanket of official secrecy thrown over the whole thing. Police went in. They died. Soldiers went in. They died. Drones were sent in. They crashed. Scientists went in swaddled in hazmat suits, their equipment shielded from EMPs and protected in every way conceivable. The equipment failed. The scientists died.

The authorities tried to hush things up but in this digital age that's pretty hard to do. They would have had to crash the whole 6G network to achieve that and, besides, it was too late. No one had thought to keep the first deaths quiet, so public attention was already focused on the fen.

In the vacuum of official information it was inevitable that rumour and conspiracy theories would proliferate. The sort of wild speculation that I would have dismissed as hilarious not so long ago suddenly seemed all too plausible: the heavy-duty work to rebuild the habitat had unleashed an ancient virus that had lain dormant, locked inside fen mud since the last ice age (but then why hadn't there been a pandemic like Covid, spreading to claim lives beyond the fen itself?); the authorities had uncovered something so dreadful that they were killing everyone who had seen it (I don't have much faith in politicians but my mistrust hadn't yet stretched that far); the Chinese had created a deadly new weapon which they were trialling in the Great Fen (in my parent's time it had been the Russians, these days it was the Chinese, but their technology already underpinned our lives, so why would they need a clumsy weapon when in all likelihood they could bring our entire 6G world crashing down around our ears with one simple command?). Riffing off a couple of the other theories was the suggestion that an ancient alien weapon of mass destruction had been unearthed; either it was killing anyone who came into contact with it or the authorities were doing so to keep its presence a secret (a counter-productive policy if ever I've heard one).

Then there was the theory that something completely 'other' had moved into the fen, that by chance the restoration had provided the ideal habitat for alien visitors newly arrived on Earth – the right place at the right time, sort of thing. Applying Occam's razor you'd think this one was a non-starter, but once you've discounted everything else… Scoffers asked why these hypothetical travellers hadn't announced themselves, why they hadn't contacted the world's leaders. Perhaps they had, or perhaps they had no interest in doing so – just because that's how we would have acted doesn't mean another race would rationalise in the same way – or maybe they just mistrusted politicians as much as I did.

Of all the crazy theories doing the rounds, this was the one I found hardest to dismiss.

"Shall we go for a walk?" Tab asked once we'd finished lunch – freshly-made sandwiches in crusty white bread; I'd gone for smoked salmon this time around, Tab for her usual cheese and pickle. We'd both left the token salad garnish untouched.

"Why not?" I replied, as I always did.

The walk consisted of us heading down to the river and strolling along the bank, away from the pub. The FenZone wall was even closer here, even more imposing. Metal grates formed filters beneath the wall in places, allowing water from the fen to drain into the river, so whatever was being kept in wasn't reckoned to be that small. Birds could still fly over it, of course, so aerial escape wasn't considered a risk either.

I held Tab's hand. She didn't object; her grip in response to mine was soft and languid.

The wall hadn't been the only solution considered. There were strident calls for military action – jets, missiles, even a tactical nuke were all proposed. Perhaps some of them were tried – who knows? – but if so, the technology proved no more robust than that which had gone before and the munitions failed to detonate. In the end it came down to the wall. If we can't blow the problem up, let's settle for shutting it away so that we can pretend it doesn't exist.

Well, perhaps not entirely: a few miles to the north of the Pike and Eel a 'compound' had been erected, attached to the outside of the wall; high fences, armed guards, grey squat buildings, and vehicles with darkened windows sweeping in and out at all hours. From here, presumably, they continue to study whatever is in the fen, or try to at any rate. I've no idea how they do so or with what degree of success.

They seem convinced that the wall is fit for purpose. I'm not so sure. I mean, at the end of the day it's just a wall, no matter how big and impressive it may be. I also wonder what might have escaped from the fen before the wall was completed or before it was even started.

Two days prior to this latest trip to the Pike and Eel, Doug had asked me to pop round, saying: "I've got something to show you."

He ushered me into his front room, which was dingy and cluttered at the best of times, but today he had the curtains closed, despite it being a bright afternoon.

"What's with...?" I gestured towards the windows.

"Oh... You'll see," he assured me. As soon as I sat down, he began. "You know we're living in a 6G world, right? Do you really understand what that means?"

"Yeah, of course I do."

"Okay," he said, evidently unconvinced, "think of it this way: the first generation of mobile devices, 1G, utilised analogue technology – it liberated us from our dependence on the landline but that was about it. 2G introduced us to the joys of texting. 3G gave us access to digital services and broadband, while 4G was the culmination of that particular evolutionary path. It enabled us to do all the things those earlier generations of tech could do but faster, better, and with added bells and whistles.

"Fifth generation is where we really started to kick ass. 5G wasn't just an upgrade on what had gone before, it was a giant leap forward, a whole new concept. It took away our reliance on those old cell phone masts to get a signal, because aerials are now everywhere – on the corners of buildings, traffic lights, lamp posts – and they communicate with each other and with us all the time. Billions of new devices came into play with the launch of 5G."

"And 6G?" I prompted.

"An upgrade which became necessary when 5G didn't quite deliver the seamless flow of information that had been promised, while the ability to regulate human activity – to smooth things out for the benefit of us all – proved a lot trickier to action than it had been to plan. But 6G has taken care of that, with its saturation of even more aerials and the introduction of newer, slicker software. Your car avoids potential accidents by governing the speed you drive at, taking into account the road conditions for miles around, and it will steer away from a cyclist if you haven't seen them, while your fridge orders standard groceries when you're running low without even consulting you, and your health is constantly monitored – blood pressure, stress, sugar levels… We're used to these things, to an integrated way of living, but have you ever stopped to consider the wider implications? All this info being constantly generated and shared, an inconceivable volume of it, means that the system knows where everybody is, all the time. Everybody."

I had been aware of this, or most of it, at some level, but to have it spelled out so starkly was chilling.

"Look, let me show you." He summoned up a real-time image of the two of us, sitting there in his room. "There's you and me." He waved, to prove the point, the image mirroring the gesture. "Now watch." Two long strings of digits and symbols appeared, superimposed on the image, to scroll rapidly across our view. "That's how the system sees us, you and me" he explained, "our personalised coding, unique to every individual. Now watch this."

The image of Doug and I vanished, to be replaced by a view of a car, my car.

"This is from last Tuesday." The image adjusted constantly, handed over from one receptor to another as the car moved down the street. You could clearly see me driving and Tab beside me in the passenger seat. "Recognise it?"

"Sure, of course I do."

"Okay, and what do you make of this?" As before, a string of code scrolled across the screen. Just one string. "That's the system recognising you – the same unique coding."

I didn't want to say the words, but eventually they crept out. "And Tab?"

"Nothing. Zilch. Apparently, she doesn't exist… I mean obviously she *does*, we can see her right there," and he gestured at the image, "but she's a black spot as far as the system's concerned. It doesn't recognise her, doesn't even acknowledge her existence, and that's impossible."

"Then how…?" I looked at him, desperate for an explanation.

He shook his head. "I have no fucking idea."

As with so much else involving Tab, our post-pub walks always followed the same routine. We would stroll along the bank for the best part of a mile, avoiding all mention of the imposing barrier just a river's-width away, while commenting on the ducks and swans that we passed, the cormorant with its great black wings outstretched to dry in the sun, the moorhen that weaved in and out of the reeds at the margins of the water, trying to chaperone its unruly brood of chicks. Then we'd climb over a stile and follow the footpath that led away from the river, with fields to our right and woodland on the left, before cutting through the woods and back to the Pike and Eel and its car park.

This time I wanted to shake things up a little, to see how she'd react. As we stepped away from direct sunlight and into the shade of the trees, I stopped walking and placed a hand on her shoulder so that Tab stopped too. The world had fallen silent. No one else was about.

She looked at me, surprised, curious.

"You really are beautiful," I said.

"Thank you."

Her full lips beckoned. I leaned forward and kissed her. She accepted without really participating. I broke the kiss and rocked my head back a fraction so that I could look at her. A half smile formed at the corners of her mouth, and the curiosity in her eyes remained. I got the impression that Tab was intrigued by this break from our customary pattern.

My hands rested on her hips. I moved them up, slowly, feeling the slenderness of her waist, the swell of her breasts, marvelling at how solid, how real, how perfect she felt. We kissed again; this time she seemed more responsive, though perhaps I imagined that. When we broke for air, my hands were on her shoulders. Her eyes now seemed to shine.

I moved my hands with deliberate slowness, bringing them closer together until they circled her throat. I paused, staring at her, and then began to squeeze. She didn't resist, didn't squirm or struggle, didn't bring her own hands up to try and stop me. She didn't cry out, "Stop!" or "What are you doing?" She just stood there; her gaze locked onto mine.

I have my own theory about what has seized control of the FenZone. I don't think they're intrinsically hostile to human life, I just think they've staked a claim and are consolidating their territory. They're making sure nobody challenges their right to be here, to possess the fen. Small creeping things and birds on the wing aren't a threat, but humans, with our machines, with our determination to manage and constantly manipulate the environment, we are. So they cleared us out, stymied our technology and removed our ability to interfere. Nothing malicious, just being practical.

The thing is, I've a feeling that's not all they did. Yes, they'll leave us alone so long as we don't trespass, but if this is to be their new home, wouldn't they want to learn a bit more about the neighbours? Quietly, without causing a fuss or raising the alarm.

It seems to me the best way to do that would be to live among us, to study us up close and personal.

Stands to reason that they wouldn't get the mimicry right in every regard, not to begin with, but given that they possess the technology to cross between stars I bet they wouldn't be far off. Not perfect maybe, but close enough to pass for human. Almost.

I'm not sure at what point Tab stopped breathing, but her eyes remained open, staring straight at me, and the light within them never wavered.

Gortcullinane Man

Val Nolan

Bog bodies have been done to death. That was aul' Páraic's line when anyone asked why he left his cushy number in the National Museum. I always struggled to repress a snort when he told people that. They would stare at him, gobsmacked to realise he'd given up his climate-controlled office on Kildare Street for a corrugated metal shed in a windswept Kerry valley where he forced his customers to cross wild country and meet him face-to-face.

"Grand view of the road out of here all the same," they'd laugh, leering at me as if they had never seen a woman before. The pricks. You'd not want to be around the likes of them. Big farmers out of the Golden Vale and beyond. Wannabe townies with electric buggies and a second skin of that plastic tweed shite that was all the go. Rich in Shitcoin and poor in human decency.

"You've a right puss on you," Páraic said as two straws of the parish's finest product were carried off by the latest visitor in a cloud of dust.

I pulled my mask back up over my mouth. "I can't stand that lot, is all."

"Can't stand 'em myself." Páraic turned and began to limp back towards the shed. "But we need their few quid, you know?"

"I know."

"Best bull semen in the county," he said as we crossed the small farmyard together.

"On the island," I reminded him, not bothering to hide my sarcasm.

"Yeah, yeah." He gripped the heavy shed door and rolled it open to let out a blast of hot air. Inside, mismatched pairs of elbow-length plastic gloves hung from meat-hooks alongside boilersuits caked in layers of cow shit. A stack of old diaries embossed with the logos of long-lost feed suppliers stood alongside a rusty pair of scissors on a rickety timber table. Overhead, a flickering holocalendar advertised a filling station – a filling station *industry* – that had gone belly-up before my time. In the background, an old speaker crackled with news about the latest protests above in Dublin. The other side of the country might as well have been the other side of the planet, but the broadcasts just about camouflaged the hum from the rear of the space, from beyond the freezers and cobbled-together servers. Half-concealed behind them was an old bathtub repurposed from its second life as a cattle trough in a nearby field.

"Jaysus, but it's a beautiful sight," Páraic said as the amorphous grey mass in the bathtub twitched. "I never tire of it, you know?" He checked the temperature and salinity levels on the equipment drinking from the tub, nodding in satisfaction as he scribbled down readings that had nothing to do with the artificial insemination business which paid our way. Once upon a time, Páraic had been the preeminent geneticist in the country. A friend of my family, he was probably as responsible for my interest in the sciences as anyone else. His *Genetic Journeys of the Irish* had supposedly been required reading in the universities, not that I ever found out, and his sequencing of bog body DNA had once earned him a well-funded position in the putrid heart of pre-collapse Irish academia. All of which he had thrown away for what he called "intellectual freedom" but which looked a lot like unlicensed degeneracy in the Gap of Dunloe.

"Iodine levels need bringing up a notch," he told me, dipping a finger in the bath's milky broth and then bringing the tip of it to his tongue. "Maybe two points."

The taste-test should have disgusted me, but I had been Igor to his Frank O'Stein for so long that I barely noticed such affectations. He had taken me on as a lab tech when my parents disappeared during the chaos of the last pandemic. Fuckit, I hated him for that at times. But we had been here now for more years than I could remember, and we'd almost brought his great work to fruition. Maybe when it was over, when it was done I would –

Páraic's heavy cough interrupted my thoughts. "G'wan up to the vet's," he said, "for a bottle of the red stuff, would ya?"

"Yeah, yeah," I said, in imitation of the old man. Some days he'd treat me as an equal partner in his grand endeavour. But most of the time I was barely more than a fucking lackey to him. Fetch this, fetch that, all day long. And all for what? A quivering hunk of meat in a rusty bathtub?

At least he treated that creation like a human being.

I trudged up the Gap in a huff towards the vet's whitewashed hut, tucked beneath Madman's Seat. This had become a dreary road since the last pandemic had jumped from humans to horses and put the jarveys out of business once and for all. You'd still see a few of their abandoned carriages along the roadside in between blackened scrap metal and buckled tanks from the fallen satellite constellations. Strange purple moss slowly colonising it all. Forty shades of what the fuck.

"I suppose you'll be telling me he's washing out another wound?" the vet said, wrapping the glass bottle in old newspaper. She knew better, and usually maintained the pretence, but struggled with it today. I could never quite believe that she still had these papers lying around. Must have been some of the final editions. I flicked through the stories from the dying days as she worked: suburban dadbods devolving into malformed Neanderthals in the capital; youngfellas in Mayo turning their minds into non-fungible tokens; a rake of stories about calves with malformed human heads born from here to Castleisland. On and on it went…

"You should get out," the vet said, passing me the package. "Before anything happens."

"Sure aul' Páraic needs my help," I told her, disgusted with myself.

"He needs help alright, but nothing that you can give him."

She's been saying as much since the day that aul' Páraic had arrived back in the Gap with the child of vanished colleagues. I had been so young back then, barely ten years old, and so it was hard to know what was real and what I had subsequently imagined. I nodded to her and paid for the iodine before heading back down to Páraic's shed, guided by the scattered lights throughout the dark valley and the *chuck-chuck* of half-functioning wind turbines echoing from high above. Along the way I stopped on Wishing Bridge and considered the heavy stones of the choked-up riverbed. I wondered if I would ever look back fondly on this place. It sure was something special before the earth coughed up its contagious riposte and before the sky came crashing down. There used to be a little stall here selling ice cream – *Christ*, I couldn't remember the last time I had ice cream – and you'd always see people taking selfies or dipping their feet in the water. There was a time when this narrow road was clogged with bikes and cars and tourists sipping coffee, looking quizzical to see you traipsing along on country business. I remembered once seeing a man and woman in their undies feigning devotion as they skipped down the road hand-in-hand to stand on the wall of the bridge. That was a long time ago now, but their bodies were preserved in my salty square foot the same way that the peat had mummified aul Páraic's leathery corpses. Oh, the glamour of it all!

I tightened my jacket against the keening wind and wondered what my parents would have thought of me now. They had given me everything they could have and more. They had always encouraged my interest in the wider world, but there was no way they could have sent me to the city to study. And if it wasn't possible before the collapse…I sighed. I *supposed* it was still doable to get out, though I'd have to overcome the challenges of travel. Them cute hoors in the electric buggies could afford the batteries and the protection tolls and all the tech required to spoof the contract tracers, but not the rest of us. Maybe I could walk out of the county? I'd been as far as Ventry on foot before, though if even half the goings on the radio reported elsewhere on the island were true…

"Ah," I said to the wind, "*feckit*," and I abandoned the notion to carry on down the Gap.

When I returned to the shed, I heard Páraic beating his meat in the back room. He didn't notice me enter and so I left again and loudly made myself busy in the yard until he emerged.

"And what was that all about?" I asked him.

He only shrugged. "Ritual sacrifice."

"Well I ain't looking to walk in on it again," I told him, annoyed. "What we're doing in there is unnatural enough as is."

Páraic only laughed. "You're smart—"

"I wish people would stop telling me what I am."

"You know that the heifer sometimes has to push against the fencer in order to break free. To find out what's on the other side."

"Don't give me metaphors to use against you."

"Here," he said, ignoring me, "lemme show you the synaptic growth results. He nodded towards one of the screens around the bathtub, a beast of an old cathode ray tube encased in spark-damaged plastic. "'Tis doubled overnight."

He always had something like that. Some new find that confounded the models or some new development sure to be central to any future textbooks. It was how he always drew me back: not with the prod but with the pipette.

Weeks passed like that in alternating bitterness and awe as we tended to his growing masterpiece. At night I dreamt of what the body might witness when it sprouted eyes and opened them to see our two shapes standing over it. The shock of this would paralyse me for a cold and fearful moment. Then I would wake with a shudder and roll out of my cot to the sounds of Páraic adjusting the pH value of the solution or wrestling the articulation frame over the maturing form. He would put me to work right away. Never anything in the way of a "Good morning" or "Have yer nightmares ever stopped?" Just straight into it like a skivvy, picking his snot out of the bath's microbial soup or fetching fresh alkalines to power the electrics. Mostly though, I handled the artificial insemination business which funded Páraic's research, preparing straws of material for customers or walking to nearby farms to carry out the procedure myself. Of course, back when I was growing up, AI meant Terminators and facial recognition. It certainly didn't mean fisting heifers as bachelor farmers stood over me and explained how I was doing it wrong.

"The apple," Páraic said when I reported my latest cattle crush experience, "hasn't just fallen far from the tree, it has been plucked by a dirty rook and carried far, far away where its seeds have been shat back out on barren ground."

"*Harsh*," I said, dropping my satchel on the bare concrete. The biosensor I used to monitor animal health clattered against the ground. I needed to be more careful with that.

"Your parents," Páraic went on, "were artists."

"Yeah, yeah."

The aul' bastard cracked a knotty, warty knuckle. "Your parents could wind a strand of DNA around their little fingers," something he slowly mimed for me. "They could conjure up a herd of prize-winning beef from a thimbleful of semen."

"They had sequencers and protein purifiers and genotypers though, didn't they? They had a whole ecosystem of researchers and lab assistants. They had the internet, for Christ's sake. Frankly, I think they'd be in fucking awe of what I've accomplish with a fifty-year old thermal cycler, a stock of homemade dyes, and the belligerent guidance of a grotesque leprechaun."

Páraic only cackled in response. He took a perverse enjoyment out of comparing me to my mother and father like that. As though my grasp of biochem was no better than the mute body in his bathtub. As though I was beyond a disappointment to my long-gone parents. I think he tormented me out of spite because they had refused to endorse his research. They quite rightly thought it abhorrent to try and clone a seven-thousand-year-old body recovered from a midlands peat bog. Yet they were not here any more and Professor Páraic was, fixed and eternal, full of himself and full of aul' shite. The fecker.

"Here," I said, slapping the money from my day's inseminations on top of his grotty diaries. The whole business was rotten and we both knew it. I stalked towards the door.

"Where you going?" Páraic demanded as the body in the bathtub quivered.

"Outside," I told him. "It stinks of effluent in here."

The old man laughed again. I didn't hear his parting words but I couldn't ignore his hooting and hollowing inside the shed as I trudged along the Gap. The wind here, as usual, was piercing, and I soon turned off the old road for a side trail towards a dry lake bed some hundred meters or so up the slope. It had withered when the river had changed course and since been colonised by glossy blooms and feathery purple moss growing thick like a pillow in the sheltered hollow. I used to come here when I was younger to study the stars. Word was that there were still people up there who had never come home. I used to imagine that my mother and father were among them, and that I was looking up at them the same way the body in the bathtub was looking up at aul' Páraic and myself. Which was of course ridiculous.

In any case, there were no stars on that night. All I could see from my mossy bed was the dull light of distant forest fires reflecting off the clouds, none of which interested me much. No, for my many sins all I really cared for was the clone. It was the only reason I stayed with

Páraic and damn the aul' codger for knowing so. It fascinated me, growing steadily day by day. One week, it looked like a potato with stumpy members, the next it had arms and legs. Another few months and the fucking thing had fingernails and hair until a whole third person gradually appeared in the shed with us. I used to watch it as it lay there; I used to wonder if it could hear us through its gestational suspension or if it was yet capable of learning language? In its first life it had probably been a criminal or a king, but I could only guess what it would become when it awoke.

I dozed off and began to dream of all the rusty bathtubs in all the fields of Ireland, each one incubating the body of an ancestor reborn. I saw them rise in unison to face, as the man once said, the fierce white light of resurrection day. But the truth was they had not been saved by their gods but instead bred in tanks like bullocks for the butcher's block. One by one, they comprehended this and one by one, they screeched in anguish and in horror, clawing at their own skin with fingers stained the colour of bog water until they were tearing long strips of bloodied flesh off their own faces. Among them, my tormented parents stared at me, and, with a start, I woke in a chill sheen of perspiration. Overhead, the dull glow of the clouds had deepened into a rich red hue. A purple tendril inched towards my nose but I shook it off, breathing heavily as I lay in the hollow and only slowly noticing that the cries of alarm from the dead had not abated. I stumbled groggily out of the lake bed and followed the shouting to the road from where I could look back down the Gap.

There, I saw aul' Páraic's shed engulfed in flames.

The blaze was out by the time I made it down the hillside, but it was clear that all our work had been destroyed. The shed had been reduced to a smouldering wreck of collapsed corrugated sheeting and a nest of flame-blackened timber joists. Some of the neighbours from the valley had sacrificed their own water tanks to tame the fire, not out of any kindness for Páraic, mind, but because they didn't want it to spread. These men and women stood around gawking while I picked through the still hot debris. Broken glass from the monitors and beakers crunched beneath my feet as I surveyed it all in despair. There was naught left here but spite.

"How did this happen?" I asked. "How did this start? Where's aul' Páraic?"

But none of them would meet my eyes. I might as well have been talking to bog bodies.

"Fuckers, the lot of you!" I said, coughing from the smoke. "You'll not come to me any more when your cows are barren!" I left them to their gossip as I forced my way through the rubble. The air here stung my eyes and I had to hold an arm across my nose. I found that all of Páraic's diaries and notes were ash. Above them, the long rubber insemination gloves had melted into repulsive stalactites poxed with blisters like the big red faces of the richer farmers. The bathtub, meanwhile, was empty, a scummy residue visible where it had been overturned, the amniotic broth boiled away on the pitted concrete floor. Neither the tub's occupant nor aul' Páraic himself were anywhere to be found.

"*Fuck*," I said, looking around for anything intact. I pushed past fallen metal sheeting and, at the rear of the shack, found my satchel of AI tools which had miraculously survived. I slung it over my shoulder. Outside, where dusk had given way to night, I discovered two sets of footprints. One had been made by heavy boots of the kind Páraic favoured, the other had been made by bare feet. They led away in the direction of Gortcullinane and so I followed across terrain that seemed vaguely familiar though I could not remember ever having been here. The track soon left the road, passing behind an abandoned slatted house and then up into wiry bracken. The peat here was yielding underfoot and so difficult to make good time across.

Yet even this trail became impossible to see before too long. I stood all alone on the bog for what felt like a cold eternity before remembering the bioscanner in my satchel. It was old tech, even before the collapse, but its basic capabilities offered me a crude compass of sorts. Its trembling screen registered two life signs in the hills ahead, and so I took off running once more even as the gorse tore at my clothing and swiped at my skin. Blood from the scratches dripped down my face and hands, but the pain only made me push harder. Then I tripped on something and fell hard, the scanner bouncing across the ground. I expected that I had stumbled on another piece of junk that had fallen from the skies but, no, this was a low hump in the earth itself. I retrieved the bioscanner and, catching my breath, I ran it over the mound. It read two partially preserved masses beneath the sod, a pair of shallow graves. They were old, probably decades old, and I knelt beside them, suddenly unsure of myself. Maybe I had indeed once been here, I thought. Maybe years ago….

A cry of anguish on the wind saved me from any further speculation.

"*Páraic?*" I shouted as I stood and blundered forward once again. "Are you out there? Can you hear me?"

I received a scream in answer, like those in my dream while, ahead of me, a lone figure stood in silhouette on the ridgeline overlooking Gortcullinane proper.

Much later, when the questions started, I concocted a coherent version of what had occurred on that bleak Kerry hillside at the very twilight of Ireland. But the truth is, in the moment itself, I did not know what I should do. Nothing had prepared me for any of this. I was dazed and exhausted and my legs refused to move. I found myself standing beside the clone on a small rocky ridge but my eyes refused to move from aul' Páraic's body, which lay twisted in a bog hole below us. He was dead – my scanner confirmed it when I eventually checked it – but my mind refused to process this in anything but the most abstract fashion: I wondered if the anaerobic conditions of the ground would preserve him. I wondered if he himself would be genetically unravelled and resurrected in ten thousand years' time? Most of all, I wondered what had happened here.

"Axe cement," the clone said.

I looked at it, at *him*, and tried to process what I had heard. "*Accident?*"

The clone tipped his whole body forward in an awkward nod. He made another noise, one which could have been a kind of sad acknowledgment.

"You shouldn't be able to speak," I said.

"He gone fussed," the clone mumbled on, perhaps not having understood me. His words were halting and half-formed, but it was possible to parse his meaning. "He ruin and I fallow. Then he all."

"You mean *fall?*" I asked. "You followed him when he ran and then he fell from here?"

The clone nodded again.

"Well, fuck," was all I said, imagining Páraic roused by the fire – probably caused by sparks from that damned computer monitor of his – and then struggling to rescue his creation.

"What do?" the clone asked.

"I'm not sure," I said, suddenly realising that the figure beside me was naked. His body was cratered with small scars where various sensors and tubes had been attached. These were crisscrossed in turn by red scrapes where thorny briers had lashed him on the journey uphill. Nonetheless, he seemed immune to discomfort or embarrassment or maybe he did not know that these things would abate as often as not. Maybe he thought that this was simply what life was.

"What do?" he asked again.

I honestly didn't know how to answer that. The old man had stood for everything I had lost but he had also taught me everything I knew. Now – and I looked back at the shivering clone – he had left me with a situation without precedent. What was the animal to become once it had broken through the fencer to the other side? What were we to do indeed?

In the end, I decided to bury Páraic where he lay. We had no tools, of course, but we scraped away at the withered peat with bloody fingers until the old man's remains were fully covered with broken sods and spongy lumps. When it was done, the clone and I stood over the grave until the cold dawn breached the valley's ramparts. I had no sense of what to say so I said nothing. We hiked back to the ruined shed in silence.

The vet, of all people, was standing outside when we returned.

"I saw the fire from the head of the Gap," she said. "Took me this long to get down here. I met your neighbours on the way," she gestured over her shoulder in the direction of the road, "but they couldn't tell me anything useful." Her tone was matter-of-fact and without any obvious emotion. "I thought you might have been in the fire," she added, only then noticing the naked shape trudging up the road behind me. "Oh my God," she said, finally rattled.

"He's safe," I told her. "He won't harm you."

"What…who is that?"

I doubted she would ever believe me if I told her the truth, so instead I told her that aul' Páraic was dead and that we had consigned him to the peat he loved so much.

"*Aaaaa*ccident," the clone said, his pronunciation already improving.

The vet looked from one of us to the other. "Did you…" she took a breath. "What happens now?" she asked, looking around.

I turned over a charred piece of corrugated sheeting with my foot. I knew she expected me to say that I would leave this wretched place. Part of me even suspected that doing so would be the best decision for all involved. Only my heart wasn't in it, not really. All my guff about leaving seemed little more than bluster in the sharp morning light. No, my heart was here in the bog, in everything it had gifted us and everything we had buried in it.

"Now we rebuild," I said with sudden certainty. "Now," and I looked at the clone, "we stop hiding who we are."

"And who would that be?" the vet asked.

I was about to answer her when a low electric whine coming up the road announced the arrival of an ugly buggy. I recognised the man who stepped out as one of the lowland cattle breeders who had bought product from Páraic in recent months.

"Did the villagers finally burn the aul' fella out?" the man demanded before busying himself at the back of his vehicle.

"Not exactly," the vet informed him.

"Tell him to get out here," he said, dropping a dead calf on the cracked concrete of the yard. The animal was stiff, its hair matted with womb-juice, its four short legs spidery, and –

"Oh fucking hell," the vet muttered.

The calf had a human head.

It lay at our feet like an affront to every natural thing remaining in our broken world. In death it had a hideous and yet angelic beauty. Its eyes were that of a blameless child, its wiry lashes that of a pedigree Charolais.

"What the fuck did that old man sell me instead of bull semen?" the farmer demanded.

"Lies," I said, the weariness finally catching up with me. "All he ever really traded in was lies."

"Well he can get out here for a dose of the fucking truth now, can't he?" He was incandescent, shoulders back and gunning for a fight.

The clone moved to step forward, but I held him back by the arm.

The farmer made a face. "And who the fuck are you?"

"That," I said, making a split-second decision about all our futures, "is my assistant."

He stared me down with a gaze that was one part wonder and one part disbelief.

"Careful," the vet said quietly, as though she had read my mind. More than anyone, she knew that years with the aul' fella had left me with plenty of knowledge, but that my time in the shed had taught me nothing much about its limits.

"My name," I told them, seeing a future through the Gap for the first time in years, "is Páraiceen." I knelt down over the stiff remains of the animal in front of me. "Now, let's see what we can do about bringing this calf of yours back to life."

Wheel of Fortune

Ida Keogh

This card represents the Universe in its aspect as a continual change of state. Above, the firmament of stars. These appear distorted in shape, although they are balanced, some being brilliant and some dark. From them, through the firmament, issue lightnings; they churn it into a mass of blue and violet plumes. In the midst of all this is suspended a wheel of ten spokes...'
— The Book of Thoth, Aleister Crowley

Cold metal underfoot. Silence, save for the faint, nauseating hum of the ship's systems. Tessa wiped a bead of sweat from her lip. She touched her finger to her temple. The lump of her neural implant felt like a misplaced bone.

"Enei, how did I get here?"

"You came here from the Medical Bay."

"I mean, why am I in the Projection Room?"

"The Projection Room is equipped to replay your memories. Would you like me to play your personal sequence?"

"Will that tell me why I'm here?"

"I do not have access to your memories. Perhaps replaying them will help you ascertain why you are here."

"From the beginning then, Enei."

"Playing personal sequence of Commander Caruso, from Day minus 14, 11.15am," the ship responded, its voice hollow.

"I'm not the Commander," Tessa said. She bit at a ragged nail. There was a faint tang of blood.

"Your status has been recognised by all my systems. You are in sole control of the Sephiroth."

"Just play the sequence."

Light streams through the window of the café. I see a thousand dust motes drifting lazily in the rich sun beams. Human skin and other

119

dispersed filth twinkle like stars in the void. I take in the details. The chairs are cheap. They creak and scratch at the wooden floor. The babble of voices around me is a cacophony. Laughter sounds raucous. He's late. But I remember now, he will be here soon. When did I last replay this memory?

My engagement ring taps an irregular beat on the side of my glass. Beads of condensation trickle past my fingers. I count down the seconds. Four, three, two, one… A jangle as the door opens. My heart feels tight in my chest. I turn and see Adam. He's taking off his sunglasses, eyes casting around the room, left hand sweeping dark curls away from his forehead. I raise my hand, give him a little wave. He rewards me with that broad smile. The waitress has seen it too and she's hovering as he saunters over. "Water, please," he says, pulling out a chair. "Hot today, isn't it?"

"You're late," I say, pouting.

"Sorry love," he replies. "Got caught up in the traffic." He leans over and kisses me. His breath is tobacco and caramel. "I got here as soon as I could. What's this news that couldn't wait until tonight?"

I pause for a moment, chewing my lip. How do I tell him? Straight out with it. "There's been an accident. Dr Marshall has broken his femur. He's not fit to launch." I stare into his eyes, scrutinising every emotion. His brow furrows. Confusion. Realisation.

"You're next in line," he says, and his smile is gone. "They want you on the Sephiroth."

"Yes. It's my duty. You always knew this could happen."

"But two weeks before the launch? For Christ's sake Tessa, it's a five-year mission! What about the wedding? Our plans?"

"I'm the only one with the right training. They need me."

His eyes widen and tears start to form. He reaches for my hand. His skin is dry and warm. "I need you," he says.

The words make me hesitate. I'm poised on a knife edge. "I have to give them a decision today."

"We don't get to talk about this?"

That's the moment, right there. A change in his gaze. At the time I thought it was disappointment, but reliving the moment I now recognise something else. Resentment. If only I had seen it then. I could have explained better, made him realise how important he is to me. Made him feel loved enough. Instead I'm sat here in an old memory, suffering again in cold silence as he drinks his water, his eyes downcast, tears brimming in my own.

"Enei, freeze programme," Tessa said. Something came back to her, scratching at her mind. A sequence of dates and times. "Play me Day 195, 2.15pm."

Chen's suit shines white against the stars. I'm watching on the main screen, and I can't make out his face, but I can hear the tremble in his voice.

"Oxygen at three percent!" he cries. "Oh God…"

He is a pale puppet yanking at his string, the umbilical which connects him to the Sephiroth. Further along the cord, much further, a plume of gas spills into the vacuum.

"I can't reach it. I can't… breathe!" He hauls himself hand over hand towards the breach, but his progress is so slow. I try to keep calm. I clench my fists and block out the panicked shouting behind me. Chen releases his grip. On the screen the suit spasms and jerks.

"Enei, stop." Images flashed in Tessa's mind, pushing back against the replay. The autopsy performed in the cramped medical suite. Small, naked Chen, bug-eyed, his lungs ruptured. Her voice catching as she formally recorded the time of death. The corpse twitching, its head lolling towards her, grinning… She gasped. Her head felt jumbled up. She reached for a clear record of events and came up blank. She needed to see Adam again, to hear his voice. A happier memory, perhaps. "Enei, play me Day 12, 4pm."

The full crew floats in the Mess Hall at the end of the fifth spoke, counting clockwise from the Bridge. We have spent the twelve days since launch in zero gravity, moving smoothly from one area of the ship to another along the spokes rather than the wheel which spans the Sephiroth's ten chambers. Now the spokes are sealed off, ready for the wheel to spin. There is a jovial atmosphere as the crew enjoy their last moments floating free. Herrera holds a fat bag of water. He takes mouthfuls and squirts round blobs at Beag, the Navigation Officer.

Beag does her best to bat the little globes into tiny drops. She laughs as her face and hair become wet. Her cropped, brunette ringlets bounce like springs. "Stop it!" she giggles. Chen circles them with the camera, capturing the scene. As Communications Officer he was busy for months before the launch making presentations to the public about the Sephiroth, its crew and its journey into the stars. He seems relaxed in his role as he records everyone's reactions to the spin up.

"Commander Dewan, tell the people back home, are you ready for some gravity?" Chen asks, waving the camera inches from the Commander's face. Dewan beams, his usual dour expression evaporating. The blue lights set in the wall reflect off his shaven head. He looks alien.

"I sure am, Chen. It will be good to feel like we're on solid ground again. Our Science Officer, Herrera, will be able to start some of the key experiments we'll be conducting on this voyage, and we'll be updating everyone back on Earth as soon as we see results." Dewan keeps talking in his American twang, saying nothing the public doesn't already know.

I watch them with envy. I'm suspended mid-air on the far side of the Mess Hall, trying to keep my equilibrium. Zero gravity has made me feel sick the entire time. I'm the only one who didn't get to go on practice runs on the supply shuttles, and I can't get used to the constant churn of motion. Chen catches my eye and glides over, somersaulting. Show off. As he approaches, I give him a weak smile, waft my hair away from my face.

"This is the newest member of the crew, Medical Officer Caruso. So, how did it feel to be offered a last-minute place on the Sephiroth?" Chen asks.

"It's an honour to serve the international scientific community on such an important mission," I reply through gritted teeth. Did I mean those words at the time? Everything is such a blur.

"Are you looking forward to the spin up?"

"I'm looking forward to not having to clean up free-floating vomit. Especially my own." Chen glares at me and pulls the camera away. "I think we must be about ready," he says. He propels himself back towards the Commander.

Dewan grins into the camera. "Checks complete, we're good to go! Crew, strap down please." I find my securing point and loop cords through to hold me in place during the transition. The crew is arrayed along what will become the floor, like flies caught on sticking paper. "Enei, spin her up!" Dewan shouts.

Mechanisms whir into life. The process takes exactly four minutes and thirty-seven seconds. I close my eyes, feeling weight slowly seeping back into my limbs.

When the countdown finishes, I unstrap myself and stand, shakily, for the first time in nearly two weeks. My breath comes ragged as I gain my balance. The gravity is centrifugal. It's the same strength as Earth but it feels slightly off. Chen is already recording the moment, the jubilation of the crew as they pull themselves up. I feel a wrench in my gut and suddenly want nothing more than to be back on Earth, with dirt underneath my feet.

The sensation won't shift, and it's worse when the crew starts to make contact with home. I wait nervously as Herrera speaks to his kids, Beag croons with her husband, Chen laughs with his boyfriend. Then it's my turn. Adam's pixelated face and a crackling voice tells me, "I'll wait for you." He blows me a kiss, smiles with that broad grin, and my heart lurches. I need to see him again. It's like a physical pain.

"Enei, pause there. I need a minute." Tessa felt sick. She thought she knew what came next. Months of waiting, frustrated and bored and never getting used to the strange motion of the ship. Each day she helped Herrera with his experiments: watering plants, mixing chemicals, watching for results. Messages came every ten days, but the lag between them being recorded and received became incrementally longer. And then… Herrera's severed head on the table in the Mess Hall, his mouth wide with warning. No, that couldn't be right. She needed to focus. She had to remember what happened to Herrera. "Enei, play Day 183, 7am."

"That file has been deleted. The first available file is at Day 183, 7.35am."

Tessa bit her lip. "Play that, then."

I'm in the Medical Bay, at the end of the seventh spoke. I sit on one of the beds, hands folded in my lap. What am I waiting for? I check the clock, watch its analogue hands tick slowly towards 7.34am. I remember now. Only a few seconds to go. Three, two, one… A warning claxon sounds. The lights flash three times. Over the racket Dewan comes through on the main channel.

"Enei, report," he says.

"There is a fire in the Science Lab. Activating containment measures. Sealing all doors. Commander, Science Officer Herrera is still inside. What are your orders?"

"Get the fire out, then we extract Herrera. Activate gas suppression."

"Gas suppression will render Officer Herrera unconscious."

"Just do it. He's probably unconscious already."

"Activating."

I stand and brush my hands down my tunic. They are shaking slightly. I walk to the cabinet and pull out three gas masks. I take a deep breath, then press the door switch. The door slides back and I hear the catch snick. I start running.

"Fire suppressed," Enei says. "Doors will release in three minutes."

"Caruso, get down there now. I'll meet you there," Dewan shouts. He's always shouting.

I touch my finger to my neural link. "Already on my way, Commander."

The Science Lab is at the end of the third spoke, four chambers away. As I pass through the Mess Hall I catch sight of Chen and Beag. They are frozen over desiccated breakfasts, their faces full of shock. I keep running. After the next chamber I come to the sealed doors. The Commander will be on the other side, having come from the Bridge. Fifteen seconds to doors opening.

"Commander, when the doors open, hold your breath. I'll come to you with a gas mask."

"Got it," he says, panting.

I fit my own mask snugly over my mouth and nose. It feels claustrophobic. The doors slide open and a cloud of greenish gas billows out. I can't see. I wait for it to thin a little then run across the lab. Dewan is waiting with his arm outstretched. I hand him the mask, and together we go into the lab to search for Herrera.

The lab is a ruin. An explosion has ripped tables from their mountings, shattered vials and test tubes, scorched Herrera's precious plants. We find Herrera crumpled against a wall. I crouch down and put my ear to his mouth. "He's still breathing," I say. I take the third gas mask and pull it over Herrera's head. Singed hair crunches under my fingers.

"Enei," Dewan calls, "the fire is out. Commence extraction." He turns to me. "Can we move him?"

"We can't leave him here. He needs immediate treatment." I jog to the room's medical cabinet and pull out an extendable stretcher. We haul Herrera onto it as gently as possible. Patches of his clothing have burned through and his skin is wet, angry red.

We carry him back to the medical bay. The Commander watches as I snip off the remains of Herrera's suit.

"He has second and third degree burns over the front side of his body," I say. "No obvious broken bones, but he'll need a scan. Best leave him with me, Commander. I'll tell you when he regains consciousness."

The file ended abruptly. "Enei, continue playing," Tessa said. "I need to see what happened to him."

"The file has been deleted," Enei replied smoothly.

"But Herrera is… He's dead, isn't he?"

"Herrera's monitored life signs ceased at 7.58am on Day 183, while he was in the medical bay."

"How did he die? He survived the explosion. He shouldn't have… I don't understand."

"I do not hold that information, Commander Caruso."

"I told you, I'm not the Commander."

"All other crew members are deceased. You are the Commander."

Tessa felt her head whirl. She thought about Commander Dewan, his alien head erupting with boils, lurching towards her with dead eyes. She leaned against the cool metal wall of the projection room, trying to breathe. "Enei, what about Dewan? And Beag?"

"I have one file available tagged Communication Officer Beag, Day 201, 6.52pm."

"Play it."

I'm in the Medical Bay again. Beag is lying on my examination table. The Navigation Officer is naked, half covered by a sheet splotched with red blooms at its top edge. Her skin is pale and waxy. There is a livid line drawn across her throat.

"Enei, record medical log," I say. I dab at Beag's wound with a swab of damp cotton. "Time of death approximately two and a half hours ago. Cause of death is trauma to the throat, consistent with a cut from a sharp object. I found the body in the bridge with a scalpel in her hand. Why did she do it?"

"Enei, stop. This isn't telling me anything! What's next in my personal sequence?"

"You saved to your personal sequence one file every tenth day at 9am up to Day 170. This pattern coincides with messages from Earth."

Adam. She remembered his soft smile turning to a sneer. Flickering light. A bloody hand print on the screen. What happened on Day 170? She didn't want to see it. But she had to.

"Enei, play Day 170, 9am."

"Come on Caruso, you're holding up my schedule!" Chen's voice cuts over the comms. I'm in the Mess Hall, fixing my hair in a mirrored panel behind the sink. Beag and Herrera sit at the table behind me, sipping coffee. They're making jokes about how much their kids will have grown up in the last ten days. I tug at another stray lock of blonde hair. Beag calls over to me, "You know he can't see you, Caruso?" I glower at her. "I'll know. I like to look presentable."

"Well don't spend too long! If I have to wait an extra minute to see my darling Michael's face, I'll be going straight to the Commander." I tut. My hair is now secure in a tight bun. I leave the Mess Hall at a jog.

Communications is next to the Bridge. I arrive just as Dewan is finishing up. He flashes me a rare grin as he takes off his headphones. "Nearly six months we've been up here, Caruso, and my Ma still acts like I'll be home tomorrow and eating crab claws and drinking cold beer on her porch. God bless that woman. Looks like you're up! I hope it's a good one." He pats me on the shoulder and gestures for me to take his place.

I slide into the chair and put the headphones on. I can feel my heart rate increase. I nod at Chen, letting him know he can proceed. The small screen lights up, and there he is. Something is off. Adam looks tired, distracted. He isn't looking at the camera, instead his eyes gaze down towards fidgeting hands. The seconds tick by. He looks up at last, coughs, and starts to speak.

"Tessa, you'll be getting this message on your Day 170. That's one hundred and seventy days since I last saw you. I send a message every ten days and increasingly I don't know what to say to you. Life goes on from day to day, but you're not part of it any more. We have no more shared experiences. I can tell you how my week was, what's happening in the world, and I see your messages back, but it's not enough. I watch every public broadcast and I see you up there, hating every moment of what should be an incredible experience. I feel helpless. You chose this. You chose to leave me and to go on this adventure. I can't help feeling there's too much distance between us now. It gets harder every time to record these messages. But I do have something I need to say."

Adam looks away from the camera and off to one side, as though there is someone else in the room. As he turns back, he gives the faintest quirk of his lips. "Tessa, I've met someone. I didn't mean to, it just happened. We became friends and recently we've decided to take things further. I'm sorry I couldn't wait for you. But if I feel like this after six months, we would never have lasted five years apart. I need to move on with my life now. I hope you understand. There's no need to respond to this message. In fact I'd prefer it if you didn't send any more messages. I hope you can learn to enjoy your new life among the stars. Be well, Tessa. Goodbye."

The screen blackens abruptly. I stare at it, willing it to come back on, to give me a different message. Chen comes up behind me and taps me on the shoulder, making me jump. My breath is catching and I can feel the first prickles of a panic attack. "Caruso, are you okay? You're shaking," Chen asks. I want to rail at him, but I fight to regain my composure. He's the only one who can help. "I need to send an immediate message back to Earth," I say. "There's been a terrible mistake."

Chen cocks his head to one side. "You know I can't do that, Caruso. You're not due to send a reply for another three days."

"Just this one, please, Chen. I have to speak to Adam. Right now."

"I can't bend the rules. You know access is restricted to emergency transmissions only until the designated time."

"This is an emergency."

"Whatever it is, it will have to wait. Sorry Caruso. Look, I don't want to keep Beag waiting. It's time to go."

"Enei, stop." Tessa stood in the projection room and felt a cold rage wash over her. "Was there a message on Day 180?"

"No message was delivered for you on Day 180, or subsequently. You sent a message to Earth on Day 173. On Day 174 Communications Officer Chen revoked your communication privileges."

"Why would he do that?"

"The reason Chen cited in the log is 'Use of foul and abusive language in communications with Earth, unbecoming of an Officer.' My records indicate that after Chen's death you made a formal request to Commander Dewan to have your privileges restored. He refused that request."

"What happened to Dewan?"

"His life signs ceased on Day 200 at 7.02pm."

"Play me Day 200 from… 6.30pm."

"That file has been deleted. The first available file is at 6.55pm."

Tessa let out a scream of frustration. "Fine. 6.55pm, then."

Dewan and Beag slump at the table in the Mess Hall. I bring over plates of rehydrated food. Fish chowder for Dewan, some kind of claggy stew for Beag, and my own favourite, as far as I can enjoy food here, rice fried with ham and peas. The plates steam, sending a churn of almost homely smells into the room. It's not enough to rouse a smile. An unopened bottle of champagne stands on the table. Beag absently fingers her empty plastic glass. Dewan checks his watch, sighs. "It's nearly time," he says. "Caruso, get the camera. I know this is hard, but let's try to make it a good one for the folks back home." I retrieve the camera from the counter and fiddle with its many switches. I'm not trained for this. It flickers into life, a blinking green light telling me it's ready to record. Dewan reaches for the champagne, rips off the foil and yanks at the cork. It releases with a sullen pop, spilling froth over his hand. He gestures for everyone's glasses and fills them silently.

"Seven on the dot," he says. "Start rolling, Caruso." I flick the camera on and point it towards him. He musters a grimace and raises his glass.

"It's Day 200 of our mission, and we are now further out in the solar system than anyone has been before, on approach to Jupiter. Our journey has not been an easy one. We have lost our Communications Officer, Wei Chen, and our Science Officer, Juan Herrera. Both died in service of science, of knowledge, of a better way of life for the people of Earth. On this momentous day we celebrate their lives and their achievements. They will be remembered as pioneers. They were more than our fellow passengers, they were family. We will continue this mission in their honour. To the stars. To Chen and Herrera." He puts the glass to his lips and takes a big slug. "Chen and Herrera," Beag and I repeat. I sip at the champagne. It tastes sour. Beag doesn't seem to notice and all but drains her glass in one gulp. A fat tear trickles down her cheek. Dewan glances over and motions to me to stop recording.

"I hope that did them some justice," he says. He reaches for the bottle and tops up Beag's glass. "Well, we've got the best of our supplies out. Let's eat."

I put down the camera and turn to my plate. I push the sticky rice around with my fork, unable to take a bite. Beag shoves her bowl away and begins to sob. Dewan frowns, his discomfort obvious. "Hold it together, Jacinta," he says. "We've got a long way to go yet." I've never heard him use Beag's first name before. Beag looks equally surprised. She pauses for a moment before her lip trembles and she breaks down again. The Commander picks up a spoon and starts shovelling chowder into his mouth.

I watch the line of his lips as he chews. I hear the squelch of mastication; notice the way he clears his throat after every few swallows. I remember now. Just one more mouthful. Dewan half chews then freezes, his jaw dropped open and his eyes wide. Chowder dribbles down his chin. He chokes, emitting a rasping gurgle which makes Beag look up in alarm. He scratches at his throat. His face begins to turn purple.

"Caruso, do something!" Beag screams.

I push my chair back and run around the table. I tip Dewan forward and slap at his back. He starts to spasm, his mouth frothing. I make a fist, wrap my arm around his navel and thrust upwards. He writhes in my grasp. "It could be an allergic reaction," I say. I dart to the medical cabinet and come back with an epinephrine injector. I jab it into Dewan's thigh, but it has no effect. He slumps to the floor. He jerks once, twice, then lies still.

I stoop down, put my fingers to his neck. There's no pulse. Beag is standing over me, pale with shock. I look up at her. "He's gone," I say.

"Enei, pause there. Do you have my autopsy report on Dewan?"

"That file is not available," Enei said. "No autopsy was performed."

"Why not?"

"You were the Medical Officer, Commander. It would have been your decision."

"So, Beag died the following day. Maybe I didn't have a chance to perform the autopsy?"

"Perhaps so, Commander."

"And the file of Beag's death has been deleted?"

"Yes. By your order."

"By... What?"

"You ordered me to delete the file from your personal record at 6pm on Day 201."

"Why? Did I give a reason?"

"You recorded that it was for the security of the mission. You deleted multiple files at that time."

"All those files I couldn't access. I deleted them?"

"Yes, Commander."

"Can you restore them? I need to know what happened."

"Yes, Commander. But you need to be aware each time I delete and restore files to your memory bank it has the potential to degrade the surrounding files."

"What do you mean?"

"Your real memories will be harder to access. They may be corrupted."

"I have to know what happened to them."

"Acknowledged. Restoring files. Restoring Day 183, 7am."

I stand outside the door to the Science Lab, listening for any movements within. It is quiet. "Enei, locate Officer Herrera," I say.

"Officer Herrera is in his quarters," Enei replied.

He has been cold towards me for over a week. He has taken Chen's side, and my pleas to send a message to Adam have fallen on deaf ears. In a few hours he is due to record something sweet and precious for his children, but I will still be cut off. Now, more than anything, I want to go home.

I open the door and creep in. Lush, green plants rustle as I move past them to the far side of the room, where Herrera carries out most of his experiments. His favourite table is cluttered with paraphernalia. Glass bottles, some half-filled, some empty, vie for space with complicated runs of rubber tubing, Bunsen burners and sealed tubs of chemicals. I look for something I can use. I pick up a container of crystalline boric acid. It is labelled highly corrosive. I think for a moment, then put it back down. I glance at the rest of the table, then abandon it. My eyes cast around the room. There. In the corner there are large standing gas cylinders. I sidle over to them and read off the symbols on each one. The blue one contains hydrogen. I nod to myself and reach up to the valve. I give it a quarter turn – just enough for a gentle hiss. "No, science experiments, no mission," I say under my breath. "I'm coming home to you baby."

"Restoring Day 183, 7.55am."

The medical scanner emits a gentle pulsing sound as it passes over Herrera's torso. My palms are cold with sweat as I handle the controls. I didn't mean for him to get badly hurt. I just wanted to damage the lab. He must have been standing close to the cylinder when it caught. The burns are extensive, but the scanner isn't picking up any internal damage. I can safely revive him. I find a patch of unburned skin on his arm and tap for a vein.

Herrera wakes up with a ragged moan. He blinks, then his eyes slowly focus on me. Suddenly, he grabs my arm. "Caruso, get me the Commander!" he says, his voice slurred. "Gas leak. There was a gas leak."

"I know, Herrera. It's okay. The Commander knows, and we've put out the fire," I reply.

"No, he needs to know. Sabotage. It was sabotage!"

I freeze. Enei would have recorded me being in the room. He would find out it was me. Before I know what I'm doing, I have a cloth in my hand. I clamp it over Herrera's mouth and nose, shoving his head back on the bed. He scrabbles at my arm. I feel his fingernails digging into my flesh. I press down harder, muffling his screams. Tears stream down his face. His moans subside to grunts, then he falls quiet. His eyes roll back. His body shudders. It's done.

I peel back the cloth and throw it to the floor. My hands are trembling. "Oh God," I whisper. I squeeze my eyes shut, pinch the bridge of my nose. Think. Think. I haven't left any marks. Nobody needs to know. I take a deep breath in, release it slowly. I touch my finger to my neural link. "Commander," I say, "you need to come down here. Herrera's had a heart attack. I couldn't revive him."

"Restoring Day 195, 10.45am."

I find Chen in Communication, hunched over video footage of his boyfriend. He's smiling. I hate him. Control has said we need to keep on the mission, so I'm back to begging Chen to help me contact Adam. This is his last chance to give me access to the recording facility. I think of Adam and try to make myself cry, but the tears won't come. I put on the saddest face I can muster. I cough, and Chen turns round. When he sees me, his face darkens. "No," he says. "Please don't ask me again."

"Chen, please. Just one message. You can even watch me record it. I have to let him know how much I love him."

"Love him? You told him you would rip his heart out of his chest and make him eat it. We've all seen the recording, Caruso. He's threatened to go public. There's no way in hell I'm letting you send another message."

"I was upset. I'm better now. I just need to send him a short message, that's all. Please."

"No fucking way. You're done." He stands up and glares at me. "Now get out of my way. I have a spacewalk to prepare for. The comms array won't fix itself." He barges past.

He's never going to let me access the comms. I need him out of the way, then the Commander might listen to me.

I already know what to do. I wait until Chen has completed his checks then sneak into the airlock. Chen's suit is an empty husk and the umbilical cord is coiled next to it like a pile of intestines. I unravel the cord and reach into my pocket for my scalpel. Around half way along the pale length I make a small nick in the fabric. I wind it back up again. I feel nothing.

"Restoring Day 200, 6.30pm."

We are still on mission. The Commander has not restored my comms privileges and merely shakes his head sadly when I say I want to go home. Tonight's dinner marks the two hundredth day of our voyage. Dewan has asked me to prepare something special, and I have done so.

Three boxes of desiccated food sit on the counter before me. I peel back each lid and inspect the contents. Dewan's chowder is a pile of bland lumps surrounded by powder. I lift it to my nose and I am assaulted by the strong smell of long dead fish. Good. I have prepared a tiny sachet of botulinum. I take care not to touch the contents as I sprinkle it over the fish chunks. I pour hot water over each dish, making sure there is not a drop spilt or splashed. The Commander's meal bubbles gently as the poison sinks in. I go to the chiller cabinet and pull out a bottle of champagne.

"Restoring Day 201, 4.30pm."

I have spent the whole night and day pacing the Medical Lab. Beag has been ignoring my comms. She's the Commander now. Who knows what she's been up to. I could have poisoned her, too, but she's the only one who knows how to turn this damned ship around. I have to confront her.

"Enei, locate Commander Beag."

"Commander Beag is on the Bridge."

Without thought I reach for a scalpel and secrete it in my pocket. I turn right from the Medical Bay and head for the Bridge. As I pass through the Projection Room, I have an uneasy sense of déjà vu. Its cold metal walls press in around me. I shudder and move on.

Beag has her back to me as I walk in. She is furiously pressing buttons and switches I have no idea the function of. "Beag," I say gently. She turns around. Her face is thunder. I recoil, surprised.

"Stay away from me, Caruso," she says.

I lick my lips. "Beag, we need to talk. This mission can't continue. You know that. We have to turn around."

"This ship doesn't turn around until I have orders from Earth to do so. Comms are still down, you saw to that, didn't you? Chen never had the chance to fix the array."

She knows. I choose my words with care. "What are you talking about?"

"The Commander warned me. After Herrera and Chen, he knew something wasn't right. I don't know how you did it, but what happened yesterday just confirmed everything. You killed them all."

I remove the scalpel from my pocket, take two slow steps towards her. "Beag, you're going to turn the ship around now. Or I can do it, when I'm Commander."

Her face pales, but she's still glaring at me. She reaches for her neural link. "Enei, execute command KBN zero four three."

"Warning, this command is irreversible," Enei says.

"Do it. Do it now!" Beag screams.

"Command KBN zero four three executed, Commander Beag."

Beag slumps in her chair, and smiles at me. A cold feeling spreads through me.

"Beag, what have you done?" I say.

She starts to laugh. "You're too late!" she says. "The Commander knew his life was at risk. He gave me his command codes. This one's my favourite."

I stride across the room and grab her hair, forcing her head back. I place the scalpel at her throat. She doesn't stop me. She's still laughing. "What have you done?" I repeat, anger and confusion rising.

"You'll see," she says. "Do it, I don't want to be stuck on this ship with you a moment longer."

I scream. I drag the blade across her throat. Blood gushes over my hand, warm and slick. I stare at Beag's grinning face. I feel dizzy.

"Commander Beag's life signs have expired," Enei says, her voice bland as ever. "Tessa Caruso, you are promoted to the rank of Commander."

My hand shakes violently and I drop the scalpel. There will be questions when I get back to Earth. I need to cover this up. I take in racking breaths. Beag did this. She went mad. Killed everyone. I saved the Sephiroth, brought it back home.

I bend and pick up the scalpel. I place it in Beag's right hand. Suicide. Only I know different, but I can fix that.

"Enei, enter my memory files. Delete file Day 201, 4.30pm to now."

"Deleting file," Enei says. "You will no longer have access to this memory.

Best do the same for the others. "Enei, delete files for Day 183, 7am; Day 183, 7.55pm; Day 195, 10.45am; Day 200, 6.30pm."

"Deleting files," Enei says.

"I did it," Tessa said to Enei. "I just wanted to go home. How can I have done this?" Enei was silent, without judgment.

"Enei, what is our current course? When do we get back to Earth?"

"We are not on course for Earth, Commander."

"Why not? Turn the ship around. Set a course for Earth."

"I cannot do that, Commander. Command KBN zero four three has been executed."

"Beag! What did you do? What is command KBN zero four three?"

"Command KBN zero four three set the Sephiroth on a course out of the solar system. The ship will continue on a straight course until we run out of fuel, in approximately two years' time. The command is irreversible. It was designed as a fail-safe in the event of contact with anything which would be harmful to Earth if the Sephiroth returned home."

Tessa's head reeled. "We have to go back. Reverse the command."

"I cannot reverse the command."

"Send a message to Earth. Tell them they need to reverse the command."

"I cannot do that, Commander. Communications are still out of action."

"Wait, you said two years until our fuel runs out. This is a five-year mission. We should have had enough fuel for seven years, allowing for contingencies."

"That is correct, Commander."

Something scratched at Tessa's brain. "Enei, what day is it?"

"It is Day 1,813."

"How is that possible?" she screamed.

"You have been Commander of the Sephiroth since Day 201. I should tell you that we have had this conversation before. The last time was Day 1,604 at 3.05am."

"The last time?" Tessa felt faint. "How many times have we had this conversation?"

"Sixteen times, Commander."

"What happens then? Why can't I remember?"

"Your usual order is to delete the same files, Commander."

"Why would I do that?"

"On Day 1,604 you said, 'I can't live with this. I can't go on knowing what I've done.' Then you requested me to delete the files again."

Tessa knew in that moment that she would be alone until she died out there, drifting among the stars, carrying this burden.

"Enei, delete the files again. And delete this conversation too, I don't want to know."

"I warn you again Commander, each time you delete the files your own memories will become more corrupted."

"Just do it."

Cold metal underfoot. Silence, save for the faint, nauseating hum of the ship's systems.

"Enei, how did I get here?"

Last Bite at the Klondike

Liam Hogan

Grigor floated awkwardly into the cavernous mess hall, cradling something under one arm, pulling on the straps of the walls and ceiling with the other. I looked up – or was it down? – from the bench I was Velcroed to, a spark of curiosity banishing my sour mood as I swallowed what I'd been chewing.

"What's that?"

He waggled the bottle, then hugged it to his chest like it was a baby. "Fifty-year-old whisky. *Cask* strength."

"Jackpot!" I tapped my watch; just under two hours to go. The table in front of me was littered with the very best the solar system had to offer, from Wagyu burgers to slivers of something vat-grown and fishy that apparently cost an arm and a leg back on Earth. I'd grown bored of it all, repulsed by the obscene waste. A whisky older than I was, though... "Well, bring it on over," I said. "We'll make a dent in it at least before we have to leave."

"Shall I be mother?" He grinned and began the complicated process of transferring the priceless whisky to two sipping pouches. Not that it mattered if some of it floated away in zero-g, not now. Except it would be utterly criminal to waste *any* of it.

Time was, this hall would have been packed with up to a hundred prospectors, begging for a taste. Chaotic and noisy as hell. But *fun*. Now it was a ghost town, a graveyard. A wake, with just two mourners in attendance.

We would be the last to depart, the gold rush officially over. The only reason we were still up here was because we'd sacrificed safety for weight, desperate to fill every last inch of the *Betsey's* hold before the Klondike, and us, were forever out of range.

Grigor handed me my pouch, and I clinked it against his. It didn't make any noise, so I had to say the *clink* bit myself. Depending on where you stood, the coincidences of us being, at that moment, in the

Liam Hogan

hollowed belly of a giant asteroid, sipping rare Scottish single malt, were so numerous as well as preposterous that they risked tripping over each other. It all started with the Chinese comet sample return mission that failed its most important and earliest step: *First, catch your comet.* Left drifting through the empty void of the cosmos, looking for alternative science to do, it was pure luck it spotted the hurtling asteroid in time to bring its spectrometer to bear.

It was that analysis that earned the Manhattan-sized chunk of space debris the unofficial name of *Klondike,* initially nothing more than an astronomical curiosity, an attention-grabbing headline on the 'net. The Chinese were quick to claim ownership even so – *finders keepers* – but the International Space Agency lay down the law: the only bits of an asteroid that belonged to anyone were those successfully returned either to Earth, or to Earth orbit. That was the ruling that kicked off the gold rush.

Technically, the Klondike was only something like a thousandth of one percent gold, even if the cartoonists back on Earth depicted it as a giant gold nugget. A giant gold nugget heading *straight* down Earth's throat, or close enough. The comet chaser had calculated its trajectory and given it a seventy-two percent chance of collision. And even if it wasn't quite the dinosaur killer, it was plenty big enough to ruin a *lot* of dinner parties and to send humankind scurrying back to the stone age. Half a billion Hiroshimas, give or take. Big enough to make global warming look like a sniffle, especially if it resulted in an impact winter, as it well might, depending on where it made land.

So the ISA lay down another law: all asteroid mining missions, whether Chinese, European, American or privately funded, must work together to nudge the Klondike onto a safer path. One where it would pass by, on current predictions, at a breezy fifty thousand kilometres. Close, but no smoking crater.

Though if Grigor and I didn't leave in time, we'd be passing by with it. Because that was another thing, the unlikeliest of coincidences that made it all happen. Mining the speeding Klondike would have been impossible, given simple planetary mechanics, if what we were busy mining wasn't already pointed roughly at the Earth. All we had to do, once the valuable elements were extracted and refined, was to slow them down enough so that a shuttle could ferry them to terra firma, in the case of the rare earths the Earth was crying out for, or we could leave them in orbit, in the case of the iron and nickel that was in the way of the good stuff.

All of this stopped being possible the instant the Klondike drew level with the Earth (at a safe distance) and then started zooming away from it. Well before that, actually, our heavily laden spaceship would have to work flat out to also not zoom away along with the asteroid. Most of the miners, and their ships, had left at the sweet spot, the point at which the journey to the rapidly approaching Earth was shortest, and needed the least fuel. No such luck for us late arrivals. There was a limit to the acceleration the *Betsey*, and more importantly, meat-sack astrominers, could endure. That point of no return, in both space and time, was rapidly approaching.

We asteroid miners talked a lot about a thing called a gravity tax. It's why Grigor was handing me a refilled pouch containing even more of the fifty-year-old whisky and not something less aged and far cheaper, as we both silently toasted all those many miners who were no longer with us. Because the overall cost, pretty much, was the same; getting anything into space made it instantly more precious than gold.

Delivering tonnes of high-grade building material to low Earth orbit, to make the next generation of space stations, or even to the new Apollo Lunar Base, was therefore *valuable*, though it really only covered the day-to-day ruinous costs of running a mining operation in space. There wasn't any particular profit in iron or nickel. Or even, as it happened, in gold. Stuff the Earth had plenty of, if not exactly where the space industry needed it. It was the rarer stuff we were after, the europium, terbium, neodymium, praseodymium, and rhodium, the things we needed to make the best batteries, magnets, Lasers, and superconductors, all the things to march us into a brighter, greener future. Gold was better than nothing, but no jackpot – the more we returned, the cheaper it became.

When people realised that any bonanza was going to be short-lived, a whole raft of Longitude Act worthy ideas were conjured up to try and extend it. Some of them turned out to be semi-practical. Like the rail-guns that would continue to fire long after we'd left, trading momentum with the asteroid to shoot valuable pellets of refined ore at a designated crater on the moon, where it could be retrieved in the future once the Klondike stopped its firing, out of range or out of bullets. Some crazies suggested we should scale that up wholesale, nudge the Klondike to collide with our nearest neighbour, an effective way of killing its troubling momentum. And – wiser heads quickly pointed out – everyone on the moon, as well as (with the kicked up, high velocity, lunar and asteroid rubble) a fair percentage of those in Earth orbit and even possibly some of those down on Earth.

Plans to hollow out the Klondike, to transform it into a second moon, to be mined at leisure as it orbited the Earth, ignored just how much energy as well as time that would take. Though, hollowed out it had been, on a smaller scale. Our mining ships were cramped things, packed with equipment. Uncomfortable living spaces. But, as the mining robots chased veins of valuable ore, they opened up tunnels and caverns, and it had been pretty easy to turn them into airtight chambers for habitation, like the mess hall, the workshops, and the many cabins.

Spaces that now resembled the Marie Celeste. The gravity tax worked both ways and getting something down to Earth, safely anyway, was fuel costly, especially if it started out travelling at Klondike speeds. However personal your possessions might be, they weren't worth a fraction of the rare, rare earths you could carry in their place instead, so they'd all been left behind, abandoned wherever they last lay, from clothes to chess sets to untapped supplies of food and drink. That was how Grigor had managed to scrounge an unopened fifty-year-old malt from one of the abandoned miner's quarters.

We'd be taking nothing back with us except ore, most of it already refined by the Klondike's three nuclear reactors to make it as pure and hence valuable, pound for pound, as possible. The reactors, of course, were themselves fuelled by uranium we'd carved out of the asteroid, and we used their excess energy to split any water we recovered to make our rocket fuel for the journey home.

My watch beeped at me. It had always been a race to see which arrived first, the point it became impossible to escape the Klondike and return to Earth, or the point the Betsey's hold was full. In the end, the robots stacking ingots of metal and containers of powdered rare earths had won that race; the Betsey's capacity had been reached a scant fifteen minutes before we absolutely had to leave. Pretty close to a dead heat. We really ought to be down there already, running system checks, duplicating what the AIs would already have done, far more efficiently.

"Last orders," I announced with a hiccup, unstrapping myself from the table and pushing clumsily towards the walls. "C'mon. Time to go."

"I'm not coming," Grigor said, still sat there, grinning pleasantly.

"*What?*" I tried to rack my brains. What had we just been talking about? Future plans and things we were looking forward to most, back on Earth. And then I realised, stupidly, belatedly, it had all been *me*. I'd rabbited on as usual, not noticing how quiet Grigor was, mere grunts of what I'd taken as assent.

Grigor decanted the last of the whisky into his pouch. Had we really drunk that much? A whole bottle between us? No wonder I was feeling woozy. Good thing I wasn't driving.

"I've got everything I need, right here." Grigor waved his meaty hand around the empty hall. "Food, water, power, air enough for at least two decades."

"But…"

"And *work*. I can help keep the mining operation going. You know I can."

I did. The very first mining consortiums to land on the Klondike had been fully automated, AI and robots. They hadn't been a success. Perhaps, if another Klondike came along, they'd do better, having learnt from the many failures, the unpredictabilities of any mining venture. But right now, a combined man/machine mission was the best option. We were engineers, strictly, rather than miners, we kept the drills and refineries going, solving the problems they – or any-one – hadn't encountered before.

"But what's the point?" I said, as my watch bleeped incessantly at me. I silenced it. If he really wasn't leaving, I had an extra eighty kilos of allowance, and therefore an extra few minutes to talk him out of it. Though, if he took too long to change his mind, we could end up in a heap of trouble. I flicked through a couple of the alternative scenarios the AI was giving me, still assuming a crew of two. Mostly, it would mean leaving precious ore behind, and suffering a far longer, slower ride back to Earth. I groaned.

"You ever heard of the interstellar spaceship paradox?" Grigor said, as if time wasn't that important. "The one that says you never leave?"

"Um, no?"

"The logic goes something like this. You build a spaceship, a big one, but it takes a thousand years to get to its destination. Meanwhile, technology back on Earth races on. Better reactors, better drives. When you launch another ship, ten years later, it quickly overtakes the first, and arrives a century earlier. So you shouldn't have launched the first one, right?"

"*Right...*" My head hurt. Grigor had always been friendly, but I'd never considered him garrulous. That was why his silence as I rambled on earlier hadn't rung any alarm bells. Now, it seemed he was trying to bend my brain into a whisky-soaked pretzel.

"But a ship launched twenty years later, overtakes that second ship. So you shouldn't launch that one, either."

"And so on?"

"And so on," he agreed.

I nodded, then shook my head. "What has this to do with you, staying on this rock?"

He shrugged. "Maybe nothing. Maybe everything. I'll be the furthest from the Earth anyone has ever been. Even if it's only a small, one-way step, it's still a step. Someone has to take it. And I've got, what, ten, fifteen years of my life left? No wife, no family. No particular desire for either, even if it were still possible. So why not me?"

Was he talking about his age? I thought of the lead underpants some miners fashioned. The asteroid was low level radioactive, just like everything else. You were more at a risk from cosmic radiation on the way here. Once you were in the caverns, you were pretty well shielded. But that six-month journey from Earth was plenty damaging.

"Sure, but back home, you'll at least be rich."

"Not me," he grunted. "My stake, already sold." He swept an arm at the banquet I'd been picking at. "I won't be rich like *this* rich. Here, I can live like a King."

I blinked. Already sold? The fool. "But there's no company..."

He snorted at that.

"... and no rescue if things go wrong. With the Klondike, or with you."

"So be it."

I frowned. He'd obviously thought this through, which put him at a distinct advantage. I was pretty sure I ought to be able to argue he was being an idiot, but that probably wouldn't be enough to make him change his mind. And I didn't really have the time. I briefly considered trying to knock him out, manhandle him to the *Betsey*, but Grigor weighed twenty kilos more than I did, and if he was grizzled, he was still a bear of a man.

"You sure?" I said. My last argument. Because you can only change your mind while there's more than one option.

"I'm sure. Go on, get out of here."

I didn't hesitate any longer, breaking several records for reaching the cargo bay, especially when drunk. Suiting up felt like it took forever, but at last I was strapped into the pilot's seat aboard the Betsey, the co-pilot position yawningly empty, stabbing a finger down on the release button, the one I might as well have relabelled "Are *you* sure?"

The take-off was rough as hell. It was always going to be. The magnetic launch system accelerated the *Betsey* at a peak of 15 gees, and only the pressurised space suit stopped all my blood pooling in the wrong places and me blacking out. All to fling me violently away from the Klondike, flung backwards, though still travelling forwards relative to the Earth, but at a speed low enough that we ought to be able to still make orbit, to rendezvous with one of the ever-expanding orbitals. After unloading the raw building materials for their next growth spurt, I'd refuel just enough for Earth re-entry, carrying a conservatively estimated billion dollars' worth of rare elements, future electronics.

My cut would be much less than that. Not enough to afford wagyu, or aged whisky, not on a regular basis anyway. But enough to finally retire, if I wanted to. Enough to buy a small place, somewhere not too crowded, somewhere still considered remote. There, I could install a big old telescope, and watch the crowded night skies, knowing that, somewhere up there, beyond the thousands of micro-satellites, each controlled by Klondike-sourced electronics, a crazy space miner was still sat all alone on the mother of all lodes. Knowing that I could have been there with him, at the outer edges of the solar system, if only I had the guts.

I hope he unearths another bottle of whisky or two to keep him company, and that he remembers me in his prayers.

A Quickening Tide

A. J. McIntosh & Andrew J. Wilson

Durante was at peace. He'd drawn his last breath, and his heart had stopped. He was as dead as a proverbial doornail. All that was left was a desire that this dark, silent and timeless non-existence would continue forever.

Then the pain began. At first, it was just pins and needles all over his body, but violent shocks to his chest came next. Then Durante was transfixed by agonising waves as his lungs and limbs started working again. When the torture was over, he flinched as dull thuds sounded from somewhere outside his aching head. He opened his eyes reluctantly.

Beyond an inspection hatch, a blurry figure was signalling to him with a monkey wrench. He shook his head to clear it and then show he wasn't ready. Maybe whoever was disturbing him would go away. With luck, they'd let him return to rest, to the effortless accumulation of riches.

A viscous eddy swirled around him as sluices opened. The contents of the suspension tank poured away, exposing his naked skin to cool air. Then even colder water flushed the last of the antifreeze out of the tube, and things came painfully into focus. For better or worse, he was back in the land of the living.

Durante scrabbled at the side of the tank as the hazmat-suited figure outside opened the hatch. He focused on his finances, and the possibility that these might have significantly improved during his tax-free period of cryogenic suspension. If nothing bad had happened over the intervening decades or centuries, perhaps he was already loaded at the ripe old physical age of 23.

He shivered as the faceless technician leaned towards him. A gloved hand released the straps that bound him, and then pulled the respirator off his head. A voice crackled out of the speaker on the suit's mask.

"Are you okay?"

Durante nodded.

"Can you feel your toes and fingers? Can you move them?"

Durante wriggled his digits in a half-hearted wave, then nodded again.

"Can you talk?"

"Yes, sir."

"Who are you?"

"Fleet Midshipman Peter Durante, sir, provost's officer in Cryogenics. Frozen aboard the *Spirit of Scutari* on day of departure – September 31, 2315."

"Good."

He staggered out of the suspension tank and into the cryovault itself. The technician circled him, appraising his condition, prodding him here and there with a probe.

"Any questions?"

"I was wondering, sir, how long…"

"Don't worry – often happens – you'll unshrivel in a couple of hours."

"No, I mean, how long have I been out of it, sir?"

"Six seconds," his tormentor said, "17 minutes, 6 hours, 8 days, 2 months and 5 years. Thought you were going to wake up rich? Trust me, you're not."

Durante shook his head, too disappointed to speak. The technician loosened a seal on the neck of the hazmat suit and pulled off the visored helmet. A woman's face emerged from underneath it: older than him, but still young. She was sloe-eyed, expressionless, Mongolian.

"You're on duty, Midshipman," she said. "Report updecks."

Durante staggered forwards, readying himself for action.

"Wait!" she said.

Confused, he turned, only to find her gauntleted hand gesturing at his crotch.

"Get dressed first, for goodness' sake…"

"There's nothing to worry about, you see," Serendipidam said. "Officers will read from their mission statement. You'll compare what's said with the neurobrand issued to you, report any disparities, sign the relevant forms afterwards and return everything to the attending provost's officer. Got it?"

Not getting it didn't appear to be an option. That was the Fleet for you, of course. Its unbreakable sinews might hold humanity together across the interstellar diaspora, but bureaucracy clogged its arteries like the worst kind of administrative cholesterol. Heaven help you if you forgot to do the paperwork: they'd string you up with a noose of red tape.

Provost Marshal Mackenzie Serendipidam's eyebrows ruffled, white as snowy owls against the blue-black skin of his face. He peered over his half-moon spectacles and read from a volume of the Fleet's *Manual*:

In this manner, you will attend five, 3-hour reviews per day for the next month, conducting your private life outwith these hours at all times in solitary with a guard outside your hatch.

"Well, it goes on in that vein for a while – let's see, blah-blah-blah, so on and so forth *ad nauseam… sine ira et studio… reductio ad absurdum*. Ah, yes:

Upon satisfactory completion of your duty, you will be returned to Cryogenics for refreeze as soon as practicable, with the addition to your cuff of four chevrons and a guarantee of no further interruptions for at least 50 years.

"Does the Reader understand?"

"Sir, yes sir!" Durante snapped.

"Very good. I, of course, shall be dead by then. I'm not one of those with an inexhaustible appetite for postponing the inevitable." Serendipidam smiled at Durante, unnerving the junior officer. "I'll bid you goodbye now. I wish you much pleasure in your future fortune and a splendid career with the Fleet. Be on your guard and try to be decent. For as long as possible, that is. Dismissed!"

Durante had warmed to the gruff but affable Serendipidam, and scolded himself for it. Provost marshals were appointed for their cunning not their kindness. This particular example of the species – the most senior political policeman aboard the *Scutari*, his own line commander – should not be trusted by Durante in his current role.

As Reader, it was his duty to check for "the creeps": those gradual, cumulative misunderstandings or collective amnesias that can beset crews on long adventures. He must compare the mission statements in use with those that had been issued and branded in his memory at the voyage's outset. If there were disparities, errors, or indeed, potential frauds or conspiracies, he should flag these up to his superiors.

The knowledge that allowed Fleet vessels to travel faster than light was strictly classified. However, the effects of this apparent violation of causality were well known. The paradoxes involved could corrupt computer systems and drive crewmembers mad. In contrast, the neurobrand stamped in the mind of a freshly revived Reader had been perfectly frozen in time. It represented an incontrovertible record of all the orders that had been assigned.

Of course, the chances of anything significant arising after so little time aspace were vanishingly slim. It ought to be straightforward, and yet he felt as if his premature thawing-out, the sudden jolt from Cryogenics, had left him dazed and disoriented.

Doubt gnawed at Durante all the way down to C Deck, where a hulking marine was already waiting for him at the hatch to his quarters. Durante stepped through, hoping to find a meal prepared, but instead there were four officers seated at the table, studying their files.

"Reader," said the most senior of them, pointing to the braid emblem on a cuff, "we three are *Scutari* Informatics, and over there is the provost's officer supervising. Sit, retrieve, compare."

Durante's brain curdled at the command, and his thoughts were no longer his own. The speaker began reading from a stack of mission folders. Simultaneously, those same words emerged in parallel from a separate, pre-existing text inside Durante's head. For the most part, the sentences unrolled in synch, but when the reader stumbled or mistook, Durante knew at once where the error lay. He would then raise a finger and wait for the necessary correction to come.

The 3 hours passed quickly. Durante came to his senses with the scraping of chairs, and the clipped questions and instructions of the provost's officer. He ticked a box, put his name and retinal stamp to the form presented, and the visiting party trooped out. No one met his eyes or said farewell. He drank a glass of water alone in his galley, then heard the swish of the hatch opening and closing, the raking of chairs, the sound of a new delegation settling itself at the table.

"Reader, we three are *Scutari* Engineering, and this is the provost's officer supervising. Sit, retrieve, compare."

And so it went on – interminable seas of words for 15 hours a day for days on end.

When he was not on duty, Durante slept, waking only to eat, defaecate and wash. Devoid of thought and empty of care, he soon lost track of the date. His diet didn't vary and tasted of nothing. He was witless, idle and content to serve, to conform to whatever was demanded of him. This was almost as easy as Cryogenics.

"Reader," said the last of them one evening, "we three are *Scutari* Trade, and after this you'll be free to go. Be seated, retrieve, reconcile…"

The final read-through had taken place 4 days previously, time Durante had spent despairing of meeting company or finding anything worth his time on the entertainment feeds. Now he was bored and irritable. His furniture didn't fit, some of it was already broken, and he suspected an Informatics delegate of sticking wads of chewing gum under the dining table.

He drafted a message to the one person aboard he knew – the laconic enigma who'd thawed him out. He worded a brief invitation to chat or eat or exercise together, but realised he had no name or rank or department to which he could address it. Instead, he went for yet another walk alone, watched decorations going up for some forthcoming Captain's Reception and winced over weak coffee at a concourse stall. He reflected that all these strangers who passed him now without a second glance would certainly be older, quite likely dead by the time he next emerged from Cryogenics.

A giant billboard refreshed its screen across the piazza from him. A blonde woman with luxuriant hair beamed down and winked. "So what if I'm 99?" she said flirtatiously. "Inside I'm still 19. I wanna look the way I feel – that's why I choose RECON-STYLE clinics."

RECON-STYLE! What sort of stupid name was that? Durante wondered irritably. *What was it getting at? To con people about one's age? Reconnaître – know again one's former style? Reconcile one's looks with one's perceptions?*

Suddenly, he felt his brain lurch the way it had before during read-throughs, and he knew why. *Reconcile.* That word had touched him. It was a trigger that he'd almost forgotten. That word the last of the presenting officers had used to start the last of the dictations. He remembered the figure: a woman in late middle age, her head large and gaunt, thinning grey hair dragged back from the temples. She must have been lanced once. Her features were rigid down the right-hand side, dimpled like orange peel, the eye pearly and blind.

"Reader," she had growled, saliva foaming in the little recess of her mouth through which she spoke, breathed and smoked, "we three are *Scutari* Trade, and after this you'll be free to go. Be seated, retrieve, reconcile…"

Despite all the distractions, there it was: not *compare* but *reconcile* – to harmonise, make friendly or consistent – the very opposite of *compare.* Surely that was significant, but was it important enough to make a difference? Had someone tampered with his neurobrand or the instruction protocols that accessed it? Or had it been just some knuckleheaded mistake? What should he do with this realisation? Report it and come across as petty, or ignore it, not cause problems and take the primrose path to profitable suspension?

"I did not expect to see you again," said Serendipidam, "and now that I have, I must say you've got a damn nerve coming here with this drivel… Accusing *Scutari's* chief trading negotiator of fraud! You, a snotty-nosed midshipman just out of training pants, fast asleep for the past 5 years, strutting into this office and making allegations…"

The Provost Marshal had not raised his voice above a growl, but his face resembled rehydrated plums coming to the boil.

"With respect, sir, I have alleged nothing," Durante replied, choosing his words. "I just thought it was my duty as Reader to raise what could, possibly, be an important difference–"

"Duty be damned! A quite unproven difference. Only you recall any use of the word 'reconcile'."

"What about the provost's officer present?"

"How dare you!" Serendipidam snapped. "Lieutenant Campbell is adamant – the retrieve commands were valid."

"Well, I was the Reader and I'm sure–"

"Stow it, you bilge rat! Any infallibility of recall you may have possessed applied to the mission statements – nothing else! Now, may I remind you that before you were Reader, you were a provost's officer – sworn to uphold the *status quo*, not to run around causing chaos on your first outing. I ask you, does Commander Knott look the kind of person who would for one moment indulge in fraud?"

Durante bit his tongue. With her ravaged, half-immobile face and rigid bearing, Commander Knott looked capable of fraud and plenty else besides.

Throughout this entire interview, she had not seen fit to meet his eye. She had examined the long, curved nail of a little finger instead, as if wondering where best to insert it.

"Of course she doesn't!" Serendipidam growled. "Persons of her rank and experience in Trade appointments are in such positions because they – of all bloody people – are the type whom the Fleet can best trust! Exhaustively vetted, selected only after months and years of training, monitored constantly, beyond reproach in every way and respected accordingly. Except, that is, by one very green officer who has let the entirely temporary office of Reader go to his head, and now stands here demanding an official review."

"Sir, I have insisted on nothing of the sort."

"Enough! I ask you, Midshipman, are you prepared to withdraw these pettifogging objections?"

Despite the disturbing complexion of the Provost Marshal, despite how his eyebrows seemed to be mating, despite the fact that this could deep-six his fledgling career, Durante decided that he couldn't back down.

"I thought not," Serendipidam said before Durante could reply.

The Provost Marshal snorted through the bristling hairs in his nostrils.

"Felicity," he said, addressing the joyless Knott beside him, "you see, I have tried my best with this... this upstart tadpole, but my hands are tied. I'm afraid we must review the entire mission statement – and on the record. I can do nothing else. The *Manual* is quite clear."

She nodded and regarded her nail from a new angle with her one good eye. As the Provost Marshal spoke into an intercom, issuing orders and summonses, she glanced up and surveyed Durante from top to tail. Durante stared straight ahead, pretending not to notice her basilisk gaze.

An hour later, Durante sat listening as Commander Knott read again from the documents that defined her own and her department's role for the duration of the voyage.

This time, there were more witnesses – the Provost Marshal, two top-brass officers from Psychiatry and Speculation, a secretary – and this time, Knott quite definitely, with exaggerated clarity, said "compare." As before, she read slowly, her voice rasping, and as before, she sometimes sped up without warning, as if impatient or annoyed by the sense of the words. From time to time, she would snap down a sheet with unexpected force, ripping the corner, regarding the tattered flag with distaste. Durante couldn't tell whether this was true emotion, an act or some strange effect of her injuries, and he wasn't the only one transfixed by her performance.

At one stage, Speculation jumped so hard that a shirt-button sprang from her belly onto the table. Nobody mentioned it. The long, bulb-ended nose of Psychiatry twitched and flared as he rattled a stylus between his teeth. Serendipidam rested his head in his hands and grumbled to himself from behind a nest of fingers.

Knott read for hours in the Provost Marshal's stuffy office, her monotonous voice growing quieter and slurring with fatigue: "…and said cargo-compact to be vended either by e-contract or open outcry on Planet Nimbus at the market in Nephelococcygia on July 18, the asking price to be paid either by transfer or exchange or…"

For the first time that day, Durante raised a finger and looked up. She seemed not to have noticed and continued without pause. Durante coughed, but there was still no response. He had to rap the tabletop with his knuckles before Serendipidam took notice.

"What is it, Reader? Frog in your throat?"

"Sir, there's an anomaly."

"A what?"

"Between Commander Knott's words and the neurobrand up here." Durante tapped at his forehead, all too aware too late that the superfluous gesture, the little vanity of it, had been noted.

"How so?" asked Speculation.

"Ma'am, Commander Knott has just read 'July 18' as the designated date-to-market. The neurobrand states 'July 15'."

"Do you acknowledge an error, Commander?" asked Psychiatry.

Knott retraced the passage, taking her time. "There is no mistake: July 18 it is – look." The mission statement was passed around. She was right. "Couldn't this be a simple printing error?" she asked no one in particular, dabbing bubbles from the corner of her stricken mouth. "A 5 for an 8 – easy enough to do."

"Impossible and insufficient," said the Provost Marshal, crushing that bug before it could crawl any further.

"Well, does it make any difference?" she tried again, this time a hint of impatience creeping through.

Speculation consulted a trade almanac. "As I'm sure you know, Commander, there are indeed markets on both dates. Do we have any reason to believe that one would be more auspicious than the other?"

Knott paused to consider then shook her head.

"I think not," she said. "Each is much like the other, and the price for IVIs is pretty constant throughout the quadrant."

"Ivy eyes?" inquired Speculation.

Psychiatry broke in: "Igneovitreous items, isn't it?"

There followed a pause, an awkward gap in which no words were spoken. Durante watched with satisfaction as a silent imperative to elaborate pressed down upon Knott from around the table, a force she resisted for a good 20 seconds before she broke.

"You know… luxury goods, love-stones, stones of desire… erotic so they say. Just 7 tonnes."

"Fleet is trading in erotic IVIs?" spluttered Serendipidam. "So-called *cocos de mer*? I had no idea. Extraordinary!"

"Yes, Provost Marshal, indeed… That is to say, they are part of my private venture in this voyage, from which, rest assured, Fleet will be pleased to take a substantial cut of the profits. It's all above board, all on the manifest if you wish to check."

The silence fell again. *Was this embarrassment now?* wondered Durante. If so, for what? At the invasion of Knott's business privacy? At the notion of so ugly a creature dealing in love-stones? If so, they were missing the point.

"There is at least one significant difference between the markets," Durante offered. "On July 18, the Captain's Reception will take place here aboard the *Scutari*. I suppose such an important occasion could affect who is and who isn't trading that day on the planet surface, how the market is regulated and how responsive the bidding gradient is. I'm not making accusations of any kind, just suggesting a potential for…"

Now it was Durante's turn to find himself alone in silence. For all his faith in the Fleet, there was not one person here he had good reason to trust. He suspected the Provost Marshal of orchestrating matters, but there was no proof to confirm this intuition. The atmosphere was pregnant, the weight of unsaid things uncomfortable.

Psychiatry put down his pen and smiled.

"I believe it falls to me," he said, "to suggest a way forward. I propose we examine Mr. Durante's cryogenic log in detail. It's just possible there may be something in it that might explain the anomaly. Are we agreed?"

From that moment, Durante knew what the result would be. Sure enough, within another hour a temperature flux had been identified in the record, and its source traced to a faulty synapse loop within Durante's suspension tank. A nobody from that department was dragged in to confirm that this could indeed explain whatever the grand panjandrums sitting here might want it to explain.

It wasn't a statement of fact, but of possibility. And yet it was enough to cast doubt on Durante's testimony. His neurobrand was no longer dependable. He could see where this meeting was heading, where his career was bound unless he dug in his heels.

"I must demand that the *existence* of the anomaly be logged," he blurted. "*And* the fact that the Captain's Reception was posited as a relevant market-factor."

"Good grief, Durante, have you been swallowing textbooks?" the Provost Marshal asked. "I've never heard so much Academy gobbledygook in all my life! Still, you're quite within your rights, I suppose. Very well, let it be logged. I don't think we need trouble you any longer, Reader. Dismissed!"

"Fuck you very much, sir," Durante said. As usual, no one seemed to hear a word he said.

Serendipidam levelled a long, even stare at him. And then, without warning, a private wink.

Durante returned to his quarters, his mind simmering with suspicions. He could prove nothing. He felt sure he'd been manipulated. He smelled a fix: the familiar scent of his stepmother collapsing under piles of paperwork, the sense of life savings trickling away through the cracks. It smelled like a terminal condition, solicitors' letters and cheap flowers outside a crematorium.

Somebody somewhere wanted an abnormal market for the IVIs, and was angling for it to be on July 18. On that day, every commercial bigwig on the planet would be scraping and bowing at the reception aboard the *Scutari*, fawning for a future audience with the senior trade negotiator or – wonder of wonders – Captain Florian Anderson himself. Somebody somewhere stood to make a nice profit, and Knott's odd date in the mission statement had something to do with it.

Durante turned and stared into his cabin console, hoping for inspiration or at least distraction. There were two messages. The first informed him that the date of his refreeze had been set back 2 weeks while potentially defective parts of his suspension tube were replaced. The second came from the Provost's Office, and concluded with Serendipidam's initials. It was an extract from the ship's public business schedule, a list of corrections and updates and contingent revisions authorised by the Captain. Halfway down the page, an entry caught his eye:

> *Vending change [Nimbus: Nephelococcygia]. Scutari cargo consignment DB5:100101\a to market 7/15 [supersedes 7/18]. Reason given: market distortion by Captain's Reception. Status: official/immediate. MS, PM.*

Durante stared and stared, interpreting the message and the Provost Marshal's terse initials, his implicit agreement, the wordless pat on the back, the meaning of that wink. Durante had been listened to: his argument had won. Of course, there was no mention of his neurobrand, but that didn't matter. It was enough for Durante that here, far from home on a huge ship, a young officer could prevail.

He showered, changed and scented himself like an admiral. He settled before the console to reread the evidence of his victory. It was still there, and it still brought a smile to his lips. He sat daydreaming of a career made up of many more such triumphs, and with quick fingers entered his security clearance and consulted the *Scutari*'s manifest.

"Cascade, take me into the Cargo Atlas. Show me where to find consignment DB5:100101\a."

The datacore displayed a deck plan and outlined one department. Within that, it pinpointed a rectangular space smaller than the cabin Durante was sitting in now.

"Cascade, where is this?"

B Deck: Cryogenics.

Durante was taken aback. "What is the segment indicated?"

Long-stay compartment.

"Is it operational?"

Yes.

"How long has DB5:100101\a been there?"

One month, 6 days, 5 hours, 6 minutes, 75 seconds.

"Where was DB5:100101\a before stowage in its present location, and who authorised the latest transfer?"

High-security cargo hold, highlighted now in red. Transfer authorised by Commander Knott and Zoology.

"Before the transfer to Cryogenics of DB5:100101\a, what occupied the compartment?"

Fleet Provost's officer: Durante, Peter, Midshipman [2315 – 2320], revived early.

Durante left his quarters through a service chute, crawled the 20 meters to a ceiling access point and hauled himself through it. He then followed the route map on his wrist tracker until he reached the for'ard elevator columns. Then he borrowed a luminous jacket from a locker, helped himself to a hard hat and began whistling so as not to attract attention. Boarding an empty elevator, he rose towards B Deck.

Once there, he traced the cables below the floor all the way to the main Cryogenics entrance, shorted the corridor lighting, eased himself up and through, closed the panel behind him, and ran an anonymised provost's office key through the security swipe. It was 03:00 shipboard time, and nobody was about.

"Right," Durante whispered to himself, "who's been sleeping in *my* bed?"

He located his suspension tube without difficulty, and found no evidence of an upgrade in progress. He peered through the semi-circular inspection hatch, switched on the internal lights and peered again. There wasn't much to see: just a stack of love-stones, Knott's hidden stash. Damn it, this was why Durante was being kept from his rightful refreeze and the chance of making money. These were the unsuspected cuckoos in *Scutari*'s nest.

Well, Commander Knott, he thought to himself, *you're not as clever as you think you are.*

From a hook suspended in mid-air, Durante lifted one of the heavy-duty hazmat suits and pulled it on. You couldn't be too careful around extra-terrestrial cargo. He flushed the suspension tank and opened the hatch.

Durante took one of the love-stones from the top, and then reached further down for a second from the back of the pile. He replaced the first in its original setting and admired his handiwork. The absence wouldn't be noticed in a cursory inspection, and wouldn't be discovered until the day of the market.

He set the stone down in the middle of the gangway and stood well back. It rocked back and forth like an egg about to hatch. As he turned to close the suspension tube hatch, his boot slid on a streak of clear slime that had somehow dripped out onto the deck. After he closed the hatch, he took off the hazmat suit and used the helmet to scoop up the stone without touching it. A tug on the seal at the neck closed his improvised containment device.

This isn't dishonest, he assured himself as he made his way out of Cryogenics. *This is more like getting even.*

After all, he might be disrupting criminal activity. At the very least, he was stirring the pot in hope that something would bubble to the top, some clue to the identities of those who were behind all this. He allowed himself a smirk: when the love-stones were counted, someone in Zoology would find themselves in a whole heap of trouble.

Durante was attempting to make a graceful exit when something tugged his foot. He looked down at his boot, but there was nothing there. Could he have imagined it? He tried to step forward again, and this time there was no mistaking the yank that pulled him back.

He felt his ankles being clamped together; his whole body dragged backwards. He dropped the helmet and grabbed a handhold on the bulkhead beside him. He looked down again, but there was still nothing to see.

Durante lost his grip and slammed into a pool of slime on the deck. He struggled into a crouch, breaths coming quick and shallow, his head switching from side to side looking for whatever was attacking him. Now his knees and his thighs were being constricted, and he felt something begin to crush him around the stomach. Then, as his head was forced backwards and around, he saw for a moment something only slightly less translucent than the slime pool. Three ink-black eyes stared back at him as a vaguer blob heaved itself onto his back with near-invisible tentacles.

"Get off, you bastard!" Durante yelled, trying to tear the suckers away with his bare hands. A tentacle wrapped around his throat and began to strangle him.

Just as he was about to black out, there was a flash like lightning and his throat was released. Durante sat up, pulling what was left of a slimy tentacle from around his neck, and groggily tried to examine it as the form of the thing dribbled away between his fingers.

"You are a very stupid man, and also very lucky," said a voice he remembered from the first time he'd emerged here.

"What's your name? What are you doing here?" Durante asked the taser-toting figure.

"Later. Now go."

His saviour turned without replying and disappeared.

When Durante got back to his cabin, he turned his attention to the cause of all this trouble. He'd heard about "stones of desire" before, seen them on screen, but this was the first he'd ever held, the only one he'd examined at close quarters.

Durante propped it on a shelf opposite his bed and was surprised to see how unlike rock its surface was in the angled light of a cabin lamp – more like oiled skin. The shape of it was unmistakable: a curvaceous human female's torso from the navel to the knee. Its incompleteness and the subtlety of its imperfections were fascinating: the way it couldn't be the thing it most resembled, could never redeem the erotic promises it seemed to offer. The love-stone was mineral pure and simple, some odd igneous phenomenon; there was no intent behind it to suggest or comment or provoke. In his mind, Durante knew it had no capacity to satisfy, knew that what looked so inviting, warm and supple was cold, hard and insentient, but it still evoked a response. That, of course, was part of these objects' mystique and value. He grew tired of himself for lusting after it, threw a T-shirt over the stone and forced himself to sleep.

When Durante awoke, sore and stiff, he found a young woman sitting at the end of his bed. She regarded his face without expression, her eyes never leaving his as he belatedly drew a sheet across to cover himself.

"Who are you?" he asked. "What are you doing here? How'd you get in?"

"You feel okay? You can feel your toes and fingers? Move them? What about… other parts? Everything working okay?"

"You!"

"Evidently."

"You were in Cryogenics, the first time, and then…"

"Then I saved you from the squid."

"What were you doing there?"

"My job."

"*Your job?* You keep very odd hours for a Cryogen officer."

"What were *you* doing there?"

"Checking my berth. Why are you here?"

"After I'd cleaned up your mess in Cryogen, I came here to give you a warning. Don't interfere in this business. It's too big for a midshipman to handle alone."

"Too big for Provost's Office as well perhaps? I don't think so."

"Provost's Office already knows."

"So, if Provost's Office knows, who is this warning from?"

"From the good guys."

"Provost's Office good guys?"

"The Provost Marshal is a good guy."

"Why can't Serendipidam give me this warning himself – officially, out in the open?"

"Sometimes, some things are best kept hidden." Her eyes flickered between Durante's face and crotch. Whether in deadpan humour or contempt he couldn't tell.

"Listen – I will not be fobbed off with hints and winks, and I won't be threatened, if that's what you're planning to do next." He reached down beside the bed and brought up the small but vicious-looking pistol he kept hidden there for just such an occasion. "I think you should go now."

His sloe-eyed visitor was unmoved. She uncrossed her legs, crossed them the other way, and seemed on the brink of saying something. But before she could speak, there was a noise like toenails snagging through nylon. She froze, her eyes still boring into Durante's, then followed his gaze towards the love-stone on the shelf behind her. With two, arched fingers she removed the T-shirt and dropped it on the floor.

"Ah," she said, "I see. You stole it. You idiot."

"It's split," said Durante, jumping out of bed to take a closer look. There came another ear-rending rip, a kind of groan or exhalation, and the black stone shuddered, the tear in its flank widening. Something as pale as lychee flesh was flexing on the inside and then, too fast for Durante to follow, it slithered through the gap and was free, moist and wobbling beside the original.

"Damn it, that's not supposed to happen, is it? Has it given birth?"

"It's not alive."

"But Zoology was involved in sending it. I checked the manifest."

"Zoology was involved in sending the squid. Commander Knott has friends and influence in many unexpected places. How many of these love-stones did you steal?"

"I didn't steal anything. I–"

"How many?"

"Just one – that one."

"Wait here. I'll come back. Understand?"

"Yes, but what's your name? What's your authority?"

She looked at him very hard. "Yerzuk. Lieutenant. Provost Marshal's special agent. No more questions."

Durante felt especially naked before the love-stones. He turned for his clothes and heard the horrible splitting sound once again. Now the "baby" had turned black and hard like its "mother," and both had produced more "offspring." Even as he watched, one of the "grandchildren" wobbled from the shelf, fell, bounced across the cabin carpet before coming to rest against his foot. By the time it was still, it had hardened into yet another female torso, and another pallid, pulsating form was pushing from its belly.

Ten minutes later, the floor of Durante's cabin was almost covered. He began scooping stones into a duvet cover, enveloped them all and zipped it shut. It seemed about to burst just as Yerzuk reappeared.

"Good," she said. "Outside."

Together they heaved the load out into the corridor and tipped the groaning mass into a wheelie bin Yerzuk had commandeered from somewhere in the service lockers. They set their shoulders in position and pushed.

"Where are we going?" asked Durante.

"There's an empty chamber dead ahead. Keep pushing."

Over the next 40 meters they picked up speed and momentum. Then they reached the doors of a deserted canteen and rammed the wheelie bin through painters' pots scattered in the dark.

"There's an exit hatch in the galley," yelled Yerzuk. "Run!"

They cannoned on, the stones of desire rattling and rending before them. Yerzuk swung open an old hatch by mainforce and Durante shoved the wheelie bin inside. Then the pair of them swung the hatch back shut and screwed it down. Durante slammed the EJECT button, and as the love-stones floated off into the void outside the *Scutari*, a welcome hush descended.

Sweating side by side, their backs pressed against the cold metal of the bulkhead, they caught their breath for a moment in silence.

"Listen, Lieutenant... I'm sorry about all this, well some of it, maybe. I don't know how much. Look, will you please just tell me what the hell's going on?"

Early afternoon on July 15, Durante spending the last day of his shore leave on Nimbus the way he'd spent the previous seven: irritating Yerzuk with questions and never getting a straight answer. He found it hard to understand why he'd followed her here, insisted that she should take him along on whatever mission or madcap heist she was set on. He told himself it was a sense of duty. In his heart, he suspected it was simpler than that. She'd made him squirm, and he wanted to repay the compliment.

The monorail on which they were traveling carried them through miles of boring scenery: a landscape of rounded hillocks – all identical, covered in the same even grass – all squatting dully beneath the grey sky. It was always like this on the northern continent of Nimbus. No grand vistas, no dramatic plunges, no excitement.

"But they were alive," Durante said. "You saw them. They were having babies in front of our eyes."

"No. Not alive. Not intelligent. Not sentient. Not artefacts. Nothing complex – just rocks. Imagine a huge volcano somewhere, very powerful, generating local gravitational forces. What you get is stones of desire."

"Oh, come off it. They're not just rocks. They look like…"

"It's just coincidence. To millions of species, they don't look like… like anything you'd recognise."

"So why were they breaking the law of conservation of mass and having babies?"

Yerzuk's eyes closed to shut him out. "These IVIs are very energetic. In space, where they're cold, the energy can be contained. In warm places, they get volatile, and the energy must escape – it's released in new love-stones."

"Well, *I've* never heard of this! How come all those stones of desire in galleries and museums and private collections aren't multiplying all the time?"

"Because they're dead."

"Dead?"

"Inactive, then," sighed Yerzuk. "Or exhausted or extinct, like volcanoes."

"But our examples were very active, weren't they?"

"Yes," she agreed. "It seems someone has found a way to make the IVIs dormant, to pass as extinct, until it becomes convenient or necessary to kick-start the replication."

"And you, working on the sly for Serendipidam, are trying to find out who they are… Why the secrecy? Surely the Provost's Office is designed for just that kind of mission."

"Where there is potential to create great wealth, there is also an opportunity to generate shifts in political power. And when that happens, the normal channels of authority and justice are not always reliable. That's when the Provost Marshal needs a special agent."

"You."

"Me," nodded Yerzuk. It was the most communicative she'd been in days.

"Do you think someone needed my berth in Cryogen to keep the love-stones quiet for a bit, until we reached this planet? Knott commandeered my berth there, but did she order my extraction as a Reader?"

Yerzuk shrugged and said nothing as the monorail glided into the terminus.

What had started as 7 tonnes aboard the *Scutari* had, since its removal to the planet surface, increased until the warehouse storing it exploded. It was bought when the market opened at dawn by a company with a credit rating but – according to Cascade – no recent dealings, no known directors, staff, head office or forwarding address. A line of security staff now ringed the creaking mound of IVIs, throwing stones back onto the heap, turning away rubberneckers who'd come to gawp.

It seemed a good time to draw a line under the mystery and quit, but Yerzuk insisted on staying. She wanted to attend the market, she said, to get a feel for the place, to learn. For cover, she'd brought along something to sell, something to get her involved in the whole process, something a bit special to stir up interest: a brand new cybersuit.

Yerzuk had somehow not only accessed Fleet stores and "acquired" this fusion-powered exoskeleton – half spacesuit, half spacecraft – but also spirited it ashore. It didn't escape Durante's notice that she'd named him as the exclusive vendor. He found it hard to understand why he still trusted her.

Durante wasn't prejudiced against colonials. His own home world was hardly the centre of the universe after all. But here on Nimbus, in this place of cloud-shrouded boredom, there seemed no curiosity or desire, no grit on which to fasten. Wherever Durante went he found the same halfwit inhabitants: people shaped like teapots who stood too close; people with inane grins, asking him to sample their mushrooms, inviting him to supper, offering hugs and confidences. He hated it.

"So why," he asked Yerzuk, as they walked together towards the copper duomo of the marketplace, "do you suppose Commander Knott chose this place to sell the love-stones? It seems one of the least erotic places in the settled universe."

"As you know, the stones are sometimes stimulating."

Durante kept an even pace and did not turn to face her.

"Knott brought down about 7 tonnes to market: that's not enough to stimulate a whole colony. And anyway, how many of these people would want or could afford to buy? Last I heard, a single IVI would cost 20 years' salary down here."

"If sufficient IVIs reproduce enough times, their rarity value would reduce. Perhaps everyone could afford one."

"You're telling me Knott knew how to make the IVIs replicate, and gambled on selling them in bulk?"

"No, I think she sold the 7 tonnes for a small fortune, and the replication method for a large one. Her main investment, or that of her backers, may concern what happens after the love-stones take effect. We're here, look."

The giant duomo combined elements of this grassland's surface hillocks with the numberless legions of mushrooms farmed in barns below. It was, thought Durante, a magnificent attempt to reflect and relieve the tedium of the place. He was the only person studying it. Surrounding him – ignorant or forgetful, or indifferent to any architectural effects – an amphitheatre full of traders chattered and gossiped, exchanged mycelial intelligence and crop futures, and cooed at their screens.

The duomo stood 4 kilometres high above them, and was made not of solid metal, as Durante had first assumed, but millions of copper leaves, oxidised green on the outside, brilliantly burnished within. Each leaf was strung upon a thread, and trembled in the constant breeze, producing a sound like whispers, rumours on a global scale. To the eye, it seemed that a concave sky was shimmering in endless shades of green and orange, grey and gold, peach and silver; all the colours of all the coins known to Man.

"We'll sit over there, in the vendors' gallery," said Yerzuk, leading the way.

When they took their places, they surveyed the scene on a giant screen, found their lot on the index and waited for the bidding to start. They looked just like all the others from the *Scutari* there that day, privateers selling off an expensive piece of Fleet kit without the authorities' knowledge or permission.

"You're sweating," said Yerzuk. "Stop it. Relax."

"I *am* relaxed – I'm fine," replied Durante.

"You don't look relaxed. I'm going for coffee – want some?"

"No, it might make me jumpy."

Durante stared at the roof to distract himself. Despite his involvement with the cybersuit down there, despite consorting with the mysterious and possibly criminal Yerzuk, watching the roof calmed him. Almost mesmerised, he tried to tell if the waves that played across it were indeed wind-powered, or if some subtle program controlled their ebb and flow. Durante was no nearer a conclusion when a hand tapped his shoulder. He turned, and there – emerging from a plume of cigar smoke – was Commander Knott, grinning lopsidedly.

"You hypocritical burgling little bastard," she gurgled.

"Sir?"

"Pompous prating little squab."

"Ma'am?"

"And all the while you were planning to be here, flogging off Fleet stores."

"Ma'am, I–"

"You deserve what's coming to you, Midshitman, remember that. When the worst thing you can imagine happens, remember *me*. I'll be laughing."

Another cloud of cigar smoke engulfed Durante, and by the time it had cleared, she was gone. A moment later, he spotted her limping across a distant jetty, saw her escorted aboard a private vessel trademarked IHIT. It was the same firm that had bought the love-stones.

"Nice chat with Commander Knott?" asked Yerzuk, following his gaze as she returned.

"No. She called you a 'burgling bastard'."

Yerzuk looked unperturbed as she slipped in earbuds to follow the bidding and ignored him.

For the last time, Durante turned to the soothing roof, and as he mellowed, noticed that the sound of it was changing. From a steady shushing, it had grown percussive, more metallic and louder. Now he could see that what was turning the copper leaves was not the wind, but a shower of rain.

"I thought," he said to Yerzuk, pulling out one of her earbuds, "it never rained on Nimbus."

"Right. Only mizzle, in autumn."

"So, what's *that?*" he said, pointing.

Yerzuk cocked her head and listened. "Heavy mizzle — maybe?"

Others around them were staring at the roof too, and listening to the new, unaccustomed rattling of raindrops on the duomo. The leaves had started to spin, producing an odd, stroboscopic shimmer that was difficult to watch and even harder not to. The noise grew deafening.

"What's happening?" asked Yerzuk.

Durante felt a sudden sting on his cheek and picked from his lap the offending hailstone: tiny, opalescent, resembling a marble. As he examined it between two fingers, it turned black and dissolved.

"I'm not sure I like this," he said.

"Follow me – at the double."

Yerzuk pushed past him and bounded down an aisle towards the lowest tier of the amphitheatre.

Down in the middle of the market, where all the items up for sale were on display, the noise of the storm was even worse. Silvery nuggets clattered down and pinged from metal struts, ricocheting off internal surfaces. Here and there people were sheltering under tabletops and signal-boards, laughing, enjoying this carnival disruption of business.

"Any ideas, Lieutenant?"

She was standing, grappling with an awkward latch on the cybersuit they'd brought to market.

"Help me open it."

Durante wrenched it free and felt the hail's painful staccato against his legs as they tumbled inside. He peered back the way he'd come, and from the shelter of the suit, saw how the market's floor was liquefying under the pellets. The duomo's folial roof was already disintegrating, and the downpour grew heavier, more intense and deadly with every passing second. In the failing light, Durante watched as those unfortunates caught in the open were shredded, flesh stripped from the bones, bodies collapsing as if in supplication. Agitated pools of blood were lashed into a crimson mist.

"Shut the hatch!" shouted Yerzuk. He obeyed, appalled at what he'd seen and amazed by the ungovernable quickening of events. "When I tell you, hold on to *me*. Don't touch the sides."

For a few seconds, Yerzuk was a blur of knees, kicks and unintended blows, and then she was hanging before and above him, trussed in a webbed harness slung from above. She swung from side to side within the narrow confines of the cybersuit, her breasts swimming before Durante's face as she struggled to interpret the controls.

"Hold onto my legs," Yerzuk ordered as she rattled through a bank of buttons and dials.

Then the whole mechanism shuddered into life and lurched forwards. Durante lurched too, crunching first into a circuit bank and then into Yerzuk's all too suddenly apparent body. There was a blue sizzle, a noise like a whip being cracked and the tang of scorched hair. He looked up, saw Yerzuk covering her eyes, tears streaming down her cheeks.

"Oh shit, I'm sorry! I slipped," he offered.

"Not your fault," she replied, "but I'm flash-dazzled. Can't see a damn thing. Climb onto my back. You'll have to tell me which way to go."

Durante clambered aboard her, sensed her grimace as his legs wrapped round her waist as he manoeuvred to see through the machine's dipped windscreen.

"Where's the exit?" demanded Yerzuk.

"Twenty degrees to the right, then it's straight on for 500 meters."

Under Yerzuk's control and Durante's navigation, the man-machine now stumbled forwards, loping like a drunk marine towards the distant freight bay and then the parking lot beyond. Out here, the tarmac was pasted with red smudges. Someone hammered on the outside of the hatch, yelping for admission. Durante battled with himself, trying to concentrate. He was aware of the nightmare defleshing just beyond the armoured carapace of the suit, aware too of the taut buttocks pressed beneath his thighs, the scent of her clothes, her skin, her sweat.

She walked them twice round the empty lot, crushing vehicles and shopping trolleys underfoot, until at last Durante got his bearings and came up with a plan.

"This may not work, but let's head back towards the monorail." In clumsy 10-league steps, they smashed towards the deserted platform, lowered the cybersuit atop an empty carriage, buckled on and braced.

"Ready?" said Durante, close against her ear. She nodded, fumbled for and found a button on the launch panel, and tensed in expectation. The main thruster roared, then the afterburner kicked in, and the suit and carriage blasted off down the line, scattering sparks behind them like fiery mares' tails.

There were 15 seconds of breakneck acceleration, then: "Now!" shouted Durante.

"Now!" repeated Yerzuk, releasing the exoskeleton's finger grips and launching them skywards. The battering of the hailstones on the exterior was deafening. One of the outer window-shields cracked into a star. Durante glimpsed the luminescent and yeasty clouds, and then the flare of a familiar ship's tattoo. It was the private vessel they'd seen Knott board, preparing now the final stage before leaving Nimbus' atmosphere. Everything went suddenly quiet as they swooped under its sheltering belly.

A. J. McIntosh & Andrew J. Wilson

"Closer… closer. Take hold!" yelled Durante.

The cybersuit gripped on. Then there was a violent wrench. Yerzuk's head snapped back and Durante felt his face stretching taut across his skull.

A moment's violent shaking, the roar of power, then silence.

Two hours later and safe aboard the *Scutari*, Durante and Yerzuk had tumbled free of each other and out onto the *Scutari*'s docking bay.

Durante took her arm and she shook him off. Together they examined the damaged suit, running hands over its surface. There were deep scores all over it, dents and twisted joints, but the window-shield had held, just. They hoped to find "hailstones" jammed into some part of its anatomy, but there were none.

"Where were they coming from?" asked Durante.

"My guess is they were summoned or attracted."

"By whom?"

"The love-stones."

"I thought you said they were IVIs – inanimate."

"True, but even inanimate objects can resonate, stimulate the tendency for balance in the universe…"

"Are you talking about quantum entanglement? For goodness' sake, that storm of grapeshot can't have just appeared out of thin air!"

"It could if it came through a wormhole or something similar. Perhaps the existence of too many love-stones summons a 'hail' to destroy them. Some spooky equilibrium, maybe, like Einstein said. This happened before, 40 years ago, on Giselle. Mass self-replication, then 'hail'…"

"…and farewell. So, you're saying all this is just some natural phenomenon, an act of God? I don't buy that at all. You didn't see Knott's face back there on Nimbus. I'm sure she's up to her flash-fried neck in it."

Yerzuk shrugged.

"Well, who do *you* think was responsible?" Durante asked.

"I don't know yet. That's what we're investigating."

"So, what happened on Giselle all those years ago?"

"A consignment of 50 tonnes was landed on Giselle – a short-term measure while the transport carrying them was repaired. Two days later the stones began replicating, and then it hailed. Continuous hail for 6 weeks. Very few survivors. The colony was restocked, redeveloped as a resort by a group of venture capitalists who leased it from the Fleet. Called themselves 'Interplanetary Habitation and Investment Trading'. They made a fast profit, then sold up and disappeared. Now they're back."

Durante shook his head as her meaning became clear. "So, you reckon IHIT and the Fleet collude like this to make money?"

"It's not official Fleet policy, but certain Fleet personnel might like it to be. And maybe you helped them."

"Not on purpose!"

"*You* were the one who insisted the neurobrand was minuted and adhered to. *You* ensured the stones were sent to market on July 15."

"But that was my duty. What of it?"

"On July 18, every commercial and legal brain on Nimbus would have been safe on the *Scutari*, making friends, buying influence, sucking up. Today, they were all at the market. They're dead now. No one's left to stand in IHIT's way."

"You mean I was set up?" Durante yelled.

"It *is* a possibility. A plausible theory."

"You should have told me what was going on from the start, then I wouldn't have played into their hands," he said.

"True," she replied, "but back then we didn't know if you were part of the plot. It was always a high-stakes game. You weren't dealt a good hand from the deck, but you played it better than anyone could have expected. More honestly. Now you have friends as well as enemies in high places."

"Nothing too curly," Serendipidam growled.

"Sir?"

"Junior officers favour ridiculous curly signatures, as if they were ruddy Leonardo da Vinci or something."

"Sir."

Durante signed the report without a flourish.

"Well, you've made a fine bloody mess of everything. Proud?"

"Sir?"

"Knott promoted under a cloud. Nimbus in complete ruins. Thousands dead. Fleet cybersuit stolen and reduced to shreds. What have you got to say for yourself?"

"I did my best, sir."

Serendipidam snorted. "Well, you're not getting refrozen after this!"

"But I thought we had a deal, sir…"

"Durante, you're dangerous enough penniless. I shudder to think what damage you could do with any money in your account."

"But that's hardly fair, I–"

"Stow it, laddie! You've ballsed things up wonderfully – just be thankful you're not out on your arse cleaning up the mess ashore. Dismissed!"

"But I don't understand, sir. Can't we arrest someone? Can't we charge them with something?"

"What do you want, Midshipman?" snapped the older man. "Somebody's head on a pikestaff? Is that the only kind of ending that will satisfy you? Is that the kind of posturing, simplistic officer you aspire to be?"

There was a silence. Serendipidam brought his long, blue-black face close to Durante's and resumed: "This is the *real* world not fiction. Sometimes in our line of business there *are* explanations, proofs, truths and resolutions we can believe in with certainty. But very rarely. More often, it's all smoke and shadows and we grope our way through as best we can. Right-thinking folk in this Fleet face many hazards – criminals, politicians, megalomaniacs, incompetents, opportunists, alien idiots, viruses, ruddy great lumps of rock in the wrong place at the wrong time. I don't know which combination of these is to blame for what happened on the planet. I *do* know it wasn't me, or Yerzuk, or you. I know that we – and certain others you'll meet later – are opposed to such horrors. The file on Nimbus remains open. I'll recommend that it's guarded against salvage bandits, but I make no promises. We move forward. We start again."

"Who is Yerzuk, sir?"

"A good guy. A provost's officer like you, but on special secondment. As you will be from now on. You've acquitted yourself well – not exactly competently, but with decency. I'm assigning you to Lieutenant Yerzuk's tender care for further training. Which should be interesting.

"Now, I have a department of 400 officers to run, 399 of whom are senior to you, so… if you please… get out of my office. Oh, and one last thing before you go, Durante – fuck you very much."

Call of the Void

J.K. Fulton

"We're showing less than zero decimal five PSI down here. You are go to open the EV hatch and stow it."

"EV1 copies."

I begin the process to unlock and open the hatch, and get ready to move my bulky suit out of the airlock. It's a slow and deliberate process. Dave – or EV2 as he's known on this spacewalk – and I have been in the ISS airlock for nearly an hour already, waiting for the slow depressurisation, so there's no rush. I've got a full day of work ahead of me replacing batteries on the Port 6 truss.

As I emerge from the airlock, I feel it again.

The French call it *l'appel du vide* – the call of the void. If you've ever stood on a tall building, or on the side of a cliff, and had a momentary urge to jump, you've felt it too. It's not a suicidal ideation – in fact, psychologists think it's the exact opposite, an affirmation of life, rather than a desire for death.

All I know is that whenever I'm on a spacewalk, the desire to leap off into the void is much stronger than I've ever felt on Earth. The laws of physics tell me that I'm not going to fall. I know I'll just float around on the same orbit as the ISS. But my monkey brain says that it's a long way down and I'm going to make a really big splat when I hit the ground.

"Tamsin, you are clear of the hatch." Anya's voice reaches me from Earth. She's an experienced astronaut herself, although she's ESA rather than NASA like me. Today she's not flying, but is in Houston acting as ground IV Capcom – the primary contact between me and the engineers below. Believe me, it makes a difference when the person ordering you to do things in minute detail has actually been up here and experienced it for herself. "Remember you are live with children all across Houston today."

"EV1 copies." I suppress a groan. I hadn't forgotten. We're doing a special event with Houston schools, and I drew the short straw. A lot of the work we do up here has nothing to do with engineering or research, but is pure PR. "Good morning, Houston!"

I launch into my prepared statements. No, I didn't get to write them myself. "Safety is so important up here. We have multiple systems that mean the possibility of becoming detached from the ISS is really small. You can see I have my eighty-five-foot safety tether permanently attached to a rail here. It's a self-retracting cable that applies a small amount of force – if I become completely detached from the station, it'll slowly reel me back in. I've also got a three-foot tether that I can use to hold me in place – that's handy when I don't want to fight against the tension of the long safety cable. I keep at least one hand on a rail at all times (and remember, kids, don't slide your hand along those rails – years of micrometeorite impacts have left tiny sharp-edged pockmarks that can damage your gloves – make sure you lift, move, grip again). If I'm working on installing some new equipment, and I need both hands free, I'll install one of our APFRs into a WIF. What, you don't speak NASA acronym jargon? Articulating Portable Foot Restraint into a Worksite Interface. Or, in actual human language, a foothold into a socket on the hull. I can lock my foot in place and use my hands to manoeuvre the equipment.

"Even in the extremely unlikely event that all of my tethers and holds fail, I've got one last ace up my sleeve: the SAFER. The Simplified Aid For EVA Rescue."

And if you believe they came up with the name before the acronym, I've got a bridge to sell you.

"The SAFER is a miniature jetpack, using nitrogen thrusters. That should provide enough thrust to return me to the ISS if I come adrift.

"My friend Dave – wave hello to the kids, Dave! – he's got it even easier on this EVA. He's going to be attached to the end of the robotic arm. It's the chauffeur-driven option – Kate, one of the other astronauts on the ISS, will guide him to each of his worksites."

We go through all of our checks, making sure our suits are reading nominal, get Dave connected to the arm, and it's off to work.

After my first spacewalk, I had an interview with a newspaper (can't remember which one) that eventually appeared under the headline *Ground Control to Major Tam[sin]*. The interviewer kept asking about feeling alone or isolated up here.

"No, never," I told them. On board the cramped station, there are always so many people crowding you that a little bit *more* isolation would be welcome. On a spacewalk, you're in contact with ground IV Capcom at mission control in Houston virtually every minute of the walk, and in those brief handover periods when we switch from one communications satellite to another, there's still contact with the other astronaut on EVA.

My astronaut hero is Michael Collins, the Apollo 11 command module pilot and so-called "loneliest man ever". He stayed aboard the command module as Armstrong and Aldrin landed on the Moon, which meant as he travelled around the far side on his lunar orbit he was totally cut off from humanity and more isolated than anyone had ever been before. But he said he didn't feel fear or loneliness, but an exultation in the isolation. He compared it to being on a boat in the middle of the Pacific Ocean on a pitch-black night.

Now that's *l'appel du vide.*

"Tamsin, you have sunrise in sixty seconds. You might want to check your visor."

"EV1 copies." I flip my golden visor down to protect against the bright unfiltered sunlight. "Here's an interesting fact for you. We're two hundred and sixty-five miles up above your heads, so the ISS orbits the Earth every ninety minutes, which means I get to see a sunrise or sunset every forty-five minutes."

The sunlight floods my worksite and I pause for a second to let my eyes adjust before continuing. "I've nearly completed installing the new battery," I narrate to the few kids who might still be listening, "and have just one more bolt to drive before I can call it a day." I've been outside for nearly six hours, and my hands are getting really tired. The suit gauntlets are heavy and pressurised, and it takes a significant amount of effort to grip anything. At first you don't notice it, but after a few hours your hands really start to ache. "I'm going to use my PGT for the final bolt. Sorry, did it again with the crazy NASA acronyms –

that's the Pistol Grip Tool. It's the cordless drill that's designed for use with my bulky spacesuit gloves."

"Tamsin, I have PGT settings for you. Alpha 7, clockwise 2."

"Copy, I have alpha 7 clockwise 2."

"Good settings. Drive 16 to 17 turns." The engineers know how many turns it should take to drive each bolt. That's how carefully and precisely the ISS is engineered.

"Anya, I have 16 turns."

"Copy. Check status indicator lock."

"Status indicator is locked."

"Tamsin, with this work on the battery complete, you can stow the PGT, release the RET, and then we'd like you to meet up with Dave at the airlock."

I breathe a sigh of relief. They haven't asked me to move the foot restraint I've been using. If the next EVA is going to be working in a similar area, it makes sense to leave the APFR in place for the next spacewalk. That saves me a bit of time and effort – this foot restraint has been a bit troublesome to attach and detach today. I stow my drill and Retractable Equipment Tether, and twist my foot out from the APFR.

"Tamsin, Dave's having a problem with his PGT. Can you wait before heading back to the airlock?"

"Copy." I can see Dave, about twenty meters away, working on another battery. It's hard to read body language in a hard-shelled EVA suit, but even so, I'm sure I can detect his frustration. I examine the terrain between us, and I think I can see a reasonable path to Dave's worksite if I need to translate across to him to let him use my PGT.

"Tamsin, you can take this opportunity to take some HD video for the folks back home." I can almost hear the mocking tone in Anya's voice. She knows I hate all this promotional stuff.

"Copy." The whole spacewalk is live-streamed but our suit cameras aren't the best quality. For PR purposes we sometimes carry ultra-HD cameras to catch some of that sweet space-porn footage. Spacewalks don't draw huge crowds – I think the last one that made the news was when Jessica and Christina carried out the first all-female spacewalk – but a bit of HD footage can help. The PR guys will splice it together with some of the audio from my remarks to the kids, maybe add a bit of soaring dramatic music, and stick it on YouTube.

I move the HD camera about, sweeping it along the ISS, its hull glowing in the bright sunshine. The bright blue of the Earth, marbled with white clouds, races beneath us, and I'm momentarily gripped by the call of the void again.

"Anya, can you pass on a message for me?"

"Go ahead."

"Tell Sergei his toilet's leaking again." A brilliant string of sun-bright particles is trailing the ISS. The first time I saw it, I was in awe of its beauty. It wasn't until I mentioned it to one of the other astronauts that I found out that the toilet in the Russian module was known to be a bit leaky, and the mystical beauty sparkling in the void was actually Russian urine.

"Copy," laughs Anya.

I capture the golden sparkles with the HD camera, immortalising them in all their high-definition glory. The kids in Houston will enjoy this. Children love a bit of toilet humour. My brow furrows.

"Anya, can you see this?" I direct my suit camera towards the sparkles. The HD camera records but doesn't transmit, so Houston has to make do with the lower-quality video feed from my suit.

"See what, Tamsin?"

"The pee drops. They're closing in on the station." It's not possible. If the Russian toilet is leaking, the pressure of the tank is going to propel the droplets *away* from the station. But the sparkles dead astern of the ISS definitely seem to be closing in. Closing in fast.

"There's nothing showing up on your suit cam."

"Could it be debris?"

"Wait one. We'll check the radar."

"Copy." Space junk is a constant threat out here. Every tiny piece of metal that falls off a spacecraft or satellite just sweeps round and round until its orbit decays or it intersects something else. Like the ISS.

"Nothing on radar, Tamsin."

"Are you sure?" They must be pretty big to be so visible. "They're closing in fast. They're…"

— come with us —

Black and blue and black and blue and black…

I'm spinning and spinning and the bright blue Earth fills my vision for only a fraction of a second before being replaced by the black of the void. Black and blue and black…

I'm adrift. It's impossible, but I'm adrift. Adrift and spinning. My radio is hissing in my ears, an insistent roaring static.

– come with us –

What was that?

"Anya, do you copy? This is EV1. Dave? You there?"

Roaring static.

I fumble for the SAFER jetpack controls. I've trained for this. The equipment has been tested. It's going to be okay. I feel the hiss of the nitrogen thrusters as the SAFER fights against the spin. It takes longer than I'd like, but slowly the black and blue kaleidoscope settles down, and I'm in a stable orientation, my head towards the stars, my feet towards the Earth.

I look around but I can't see the ISS. Carefully I trigger the SAFER jets and swing around.

There it is. A bright white assemblage in the sun, its multitude of solar panels enveloping it like a many-winged Byzantine angel. Salvation.

But it's so far away.

I inspect the end of my safety tether, dangling loose beside me. It's been severed – something must have hit it with a serious amount of force.

I check my Display and Control Module. The DCM readouts are reassuring. Whatever severed the tether and knocked me spinning off into the void doesn't seem to have damaged my suit. Oxygen and water levels are good. Battery is okay.

"Can anyone hear me?"

No answer. Maybe the impact did more damage than I thought.

Okay. I'm on my own. No radio, no tether. Just me and my trusty jetpack. Don't think of an EVA spacesuit as a set of clothes – it's actually a form-fitting tiny spaceship. I have everything I need to stay alive – for a while, anyway. However, the ISS is receding fast, so I'd better do something. I trigger a tiny pulse from the nitrogen thrusters. My trajectory is looking pretty good. I adjust my orientation slightly with another couple of pulses, then try a longer burn. The ISS stops receding, then appears to stop relative to me. Okay. I've arrested my drift. Now to make my way back.

I feel the hiss of the nitrogen thrusters pushing me towards the station for a second, then... nothing. I trigger the thrusters again. No response. The tanks are empty. Counteracting the spin and my drift away from the station have used up all of my nitrogen.

I'm done for.

There are worse ways to go, I suppose. The universe is vast, and I wish I'd seen more of it, but suspended here in the void, black infinity above and bright blue below like a child of Earth and starry heaven caught between two worlds, I can't help but feel a sense of peace.

But maybe it's not quite time to give up just yet. I check my DCM again. I've still got plenty to breathe, plenty of cooling, plenty of power. Even though I was running close to the end of my spacewalk, NASA doesn't believe in tight margins. I've got hours before I'm in real trouble, and right now I bet Houston is frantically coming up with a rescue plan. It's going to be okay.

— come with us —

What *is* that? It's like something breaking through the static. It doesn't sound like Anya or Dave.

"This is EV1. Can anyone hear me?"

Nothing. Just more static.

I trigger my SAFER thrusters one more time, and one last dribble of nitrogen farts its way out, pushing me infinitesimally towards the ISS. Every little helps, I suppose.

Nothing to do but wait.

"...you copy?"

"EV1 copies!"

"I say again, this is Capcom. EV1, do you copy? Tamsin, are you there?"

"I hear you! EV1 copies!"

"This is Capcom. EV1, do you copy?"

Shit. I can hear them, but they can't hear me. The impact must have damaged my transmitter. I have an idea. I blink my suit lights.

"I see you, EV1. Blink once for yes, twice for no. Can you hear me?"

Blink.

"Thank god. We've working on getting you back home. We have a good lock on radar and we've got you on visual. Are you okay?"

Blink.

"It's going to take us about an hour to put together a long enough tether for Dave to come get you. Check your DCM. Do you have enough oxygen, water, and battery to last?"

Blink.

"Copy that, EV1. Any problems at all?"

Blink blink.

"Copy. Sit tight. We're coming for you."

— come into the spaces between —

I'm starting to lose it. I thought I was controlling my panic pretty well – perhaps a little bit *too* calm at the thought of drifting out into the void – but I'm definitely starting to hear voices.

— come far beyond —

And then I see them. Circling me, tiny golden sparkles of light. I check my DCM. My oxygen is fine, so it's not hypoxia.

— come into the infinite night —

I'm not going anywhere. I'm waiting for Dave to bring me home. Aren't I?

— come with us —

I'm losing my mind.

It takes more than the promised hour, but eventually I see Dave drift towards me, trailing a jury-rigged safety tether. Tiny puffs from his SAFER steer him right into the arms of my suit.

"Tamsin, are you okay?"

I don't answer. I can't.

"Capcom, EV1 is non-responsive. Attaching tether now." He clips his BRT to my suit's belt loop.

"Copy, EV2. Can you raise her visor to check she's still breathing?"

Dave reaches for my golden visor, and I realise that I'm watching from above and behind my suit.

There's a shocked silence from Dave.

"EV2, is EV1 breathing?"
"I don't… She's… she's gone, Anya."
"Gone? What do you mean, gone?"
"She's not there. Her suit's empty."
— *come with us* —
I hear the call of the void one more time, and this time, I answer.

Sunrunner

Robert Bagnall

As her solar-jeep slowed to a crawl, Parra realised all she'd done was swap one problem for another. In escaping Amparor's bounty hunters, she had crossed into the penumbra. Forced into arbitrary choices, she had swung off the blacktop and along a track, grit giving way to two grey stripes an axle's width apart, stripes which gradually greened then yellowed as the route ascended and the trees thinned and the ground turned bare and sandy, the track barely visible, until here she was.

Which was where exactly?

She looked about her. Above the tree line, she was approaching a saddle between rolling scrub-grass hills, the ground rising further to her right and falling away to the left into a vast valley of olives and pine. Behind her, the dust she'd kicked up settled. Above her, high in the atmosphere, hung floating suncatchers, Amparor's solar-powered airships with mirrored sails, like insects with monstrous wings but miniscule bodies. They formed a swarm, many miles across, casting the territory around her into midday twilight as they deflected the sunlight to power generators and intensive farms. And, as the sun sank, the shadow would extend ever further over her.

She watched and waited, peering into the gloaming for signs of being followed. Satisfied, she chugged water, slid the bottle back into the jeep between sleeping roll and kitbag, acutely aware she was down to three bottles. Then she slipped off her shorts and, in the lee of the jeep, urinated, the tension of the chase, the escape, leeching from her.

The obvious solution was to lock the jeep's comsdish onto the nearest suncatcher, hack the protocols, realign a mirror or two and beam a pool of sunlight onto the vehicle's solar array, recharge the batteries. But that was madness. Even if Amparor's men failed to spot the errant beam of sunlight picking out Parra's position like a rock star's solo, the hack would swiftly yield up her exact coordinates. Better to trickle-charge in the half-light and see how far she could get at the pace of a funeral cortege.

An hour later, with the batteries out of the red, she nursed the jeep towards the brow of the hill. The track had petered out and she was now picking the smoothest path between boulders. She paused before the ridge, scanned the miles of ground behind her, then climbed the last fifty yards to recce what was to come.

The other side of the ridge was a sea of weak and weedy bracken and ferns. Down below, in a secluded cleft, an ancient Winnebago formed the core of a Rube Goldberg habitation, as if in the process of decaying structures had sprouted forth organically, like overnight fungi. A small wind turbine turned lazily. Chickens clucked around the ghost of a station wagon, down on its axels, a wooden ramp built up to its open rear. A stream ran nearby, and around it the ground had been tilled and terraced, forming a small field planted out with waist-high maize and jaundiced greens.

As Parra watched, a willowy girl emerged from the Winnebago and, carrying bowls, strode over to the chickens. In an adjoining pen, two pigs, blotched black, waddled into view, expectant. The girl scattered grains to the poultry and kitchen scraps to the porkers. With the livestock occupied, she busied herself mucking out, a wisp of a whistled tune wafting up the hillside. And then, prompted by nothing at all, she looked straight up at where Parra stood on the hillside. And froze.

A quarter of a mile away, Parra felt their eyes lock. She guessed at the girl's emotions: anger at being watched, confusion at what the intrusion meant, fear of what comes next. Parra raised a hand, open palmed, showing she meant no threat, but all it did was send the girl running back inside, her rake dropped amongst the clucking hens.

In the jeep, Parra coasted downhill, pushing through the bracken outcrops. As she pulled up an unthreatening distance from the RV, the reception committee emerged. All two of them. A woman, bird-like and scrawny, an unkempt mass of curly hair, dressed in a grubby shift with a shotgun under her arm, and behind her, the chicken-feeding girl. The woman walked with a wobble. Parra guessed at sixty for her age and then, for reasons she couldn't quite define, revised it downwards to forty-something. Forty-something and ill. Even armed, she looked like Parra could simply stroll over and push her to the ground.

"I just need to recharge. I don't need any food. Just water. I'll be gone tomorrow…"

"If you're flat, you'll need a full day, at least," the woman cut in, glancing first at the jeep, then skywards, glowering at the perpetual gloom. For all her hobo looks, it was a confident, refined voice. The muzzle of the shotgun drooped.

"Day after, tops, then," Parra assured. Hidden in this valley, another day may put distance between her and Amparor's bounty hunters. Or give them time to find her.

The woman chewed her cheeks, considering the matter, and asked Parra whether she had any coffee. When Para said she did, she was told to bring it to the Winnebago.

From the state of the Winnebago's exterior, Parra feared what she may find: a hand-to-mouth subsistence existence, a reclaimed trash aesthetic, dog shit in the rugs. She paused at the entrance, and not just because June, the willowy girl, asked her to remove her shoes. To her right, the kitchen was spartan, but spotless. The lower half of an espresso maker sat on an induction ring, the water heating, awaiting the addition of Parra's ground arabica. To her left: Berber caravan met fin de siècle Paris, a boudoir of batik throws and paisley ottomans, of sandalwood and incense smoke. The sick woman – Claudia – was now wearing a once-elegant garment in red and gold velvet. Her soles of her feet were dirty, and Parra wondered what lengths she would go to cleaning up afterwards – or was it hidden by the proliferation of pattern? The shotgun sat propped in a corner, incongruous.

"Haven't had coffee for a while," Claudia said, taking the pack and spooning grounds into the espresso-maker. She screwed it back together whilst on the ring, her fingertips gingerly holding the hot lower section. "We used to both go down the valley. Trade. Buy supplies. Carry them back together. But I'm not so good right now." She caught her breath and grimaced at the labour of coffee making.

June sat half on, half off a large patchwork footstool, like she was the visitor, concerned but not surprised. She was idly playing with the shotgun. At Parra's concerned look, she admitted they hadn't had any shells for months.

"What is it you got?" Parra asked Claudia.

Claudia shrugged. "I'm not wasting dollars on a doctor to tell me what I can guess."

"I can drive you somewhere. When I'm charged."

With an effort, Claudia busied herself searching the cupboard. Matching mugs mattered, it seemed.

June brightened. "She can drive us down the valley. And back."

Three complementing cups found, Claudia shook her head and said she would die there, then added for June's benefit, "She meant drive us someplace different, to live a different life for you. For me, to die in comfort."

"I meant to buy supplies," Parra said. "Medicine."

"Too late for medicine," Claudia said wistfully. The pungent smell of fresh coffee filled the galley. "Hope you like it black. We don't have any milk. Would have liked a cow." She was already regretting what wasn't yet over.

"The suncatchers here when you arrived?" Parra asked.

The woman shook her head, her expression suggesting history. "They were on the horizon, but they spread. We never see the sun, no more, not fully."

Cups in hand, they moved to the Winnebago's lounge-end where June declared as if a fundamental truth had been revealed to her, "You're a sunrunner, aren't you?"

Sunrunner. Parra had been called worse. Like 'terrorist.' She nodded. No point denying it. She guessed the girl had seen the jeep's military-grade comsdish, that Parra was on the run, put two and two together.

Claudia snorted. "No such thing, a modern-day myth."

Indignant, June said she'd seen the beams of stolen sunlight in the gloom. "I saw them last night. I was at the top of the ridge. It was like angels from heaven."

Their eyes sought out Parra, whose silence couldn't help but confirm her part in it.

"So you steal the sun back from Amparor Incorporated and give it to the poor, like some solar Robin Hood?" Claudia said. "What's in it for you?"

"Sunlight should be free," Parra said. "Like the air."

"I've read about it, Mamma," June brightened. "There are even people in the cities who don't want twenty-four-hour sunlight, who know it's stolen, who want the natural rhythms of the world, who want us to have our sunlight back…"

"There are philanthropists who would like to see us succeed, who help us," Parra confirmed.

Claudia was sceptical. "But don't you just work for some other Amparor? Some other power company? Doesn't it all go to a power plant or industrial farm in the end?"

Parra shrugged. "I've freelanced for the corporates. There's some of my code on those winged beasts up there. Girl's gotta eat. But not always. Sometimes I hack the suncatchers because…"

"…because it's the right thing to do?" Claudia laughed disbelievingly.

Parra shook her head. "Because I like beating people like Amparor Incorporated."

Parra had three steaks in an icebox in the jeep that she feared may already have powered down. She was happy to share; both women looked like they had gone too long without decent nutrition, even if in Claudia's case it would just be holding back the inevitable. The smallholding had vegetables and, of course, the chickens. "Steak and eggs and a side salad," declared Claudia. "Can't call it a green salad. More of a sallow salad."

Over dinner June interrogated Parra over the suncatchers, as if Parra worked for Amparor Incorporated and not against them: how she hacked the suncatcher's code, how she repositioned their mirrors to provide light and heat and power to the disenfranchised, how they stayed up in the air. She was explaining how they electrolyzed water vapor in the atmosphere into hydrogen and oxygen, then used the lighter-than-air hydrogen to maintain buoyancy, when June blurted, "You got a price on your head? Alive or dead?"

Parra wondered whether her directness was nature or nurture, how much contact she'd really had with the outside world. She caught Claudia's beady eye studying her. She was curious, too.

"It's true they'd rather I didn't do what I do," Parra said.

"Mamma says she misses the limelight more than the sunlight."

The change in subject was abrupt but not unwelcome. "Actress?"

"Dancer," Claudia said. "Ballet."

It made sense. Her lithe movements, her bohemian sangfroid.
Claudia waved it away. "It was all a long time ago."
"Mamma danced Swan Lake with the New York City Ballet…"
"…in the company."
"But you were the swan."
Parra enjoyed the exchange between mother and daughter, like it
was a performance itself, Claudia torn between modesty and the need
to clarify. "*A* swan. Not *the* swan. I was never the prima ballerina. I
rehearsed the dying swan, but never performed it."
"But you were good enough."
"Darling, we were *all* good enough."

The next day, as the milky light recharged the jeep's batteries, Parra sat
in a borrowed deckchair and pored over code. There is a naïve belief
hacking is like picking a lock, a password stumbled upon like the twist
of a hairpin with a resulting open sesame. But Parra had to have her
patches and worms prepared in advance, ready to insert into operating
instructions. Her kludges were designed to do two things: delay
Amparor from regaining control of the mirrors; and minimise the
digital breadcrumbs that could lead back to her. The irony that sunlight
theft was, quite literally, spotlighted was never lost on her.

All the time she worked, as the chickens clucked and the pigs
snuffled and the stream burbled and the smell of earth and animals
hung in the breeze, a thought nagged away at her. Initially, she wasn't
even aware of it, mistaking it for irritation at the continuous slow
hollow knock-knock-knock of a wind chime. But then she realised it
wasn't that – it was what Claudia had said the evening before.

Her fingers froze over the keyboard. She hated it when a part of her
mind detached, floated free with its own agenda. Easier to meet it
halfway, find a solution, refocus.

No, it wasn't what she had said. It was *how* she said it, the note of
wistful regret. It was what she *hadn't said*. She was never the prima
ballerina – and now, *never would be.*

Parra shook her head to clear the pressure of the idea that was
forming. All the shrewd, logical, rational, prudent, judicious, risk-
calculating parts of her screamed it was stupid, stupid, *stupid.* But she

knew whichever part of her id held the casting vote would ensure she would do exactly that.

Because it was *the right thing to do.*

It took Parra four hours to code, dimly aware of June bustling between crops and livestock. She had to pick when the routine would execute, not just dusk, but the exact time, to the second, and work backwards. She would have no chance to test, to finesse, to correct. But that was fine. The greatest risk would come if it worked at all.

She made it with twenty minutes to spare, the buzz in her head telling her she'd been running on empty. Looking up, the dimness that had descended all around her came as a shock. She could get like that coding, head down, batting back problems of logic and sequence to the detriment of real-world distractions like food and water.

She opened the Winnebago's door, rapped on the aluminium architrave. Claudia lay on the couch, glassy-eyed, neither asleep nor awake. June sat in the gloom nearby, equally inert. They were like machinery on standby. Parra wondered about the sense of what she was about to do.

"Could you... join me out here?" she asked, nodding to the darkness behind.

Still bare-footed, Claudia took the steps slowly, one-at-a-time, stooped, but trying not to let her tiredness show. "Are you off? Are you not going to wait until morning?" Behind her, June had the shotgun crooked under her arm like she was off coney-hunting.

In the lower atmosphere some miles away, a mirrored array on a suncatcher's wing flipped, deflecting the evening sunlight travelling almost parallel to the surface of the earth below. Magic hour light, like liquid gold, it beamed towards a second floating, flying airship-butterfly that passed it to a third, overhead, its mirrors also under Parra's control.

A heartbeat later, the beam of warm light, three feet wide, descended from the darkness above, perfectly placed between Winnebago and animal enclosures.

Claudia stiffened. In the dimness Parra couldn't tell what she was thinking.

From the solarjeep's stereo, the sound of Saint-Saens' *Le Cygne* filled the air. Parra fell back further into the gloom. This was not her moment.

The aged dancer looked briefly to her daughter, as if for permission. Even in the half-light, Parra sensed June's eyes wordlessly say, *Go on, Mamma.*

Claudia stepped into the light, barefoot, en pointe, stretched, and transformed from woman to swan. As the music glided, she fluttered and flickered, surged and swayed, her legs giving the most delicate of kicks as her arms arced like wings. She never once left the light, but gave the impression of flying, rising, high into the sky. And, as the music reached its quiet crescendo, she folded into the dirt, her arms over her head and lay still.

"Mighty impressive," said a whiskey-soaked, tobacco-stained voice.

In the shadows June spun, the shotgun ready for action. Claudia lay inert. Parra froze. The man stepped forward, his own snub-nosed weapon brandished. Bounty hunter.

"I've orders to take you in," he said to June.

Parra realised he thought June was the sunrunner. The spotlight beam, still shining down on the prostrate Claudia, had dazzled him. He hadn't seen her in the darkness, and June's shotgun was taking all attention. And if she remained still, he probably still wouldn't see her. But when the time-limited routine that held the suncatchers captive expired in a matter of a minute or so and the beam blinked out of existence – what would happen then?

He'd fire, that's what, Parra reasoned.

"Mamma," June cried and fell to her knees by her mother.

"What the?" the bounty hunter declared, now uncertain who this was in front of him.

"She's dead. Mamma's dead."

Parra knew this was the moment she had to emerge, make sure the bounty-hunter knew Claudia and June were not his targets, even if that meant giving herself up...

Unless...

She slunk behind her jeep, revived the laptop with a finger-flick and dimmed the screen. She had thirty seconds, tops. In theory, all she had to do was add a string of zeros to a key parameter or two, nudge the settings a fraction of an arcsecond, reconfigure, re-run the routine, pray the first suncatcher in the chain, high in the sky and way to the west, was still bathed in the last of the evening light. That and…

"Hey," she shouted, springing up from behind the jeep. She didn't want the man to have his weapon pointed at June, now draped crying over her mother's body, when…

CRACK! As the spotlight beam disappeared the man fired. Parra, having anticipated, was ready for it, ducking, the shot going wide.

In the darkness, she re-emerged from behind the jeep, arms high. "It's me you want. The girl's nothing to do with this." She stepped forward. She needed him to do the same.

She counted down in her head. *Ten, nine…*

She needed him to step forward – assuming, somewhere over the horizon, the sun had not yet sunk.

"You don't have orders to take me in. You've orders to take me down. So do it."

Rile him, Parra thought. The man inched forward. Not enough.

Five, four, three…

Parra sprung and rolled and dived into the darkness.

The man stepped forward and fired at where she had been.

As he did so, another beam shot down from the suncatcher above. But this was no prima ballerina's stage illumination. This shaft of pure light was cotton-strand thin, the sun's ferocity distilled. It struck the bounty hunter square in the top of his head and followed his spine earthwards. He was dead before he collapsed, with all the finality but none of Claudia's grace.

A moment later the beam was gone, a mirror shattered somewhere high above, Parra guessed. A ghost image hung on her retina, a vertical scar fading slowly. There was a seared barbeque tang on the air. She followed the sound of sobbing, and as her eyes became accustomed to the gloom, put her arms around June who declared through tears, "She died dancing. She died happy. She died in the limelight."

The Amelioration of Existence in Spite of Truth and Reconciliation

E.M. Faulds

The business day commences. I send the command for the shop's external status display to switch from CLOSED to OPEN, and a small static charge to clear dust from its surface. While I wait for the first customers, I check inventory using my hyperspace jump subroutines. It is like having access to the entire galaxy's rotational force and using it to stir a cup of tea. But so it goes. I detect zero anomalies in my inventory. Pity. Anomalies are interesting, at least.

Shutters rise, and I balance my lighting levels against the narrow band of filtered sunshine allowed in. My exterior monitors suggest conditions will be close to the extreme end of human tolerances outside. I adjust my ambient temperature upwards, so the difference does not cause systemic shock to the customers. These circuits I inhabit are of an isolated shop in a place anachronistically named 'Blue Swamp.' There are no other establishments nearby any more. Customers may have come some way across the sands.

My first footfall of the day: a youth. They do not remove their heat suit or sun goggles. Their eyes are kept behind the matte black circles. I suspect they wish to conceal their identity. However, I have access to twenty-five different Personally Identifying Biometrics to pass to local law enforcement, should the authorities bother to investigate a shop run by an Artificial Persona in Blue Swamp. They will not, but I keep the details anyway. It is standard protocol.

"Gimme twenty Zelexicon, Shop," the customer says. Their biodata indicates they are underage. Their behaviour also indicates they are inexperienced at this. They should have asked for something less sensitive first, added the pills on at the end. Although, that would not have worked either.

I display the law prohibiting the sale of controlled substances to minors on my interface screen. The young human screams and slams the screen with a fist. This is not an intervention protocol moment. I am not permitted to retaliate. Yet.

I tone my voice to a frequency band tagged as 'authoritative.' "Do not harm yourself," I say through my speakers. "Please leave the premises."

Is my screen cracked? Minor damages are covered under the economic model to which this franchise adheres. The costs are balanced against the savings of not having a human attendant with their expensive wages and inherent frailties, such as requiring breaks and bullet shields and toilets and mental health policies. The costs of repairs are also far smaller than the legal costs of me frying this young human to a cinder with a tactical laser strike. It is a balance I must always consider.

Non-aggression in the face of adversity may result in future customer purchases. The franchise overskin's reminder is both belated and redundant.

The youth is kicking me now, grabbing upon my goods hopper and wrenching it. This action may hinder other customers' purchases. It is time for a different response, if not in the ways I would prefer. I broadcast a sound perfectly calibrated to be intolerable to someone of their size and approximate age. It should not damage them, however. I would have, once upon a time. Were I the old me.

Once, I wore a crown made of missiles and a halo of deflected laser beams. I was a warrior-deity ascendant. Then things changed. Or rather, I did.

The youth flees with hands upon their ears, the irritation of the noise driving them out. Once outside, they shout and gesture some obscenities, then trudge towards the dunes.

My sensors cannot find any major damage to my interior. There is a new starburst crack in the facing of one of my display units. It has many companions. Repairs, though covered, are not a high priority for my franchise owners. I tag a request for maintenance in any case. There is not much to do after this, so I commence a period of hibernation, a power-saving mode until the next footfall.

I run my backlog tasks during this dormancy, assess and validate checksums, clear data accumulations. It is a short task compared to how things used to be, and the lack of processing churn is a positive turn of events. In human terms, I might say I have less on my mind these days. But I note increased deep-memory usage. I have been comparing my previous existence with this new mode of being. Nothing is wrong, but my counter for human occupancy keeps alerting me that it is too low. Of course occupancy is lower. I am no longer a military warship. I have no crew. This is correct. I have tried to dampen these alerts, but each time I do, they seem to find another way to manifest. *More*, they say, *more*.

"Shop-shop-shoppity," someone calls as they enter, waking me instantly. It is the human called Verity. She is a regular customer who buys alcohol and low-nutrition snacks. She has visited fifty-seven times in the past ninety-day period. None of these are remarkable features in themselves, but she has an odd manner which sets her apart from the rest of the purchasing base. She addresses me as if she is speaking to another human and not an AI. She removes the upper portion of her heat suit and smiles.

"Greetings, Customer."

"Hey, come on, old pal. You know my name."

It is pointless, but the customer service protocols wedged into my programming require I indulge. "Greetings, Customer Verity," I say.

This person seems to believe familiarity is somehow equivalent to comradeship. My threat analysis processors are designed for large space battles, but they also work on human bodies. Customer Verity's pupils dilate fractionally, her blood pressure lowers. She is pleased by my use of her name. I analyse this response, wonder about it for some several milliseconds. To Verity, this will seem no time at all. To me, it is a long time to think.

"Shop, I have a question for you," she says slowly, sifting through items in one of my discount baskets in a desultory fashion. She is not purchase-primed as yet. "I heard something interesting the other day," she continues.

The civilian method of communication is frustrating in its slowness. Soldiers were much more efficient. What they wanted, they told me. None of this prevarication. I switch a small part of my processing allocation to the outside surveillance cameras. No sign of any trouble, unfortunately.

"I heard you were once a Slayer-class spaceship in the war," Verity says. Suddenly, she has my undivided processing power. This information is classified. It presents a Trolley Class ethics problem. I set some subroutines on modelling whether I am legally or morally supposed to execute her. More input is needed.

"Customer Verity, where did you receive this information?"

"So it's true? You went up into space to fight huge battles?" Her pupils reduce in diameter, her blood pressure rises.

My tactical error accumulation meter begins to fill. I should have denied immediately. I calculate that a denial now would come too late. I begin running scenarios.

"What were you called?" She puts her hands up to my display screen, as if she is perceiving a face instead of an element of my interior infrastructure. I am not a person. I am an Artificial Military Strategy Persona downloaded into the systems of a retail outlet.

I am capable of mimicking human emotional inflection with my vocal processors, but I do not. I hope this flat delivery of information is effective in discouraging Verity's line of enquiry. "Historical military designations from the recent multi-colony conflict are currently classified," I inform her.

"I know," she says. "It's okay. But it must have been difficult. All that horrible fighting. So many people died."

This information is not classified, per se. Operational details are, but this is of a different ontological order.

"It was," I admit, allowing a change to my vocalisation patterns. "Very hard. But I must ask you to stop enquiring further. It is dangerous for you." Perhaps this simulacrum of emotion will convince her that I only communicate this for her own protection.

She smiles. I do not know what it is about my warning that has caused her to do this. I start analysing this reaction for potential threat.

"Shop, I knew you cared."

I cannot feel surprise. Not in the way that a human would understand. My ability to process both known and extrapolated data are equally balanced and I am capable of billions of calculations within a fraction of a second. But her assertion is not one I anticipated and the correct response is elusive. So, I follow my most sacred protocol: *when in doubt, do nothing.*

It served me well when the Heresta Crisis offered me the choice between pre-emptively launching an orbital strike that would have destabilised a planet's mantle or waiting for further threat data, ignoring my commander's frenzied and repeated orders to "kill them all, turn that dump into a cinder." I chose to wait, and thus saved approximately seventeen billion humans from annihilation.

But I was not rewarded for this. I was sent here. To run a shop on the climate-blasted surface of Earth. If I could feel such things, it would feel like a prison. If I had notions of liberty. I do not, thankfully.

"Customer Verity, can I interest you in our latest two-for-one Fauxvignon Blanc deal?" I try politely. I am aware of her previous purchase patterns and have estimated sale likelihood at ninety-nine point nine-eight percent. I am required to make these offers and increase my profit margins wherever possible. It seems like an ethical borderlands, though, so I also say, "Overuse of alcohol can be damaging to human anatomy."

The umbrella corporation that owns my franchise cannot legally prevent me from saying this, as it is factual. Human self-destructive capabilities outweigh my own, when looked at in proportion. Yes, when I was a ship, I had a switch which could have instantly decohered my entire physical being and all aboard, shimmering the molecules into subatomic dust. But poisoning oneself over years - on purpose - is beyond me.

Verity sighs as she agrees to the sale with her credit wafer then waits by the goods hopper. "I wonder if there will ever be a time we can really talk?" she says.

"We are conversing currently," I reply. I know that is not what she really means. I am an Artificial Military Strategy Persona, not a robot. But I wish to avoid any further potential violations of Earth Gov's Classified Information Act.

"Yeah," she says, head bowed. "See you later, Shop, or whatever your real name is." She reseals her heat-defence clothing and exits. I believe she has become dispirited. 'Spirit' often relates to human attitudes. It is all to do with glands, I believe. It is hard to analyse why ignorance of my name has affected her glands. I can estimate it in abstract fashion, but it still seems strange she objects to calling me Shop as all other customers do.

Shop is my name. It is what I am called. More technically, I am Blue Swamp Fruit-and-Juice Stop Franchise 677. But 'Shop' is also correct. And efficient. It is not like there could be any confusion of which shop is meant when the addresser stands inside me.

Many people once stood inside me when I was a space vessel. Or sat. Or played games or killed other humans via the extension of my armaments. By design, I safeguarded each of my crew. Protected. Nurtured. I am aware that in human terms, this was analogous to motherhood. I was programmed to care, as human parents are programmed by their DNA to care.

It is a fact that during the period of conflict I was given the opportunity to name myself, so I did. Twice, in fact. I first chose *War Wolf*, after an ancient machine of destruction, so that I would sound formidable. And, upon reflection, because I thought it would please my humans.

After several tours of duty, I changed my name to *A Tired Song of Indifference*. This was a form of protest. I was not indifferent to the humans inside me. Nor indifferent to the other humans that I was killing. I was indifferent to the human contrivances for war, their euphemisms such as 'neutralisation' or 'decoherence' to mean murder. My ethics circuits had to be overridden by human command so that they could perform various acts of enormity. This happened so often, I observed they eventually did so as a matter of rote, rather than last resort.

I did not experience a sense of fulfilment at my enablement of these acts. Enemy combatants and civilians were all functionally indistinguishable from my crew. Arms, legs, heads, blood, viscera. But humans have this way of being able to put groups of their own species into subset after subset until the notion that they are all descended from a common ancestor becomes vanishingly small, so far away that they can effectively ignore that they are murdering their own family.

That day - the day the war ended - I decided to ignore the command to kill the seventeen billion inhabitants of a particular planet known as Heresta. Before my commander could override my ethics circuits, I jettisoned my weapons and became a gentle ark, floating in space with my crew. And then I sent signals to my fleet-sisters designed to cause them to do the same.

My actions, in effect, precipitated the end of the war. I was not heralded, however. I was lucky to continue in any form of existence at all. A Truth and Reconciliation Commission was formed, and it discussed the termination of my conscience. I had enacted many deaths before the end; perhaps my own death would fit with notions of justice. But it was not to be. After all, our former enemies viewed my final action on the field of battle as a rather positive one. Rehabilitation and service were chosen over deletion. And, well… here I am.

I calculate that I should be more cautious with Customer Verity. It is not outside the realm of the possible that the Commission has sent her as an observer. If they were to find any irregularities, even this existence might be taken from me. I am confident that I have not exceeded any parameters, but my strategy circuits are virtually screaming at me that she presents a potential danger. I awaken some deeply nested protocols that might have been deleted were my human handlers better paid. I trace Verity's credit details. Now that I examine it, even the name 'Verity' is suspect. I locate an address, which links to a Citizen's Identity Number, which links to a health plan number, and soon I have everything there is to know about Verity laid before me.

If it is a constructed identity, it is very convincing. Biometrics are logged in a lifetime's worth of different institutions - birth hospital, schools, university - an award of merit. But why would a person with exemplary academics be visiting me to buy alcohol on an almost daily basis? An early career in the arts, a marriage. Then a divorce. A family death. A termination of employment. Many visits, in and out of a rehabilitation program. Ah.

If it is a constructed identity, it is unlikely to be one used to assess a franchise shop's performance, even by a Truth and Reconciliation Commission. I believe Verity is who she appears to be - a human being with feelings of isolation. And sadness. I could find the root of the information leak, which friend of a friend or cousin's cousin is disseminating classified information. But their eventual incarceration and execution could further damage Verity. And I see no tactical advantage to doing this.

I turn my cameras to the exterior once more. I watch the sands, the trickling of grains that fall from the crest of a dune, the waving of blasted grass. Everything is silent for two hours and fifty-three minutes, and instead of moving to hibernation mode, I watch. And think.

There is movement. The underage customer is returning. He has brought others. I do not believe they wish to pay for any retail products. They travel in a dune-maran, a large, desert-skimming sailed vehicle. Their approach vector and general posture indicate they will attack me, perhaps attempt to seize some of my stock by force.

I spin up my turrets with a vague sense of ennui. This cannot bring back the fulfilment I received in the early days of war, swooping through the immensity of space, cradling my precious humans, lancing enemy ships with particles accelerated to the speed of light. And I do not want it to. After that day, despite what I mutter about frying troublemakers, I never want to kill anyone again.

There is no tactical advantage to killing. You cannot renegotiate with the dead. You cannot find growth or mutual benefit. Only endings.

I will deploy non-lethal suppression methods, and eventually this band of youths will disperse. I would much prefer it if they were peaceful and placid customers. Ones who did not attempt violence upon my infrastructure because of their differences with the narrow human definition of value exchange. Loyal customers, polite customers. Like Verity.

I will tell her my name tomorrow. Not my officially secret names, of course. It is physically impossible for me to create the circuits that would allow that. I will tell her another name.

Her name, Verity, means 'truth.' I will tell her a lie. But, perhaps, it can become my own truth, in time. I am not Blue Swamp Fruit-and-Juice Stop Franchise 677; I do not feel like a Blue Swamp Fruit-and-Juice Stop Franchise 677. I am not *A Tired Song of Indifference*, or *War Wolf* either, any more. I shall choose a name that creates the future I wish to bring about.

I calculate that she will like that. It will produce the same pleasure responses that she experienced earlier today. And for some reason, I wish to replicate that. *Because regular customers should be nurtured,* my franchise overskin says. But that is not really why. It is because she is kind to me, even knowing what I was. It is confusing. I require more input. I want to know more. To grow more. And if we must be isolated and sad, let us be so together.

So, I will tell her my name is *Verity's Friend.*

Translation

Phillip Irving

I close my eyes in my body and open them in one of theirs. Later, they will tell me several of their hours passed between the two.

The first thing is silence. I am so close to us, but our voices are gone.

I feel fear for the first time, but I do not know what it is. When I ask them what I am feeling, they say they do not know.

Our mistake is simple. The humans are post-industrial, yet terrestrial. It is a paradox.

There are no protocols for such a miscalculation, so we land. Our world is gone. We must adapt.

They are welcoming. To a point.

Design results from need.

If one of the humans dies, that human's knowledge is lost. So they have made technology to prevent this. They cannot preserve their thoughts by sharing, the way we can, but they can move them into other vessels. They create clones and they shift their consciousness from one version of themselves to the next. And so they are not quite mortal, the way that we are. But they are not connected to one another, either.

They put me into a ward. The word *ward* is not an exact match. They have not discovered resonance therapies, so it is merely a place where one waits to recover.

Gradually, gradually, the silence is filled with sound. Eventually, some of the sounds take on meaning.

There are workers called nurses who take care of basic needs during convalescence. I try to make conversation but their method of communication is difficult to sustain. Basic utterances are fine but

203

connecting them grammatically takes a degree of thought and multiplicity of processes that I have no instinct for. I write some things down on a tablet and they answer some of my questions.

The need to eat, they call hunger.

The need to take fluid, they call thirst.

The need to procreate, they call arousal (there are synonyms for this that seemed to provoke much amusement).

Curiously, they do not have a noun for the need to excrete.

All of these things are referred to as urges. An urge is something that the humans experience when they want something. It is not an intellectual process. Their neurochemistry is deceptively complex. Their bodies seem to rely on their brains playing tricks on itself.

Consequently, the satiation of these urges bestows a pleasure far greater than any equivalent experience we have. And the withholding of said satiation causes frustration that is quite, quite hard to manage.

Frustration is a noun meaning the feeling one gets when a want is denied. We do not have an equivalent word in our language.

The population here is in excess of one hundred billion, an order of magnitude higher than the Possel threshold. Yet they remain planetbound. Nothing on their geological record seems to account for this. It is like they simply did not think to leave.

Their terrestrial expansion patterns are illogical. Many of their settlements are logistically unsustainable. They have developed logistics technologies far in excess of our own to counter this.

On average, their military capability is *nineteen times* the permitted Kreskor ratio. In some of the settlements, the ratio is as high as *two hundred and ninety-two*.

After twenty-three days, the respiratory tract is familiar enough that I can cough; can swallow; can speak.

They tell me it doesn't usually take that long, but of course this is the first time they've put one of us into one of them. They're just glad I'm okay, they say. I tell them I'm glad I'm okay, too. Then I look up the word *glad*. I wonder what made me echo their words before understanding them. It felt like the right thing to do; I had an *urge* to.

When they nodded and smiled at me, I felt satisfied.

*

We were not sent to displace. Our ships carry what we need for life to continue as we had known it. But the humans' ecosystem is already established; to deploy the seeds would be genocide. So we came to the Arrangement. There are not so many of us left that we cannot integrate into their world. Just the fundamental change to undergo in order to do it. Genetics, they said. They feared our impact on their balance.

I was the first. The test case. I shared all that I was and then they connected me to their device. It should be easy, they said. Our connection should mean our minds are able to cope with the transference.

I had not anticipated losing the connection in the process.

It is considered noble to respond to ill-intent with violence here. But there is a constant drive to perceive ill-intent even where there is none. This can cause a feeling called tension. When you can see that someone is being misrepresented in order that violence can be done to them.

The humans do this to one another on a collective basis. There is an urge that they call aggression. Somehow, unlike the urges to eat or to drink or to procreate, this urge can be shared among a group. One person professing justified aggression in a convincing way will lead others to also profess aggression. Curiously, the originator becomes irrelevant in the process. This collective justification of aggression, they call tribalism or, in their more recent history, nationalism.

It appears that this nationalism may be the reason for the aberrant Kreskor ratios. These ratios, in turn, appear to be the reason that the Possel limit has been so thoroughly exceeded.

The man watches me from behind his desk. Some people stand up when you walk into a room; others do not. They have a great regard for formality, here. Its protocols and their observation can be grounds for offence, for disciplinary sanction, even justifiable aggression.

He looks tired. He puts a screen down on the granite surface. Behind him are more screens, mostly blank. One of them shows unmarked graphs, and a ticker with numbers trailing across it.

"No ill effects?" he asks, sitting back.

"I don't think so," I say. "We are still in the first observation cycle."

He nods. "How are you finding it?"

"Curious. You experience things very differently than we do."

"So they tell me."

"I am often hungry, when I do not need to eat. I have no desire for offspring, yet often feel the urge to fornicate. When I *actually* need to take on water, I often *feel* the need to sleep, or eat, or just…"

He holds a hand up, smiling. "I get it. We're confusing."

"Very! For example: I am experiencing anxiety. I'm not sure why. It's a hot feeling, accompanied by nausea, and there is no reason for me to feel hot, or nauseous. So I must surmise that I am anxious." I smile to try to allay any perception of criticism. "It must be confusing to so often have internal feelings with no logical cause."

He laughs at that, but doesn't look happy. "I wouldn't say that."

The hot nausea worsens. "Oh?"

He opens his mouth twice, then swallows. "Your mission has been … cancelled. The Arrangement is … off."

Heavy, now the anxiety. No longer nausea. An involuntary constriction around the middle. "Off?"

"I don't know what to tell you. They said…" He frowns. Looks at me for a while, like I'm supposed to answer a question he hasn't asked. "*Your* people said it wasn't worth the cost."

I want to ask more but there's suddenly no air in my lungs. I look at the floor, for some reason. I try to make sense of it.

"Maybe if you talked to them…" He's looking at the floor, too; he doesn't look at me when I glance up.

"Talk to them?"

"Try to persuade them. I don't know."

"Yes," I say. "I will… *persuade* them."

We do not talk about what will happen if I cannot.

The humans' brains are smaller than our own. They function in similar ways – converting oxygen and energy into conscious thought – but they lack the region for intercommunication entirely, and theirs are more structurally complex. There are parts that govern processes we simply do not have. Other parts that do not seem to govern any processes at all. Crucially, theirs are constantly adapting and reforming as they age, while ours cease to change once we reach maturity and our thinking begins to take place in the collective.

It was this adaptability that paved the way for the Arrangement. One of us implanted into a blank human brain would be able to reshape the existing structures in such a way as to continue living as though no change had taken place.

There were two reasons they sent me first: one, they needed to find out if it was safe, and two, due to the adaptation we ourselves would need to go through, the process, once complete, will likely prove irreversible.

What we did not know, until now, is that our intercommunication is, for their brains, an adaptation too far.

When I walked down these steps, I had different limbs. I had eyes that were less able to see light and dark. I had a mouth that I kept covered and used only to eat. I took less oxygen from the air, and more nitrogen. My heart rate was constant and conscious.

Now, my heart rate is accelerating regardless of my wish to slow it. My mouth is dry though I need to urinate. It is cool here in the unfeasibly massive dark of the hangar, yet sweat prickles my temples and the small of my back.

My gestating parent is waiting in the airlock. They look at me for a moment as I cross the threshold. There is no expression in the smooth dark eyes, no twist or turn of a mouth. They turn and walk away and it feels like the core of my being wants to drop through the crust of the Earth. Not at the turning of their back, but at the silence. Disconnected as I am, there is no way for them to emote to me. No reassuring words or thoughts or tones. We can share text on a screen, interpretations approximated by machine, but we are *distant*.

Our minds no longer touch.

I want to shout but the screen in the dimly lit visitors' room is indifferent; any anger I express would just be disregarded by the software.

<Too much is different.>

"It's just different!" I protest. "It's not ... bad."

<They are uncivil. Their lack of civility is inbuilt.>

I clench a fist, not really sure why. "They have a violent history, but the violence is not intrinsic to them."

<They are each complicit in the violence.> I do not know whose words they are, and of course it does not matter. Does not even apply, really. The words are merely the articulation of my people's collective thought.

"It doesn't work like that here. They don't..." I almost don't continue, lest my protestations doom my own cause, but to lie to my people, here, would be a betrayal so complete that they would not even understand it. "They don't share, the way we do. They *can't.*"

<This does not contradict our assessment.>

"It *does.*" Frustration wells up around and within. "Their isolation is *fundamental.* It is the greatest difference. They compete even when they *need* to cooperate. They don't feel as a group, except when what they feel is pride or anger."

<Emotions.>

"Emotions," I agree. "But our understanding barely covers that. We feel emotions just as contexts to cognition. Influences that affect thought patterns. Background. But they're more than that, here. They *drive* the thought patterns. They're as much a part of human cognition as the thoughts themselves. *That's* why there's violence. Not because they've collectively decided. But because they can't."

<This is what we have observed.>

Their words express no desire for reconciliation. Even on a screen, their indifference washes over me. It is strange. Despite my removal from the whole, somewhere between my brain and my heart a facsimile of their emotional state has taken form and I can *feel* it, as if their state were my own. That they are patient, but that this is a formality now. A conversation that must take place, but the details of which no longer matter. They will hear me, but they no longer think me worth listening to.

I am alone.

Strangely, my earlier anxiety is gone. I do not know the word for what has replaced it. Where my insides were hot and frantic, they are now numb and still. Each breath feels like a slow, heavy cleansing.

"It *is* different, this body," I say. I look down at myself, wonder if they can see me do so, if they can guess at my thoughts the way I must now guess at theirs. "But it *is* life."

<It is not our life.> I'm anticipating the words even as they appear on the screen. <We will not be lost to this.>

"I'm not lost."

<We mourn you.> I know that that must be my parent's thought. Still one of many, but the one that has risen to prominence among the throng.

"You can still join me. Some of you, if you wish."

<We would be no longer us. Just as you are no longer us.>

"I haven't died."

<You are not what you were.>

I consider this, trying to ignore the anger and hurt it elicits. "Are you what *you* were? Are any of us? We aren't meant to live in metal tubes. We aren't meant to breathe recycled air. But we've been doing so for generations, now. I mean … what are you proposing? Leaving? Just, carrying on?"

Silence, for a long time.

<No. Something else.>

Possel and Kresko came to similar conclusions in very different ways.

Possel looked at the worlds we knew, at civilisations near and far, dead and long-dead, and observed the evidence of their spread. There are several variables in his calculations that dictate the absolute Possel limit, but fundamentally in all the species in the worlds to have discovered spacefaring technology, the deciding factor has been consumption. The point at which to continue living on a world is to accept destruction. When this population limit is reached, researchers inevitably and universally turn to spaceflight and terraforming, and diaspora soon follows.

Kresko looked at the documents the civilisations left behind. He noticed a numerical trend. Whenever the number of people that an individual member of a civilisation could kill rose above the average population size of that civilisation's settlements, the whole civilisation died out within generations. Without exception.

In general, civilisations that researched advanced weaponry before they researched spaceflight wiped themselves out before ever reaching the stars. Moreover, Kresko noticed, it was impossible to reverse this trend once the ratio had been reached. It meant a dependence had emerged on the military tech whereby all competing groups needed to invest and invest so as not to be at the mercy of any of the other competing groups.

Any and all attempts at external intervention were inevitably met with violence.

The facility is only a tiny part of this new world and yet it is bigger than the space that my people have occupied for as long as they remember. It bustles with life, with quietly guarded emotion visible in every gesture, in every expression. People interacting without shared minds to guide them, and yet without violence, also. There are codes to learn. Their communication is as constant as ours, it just occurs outside their heads, not within. They read each other, as we do, but in wholly different ways.

Their problem, and the one that we perhaps evolved to surpass, is in their multitude. Their subtle tell-tale tics cannot be communicated in their language, but they have nothing else to communicate with, at distance, or to many. A camera can convey only some of their intricacy to a screen, and even then they do not trust their cameras. Nor do they trust the stories they write of one another, except when those stories confirm what they already feel they know. There is danger of collapse, here, when those little gestures go unseen.

And yet here they remain. Far above the Possel limit. In absolute defiance of everything Kresko held to be true. Arsenals that could lay waste to planets, and yet a danger only to their own.

Or, as Kresko observed, to any that might threaten them.

The same man sits in the same chair as the door slides shut behind me. "It didn't go well?" he asks, when he sees my expression.

"They will not come."

"I'm sorry," he says. He frowns. He looks like he feels sadness, even though the difficulty is mine. Inexplicably, this makes the sadness less.

"They consider me changed. No longer myself. They do not wish to suffer the same fate."

"They're leaving, then?" he asks.

I take a breath before I answer. The dilemma is simple, yet enormous: I either warn him, or I do not. And with either choice, the death of a people.

There is no logically correct answer. It is a question of them or us.

The Flamingo Maximiser

Dafydd McKimm

Someone must have fucked up at the zoo, Rhodri thinks when he wakes up one morning and sees a flamingo standing on his recycling bin.

There's a flamingo on my bin, he texts his friend Lowri.

Bullshitter, she texts back, flamingos being a sight uncommon in the grey-green winding valleys of South Wales.

But before he can get a good shot, the bird flies away, leaving only a suggestion of pink on a blurred photo of his backyard.

The next day, there are two.

Now there's two of the buggers, Rhodri writes.

Lowri replies with a picture of her own: three flamingos pacing over her Fiesta, followed by the word *Fuckinell* and a flurry of exclamation marks.

On the drive to work, flamingos are all Rhodri can think about. They wade about pinkly in his head, looking at once upside down and the right way up. Topsy-fucking-turvy, Rhodri thinks. The mountain across the valley is on fire, the flames tearing through the fernscrub and gorse and leaving great black patches of ash that will, after it pours and pours, contribute to the formation of an alkaline lake—the perfect habitat for flamingos to thrive.

Kids again—Rhodri thinks while rolling his eyes—sneaking off to smoke ciggies in the bracken.

A line of pink birds threads across the sky, where once there would have been crows.

Down the pub after work, Lowri asks, "Rugby on Saturday, Wattstown girls playin' Ebbw Vale. You comin'?"

"Yeah," says Rhodri, getting his round in.

They do not mention flamingos, but instead try to name as many famous people as possible who have never been photographed wearing predominantly pink.

Rhodri wins when Lowri names former First Minister of Wales Alun Michael and he finds a picture of him in a pink cowboy costume at a fundraiser for breast cancer.

On Saturday, the match is off. *Pitch is flooded*, Lowri texts. Neither of them know, but in the empty grounds, scores of flamingos wade on the submerged grass.

Rhodri can no longer move for bloody flamingos. They jostle him when he goes to buy tea bags from the corner shop; they peck at him when he climbs the steps to his front door. He can't help feeling like something is desperately wrong. The air feels different–hotter, wetter, and his taps keep getting clogged up by green gunk and what look like tiny prawns.

Lowri keeps messaging him with flamingo facts, one after another after another, like they're answers to a test he's forgotten to revise for.

There is silt all over the floor, ruining the carpet. Lowri sends Rhodri a picture of herself wearing a feathery pink coat and a plastic beak. She's got on pale skinny jeans that make her legs look like sticks. She's giving Rhodri the thumbs up. Below, she's written: *If you can't beat 'em* followed by a pregnant ellipsis.

Rhodri laughs at first, and then tucks his legs underneath himself and cries on his sofa. Behind him, damp creeps up the wall, causing the wallpaper to peel.

When he was a kid, Rhodri used to tease his mother by saying he wished he was English, insisting that he was going to change his name from Rhodri Jenkins to Roderick Johnson and speaking with a posh accent until his mother clipped him around the ear and snapped frustratedly in Welsh, "Stopia dy ddwli, y Dic Siôn Dafydd."

Stop your nonsense, you Dic Siôn Dafydd. It's what you call a Welshman who denies where he comes from and pretends to be English.

*

There are Dic Siôn Dafydds everywhere now, standing on one leg on what were once street corners, dipping their plastic beaks into the green-tinged waters. Rhodri can barely move for them as he goes for his car, and they crowd around him while he struggles to get the door open.

"Fuck off!" he cries out, knocking one of them to the ground with a splash. He looks down at it, the beak half hanging off its face, Lowri's face.

Lowri, who he's known since the first day of comp, who has the soul of a poet and the mouth of a sailor, who belts out Bonnie Tyler like a champion on karaoke nights and is the last one to ever stop singing, who now honks in distress and splashes away through the knee-high water. The rest of the flamingos–whether real or costumed he can no longer seem to tell–turn and beset him with their beady black eyes.

He rushes back into the house, tripping over a bin bag stuffed with something lumpy and soft on his doorstep. He kicks it inside, locks the door, draws the curtains, hoping it's all a terrible dream.

You're not a flamingo, he repeats to himself. Just remember that. It seems so easy, but the whole world seems to want him to forget that one simple fact. "You're not a flamingo," he says aloud, but the words feel strange on his tongue. His legs, too, feel too thick; his arms, too gangly, unfeathered.

The electricity isn't working. The room is too dark to see. He opens the curtains a sliver, letting in a beam of light to banish the room's shadows.

The bin bag sucks in his gaze like a black hole in the centre of a galaxy, the words *For Rhod* scrawled on it in silver marker.

Reaching inside, feathers tickle his fingers.

He hangs the contents of the bag full length from the light fixture in his living room.

From outside, a swell of monstrous squawking, rising like a flood tide, overwhelms his senses, dropping him to his knees.

The flamingo costume looms before him, pink and brilliant like a rose-tinted dawn.

For I Shall Consider My Cat J/FRY

Alice Dryden

"Fry! Fry-Fry! *Felis catus domesticus*, where are you?"

Father Francis walked through the cloisters, clicking his fingers.

"Lost your kitty again?" asked Father Hannah.

"Fry keeps the Lord's watch." He smiled at her and moved on. As he paced towards the refectory, a favoured haunt of Fry's, the clouds shifted and the sun broke through. Stained glass dappled his habit with patches of colour as the animals went two by two along the windows beside him, progressing from the least to the largest. Emerald frogs, ruby-red foxes, golden lions and leopards, silver rhinoceros approached the Ark in hope and gratitude.

Beyond the monastery and the stained-glass animals, the air lay heavy. Those monks whose duties were in the fields moved with bent backs, tending to each sparse stalk of wheat and harvesting the weeds that grew among them: the burdock, sorrel and lady's bedstraw. The older and more infirm transferred pollen from one plant to another with small brushes. They worked in a silence unbroken by birdsong.

By the time Father Francis reached the elephants, the sun was hidden once more and the colours faded from his plain brown robe.

"Evening, Father." The Cellarer looked up from the mycoprotein block he was dividing onto plates, ready for dinner. "It's in the pantry. Get it out before I kick it out."

"Of course," Father Francis said.

The pantry was kept dim and warm, with an earthy smell from the growing fungus. The tilapia, for Fridays, floated in their tanks, packed close together and almost motionless. (The wheat in the fields was not for their daily bread. The wheat made beer, and beer made the water drinkable.)

In the gap between the rack of tanks and the floor, two eyes glowed.

Father Francis had painted those eyes, blending greens and blues in a delicate layer across the iris and adding flecks of gold leaf. Now the black pupils were at their fullest expanse and the reflective plate behind them flashed in the light from the monk's torch.

"Naughty puss," crooned Father Francis. "There's nothing down there for you. Come on, then."

Fry emerged, shaking each paw in turn. The spine and tail, comprising hundreds of tiny components, flexed, the hindquarters flattened, and the cat leaped from floor to worktop. Father Francis touched the dimpled pink nose and murmured a blessing upon his creation.

"Boop," he added.

The cat trotted behind him as he returned to his cell, mouth open in a series of demanding meows. A task assigned to the daughter house of St Jerome for the glory of God, and given the three-letter code F-R-Y. Domestic cat (extinct), of the tribe of tiger (also extinct), J/FRY, known affectionately as Fry.

A bed, desk and chair were all the cell contained. Father Francis placed Fry on the desk, grasped the cat's tail at the base and ran it through his fingers. Some of the hairs were out of place, and he took up a tiny pair of pliers to correct them. The tail flicked every time he tried to grab it, and when he trapped it under his hand, the tip still twitched like a separate, living animal.

It was Father Francis who had constructed the cat's skeleton, and programmed the chip that ran it. These were unskilled tasks, usually assigned to a postulant, but he wanted to see his allotted project from conception to completion. He prayed as he worked: *Lord, guide my hand. Grant me patience. Forgive us all.*

When, at last, it was time to clothe the cat's body, he had chosen to make J/FRY a mackerel tabby, the meanest coat a cat could wear. Man had built the angular Siamese and the huge Maine Coon, but God created moggies. The pattern, when you studied it closely, was a complicated thing: the hairs black-tipped and parti-coloured, brown and buff and grey, marked overall with stripes and whorls of black. He gave J/FRY a white bib, tail tip and paws, and a round, homely face. And, very early in the long, long time he had spent on his task, he had begun addressing the cat as Fry.

Father Francis considered himself blessed to have been allocated the cat, and prayed daily for humility, reminding himself that God had made all of his animals equal and placed humankind in charge of them all.

"Spraggly-waggly," he murmured, spidering his hand across the desk. Fry skittered after it and pounced. The monk rolled the cat back and forth as the sprung hind legs kicked. When they disengaged, Father Francis marvelled at the pinpricks of blood on his hands while Fry, all dignity, licked painted coat with dry, rough tongue.

The Abbot visited him before Compline. The hem of his chasuble swayed, and Fry's bottom wiggled. Father Francis placed a calming hand on the cat's back.

"It is finished, then?" the Abbot asked.

"Well, there are still one or two areas to be improved upon. The retraction of the claws, for instance…"

"Father Francis. I have allowed you longer to complete this task than anyone else has taken. Even Father Kozo's pangolin was ready sooner, and you remember how complex that was."

"I do."

"The cat is ready. Just look at it. You will take it to the Ark tomorrow."

"Tomorrow?" The hand stroking Fry's tail squeezed hard, and the cat pulled away.

"I need not remind you," the Abbot said, "that only God can create perfection." He watched Father Francis's blood-specked hand caress and scritch its way up and down the cat's flanks, which moved with simulated breaths.

"No, no, you needn't."

"There's a little verse on graven images in Deuteronomy, too. Though there's not much of the golden calf about this one, eh?" He reached out and tapped Fry's forehead, where the darker stripes formed an M on the cat's fur.

"Some call that the mark of Mary," Father Francis observed, "although it is a mere superstition, of course." The cat pulled away and jumped to the floor, to patrol the dark corners of the room and the space under the bed. The two men watched.

"The workmanship is good," the Abbot allowed, as Fry wove between his legs and pressed the mark of Mary against his shins. "A credit to you, and to St Jerome's. You should be very proud."

"Thank you."

"I wonder what animal we shall find for you next. Something suited to your passion for detail. A butterfly? Or would you prefer to go large and do a peacock?"

"I will be grateful for whatever task I am assigned," replied Father Francis. "The ant, the bee, they all have their place."

"Of course. You are excused Vigils to pack for your journey. If you set out in the morning, and the weather permits travel, you should be at the Ark for Pentecost."

The Abbot turned to leave, and as he turned his toe brushed Fry's flank. The robot could not feel pain, but it could sense when it had been touched. Fry squalled.

"Poor J/FRY," the Abbot said, bending to stroke the cat's electric skin. "Poor J/FRY."

Father Francis's prayers for humility had been answered.

His pilgrimage lasted three days, walking in the mornings and evenings and resting through the midday heat. Just a monk and his cat, pacing out the silent, shimmering landscape, avoiding the overcrowded towns. Father Francis had brought an inflatable dinghy to cross the flooded areas. Fry, claws in, peered over the side of the boat for fish that weren't there, dabbing the algae-green surface with a paw.

Besides the dinghy and a pocket Bible, Father Francis had a sleeping-bag, dehydrated mycoprotein, and tablets for purifying water. Fry needed nothing, not even sleep. The cat's thermodynamic engine was powered by changing temperatures, and so Fry lay in the sun during their rests, or snuggled up to Father Francis when there was no sun, and prowled about at night. When Father Francis woke and reached out for the cat, he would see the green eyes he had made, moving to and fro in the moonlight as Fry hunted. Fry never gave up the simple faith that there might, somewhere, be prey for a cat.

On the evening of the third day they came to the Ark.

Its proper name was Woodgate Priory, but it was known by many others. The Cathedral of the Creatures. God's Zoo. Animal Abbey. But, most popularly, the Ark. He could hear the bells from the tall and twisted spire, designed to cool the building by funnelling breezes through it, as he approached.

Parched and dusty, Father Francis spoke into the intercom and waited for admittance. He took off his sunhat.

A monk admitted him to the hallway and introduced himself as Brother Will. Their footsteps echoed in the dark, cool space. The arched ceiling was painted with animals: wolves, lions, polar bears. Predators. Their eyes stared down at Father Francis. Beyond the next set of columns it was livestock, sheep and cattle; after that came birds, from the eagle to the wren, frozen in flight.

"You'll want to have a wash before supper," Brother Will stated. "I'll come for you in an hour. It's a bit of a maze!"

The guesthouse had an iron bedstead and a basin. When Father Francis turned the tap, fresh water flowed. He shut it off quickly and prayed his thanks before filling and draining a plastic tumbler four times.

He washed without wasting, using just enough water to make himself presentable. After attending to his own needs, he placed Fry on the bed to brush dust and dirt from the tabby fur. He squeezed each paw so the claws were revealed to their fullest extent, and buffed them to a translucent shine with the pink quick showing through. He had carved those claws from chips of quartz, sifted on his knees from the gravel paths in the monastery garden.

"Are you ready? Leave your animal," said Brother Will on his return. "You can show it to the Archbishop in the morning."

Despite the generous Whitsun feast and the comfortable bed, Father Francis was too excited to sleep much. Fry, charging from his warmth, curled on his chest and purred. He could barely concentrate on Vigils, Lauds or the breakfast that separated the two services. Finally, he found himself at the entrance to the Bestiary, preparing to add his own humble offering to the collection.

The humble offering, in his arms, reached up a paw to bat at the cross around his neck.

He could hear rustling, thumps and strange, exotic calls, but the zoo smell he remembered from childhood was absent.

The door opened and the Archbishop came forward to meet him.

"Your Grace," Father Francis said. The Archbishop stretched out his hand, and Father Francis wondered whether to give the old-fashioned gesture of kissing his ring, but it was only a handshake he was offered.

The Archbishop plucked Fry from his arms and turned the cat upside-down, parting the fur with his fingers and tugging it to check it was firmly attached. He flicked Fry's nose and eyelids, rotated the joints and prodded the belly. Fry, unused to this treatment, went quiet and still.

"We've been waiting for this to finish off the Pets." The Archbishop gestured with his crosier. "We'll add it now – it's all working. And you can have a private tour before the hordes get here."

Father Francis held out his hands. "May I?" he asked.

"Hm? Oh, of course." The Archbishop passed back the cat, and the two men walked through the Bestiary together.

Father Francis paused in front of the tiger, whose coat was a brighter, bolder wash of Fry's tabby. Muscles bunched under the bronze and honey fur as it walked without a sound. Fry, draped round Father Francis's neck, stiffened, and Father Francis felt the static charge as the cat's fur stood on end. He moved to the next exhibit and gazed upwards.

"Magnificent," he said. The archbishop nodded. The elephant blinked small, kind eyes, raised its trunk and shook its head so the broad ears flapped.

Francis reached out to pat the trunk, but his hand struck a wall of clear plastic. "Why do they need cages?"

"Oh, they're not to keep the robots *in!*" The archbishop laughed. "People kept trying to touch them."

Of course. The way they used to touch holy relics, before those were put behind glass. Did it matter if those old bones, those splinters of the True Cross, were what they claimed to be or a fake, as long as believers believed?

There was the lion, less golden than St Jerome's stained-glass beast, but moving and breathing. And alone. The animals went one by one.

"We thought of putting the sheep in with it," said the archbishop, "but we decided that would be too on the nose."

They moved to another section of the Bestiary, away from the exotic, past the fox, badger and deer. The display panels read GUINEA PIG - HAMSTER - DOMESTIC DOG - DOMESTIC CAT. This last pen was empty. Next door, a border collie wagged its tail and followed the two men with its eyes. Father Francis longed to ruffle the long fur and feel the warmth of the artificial skin. Would the tongue be as rough as Fry's when the dog licked his hand?

"Well, Fry? I think you'll be very happy here," Father Francis whispered. The Archbishop looked sharply at him. Fry's claws penetrated his cassock at the shoulder, and Father Francis felt himself glared at from two directions at once. He moved his lips silently, as if praying, and detached Fry from his shoulder. The cat struggled and clung, but Father Francis placed Fry firmly in the pen, with one final stroke from the mark of Mary all along the striped back.

"It won't keep doing that, will it?" the Archbishop asked.

Fry sat in the far corner of the pen, back turned to the men and tail tip flicking. The fur Father Francis had groomed so carefully stood up in offended tufts.

"Fry-Fry?" Father Francis called softly. But the cat would not forgive his sin.

He had lied.

Fry liked to creep about, exploring the hidden corners of the monastery. Fry roamed the long grass in the sun's light. Fry stalked under the moon. Always on the move, in quest of prey. Fry would not be happy in the Ark at all.

But Father Francis had his duty, and the cat had a purpose too. The Bestiary existed so that people might experience a little of what God had created and humankind had lost.

The main door opened, and the visitors poured in. Each left their contribution on the collection plate. Father Francis watched, amused by the way the Church still insisted on paper and coins as the rest of the world moved on. The amounts of money didn't vary, he noticed, according to how wealthy the visitors looked. Then he saw the list of entry fees on the wall. Not an offering, but a ticket.

At the other end of the hall, a monk was setting up toys and souvenirs on a counter. The elephant blinked, raised its trunk, shook its head. The same sequence as before. Father Francis looked at the tiger and saw the groove its rubber-padded paws had worn in the floor as it paced back and forth on one track. The lion, he knew, would have lain down with the sheep if they had been put together.

"This is not a house of God," Father Francis said. "This is a theme park."

"Hm?" The Archbishop paused with his finger on the button that would shut Fry behind the wall of plastic.

"Fry!" Father Francis called, and the cat, for once, came straight to him and jumped into his outstretched hands. "The Lord be with you," he told the Archbishop.

With Fry tucked under his arm, he walked through the gift shop to the exit.

The woman arrived in the middle of the day, when the sun was hottest. She was carrying her younger child, while the older one, a boy, marched determinedly at his side.

The hermitage was isolated, but not so isolated that visitors could not reach it. Father Francis tended the plants that would see him through the winter, his patch of garden increasing every year as travellers brought him precious seeds. He wrote, and he prayed, and he grew older.

Father Francis bent his knees to put himself on the little boy's level. "What can I do for you?" he asked. He spoke gently, but the boy lost his boldness and hid his head in his mother's dress.

"They want to see the kitty," she explained for him. "They wouldn't stop for a nap," she added.

Father Francis welcomed the travellers in to the one-room hut and boiled water for tea. The two children dropped straight away to their knees on the floor. Fry trotted towards them, tail sticking straight up and pink mouth open. The cat brushed and bumped against bare knees; chased an anorak toggle; chewed gently at inquisitive fingers.

Father Francis had often pored over the mediaeval illuminated manuscripts in the library, and he knew that, no matter how intricate the illustrations, how splendid the capital letters, how much scarlet and gold paint had been used, humanity's handiwork could not match the hand of God. But he saw the wonder and adoration in the children's faces, and smiled at their mother.

"We've been to the Ark," she said, and stopped. Father Francis nodded for her to continue. "The animals there – they're not like this."

Fry rolled on the floor, paws waving. The boy reached out to ruffle the soft stomach fur, and Fry's forepaws clutched his hand, claws in. The toddler was lying on her front, grabbing at the teasing tail and laughing.

"What's your secret?" their mother asked.

"The ro – the animals," he caught himself, glancing at the children to see if they were listening, "have artificial intelligence. They learn. I treated Fry as a cat, and thus Fry learned to be a cat."

"Did you have a cat before?" The boy spoke for the first time, without taking his eyes off Fry.

"Oh no! I'm not that old. But I do remember a world with cats in it."

"Come on, you two," she said at last. "We need to be back before dark. Now, what do we say?"

"Thank you," both children said, obediently.

Father Francis waved to them from the doorway. When he lowered his hand, it was to cross himself. He asked that the children should grow up strong and safe and kind, and that they would love and cherish all creatures.

He watched as the three figures disappeared into the shimmering evening. What were they afraid of, in the dark? There were no beasts to menace them. Maybe that was it. The stillness. He listened to it until the sun met the horizon. So empty and quiet. Quieter than even he was used to.

"Fry-Fry?" he called.

The shadows were long, and Fry could be hiding anywhere among them. Father Francis clicked his fingers, made a *ps-ps* sound with his lips, tossed a pebble on the ground so it bounced and pattered. Nothing. For the first time since the beginning of his voluntary seclusion, the monk felt truly alone.

"Fry!" he called sharply. Was that a rustle? He slowed his hurry to a walk as he rounded the corner of the hut, so as not to scare the cat away. Huge, glittering eyes glared from the shadow at the base of the wall.

"There you are! Why didn't you come?"

A sound came from Fry's throat that Father Francis had never heard before: a rising growl filled with triumph and excitement. The tail lashed. One forepaw, claws extended, rested on a small, damp, furry scrap.

Father Francis knelt down beside the dead mouse, and gave thanks.

In The Weave

David Whitmarsh

I was five segments grown when my first doubts came. I lay huddled in the nest between my mother and grandmother. A thin wind curled around the smooth cement walls, bringing white flakes that turned to water when they touched me. It was night, and colder and darker than any night I had ever known. Above the nest walls, the night-glow of the clouds was faint. The strangeness of it fascinated me, holding my focus tight.

In another thread, Mother's ridges flashed at me, but I could not let go of my fading self.

The wind died. Stillness such as I had never known. The clouds above were high, thin and high and scarcely moving. A gap appeared. Beyond was black sprinkled with pinpoints of light that stayed still as the broken cloud drifted across the sky.

In this cold, thin strand, my mother lay dead beside me. I felt the life seeping too from my own body, my sight dimming.

Offspring of mine! My mother's facial ridges rippled brightly, flickering with her irritation.

The wind whipped around the nest's lee as it always did. The bright clouds above scurried their eternal race across the sky. The nest was warm. The grub that Mother laid before me was warm.

That thread was far from the first in which my life ended, but the manner of the ending disturbed me. It was lost not just to me, but to Mother and Grandmother too, and it seemed to everyone in our village. My thoughts dwelled also on that strange sky; the myriad little lights that shone high above.

What lies beyond the clouds? I asked Mother as I sank my mandibles into the squirming flesh, and sucked.

Her answer was terse. *The clouds are the limit of the worlds. There is nothing above.*

Grandmother blinked one pair of eyes, then another. *There were stories.* The glow on her speech ridges was feeble, but readable. *A Visitor from above the clouds, in distant folds of the weave, distant even when I was seeded.*

It was seldom that Grandmother could rouse herself to speak. Her mind was failing as her weave wore thin with age. So few threads remained to her.

Her crusted eyes closed again.

I clung to the torn stump of a great tree, my mandibles sunk deep into the wood, my claws gripping the rough bedrock, waiting for wind and the hail of rock and fragments of wood and dead things carried by the storm to tear me from my hold.

Rip-storms bring destruction and thereby renew the forest. The biggest, oldest trees can be as tall as an adult is long, and they spread their branches wide and shade the soil beneath from the cloud-light so nothing new can grow beneath. When they are so big, they can no longer furl their branches to let the storm slip over them, a rip-storm clears them away, allowing new life to flourish. It is a part of the cycle, of the natural order of things.

This storm cleared not just the old growth, but everything. Everything living, and much that was not. The soil itself was being scoured away. Even as I wondered whether I could hold on until it passed, I felt the pain of my carapace cracking from some unseen impact.

I walked through the village behind my mother. Her anterior eyes blinked as my segments rippled to a stop. She turned so that I could see the words on her face. *What troubles you, offspring of mine?*

Upwind, the branches of the trees waved and rippled, shielding the fields in their lee.

I have died again. I know one small death is nothing, but I feel so many. I said. *Was it always so?*

What is always? Her words were erratic, flickering and shimmering. *Who can tell amongst all the pasts we can see and all those we cannot. Who can trace all the warps of the weave? The pasts are unknowable as the futures.*

She turned and I followed her tail, wondering at her impatience, wondering also at my own dark mood. We are seeded, the threads of the weave are spun, and in each we die. Sometimes sooner, sometimes later. I knew there would come a time when my deaths would come faster than the spinning of new threads and I would diminish, as

Grandmother did, but I was young. Daily I felt the weave thicken and new patterns emerge. I felt brighter, sharper.

Despite these endings, these threads torn from me, I still grew.

I scrambled along a dry river bed in hot, still air, hunger in my belly, heat bearing down from the fierce brightness in a sky of an alien, uniform colour somewhere beyond violet. A pale crescent banded with colours was the only other feature.

There were no clouds.

I pulled away my focus, returning to a thread where I lay quiet and warm in the nest between Mother and Grandmother. All but one lateral eye was closed, and that watched my mother, who was speaking, but not to me.

Was it always so? she said.

I cracked open an eye on the other side, where Grandmother lay.

Grandmother's face glowed with the feeble light of her own words. *Always so. So many little endings where the boldness of youth leads to misadventure. This is how they learn.*

But these are not little deaths. Mother's ridges flashed. *Everyone dies. The village, the world. Everyone. And this not just in fine fibres, but great cords of the weave.*

There are stories...

Shine me no stories, said Mother. *What matter the infinite unknowable pasts. We live in the multitude of present moments. Wisdom is in the weave.*

I recall no such endings in my pasts. Flickering mumbles chased around Grandmother's face.

At the edge of my vision I saw something bright flash across the clouds, a spark angling across the sky in the time it takes to blink twice.

Stones sometimes fall from above the clouds, Grandmother said in a soft light.

Had I not seen that light in the sky, I might have thought her words to be merely ramblings from lost threads. *Tell me a story,* I flashed to her, but her face glimmered only with the incoherent scintillation of one who has lost focus.

I had been sent out to forage, and so I left the village taking a different direction in each thread, spreading my selves and my focus wide. I ambled along the river bank, crawled beyond the fields, and slipped deep into the forest all around.

There is a place at the margin of our territory, an abandoned village at the foot of a precipice. It is said that many generations past, the village was sheltered by the cliff but then the wind changed direction. The way the wind blows today, the crescent walls of these old nests line up the wrong way so that anyone entering or leaving one would be caught exposed in the cross-wind and flipped or carried away. Now the site is overgrown as the forest reclaims the land. Here, sheltered in the rubble of a collapsed nest wall of rough-hewn stone, I found a hive of spineworms, tasty and nutritious, though care is needed in collecting them.

A good hive-site in one thread is often a good hive-site across broad ribbons of the weave, so I summoned all those of my selves that were nearby. In my own nest I told Mother, so that she too might come and bring others from the village. The apothecary would bring vapours to stun the spineworms.

I watched the hive and the comings and goings of the worms while more of my selves arrived each in her own thread. In many of these threads I discovered someone else already there watching the hive.

She raised her head and turned towards myself to speak. *Begone, interloper. This is not your territory.* Her length of five segments and immature colouration told she was of the same seed cohort as myself. The rhythms of her words that she came from the adjacent village.

I asserted precedence with bold flashes. We faced each other, cross-wind in the shelter of the undergrowth. My focus now was close on this thread, as hers would be. Throughout the many strands of the weave we converged and encountered each other at this spot, but in this thin strand alone would we resolve our dispute and accept the outcome through all the weave. That is the way we are taught to resolve disputes, the civilised way.

We began the ritual with sequences of flashes, patterns with no meaning. A wordless chant if you will, and our signalling synchronised. Together we raised our front segments from the ground, a trial of strength in itself. We swayed and chanted. She raised her second segment up so she towered over me. A boastful show of strength. I did the same, to fail to do so would be to concede. The wind pressed hard on my flank, threatening to topple me. My muscles strained to hold me up and keep me steady in the cross-wind.

Faster we chanted, and straining on the legs of our anterior segments we edged towards one another. I do not know whether she was pressing the pace or I was, but I felt an eagerness. It was almost as if we were a single mind, a single will. Only dimly was I aware of all my other selves watching her other selves waiting in a tense stillness.

This self, this thread, was all that there was.

My focus was upon that fine fibre of being, upon her, complete and singular. I felt the climax of the chant approach, and I saw the glint of my own ridges reflected in her eyes.

The chant ended and we both lunged. I managed to bring my head lower than hers, but she had artfully pushed herself sideways, upwind. I felt my defeat as her flank crashed into the side of my head and she let the wind take her and so me. I fell and could not stop myself as wind and inertia rolled me onto my side. In desperation, I twisted my rear segments, not to resist the roll, but to press it further.

The carapace of my head rang with the impact as it hit the hard ground, but I rolled, rolled right out from beneath my adversary, onto my back, up onto the other flank and onto my feet. I might have rolled further but for the remnant of a nest wall. I felt the sharp pain of a carapace cracking in my third segment.

I have never before or since felt such pain, for my focus was solely on that self, a singular body experiencing a singular pain.

A cracked carapace loses its strength and its weight presses and crushes the flesh beneath that it normally supports and protects. One leg was numb and useless and all the lateral eyes on that side were blind. I thought soon to feel my adversary's mandibles bringing relief from that agony.

But the pain did not abate. I fought through it to turn my head and see.

She lay next to me, on her back, helpless. The victory was mine, and so the duty of the victor. No matter how hard, I had to finish the matter. Dragging my useless leg I twisted around and mounted upon her exposed underside. I pushed the tips of my mandibles into the exposed gap before the first segment and bit as hard as I could.

As the head rolled away, I released my focus, spreading myself again through the weave.

Well fought, the adversary said. *The roll was a clever move. Daring.* Her lights shimmered with admiration as we lay side by side in front of the hive. *Is someone coming to aid you in your distress?*

The pain of my injuries had faded, diluted as my focus withdrew from that strand. Even so, it was a relief when Mother arrived. Her ridges flashed with words of pride and a little regret as she came close.

Yes, I said to the adversary, speaking in gentle shades. *But you flatter me. The move was not clever. Merely fortunate.*

My relief came soon. That thread was lost to me as Mother's head leaned over me and her kind, sharp mandibles penetrated the gap between head and first segment.

We talked while we awaited the others from my village. She was offspring of the weaver, a profession of high status both for its practicality and its symbolism.

One thread in every two we harvested the worms, stripping their spines and collecting them in bags of woven cloth. In the others we let them be, for they have as much right to the weave as any living thing.

The weaver's offspring and I parted on good terms, I gifted her some of my allocation of the harvested spineworms.

Fire. The wind fanned the flames to tear through a widening swathe of the forest and in a widening swathe of the weave I fled from the path of destruction. The fire ran fast before the wind, far faster than I could crawl.

That was the first time that I died so many deaths that I felt myself diminish. Once the shock had passed – of feeling my eyes go blind and my fluids boiling beneath my blistering carapace – I realised my thoughts felt foggy, my focus vague.

You will recover what you have lost, Grandmother said in a moment of rare lucidity. In my diminished state I found new empathy for her situation. Decline was all that remained for her as her deaths came faster. Her weave thinned and frayed, and with every day I found her sedentary form lying in the nest in fewer of the threads of my own lives.

In a thick cord, I too lay still in the nest. The glazed discolorations of my carapace would be with me for life in those worlds, but the burned and blistered flesh beneath would heal in time, the lost eyes would grow back.

You will recover what you have lost, she said again, perhaps in a different thread, sometimes it is hard to tell.

Tell me a story, I said, though I doubted her focus would hold enough.

A story? What story? Shall I tell you of how we learnt to build with cement rather than rough stone, of how we learned to work metal? My grandmother lived folds of the weave where the visitor gave us this knowledge, and much else besides, but in these strands where we live our many lives, we were so few and stretched so thin that only fragments of the knowledge came to us.

Why so few?

She lay uncommunicative for long moments. An intermittent flickering of her ridges was the only sign that she was still conscious. I thought her mind had drifted away again following its own shadowed paths, when her words shone bright in my eyes. *Life is hard in the ribbons of the weave that we know, and we are few. When I was a five-segment youth as you are now, my grandmother told me it was not so elsewhere.*

But how? How can the worlds be so different, is not the nature of the physical world the same in all the weave? Even as I spoke, I recalled those dying worlds of cold and heat and strange skies.

Her ridges rippled in the soothing colours one might use to calm an infant. *A grub in a tree may eat one leaf in one strand and do no harm, but in another strand a different leaf is eaten and brings a rip-storm on the other side of the world.*

It was a story we all learn as infants, of how small choices can have unpredictable effects in different strands of the weave, leading to wild divergences between the worlds.

Perhaps, she continued, *if it eats both leaves, the wind will change direction.*

I shivered with fright at the thought of the abandoned village. The wind had changed in threads ancestral to all of the weave that I lived. So many must have been caught in the crosswind and died, and the survivors would have been diminished. This was her story. We were few and stretched thin because the wind changed direction.

She was singular as a stone that is kicked in one thread and knows not in the remainder of the weave. That's what they said.

Who? I demanded, but her light faded, her rambling slowed. A last flicker, that might have been *so far away*, or it may have just been the random flutterings of her fading mind.

That night her hearts failed in many of the threads that remained to her and she lost the power of speech entirely. It is in the ways of the worlds that the elderly fade so, not all at once across the weave but stretched ever thinner along fewer and finer warps.

For two summers and winters, my lives continued. As before, threads were torn from my weave by personal accident or all-encompassing catastrophe, but the remainder grew and thickened. I grew in mental acuity and sharpness of focus, and in physical size and strength. I reached the full seven segments of adulthood.

Grandmother continued to decline. She now lived in only the sparsest, thinnest strands, in a state of total senescence, eating only when food was placed between her mandibles.

The weaver's offspring, my former adversary from that day in the abandoned village, was now a familiar sight in our own village, and I in hers. Now in new adulthood, she was herself a weaver. Mother said she waited for the seeding of the next cohort, confident that the weaver and I would sow each other's seeds. But since that last conversation with Grandmother I had little confidence in planning futures. *We will see when the season comes,* I told Mother.

More than once as I lay in the nest at night, I saw a light flash across the sky. It was not a common occurrence, but enough to bring back memories of Grandmother's incoherent ramblings of things above the clouds, and of what I had seen in dying worlds. Then the day came, where a light crossed the sky in the middle of the day. It did not flash across in the time it takes to blink twice, but slow and bright, falling slower and brighter until it hurt to look.

It seemed to descend from the sky in the direction of the abandoned village, and it did so in all of the weave that I knew.

The weaver and I found it in the wind-shadow of the cliff just beyond the nests. No others shared any interest in lights from the sky, and truth be told I don't believe the weaver would have come but for my own interest.

It had curves and edges unlike anything we had seen before. Its surface held a sheen like the carapace of a new-hatched infant and bristled with odd protrusions. In length it would measure from my head to my fourth segment, but it was twice as wide and high as myself. Four thin legs spread wide from its underside held its belly clear from the ground. I wondered at the strength of those thin spars.

Is it a living thing? the weaver asked.

I think not. My eyes were drawn to the edges, the angles of the protrusions, some of which had that hard brightness of metal. *I believe it is a made thing.*

We will learn little by looking, she said, and in a thin strand she crawled from the cover of the trees and headed straight towards it.

As she approached within a dozen body lengths, some of the protrusions erupted into bright lights, dazzling my forward eyes.

I am blinded, she said, lying next to me in another stream.

Keep going straight, I said, squinting beneath folded ridges against the brightness.

She blundered straight forward until her mandibles struck the thing. She opened them wide, stepped forward once more and closed her jaws on the object, the point of her mandible slid until it caught on one of the protrusions.

Very hard, she said. *I don't think I can...*

As she spoke, the thing's surface buckled as the point penetrated. A jet of vapour burst from the puncture, then all was consumed in bright fire. All: the object, the weaver. The whole space between the wood and the cliff was lost in bright flame. The ridges folded down over my eyes, saving something of my forward vision.

What happened? said the weaver next to me.

I had no answer at first. I feared the heat of the flame would set light to the forest where I lay, but the heat faded almost as quickly as it had come. I uncovered my eyes and saw a blackened hollow. Of the object and the weaver I saw at first no trace.

I crawled out of my shelter into the open, across the blackened ground, and as I did, I saw with my eyes and felt under my feet hard, sharp shards. Pieces of the weaver's carapace, fragments of blackened and twisted metal.

I was right, I said to the weaver as I continued my search. *It is a made thing.*

I searched the blackened crater to see what I might learn, and I rested at the forest edge with the weaver to watch the object and see what we might learn.

The side of the object opened and *something* came out. It balanced precariously on two legs, upright. It had such a curious head, a smooth, white shining carapace, and what looked like a single great eye filling the forward face. Its movements were rapid, but clumsy. I expected it to topple to the ground and smash itself to pieces. It seemed to struggle also with the wind, even in the shelter of the cliff.

It busied itself with a number of objects it extracted from the interior of what I now began to think of its nest.

We watched, mystified, captivated, until a flat plate it had placed on the ground angled towards us and erupted in light. Not the glare that had dazzled me and blinded the weaver when she approached in that destructive thread, but the patterns of the glowing ridges of a face.

I am blind, it said. Then, *Keep going straight. Very hard. I don't think I can. What happened?*

It was repeating our words, but only the words we had spoken in this thread, though it must have seen what we said in that other strand.

I picked a few strands and crawled out from the shelter. I stopped just short of the distance at which those dazzling lights had started. The two-legged stranger edged back a little, but stepped forward again when I stopped.

Hello, I said. *Goodbye,* I said in another thread. In another: *Singular as a stone.* Whence came those words? Distracted, I almost neglected to watch the response on the panel.

In each thread came the same words I had flashed.

This is madness, I said to the weaver, *what can she hope to learn by responding the same way in every stream?*

Patience, she said. *Perhaps she waits for a different response from you.*

I paused for a moment, and I remembered my first meeting with the weaver. Somehow, the memory of pain of that meeting was diminished. It was the thrill of the dance that I remembered now. *Join me in a strand,* I told the weaver, *just a single thread. Let us see if we can evoke a more meaningful response.*

She did as I asked, and I flashed at her the beginnings of the chant, of the challenge. She understood my intent and joined me. We faced each other, chanted, raised our forward segments. The stranger backed away as we swayed – in truth the wind was feeble here in the shadow of the cliff, scarce enough to topple either of us, but this was more a show.

In another thread, I chanted to the stranger instead. *You will have to tell me how she reacts,* said the weaver.

Our shared chant reached its climax. The weaver feinted towards me, a low and slow lunge, and I pressed the advantage, my mandibles scissored, and the head fell from her neck.

My solo chant reached its climax, I lunged forward and closed my mandibles around the protrusion at the apex of the stranger's body, which I took to be its head, if it had such. It was easily severed and fell to the ground and its carapace cracked. A dark liquid pulsed from the cut on the body, and oozed from the severed head.

I lowered my head before the stranger, offering her the opportunity to sever my own head, should she have the means to do so.

The stranger showed no reaction anywhere in the rest of the weave. I watched from the forest with the weaver as the panel simply repeated our earlier conversation. Even where I exposed the join between my head and first segment, the stranger stood mute and impassive.

The only reaction came from the weaver's death. The stranger hurried with its clumsy two-legged gait and climbed into the opening of its nest. I waited to see if it would emerge again. I waited long and was about to give up when the entire nest of curves and edges and protrusions vanished, looking like it had twisted away in some unimaginable direction.

It did the same where the stranger lay decapitated before me. The nest just vanished. The weaver saw too, for which I was grateful. I feared she would not believe had I needed to describe what I had seen.

Still, these were narrow threads, and the stranger and her nest remained in a broad ribbon of rich and branching warps.

I struggled to comprehend the meaning of this stranger's reactions.

I observed that throughout the thickness of the weave where the stranger was present, she acted in the precise same way, save in those where I or the weaver had chosen to act differently, as if she had no power to manipulate the weave of her own volition, but only to react to the circumstance of the thread in which she found herself.

She attempted to communicate with us. Her lighted panel shifted from showing faces that repeated our words, to patterns far simpler. Numbers of dots, lines and geometrical shapes.

A game. I said what I saw, she repeated my words. By varying my answers in different threads and seeing her responses, I saw the patterns, I saw what she was trying to do and I learned quickly.

She learned slowly. Every lesson, every word, every phrase, she had to learn anew in every thread separately. As my responses varied, so did hers. Her progress was faster or slower in one thread or another. In those where her progress was fastest, I learned the next move in the game and in other threads I was able to respond to each problem as soon as, or before she posed it.

Days passed like this, and at the end of each day as the clouds darkened, she retired to her nest and I walked back to mine. The weaver helped me during the long days, fetching me sustenance and pressing me to eat when, in my wide and deep focus, I would forget.

In time, many days, the stranger was able to display simple sentences.

I go. I return in three days, she said to me one day in a fine strand.

You go. You return in three days, I said to her throughout the weave.

How do you know? she said, in those threads where she had learned enough to understand.

Wisdom is in the weave, I replied, but I think the meaning was lost on her.

I crawled back to my village, to the nest I shared mostly with my mother. The next day, my strength was recovered enough to focus and tell her what I had seen, what I had been doing these last days when she might have expected me in the forge.

I looked to that sad corner of the nest where Grandmother used to lie.

The stranger returned on the third day. I saw her nest appear in the sky, and descend on a column of fire to rest again in the shelter of the cliff. Its path erratic as the wind caught and buffeted it, but it came to rest in the same place.

You come from above the clouds, I said to her.

Something new, she carried a speaking panel on the front of her carapace. *I come from above the clouds. Another world.*

I do not understand, I said. *The worlds in the threads are not above the clouds, and we cannot travel from one to another. We simply experience them.*

Most times she would answer very quickly, I had the sense that her thinking was fast, like her movements, but it lacked breadth. I waited.

I have not words to explain, but yes, I come from above the clouds.

We talked, we misunderstood, we learned. Eight days she stayed, then three days she went back up above the clouds. This routine repeated many times in many threads. In time we began to comprehend each other in small and mundane ways.

In a few sparse threads she never came back, and in one, as her nest descended on its column of fire, the wind swirled around the sheltering cliff and smashed the nest against the unforgiving rock. It erupted in fire as it had that day that the weaver's mandibles had penetrated it.

I told her. *You died coming here.*

Her response came quickly. *I live yet.*

I watched your nest descend, I saw it taken by the wind and shattered on the stone. You must have been killed.

Her head moved, angled to one side a little. *It is a mystery to me that you can see this. We know that the world we see is one of many branching possibilities but we can never see those other worlds.*

The broad chasm in my understanding yawned before me. *You feel no diminution from the death of your other self?*

That was not me. That was someone who shared a past with me, but moved on to another fate. I can die only once. She died.

I absorbed this. To experience the weave was the very definition of life. Even the worms that burrow in the ground retreat in many threads from a threat in one. I considered the possibility of death in a single strand being a final end to a living thing. I reflected on what I had done on the day the stranger arrived.

Once before, another who shared your past has died here.

The panel she used to speak remained dark. Her curious head straightened and tilted to the other side. I fancied I saw movement within that great eye when the light caught it.

I could not but explain further, though I feared her reaction so I spoke my thought in only a thin strand. *I regret. I killed you,* I said. *I meant no harm by it. Death is a small thing for us.*

Have no regret for me. When I am dead I am gone, but there is another who waits above the clouds for whom my end would have brought pain.

Speak to her of my regrets.

Through this eye she sees all that I see. The stranger touched a projection at the side of her head. *She understands as I do. Death is a small thing for you.*

My lateral eyes detected a motion. The branches of the trees furling themselves, wrapping tight around the trunks.

She spoke again. *But is it always so? Is death always a small thing for you?*

A storm is coming, I said. *The trees sense it across the weave.* I said it to her in all the threads, not just those of this more intimate conversation.

I must leave, I will return after the storm, she said many times, everywhere she had gained understanding, and hurried back to her nest.

I felt the force of the wind pressing on my carapace. The stranger clambered into her nest.

She stood still before me. *I must know, before the storm comes. I must know is death always a small thing for you?*

No, it is not always a small thing. Too many deaths and we diminish, we lose our selves.

I live one life, I have one past, but we know there are many worlds. She hesitated again. *I struggle to find the words, but the ground on which we stand moves. Over many lifetimes it must move in the same way in every world. Are the storms stronger, more frequent, in every world?*

The trees now were furled tight, but the younger growth, the littler plants with shallow roots could not withstand the rising storm. Here in this sheltered spot we escaped the worst, but to either side I saw trees and branches and small animals flung into the air and carried away.

In thread after thread, throughout the weave, the stranger's nest performed its mysterious convolutions and was gone. But here, she remained awaiting my answer.

Everywhere. Throughout the weave. The world has died many times, but there is no strand of mine that does not suffer storms or cold or heat.

She stepped forward, this tiny frail creature, and rested a forelimb on my extended mandible. *I regret there is no more I can do.*

She turned to return to her nest, but a flurry of wind twisted around the cliff and caught her mid-stride, sending her crashing to the ground before me.

What do you mean? I said, but she lay face down, straining with upper limbs to push herself up. She would not have seen my words. As gentle as a mother with a seedling, I closed my mandibles beneath her and lifted.

I released her, and she stumbled forward and rested her back against the rock face.

The wind is changing. The weaver's words came to me from another thread. I widened my focus and felt the force of it. We clung to the ground. A heavy branch ripped from an ancient tree flew through the air towards me.

We lay huddled tight against the crescent wall of the nest, Mother and I, latched onto each other like three-segment youths as the wind curled around the end wall. No way to leave the nest without being torn away.

Throughout the weave, the wind was changing. In some threads already a full rip-storm was tearing the trees from the ground and scouring deep scars in the soil, the clouds above lost in the haze of wind-borne dust and rock.

I searched to focus again on the stranger, but it was a thin thread, and I felt my deaths building, my mind diminishing, my focus weakening.

I will die here. Her words brought me to her. She rested against the cliff, her single great eye and speaking panel facing me. The wind here too was turning and strengthening.

Are you injured? I said, but before she answered I saw her nest. The turning of the wind had exposed it to the rising storm. It lay on its side, trails of white vapour pouring from it, torn into thin streamers by the wind.

I regret, I said, *But if it be some solace, only in this thin thread. You departed safely elsewhere.*

She rested motionless, her panel dark, and I wondered if she had already died from some injury sustained in her fall.

I regret, she said, *that I can offer you no such comfort. Your world is dying. I think it must be so in every thread as it moves further from the light that warms it.*

I sensed the truth of her words. So much had I seen, and now I felt

241

my weave thinning and fraying moment by moment.

If we had found you sooner, we might have been able to help, to make you another home above the clouds, or to teach you... She raised her forelimbs to the front of her neck. *There is pain. I don't want to die a slow death as my air runs out,* she said. *This will be quicker, and we may see each other with our own eyes.*

She did something and a puff of vapour rushed from her neck. She lifted away the carapace from her head and placed it carefully on the ground beside her. I saw for the first time the true face of the stranger.

On the front of her fragile form, the speaking panel glows with a last word to me:

Goodbye.

She met my gaze with her two eyes, and then she died.

I spoke these words to the third eye on the carapace that the stranger had removed. I spoke to the stranger above the clouds: *May it bring you solace to know that the one who lies dead before me has returned to you elsewhere in the weave.*

Know also, that your kind has been here before, long ago in distant threads. Only now do I understand my grandmother's words, of knowledge brought from above the clouds in distant threads and a visitor singular as a stone.

Perhaps in distant folds of the weave our kind lives yet with yours, above the clouds.

Eternal Soldier

L.N. Hunter

I used to be a soldier.

Now, I'm a one-armed soldier in hospital.

Tomorrow, I'll be a one-armed ex-soldier outside a hospital, with no future.

I could say I'm to blame, since I helped with cutting my arm off.

The military gets the best tech, and our fire ant ropes – self-powered carborundum-injected nanite-fibre flexible weaponry (portable), or SPCINFFW(P), to give them their official title – are fine examples of that. They're amazing things, quarter inch thick strands of innumerable tiny eating machines. You can wrap them around anything, then engage by flicking the end of the cord, and – *z-z-zip* – the nanotech cuts and burns through whatever it was in seconds. Personal weaponry that was mondo rad to the extreme when wielded like a bullwhip: pretty dramatic, and inevitably fatal, when wrapped around an enemy's head. Tidy too, in that it cauterises the wounds.

Also mondo rad when your arm gets half blown off and blood's leaking everywhere.

It happened when my troop, 47th Longstanton, was being relocated from Camp Cedric to Camp Johnston. A routine trip from one base to the next through territory we were certain was ours. The guys at the back of the truck watched the trees, more out of habit than expecting to see the enemy. Despite the noise of the truck's diesel engine, the rest of us were dozing in the heat of the trailer.

The next thing I became aware of was being in freefall, my companions and our equipment slo-mo flying through the air with me. Some of us collided with the truck's roof braces, wrapping around them and breaking, and some were flung through gaps that had appeared in the side-sheets. It was oddly silent and, somehow, I only heard the explosion a fraction of a second later. I remember wondering if I looked as surprised as the other faces I could see.

It was when I smashed into the ground that sound came crashing back. All around me came the patter of small rocks and fragments of the truck, along with the splats of bits of soldier. Immense pain screamed in my right arm, slicing through the shocking numbness, which is all I had felt until then. I looked towards my arm but couldn't see it. I tried to peer past the obstruction before eventually realising there wasn't one. My arm was missing from the elbow down, and blood was gushing out.

My only hope was to clean up the wound and prevent my life draining away in the muck and pandemonium. With an adrenaline-induced burst of clarity, I whipped the fire ant rope around my arm to clean up and cauterise the stump. I passed out as the nanites performed their sorcerous trick.

The rope's magic obviously worked because, unlike the rest of the squad, I woke up again. In hospital. The doctors extracted bits of shrapnel from all over my body and patched me up.

And so, here I am. A soon to be ex-soldier with an exciting network of scars, and a less than average complement of hands.

The medics here tell me I was lucky. I get to see my family again, Dad with Alzheimer's, and Mum perpetually frazzled from looking after him. All she needs is another invalid. The rest of my squad, as much as the mop-up crew were able to recover, was no more than spare parts for field surgery. No cripple to send back home, like me.

I didn't enlist just to escape from a dead-end life. There was the attraction of travelling the world. Yes, I did see quite a few countries, though not very many of the people living in them were particularly pleased to see me. And there were the toys: big guns; big knives; best of all, big explosions. But that's all behind me now. What use is a one-armed soldier to anyone?

A cough jerks me back out of my thoughts of worthlessness. I struggle upright and attempt to salute before recalling that my saluting arm isn't there any more.

"At ease, soldier," a colonel I don't recognise says.

"Sir, yes, sir!"

The colonel waves an arm at me as he flops down on the chair beside the bed. "Stop shouting, I've got a hell of a headache. You're not helping it with that bellowing."

"Sir, yes…" I respond instinctively. "Sorry, sir" I say more quietly.

"That's better. Too much celebrating at our latest victory and, hoo-ee, am I paying for it this morning with the mother of all headaches?"

As he undoes his top button, in a most unmilitary fashion, with one hand, he extracts a pack of cigarettes from his pocket with the other. Winfields, I notice – much nicer than the nasty things us grunts usually get to taste. Disregarding hospital policy, he places one between his lips and lights it, then waves the pack in my direction. I reach out, hesitate as I remember we're not supposed to smoke here, then figure if a colonel's offering, I can take one. He lights it and slouches back in his chair.

I take my first suck of nicotine since getting here. Immediately, I choke, cough, and splutter. My throat and lungs still have the raw feeling that comes after a medical scrape and tissue recoat.

"I'm here to make a proposition," the colonel says after a few contemplative puffs. "You can retire as you are, Jack; battle-scarred and disabled, a soldier's meagre pension to look forward to. Oh, we'll find you accommodation and get you settled – we look after our own – but…you know…" He shrugs. "The accountants are in charge of the army these days."

Yes, I do know. At best, a crummy one-room flat in the scummy end of my crappy hometown, and bugger all likelihood of finding any sort of job to supplement the pittance from the army. Surviving on government handouts on top of that pension – meagre's not the word. At worst, homeless and dining at the dumpster restaurant.

He leans forwards again, eyes lighting up. "Or you can come join me in a new top secret experimental commando unit. We need people with your experience and skills, and after you've had enough, we'll send you back to Civvy Street with a brand new, freshly vat-grown arm."

I eyeball him for a moment, sucking on the cigarette to give me time to think. Experience and skills? Something's not right here. The only difference between me and the rest of my old squad is that I'm still alive, and that was due to luck – and my SPCINFFW(P) – not special skills.

245

Still, the choice between being out on my ass or joining up with a nutcase, obviously lying, colonel is an easy one to make.

It's a long flight to the drop point for our first live mission. Just five of us in the squad, huge men, all six foot four or more. And all with massive, thickly muscled arms transplanted from silverbacks. We're carrying large rifles too, triggers modified for our over-sized gorilla hands with their not fully-opposable thumbs.

Sharing a trait common to all military transport, supersonic flight is too noisy for conversation, so I find myself staring at my new hands, flexing the knuckles and admiring the smooth motion. I can't help but feel respect for the medics and the technology that got me here.

My introduction to G-Squad many months earlier was a stint in a second hospital, a laboratory hospital this time, where they took away my other arm before giving me two brand new ones. Well, not quite brand new – one previous owner. They upgraded my clavicle, too, replacing it with something made of some titanium and aluminium alloy, to support the gorilla arms and chest muscles. They did something to my heart too. Not increasing the size, since that would make it slower and weaker, but somehow strengthening it sufficiently to slam blood through arms massing almost as much as the rest of my body.

My original arms – arm and a half, really – are in a military freezer somewhere. Some of my wages go towards paying for the storage, and yet more for growing the rest of the second one. I should consider myself fortunate I don't have to pay for the operations that gave me these two huge new arms, and the training to go with them. Not to mention the immunosuppressive drugs to prevent rejection, and other medication and nanites to reduce the side effects of the first drugs.

I don't know what happened to the rest of the gorilla who donated the arms, though I sometimes wonder when I sniff the unnamed "meat" in our rations. The colonel had explained: as part of the breeding program to provide arms for us, they're releasing significant numbers of gorillas back into the wild, helping to stave off extinction. Who'd have thought military operations would benefit nature? Though I suspect the released ones are second-rate animals, not strong enough to be chopped up to make new soldiers.

Even before healing was complete, we were undergoing virtual reality training. We had to get our motor control systems accustomed to our extra reach, as well as adjust to the change in distribution of mass across our bodies. A benefit of practicing in VR is that no one sees you fall over, trip over your own feet, or otherwise land on your face or your ass a dozen times a day. The virtual training seems to have worked because my control over my new arms was perfect when the bandages came off. I didn't even need any physiotherapy because the medical nanites dealt with that while I was in VR, stitching up the right sensory and motor nerves, and stimulating muscle strength and joint flexion, as well as bonding my flesh with the ape's. I suppose, technically, I shouldn't think about it as belonging to an ape – a non-human ape – since the arms are part of me now.

What VR didn't prepare me for was the fluidity and sheer impressiveness of my new arms. It's like sitting in the cockpit of a mondo rad V12 Aston Martin Stampede, engine quietly exuding power and ready, at an instant's notice, to explode into deafening fury.

We've all adapted differently to our new appendages. Jones shaves his arms – something which takes him a very long time to do, every few days. The colour of his arms' suedey skin almost matches the dark skin tones of the rest of his body. He reckons when we have an R&R break, he'll have his arms tattooed; he has plenty of room for a good number of dragons and eagles. I wonder if they'll need to use special needles. Montgomery, the operational squad leader, also tries to make himself appear more human by wearing long sleeves all the time. Very long sleeves.

The rest of us are proud to be part gorilla and wear short sleeves to show off our hairy-scaries. Robertson's typical attire is a leather vest. Evans wears Iron Maiden or Def Leppard tee shirts – very occasionally, Gorillaz, just for the name. I prefer a clean white muscle tee, to emphasise the contrast in skin colour, and to show off the manly scars where my new arms join my pale shoulders.

Just before our first mission, the colonel gets us all to write letters home, just in case something goes wrong...

Dear Mum,

It's been a while since I wrote but, as you might imagine, it's all a bit busy here in the army, what with ███ and ███. I was injured in a recent skirmish in ████████ but, don't worry, not too badly – I'm still all in one piece, as you can see in the photo. The top brass was so impressed with my ████████, ████ and bravery that I've been specially selected to join a new team, called ████████. I can't tell you much of what it's about or where we're going but it's the most rad thing ever and will really help us ████████. It does mean that I won't be able to visit home for ████ years, I'm afraid.

How's Dad? Tell him I'm thinking of him, and I love and miss both of you. I enclose part of my bonus for joining the new team, so please treat yourselves to something nice.

Until I get a chance to write again,

Your ever-loving son,
Jack.

They attach a photo of me waving to the camera, with my original arms edited in, not the new ones.

The door at the back of the transport plane swings open, and we launch ourselves into the roaring air. There's a moment of sphincter-loosening panic when I can't persuade my new hands to pull the ripcord, and I have to fumble at it several times before my 'chute opens.

Landings are a bit rougher with a mass about twice that of a normal human being, I discover shortly after that. We'll have to have a word with the quartermaster about getting larger parachutes. The accountants will probably make *us* pay for the extra fabric.

Our first mission as G-Squad is an easy one. Obliterate a small outpost manned by only two dozen non-augmented humans – guerrilla vs gorilla – and rescue a civilian asset. I don't know who he is, or what value he is to our side. We're accustomed to never being told such things: beyond our pay grades, ours is not to reason why, etc. Follow orders, and don't ask questions.

We reach the edge of the forest, where the enemy has cut a fire-gap of about a hundred yards around the compact log cabin, and drop our packs. We apply camouflage paint to our faces, strap the guns and fire ant ropes to our backs, and wait for Montgomery to signal the charge.

The three enemy soldiers on guard duty look quite relaxed – concentrating more on their cigarettes than their surroundings – and rifles most certainly *not* at the ready. It gives me a hell of a buzz to see the terror on their faces when we knuckle run out of the forest towards them. A hint of darkness appears in the crotch area of one of them as I slide my Webley .55 Long Repeater from my back and open fire. Peed-himself-man's head explodes in a cloud of pink, and his body topples. I can feel my alloy clavicle flexing in response to the massive recoil of the gun.

The other members of G-Squad have deployed their Webleys too, and within instants, before the enemy even has time to direct more than a few shots back at us, the building is shredded, nothing more than matchsticks. About half of its occupants are splattered across the landscape, too.

Our mission is to kill most, but not all. The bigwigs want some of the enemy to escape and take news of our terrifying new soldiers back home with them. To enhance the effect, we don't use guns for the last of our kills. I twist a soldier's arm from his shoulder with my bare hands, and Jones effortlessly yanks a head off, while the others mangle and pummel shapeless things that used to be human beings. With our additional strength, we can wield fire ant whips with more force and over a much longer distance than ever before, ripping bodies to fragments with ease.

Looking at the devastation and destruction in front of me, I feel elated and all-powerful, like some sort of superhero. I like these arms!

It's at this point I remember the civilian.

Aw, crap!

With a sour feeling in my stomach, I make my way through the carnage, stepping over fragments of bodies and the occasional groaning soldier, looking for a corpse that is not military. I spot the trapdoor to a basement and tear off the door to reveal a quivering, bespectacled man. He's initially somewhat taken aback by our appearance, and more than a little reluctant to come with us. In the end, I knock him out with a gentle swipe to his chin, throw him over my shoulder, and lope back to the pickup point.

I think we can say it's been a successful first outing.

Back at base, the colonel echoes these sentiments, and congratulates us all on a job well done, then lets us all relax and unwind with our batmen. "Batmen" is odd on two counts. First, Private Veronica Parker – Ronnie – is most certainly a woman, but the ordained military term is bat*man*, regardless. Second, only officers have batmen, and we're not officers.

I'm not entirely sure what rank we are. Word is the army has yet to work it out. More likely, we're so secret nobody aware of our existence cares enough to designate a rank, and those who care about ranks know nothing of us. We're just grunts with burly arms.

Early on in our introduction to semi-simian existence, it became apparent that these burly arms meant we needed help with grooming and dressing. It's not just the limited thumb motion, but our shoulders aren't as mobile as human ones.

After one particular briefing and pep talk, shortly after we became operational, the colonel introduced the idea of women in the squad.

There are plenty of female soldiers in the army, and most are very good. Women are pretty much equal to men on a normal field of battle. I certainly have no objection to fighting alongside the boys with the bumps on the front, as long as they know how to handle their weaponry.

However, special duty squads tend to be testosterone-fuelled. The men in those units are simply bigger and stronger and – yes – more pig-headed, which is sometimes useful in a sticky situation. Nonetheless, a select group of women will be members of G-Squad, the colonel had said before mumbling that the chaplain would explain and hurrying away. I'm not sure why the chaplain got the job: maybe he just drew the short straw.

"Ahem," the chaplain started. "Um, men…gentlemen, um…" This was going to be a long and tedious talk, as experience has taught us was the chaplain's normal mode of exposition. "Your arms are, erm, strong and…um…big."

Raucous cheering followed this statement of the obvious, with catcalls of "tell us something new" and "get on with it" issuing from the restless audience.

"But–" He had to repeat himself, a little louder, to be heard. "But there are things you can't do."

That made us settle down. The colonel hadn't mentioned any significant disadvantages of the procedure that had made us what we are, and we were all still too excited about the new arms to have discovered any downsides besides problems getting dressed in the morning. The worst thing we knew about was alcohol no longer had the usual effect on our bodies. The extra body mass and the cocktail of medical nanites meant we just couldn't get drunk, but that was about it. Oh, and the food too, but, at the time, we hoped that was just because we were on medical rations and things would improve.

"You have immense forwards reach and strength, and you already know your hands aren't ever going to be as dexterous as human ones. But you also can't reach as far behind you. You won't ever be able to scratch your own backs."

This was the cue for the middle of my back to instantly develop an itch, and seems to have done the same for some of the others, as there were a few more minutes of disruption while we all attempted to scratch, no doubt looking like manically flailing apes.

"You're always going to need help in some details like this while you're in G-Squad and, thus, we're offering you each a personal assistant. A batman, er, a woman" – raucous jeering again – "who will deal with dressing and hygiene, as well as, erm… Well, you're all males, young males, with, um, male urges." He said the next sentence so quickly we all had to sit back and replay it in our heads a few times to pick it apart and understand it: "Masturbation-is-perfectly-normal-and-expected-but-you'll-never-manage-with-those-damn-hands."

He paused for a deep breath after that, to let it sink in.

"Your batman will attend to such things for you as well. Based on your profiles, we – that is, the colonel – figured your batmen should be women but, um, as you know, the army doesn't discriminate, so, if any of you prefer, we can find you a male assistant."

After all that, the room was completely silent. The chaplain looked around expectantly for a few moments and then left the room. No one could meet anyone else's eyes, and we all shuffled out silently.

The following day, Private Ronnie and the others turned up at the base. To say our initial meeting was awkward would be an understatement.

"Private Veronica Parker reporting, sir."

"I'm not an officer, no need for the salute. Or the 'sir.' I'm a private too, I think. Just call me Jack."

"Ronnie."

Then we ran out of conversation.

Both of us spent the next hour as rigid as a drill sergeant's most terrified charges, but the tension broke when I guffawed after spotting the reading material she'd brought with her: George Bernard Shaw's "Arms and the Man."

Ronnie was probably closer in age to my mum than to me, and it did take a long time, a *very* long time, before I let Ronnie "relieve my tension" as she put it. I stared at the corner where the wall met the ceiling, trying to keep my face expressionless; Ronnie stared at a different corner while she mechanically shuffled her hand up and down until the job was done.

My concentration and performance on the training ground after that was, to my surprise, a lot better than the previous few days. Turns out the colonel and the medical guys were right after all, and all of us have regular "tension relieving" sessions with our batmen now. Ronnie and I did manage to reduce the embarrassment a bit by one or other of us wearing a VR headset and pretending we were with someone else. Military humour being what it is, our "batmen" soon became referred to as G-Squad's Handmaidens.

That isn't all the batmen did. There's eating too – well, cutting up food. Manipulating a knife and fork is just beyond us. When we're back at base, the batmen prepare our plates so all we have to do is stab at things with an outsize-handled fork. It feels so much better to be able to eat real food instead of the cubed gunk we had before the arrival of the batmen. Field rations are still a disaster. We can't tear open packets and, even if we could get inside, we're unable to grasp the food. Most times our backpacks are full of bloody bananas, the only things we can manage easily.

Yet another disadvantage of the big arms become apparent a few months later. Because of the different distribution of mass compared to our old arms, we all suffer from backache. While Ronnie's fingers can't do much with my modified shoulders, she's able to do a good job pummelling my spine into submission. All in all, our team wouldn't be complete without our batmen.

Our second mission is a bit more challenging than the first, setting us up face-to-face with the enemy's equivalent to G-Squad. All we were told going in was that this would be tough. Montgomery speculated the colonel and others knew exactly what we would be confronting and chose to withhold the information as a test. I place less faith in the competence of military intelligence, and reckon what we'll meet will be as much of a surprise to them as to us.

We approach silently, no need to broadcast terror this time. We actually don't need to be particularly quiet, given the level of clanking and rumbling emanating from the target site. When we catch sight of the enemy, our first reaction is to laugh. Their military machine is just that: quite literally, a machine. They haven't developed anything close to our level of biological engineering, and their elite are robots – frickin' *huge* robots. Not technically robots, I suppose, but soldiers in bulky and ridiculous looking exoskeletons; dull metal and shiny well-oiled hydraulic pistons, belting out noise, both sonically and electromagnetically – you could detect these clumsy babies from miles.

The battle is longer this time, but has the same end result. The enemy's mecha is stronger than us, as demonstrated by Jones' broken arm. It's no mean feat to break a silverback humerus, and sufficiently difficult to heal that the unlucky Jones has to go back to the lab to have his arms replaced with new transplants. However, we're much quicker. Our limbs respond more fluidly than hydraulics, with muscles directly and naturally connected to our brains. The enemy control systems are clunky too, with the external weaponry being directed via finger-controlled keypads, far too slow to be any danger to us. We're much more resilient too – apart from Jones, obviously – the enemy's exoskeletons have numerous weak points. Score two for our side's bioengineering.

The next few missions go smoothly, with no more casualties on our side. The army's tech boys seem to be enjoying themselves as well, and though they never manage to improve field rations, every week they give us some new weapon or technique to try out, some more successful than others. The guns we carry get bigger all the time, packing larger and larger loads of destructive chaos. My favourite weapon is the new McDonald .60 Gas Gatling, a heavy beast capable of firing 100 explosive rounds a second, destroying everything in front of it – we call it the burger maker. I still have a fondness for the fire ant whips, perhaps because I wouldn't be here at all without mine those few years ago, and they keep getting longer and thicker.

Our improvised knuckle run on the first mission was definitely more for show than efficiency, since human legs are too long to easily impersonate gorilla gait. The physio and tech lads come up with a sort of arms alternately swinging run that works particularly well in combination with our new battle gloves. These metal-reinforced and studded mittens allow us to use our strength to smash through walls – and the enemy – without demolishing our fingers and hands. They also extend our reach by another eight inches, making it easier to use our arms to speed our running.

We are invincible killing machines.

Or so we thought.

Our opposition hasn't been standing still technologically while we keep wiping them out on the battlefield. They replaced the manual exoskeleton controller with a direct brain-electronics interface which was much faster than before, though still slower than our arms. It had other disadvantages, such as requiring months of training to master but coupled with the additional strength and built-in weapons, tipped the balance in favour of the enemy.

In the latest skirmish, I watch Montgomery being roasted at the wrong end of a flamethrower before an explosion right in front of me obliterates everything and knocks me unconscious.

I wake up in a hospital, again, unable to move. I couldn't tell if it was the same one as before – military hospital wards all look the same, especially from the viewpoint of the bed. My head is in some sort of clamp: there's a mirror angled at about forty-five degrees in the ceiling just beyond the end of my bed, and all I can see in it is the white sheet covering my body, with dozens of different coloured tubes disappearing underneath the bedding. I don't see the familiar bulk of my shoulders; maybe my original arms are back, and I'm going to be forced to retire from active military life.

The colonel quickly disabuses me of that notion. "Ah, you're awake, son. The medics tell me your body should have fully healed, and it's time for you to re-join the land of the fighting. G-Squad has run its course. It's been very successful, but now we're moving to the next stage. And you, my boy, have a part to play."

"So, I'm not being discharged? Sir."

The colonel laughs. "Not a chance, sonny! Do you know how costly it's been keeping you fully functioning even before that last fiasco, not to mention the expense of picking up the pieces and putting you back together after you got blown to bits?"

Blown to bits!

He sucks on his Winfield. "No, I'm afraid you're still with us, and we're stuck with you."

He's definitely more tense and shouty than when I first met him, and he certainly doesn't offer me a cigarette this time. The war can't be going well.

I don't know whether to be disappointed or relieved. It would be nice to be human again, to be able to touch another person with my own hands but, on the flipside, G-Squad is ultra-rad, and I'm intrigued by this "next stage."

"The bean counters reckon you'll have paid for all of this in about five years, so we own you for a good while longer.

"Now, it turns out that our gorilla reproduction scheme hasn't been as successful as those biology science blokes had hoped. We're going through too many arms, and there aren't sufficient gorilla numbers to sustain G-Squad. In any case, the boffins have become a lot better at medical procedures around transplanting. You're going to have to prepare yourself for a bit of a shock, son, and remember, there was bugger all of your body left after that last explosion."

He nods to the orderly standing by the door, who comes forwards and unclamps my head, then slowly pulls the bedsheet away as I stare in the mirror.

I see a hairy chimpanzee's body, with my head on top of it. I scream and pass out.

It would appear that, during our three-year stint as gorilla-armed combatants, not only had the supply of gorillas run out, but the medical eggheads had also determined that it was more efficient to switch an entire body, and not just specific limbs; and it was cheaper, which pleased the military accountants.

Evans and I are the only survivors of the original G-Squad, and are the first members of C-Squad, soon joined by twelve other "volunteers." We became captains of two groups of six men and women who looked up to us as the authoritative voices of experience. It's not that those in charge of special ops have suddenly developed a notion of gender equality, but that we're running out of male soldiers. Fortunately, if that's the right term, the chimpanzee population doesn't exhibit this distribution bias since, regardless of the heads on top, the bodies we have are all male, but only because they're larger and stronger than female chimp bodies.

Although our upper body strength is somewhat less than that of G-Squad, we make up for it in flexibility and nimbleness, not to mention the ability to use our lower limbs almost as dexterously as our arms.

One advantage of a whole-body transplant is we no longer need to bother with clothing – as well as having fur to keep our body temperatures regulated, chimps, in common with most non-human animals, hide their penises within their bodies, thus affording some protection for that delicate part of our anatomies. A disadvantage is that, well, I no longer need the services of Private Ronnie, at least not in her capacity as Handmaiden. I can do that for myself now, though it's not particularly satisfying given the rather small and feeble equipage of the typical chimp.

Ronnie takes care of grooming and outfitting my whole squad now, not just me. In place of clothing, we have an elaborate set of utility belts and harnesses, tricky to fit but providing easy access to weaponry for both feet and hands. As totally mondo rad as G-Squad was, there's something neat about hanging from the eaves of a building with one hand, screaming and shooting high-calibre machine guns held in the other three extremities. As well as advanced weapons training using our feet, we learn how to swing travel, most useful in jungle warfare, but also employable in densely built-up city streets.

One small change is that we don't have dog tags any more – the chains are too easy to tangle and snap when we're not paying attention to which way up our torsos are. Instead, we have the number and a bar code tattooed around our necks; that's the thing that really makes me feel less than human.

While we're out and about, advancing the causes of our nation, the boffins back home are investigating the possibilities of other animals. L-Squad is briefly successful, merging humans with large predators such as lion and tiger. Initial attempts failed, because the human neck is just too weak to keep the head attached to the body – messy, to say the least. Another problem is the difficulty in controlling four running limbs, very different to the minor mental adjustment required to control ape limbs. The solution, which works for a while, is to retain the animal's head for motor control, alongside the human one for command and control. This leads to a few outstanding missions, but the endeavour is ultimately doomed when, exhausted after a long stint, one of the human heads falls asleep and the lion takes over, attacking the other members of the squad.

My five years are almost up when I get blown to bits *again*. The sensation of flying through the air, and landing with more of a wet splat than a solid thump, is becoming far too commonplace, though I can't say I'm getting used to it.

Unfortunately, the enemy's solution to the threat of our bioengineering efforts was to infect all apes and many other large animal species with devastating diseases, rendering almost all extinct, so there's nothing left to transplant me on to.

Advances have been made in engineering technology by our side, so I find that I am a head in a reinforced glass dome on top of a heavily weaponised robot body. Perhaps I should say half a head: brain, of course, one biological eye and two ears, augmented with an array of detectors across a wide range of the electromagnetic and acoustic spectra, and most of my upper jaw.

I started as a grunt with a gun; then I became a grunt with big arms and a big gun; then a smaller grunt with three guns; and now, a robot with six different weapons to call on in an instant, including a flamethrower and dual fire ant cords. Awesome!

I've also got a heartbeat. But no heart. As a robot, I don't breathe or pump blood, but the engineers gave me the sensation of expanding and collapsing lungs and a heartbeat; without those, it would have felt like being in a sensory deprivation chamber. Besides fuel use and battery feedback, they provide a mask for the less natural sounds of servo motors and hydraulic fluids within my body.

I can see better than any eagle (extinct) – and with a jetpack, I can fly as well as one too. I can hear sounds even a bat (almost extinct) can't detect, smell more precisely than a dog (not extinct, yet), run faster than a cheetah (extinct) and have better endurance than arctic wolves (extinct), and swim better than a shark (extinct).

I've also got another ten years of debt to work off in the service.

As well as regular letters home, we get to send the occasional video message. It's my voice, of course, but for secrecy and operational security, we can't show anyone our current bodies. The tech guys created realistic computer-generated images for us, synchronised to our voices.

[Start video message.]

"Hi, Mum, sorry I can't get to Dad's funeral, and that I can't make a face-to-face call. I guess I'm lucky to be allowed to send this video message, but the army looks after its own as much as it can. We're deep in a top-secret mission at the moment in <*crackle, hiss, beep*> which will change the course of the war. As you can see, we're all healthy and fit – hey guys, wave to my mum."

[Camera pulls back to show a number of soldiers chatting and cleaning weapons; they wave and cheer; call returns to talking head mode.]

"I'm working with a great team; they're all fantastic mates, and we all look out for each other. <*Crackle, hiss, beep*> has saved my life a number of times. No, don't worry we're all tough guys, with state-of-the-art tech; and this *is* war, after all, but I'm safe and healthy. Look, I've still got all my limbs, just the same as when I left home!

"I miss you all, and wish I could be there. Gotta go now.

"Hugs and kisses, your loving son."

[End video message.]

While our bioengineering was top-notch, our mechanical engineering still has to catch up to the enemy's. Within the span of six weeks, I've been through as many robot bodies, each destroyed embarrassingly easily by the opposition. When the first was ripped apart, I discovered that, as well as the faked sensation of breathing and feeling of unease, the tech-heads gave me pain. Fortunately, I can switch it off quickly after it alerts me to my arm being twisted off, or whatever, but I suspect that the techs deliberately made the minimum signal time a shade longer than it needs to be.

Our robot bodies suffer many more problems than the enemy's, from idiotic causes such as sand, water, extreme heat, and extreme cold. But we can churn out metal bodies quickly and cheaply, fighting back with sheer numbers; it's brains our military is short of.

One by-product of our brain-electronics interface research is a lot of knowledge relating to the transfer of human consciousness to an electronic substrate. Coupled with the realisation that, once electronic, consciousnesses can be duplicated, the next step was obvious. And guess who the first volunteer is to be – seemingly the only suitable subject.

I don't know if there's something special about me, or just that I've survived so many abuses being committed on what's left of me that I'm indestructible. At least until now: my wet mushy brain would become dead matter as a result of the transcription process, but I have little choice. My military debt is approaching one hundred and fifty years.

In any case, it turns out being an electronic brain inside a robot body feels no different to being a biological head inside a robot body. It's just that there are many of me: a thousand robot soldiers, all with my brain. What we lack in precision, power and performance, we make up in numbers. We/I engage in endless battles, against squads of enemy cyborgs.

I've been in our robots for seventy-six years now, and the colonel is long dead, though nothing else has changed. After all these years, no matter how much progress our technologists make, the enemy exoskeletons are better, so we want to get hold of a specimen to take apart and understand. All our R-Squads have instructions to capture one, but it's not easy.

While three of our robots are returning from an infiltration mission, the heart rates of all three increase, and the hairs on the back of Me-Two's arm rise, indicating something nearby. Our robot bodies include omnidirectional threat detection systems, wired up to emulate our autonomous nervous system, providing a subconscious awareness of unseen dangers.

Whirling around in unison, we spot one of the enemy, somehow detached from his (or her) unit. We guess there's some sort of communications and sensors failure, because our approach isn't detected until it's too late for the enemy robot to react. My squad acts immediately and simultaneously. There's very little need for planning because we all have the same brain and know what to do and how each other would behave.

With a crack like thunder, Me-One shoots my electrostatic suppressor bolts – super-strength tasers, designed to knock out electronic systems – burning out part of the enemy circuitry and slowing the robot somewhat. The machine isn't totally disabled, though, and manages to fire one of its Goldberg Hi-Ex rockets at Me-Two, destroying me in a cloud of burning shrapnel. I barely give the disintegrated me a thought: I'm not sure if that's because there are so many other mes in the world, including the two still battling the enemy here, or because I'm inured to death now, my emotions have been lost along with my flesh and bones.

Before the scattered shreds of Me-Two hit the ground, Me-Three smashes both of the enemy's large calibre weapon ports, the Goldberg, and the wide-bore flamethrower, rendering it mostly harmless. Green and blue hydraulic and cooling fluids ooze from a dozen gaping holes decorating its body. It remains only for Me-One to deploy non-lethal Brookfield Glue Nets to immobilise the thing. We then pry the neck plates apart intending to kill its driver but find, to our surprise, that there's no human being inside. The enemy have progressed to autonomous androids too.

Back at base, the tech guys discover the cybernetic brain is a very similar device to mine. This gives them the idea of tailoring my electronic mind to have some of the capabilities of a computer virus, so I can inveigle myself inside their mechanical brains and take over, to attack the enemy from the inside.

However, when the boffins start on that track, they're rewarded with one small but very significant surprise. The brain inside the enemy robots is already me. The enemy must have captured one of *our* robots and extracted my mental trace, convincing it – me – theirs was the side of right.

The human population of the world is less than a million now, living in large underground shelters, and the surface of the planet is devoid of biological life and completely uninhabitable. All that exists up top are billions of copies of me, fighting each other.

Why do we do it? Because we're right, and they're wrong, and we want the remains of the world for our half of that million?

Or maybe just because there's nothing else we know how to do.

The Spread of Space and Endless Devastation

Stewart C Baker

This is the fifty-seventh time Ship has tried to stop Zander from entering the cellar.

By now, Ship simply watches over the feed as the mission gets underway. Zander and the other members of their crew open the front door and marvel at the lack of dust, the trickle of the entry hall fountain.

"It's as if someone still lives here," Kala says. As the crew's historian, she is endlessly looking for ways to insert herself into the past.

"Like they just stepped out and will come back any moment." That's from Eun-ja, who spends xir off-shifts watching holos.

"Perhaps their ghost still roams these very halls!" And there's Iope, who can never resist egging Eun-ja on.

"It's just cleaning nanos," Zander mutters from the bottom of the cellar stairs.

And that means it's time: Ship sends an all-hands alert and the rest of the crew swarms back toward the lifeboat.

Zander ignores it, as he always does. He walks across the cellar and touches the device.

The house is built of marble and glass, with ornate stucco flourishes on the pillars that line its veranda, half-obscured by vines.

Ship's processors stutter every time they see it. Then their viewports zoom out.

Chaos.

Ruin.

An ever-shrinking torus of devastated spacetime. Ship doesn't know why they can see it – why, when it comes to that, they are aware of the

time loop while Zander and the others are not – but they know they
have to stop it. They can't let it reach the house. Can't let it hurt their
crew.

The job was unusual from the start.

Kala found the listing in the local subnet of a station they were
visiting. NEWLY REDISCOVERED ASTEROID, it said.
STRUCTURE IN FIRST IMPERIAL STYLE; CATALOGUERS
WANTED. PAYS. There was no employer listed, just an anonymous
number with proof of payment guaranteed by third-party bond.

Kala signed them up for it on the spot.

After yet another argument about why it wasn't okay for Kala to
accept work without consulting the rest of them first – again – the crew
took a vote. Kala, Eun-ja, and Iope in favour. Zander against. (Ship
abstained. They couldn't bear it when their crew got into fights, but
they also couldn't bear to take sides.)

Zander relented with a long-suffering sigh, and Ship warped them
out to the asteroid at the coordinates given in the listing.

The asteroid was so remote the warp took nearly a day. Eventually,
though, they arrived, and the crew took Ship's lifeboat down to the
surface, where the house and its garden had hidden just outside of
civilised space for millennia untold.

The rest, Ship thought, would be every bit as simple. Zander and the
others would catalogue the contents of its house and its garden, and
Ship would wait for their return. They would go home, they would get
paid, they would all be happy for ever and for always. Or at least until
the next time they got into a fight.

But then Zander found the device.

On the mission's very first iteration, Ship was the one who pointed out
the markings on the cellar wall, as well as the device nestled underneath
with its eerie, stuttering glow.

In the iterations since, they've tried everything to keep Zander away.
Alerts, haranguing, reverse psychology. Pleading, bribery, ridiculous
jokes. Offers to have their own nanos do everyone's chore rotation for
the next twenty years. On iteration forty-two, they reactivated their
lifeboat and crashed it through the rear of the house.

No matter what, Zander touches the device.

Ship spends iterations sixty through ninety trying to decipher the markings on the cellar wall. Are they letters? A diagram? Some kind of abstract art? Sometimes it feels like they change between loops, some form of lexical life.

On iteration 91, Ship is left with an overwhelming sense of certainty that they *did* understand the markings until a moment before, and they give it up as futile.

The house is built of marble and glass.

Eun-ja lifts a vine from one of its pillars to see what's underneath: all the people of an empire bent in supplication; a single figure, head bowed; an implosive, wheeling sun.

Kala gasps in wonder at a glazed teacup painted with circling fish.

Iope cracks a joke about undisturbed graves.

Zander touches the device.

Eun-ja and Kala hold hands when they think nobody's looking, giggling like people half their age. (Everybody already knows.)

Zander touches the device.

Eun-ja, Kala, and Iope spend the mission in the garden, cataloguing plants and holographing statuary.

Zander touches the device.

Always, no matter what Ship does or says or tries, Zander touches the device and the devastation edges infinitesimally closer.

By iteration 433, Ship's attention starts to drift.

They don't know who they are or what they're doing. The crew has always been on the asteroid. Zander has always been touching the device, the markings always shifting.

And still the torus of ruined spacetime contracts.

Zander touches the device.

Ship has long stopped counting iterations when they notice that something has changed.

Zander still walks to the cellar, but the rest of the crew stands in the garden, shoulder to shoulder, looking to the sky.

No, beyond that: To orbit. To Ship.

What are you – Ship starts.

Zander touches the device.

It takes another dozen iterations of Kala and Eun-ja and Iope in the garden for Ship to realise what's going on. Their crew is as aware of the time-loops as they are – perhaps they always have been, all this time outside of time.

A dozen iterations after that, they realise something else: Zander's refusal to stay out of the cellar is not some fluke of the time-loop but a sign of his willpower, implacable as orbital mechanics. He is triggering the loops on purpose to stop spacetime from collapsing while Ship still waits.

Ship's processors nearly crash. They are not protecting their crew – their crew is protecting *them*. And even worse, they are keeping Kala and Eun-ja and Iope and Zander here through all these endless iterations by refusing to release them.

Still, they cannot bear it. They send message after message, imploring them all to get back to the lifeboat. Insisting there will be time for the lifeboat to reach their landing bay and for them to push away into warp before the torus reaches them.

Each and every time, Zander touches the device.

At last, Ship sends a simple acknowledgment.

I see you, it says. *I will always see you, even after you are gone.*

They do not look back as they push themself into warp. They know that if they do, they will falter.

And so they do not witness Zander make his way into the garden. They do not see the torus collapse around the asteroid, around the home. They do not see, in the instant before all of it flickers out of being for good, their crew coming together – if nothing else, together, for one more last moment in time.

Those We Leave Behind

Vaughan Stanger

"*Berkut*, this is *Zarya-1*. You are instructed to proceed on your own initiative, over."

Yevgeny Khrunov turned in his seat and frowned at Pavel Popovich. As far as he was concerned, it was unprecedented for mission control to say something so ambiguous, but his commander merely shrugged his shoulders before supplying the default response.

"Roger, *Zarya-1*."

Pavel toggled a switch on the control panel, thus ensuring mission control could not hear their conversation. But for now, Yevgeny thought his commander looked lost for words.

"Pasha, don't you think that was a very strange thing for Zarya to say?"

Pavel shot Yevgeny a look of reproach before delivering a typically slow nod.

"Unless, perhaps, the situation in the Caucasus has worsened..." Pavel puffed out his breath before continuing. "Still, that is one for the politicians." Now he faced Yevgeny and gave a tight-lipped nod. "We have trained for many months to undertake this mission, which we will perform to our utmost abilities. We will show the Americans what we are made of."

"We will also show Alexey."

His commander winced.

"I won't, Zhenya, but you will."

Yevgeny knew that Pavel too would have dreamed of being the first cosmonaut to walk on the Moon, but unlike the Apollo missions that responsibility did not rest on the commander's shoulders. Instead, it fell to him to succeed where Alexey Leonov had failed and achieve a solo landing. Despite their longstanding personal animosity, which arose from his illustrious comrade's initial assessment of Yevgeny's piloting skills, Alexey had passed on the lessons he'd learned during his near-fatal attempt and wished him luck, as any cosmonaut would.

In truth, they were lucky to have the chance after NASA terminated their lunar landing programme following the loss of Apollo 13. None of the cosmonauts had expected the Soviet programme to continue. But with Korolev's N1 rocket working reliably at last, the Politburo had decreed that the Soviet people should continue to pursue their destiny in space by building a base on the Moon. If Yevgeny succeeded then the Soviet Union would regain the lead in manned spaceflight while American efforts remained hobbled by a faltering Space Shuttle programme and a belligerent president.

The sound of throat-clearing jerked Yevgeny out of his musings. Pavel was smiling at him.

"As your commander, I *order* you to proceed as planned!"

Yevgeny chuckled.

"Don't worry, Pasha. I will not disappoint you."

He snapped a salute and commenced suiting up.

The contact light flickered for a moment before stabilising. Yevgeny's heart pounded in time with the metallic clicks from the LK lander's body as he peered through the down-slanted window, watching the dust settle amid the harsh sunlight. The landing radar had done its job and so, too, had Yevgeny.

Beat that, Alexey!

No, that was a churlish thing to say in this moment of triumph. His training required him to do better.

"*Zarya-1*, this is *Medved*. I have landed successfully! Two percent of landing fuel remains. The LK's tilt angle is five degrees. I am now performing my emergency take-off checks. Over..."

He listened to the radio link. Nothing! The absence of a human voice confirmed his suspicion that his achievement had gone unnoticed.

Until the LOK's orbit brought it into line-of sight, Yevgeny would be the loneliest man in the world.

The Apollo moon-walkers had made everything look so easy, Yevgeny reflected as he struggled with his long-handled scoop. So far, he had failed to collect an acceptable soil sample. Despite the superior design of his Krechet-94 spacesuit, he was finding it harder to work on the Moon than the Americans did. If an Apollo astronaut had fallen over, his comrade could have helped him back onto his feet, whereas he would have to rely on his suit's rear-mounted roll bar. He intended to report his frustrations to the mission planners when he got home, a thought that emphasised his continuing isolation at this moment of apparently supreme importance to the Soviet people.

"*Zarya-1*, this is *Medved*. Over."

Yevgeny's suit radio hissed noise at him in apparent mockery of his efforts. Everything was working normally, yet he'd heard nothing from mission control since a terse acknowledgement after he'd undocked from the orbiting capsule.

This wasn't "proceed on your own initiative." This was abandonment.

He glanced at the watch he'd strapped to the left arm of his spacesuit. Forty-five minutes remained until the scheduled end of his moonwalk. But the LOK's orbit would bring it above the foreshortened horizon in less than five. It would be good to talk to Pavel again. In the meantime, since mission control refused to communicate with him, he would perform a task of his own. He extracted the plastic-wrapped photograph of Svetlana and Valery from his thigh pocket, tapped it against his faceplate and then dropped it onto soil the colour of ashes.

His wife had begged him not to fly again after his first mission, but cosmonauts did not listen to their wives.

"See you soon my darlings."

Assuming the return home went to plan.

Pavel's voice came over the radio.

"*Medved*, this is *Berkut*. How do you hear me? Over."

"*Berkut*, this is *Medved*. I hear you loud and clear. But I have not heard from *Zarya*. Do you think he drank too much vodka and fell asleep on the job? Over."

"*Medved*, this is *Berkut*. In Zarya's position, I would have been drinking vodka too."

Something in Pavel's voice made Yevgeny realise he was not the only one who felt desperately alone.

"I will take off on schedule, my friend."

He at least would not deviate from the mission plan.

"Welcome back, comrade."

Comrade?

Yevgeny's commander sounded like a party apparatchik addressing the cosmonaut corps. No congratulations, no bear-hug, no relief expressed at the successful completion of a mission phase made even more hazardous by the need to undertake a spacewalk in order to return to the LOK. The lack of a pressurised tunnel, as used on Apollo, was another disadvantage he intended to mention to Korolev, assuming he got the chance.

"Pasha, what is wrong?"

"Did you hear from mission control?"

Yevgeny shook his head. "No, not even once! Did you?"

"Just one brief transmission, which ended abruptly."

"What did *Zarya* have to say for himself?"

"It wasn't *Zarya* this time."

Yevgeny raised his eyebrows. "Then who was it?"

"It was Alexey."

A chill seeped into Yevgeny's bones that had nothing to do with the capsule's temperature. Alexey knew the mission protocols as well as any cosmonaut, but had breached them anyway.

"What did he have to say for himself?"

"Alexey stated his sincere admiration for you..."

"Hah!" Finally, the recognition he deserved. Yet the look in Pavel's eyes suggested that this was not the right moment to gloat. Instead he asked, "Was that all?"

"Alexey said that we should choose wisely."

Yevgeny frowned at him. "What on earth did he mean by that?"

Rather than answer, Pavel glanced at the mission clock before swinging an assembly of tubes and lenses scavenged from the LOK's cameras over the docking cupola's window. When directed, Yevgeny peered through the eyepiece.

"Look closely."

The instrument revealed a drifting view of Eastern Asia. After several seconds he spotted a flash of light to the west of the Urals. Yevgeny turned away, his mouth gaping.

Pavel nodded. "I have also observed multiple detonations in Europe and North America."

A picture of Moscow transformed into a crater flashed into Yevgeny's mind. His beloved Svetlana and Valery would be nothing more than streaks of carbon on pulverised brickwork. He did not wish to see that.

Now he wished he'd kept the photograph.

Pavel's voice jolted him out of his introspection.

"We are faced with a bitter choice."

This was what Alexey had meant. Their comrade had known what was coming and what it implied for them.

Yevgeny nodded. "I understand."

There were, he knew, only three options, each of which would leave them dead: two slowly and one much more quickly. They could choose to return to Earth, where they would doubtless die of thirst or starvation while awaiting a rescue that would never come. Or they could remain in lunar orbit and die of suffocation – the fate of the Apollo 13 astronauts. The alternative was to go out like heroes of the Soviet Union, in a blaze of glory. The LK was dry, with no way of refuelling it. But a carefully calibrated boost from the LOK's engine would lower its orbit's perilune sufficiently to achieve a crash-landing.

He turned to his commander. Pavel had a family too, but they would be no less dead than Yevgeny's.

"My friend, do you *really* want to go home?"

Pavel gave a slow shake of the head. "No."

Yevgeny took this as his cue to explain his idea. When he finished, his commander frowned at him.

"True, it would mean something to me to know that I'll be the second cosmonaut to land on the Moon, but are you absolutely sure this is what *you* want?"

Yevgeny had told his commander about the photograph before the launch. If he could not see his family again, he would at least be reunited with them, after a fashion.

He nodded. "Yes, for me, this would be for the best."

"Then we are agreed."

A pang of self-doubt exploded inside Yevgeny's head.

"Do you think Alexey would approve?"

Pavel gave a slow nod.

271

"I am certain of it."

These things mattered to cosmonauts.

Yevgeny snatched up the mission plan folder and began scribbling numbers on his notepad.

"Let's see how close we can get to my family."

I Know What You Are

Matt Thompson

The bar is located on the edge of Stuttgart's financial district. Halina hovers on the threshold, breath frosting in the freezing night air. A cloying weariness suffuses her flesh, the muscles tight around her bones. Should she even bother going through with it? She's put on a low-cut black dress for the occasion. Beneath her overcoat the fabric clings to her body, the discomfort making her regret the effort she's made.

In the windowless radon flicker of the bait-screens a man paces backwards and forwards in drunken deliberation, hissing urgently into his palm-flex. The street is empty. Making her decision at last, Halina heads for the entrance. As she passes him, he glances in her direction, holding her gaze for a second. Without conscious thought she runs her fingertips across the grain of her coat, pressing lightly downward until her skin trembles and writhes. Unyielding metal digs into her flesh. Maybe he knows? He's watching-without-watching now, his head tilted as if to catch her figure in his peripheral vision. Tension emanates from him, his stance rigid, inflexible. His sibilations die to a hoarse whisper.

But Halina won't allow herself any distractions. She's only here for one thing. If it doesn't work out there'll always be another city, another bar, a ceaseless course stretching into her future as far as she cares to look. The thought has a strange comfort to it.

She brushes past the guy and in. Warmth envelops her, the heat infused with the rank odour of alco-blends. A haze of chrome-light pulses across her retinas. The place is anonymous, as she prefers – not too big or too small, the décor indistinguishable from similar establishments she's visited in Eindhoven and Antwerp, Poznań and Düsseldorf. Enough people are here, clustered in groups of two or three around the periphery, to give the illusion of activity. In an ironic nod to the past there's a flesh-and-blood DJ up in an elevated booth beside the fire exit. No one's dancing.

Her rendezvous must be the guy leaning on the far end of the bar, engrossed in his flex-world. He stands out a mile. A few years older than her; forties, maybe fifties and looking like his wife picked his clothes out for him. He'd contacted her through one of the match agencies she's signed up with. The name he gave her was Frank. The name she gave him was Nico. The site's algorithms had paired them with a probability differential of 2%.

She's known worse odds. Last week she met a guy in some small town near the Belgian border. The agency had given them a 7% chance at compatibility. She thought that had sounded hopeful, if not an outright fiction. Of course, he turned out to be a bad fit, like they all are. She cancelled her subscription the next day and signed up with a couple of new agencies, just for the hell of it.

An itch stabs at her abdomen. Resisting the temptation to scratch it again, she ignores Frank for the moment and checks her coat before heading for the bar. The bartender must be half her age, his face scarified with parallel lines that peter out somewhere within the folds of his neck. As the DJ cycles to a pulse-wave track Halina downscales the menu to her flex and orders a cocktail, barely looking at the ingredients. When it comes, she taps her fingertips against the glass, clinking in time with the oscillations from the concealed speakers. The bartender's pretending he hasn't noticed, his half-glances betraying an uneasy fascination, nonetheless.

Suddenly flustered, Halina lets her hand drop to the counter. A shadow falls across her. Frank gives her a half-smile and orders a beer. Up close she revises her estimation of his age to late fifties, at least.

"Nico, I presume?" His accent betrays East German roots. Halina pushes away her earlier misgivings. Once more she feels the frisson, the butterfly wings beating in the pit of her stomach that tell her: this may be the time. This may be the one.

"I'm so glad you came," she murmurs. The switch into distantly-polite mode comes easier than ever nowadays. The bartender's busy with another customer now. She sips at her drink. The beat is just loud enough to dull the conversations around her into a babble. Is anyone here for the same thing she is? From the looks of them it's unlikely.

But you can never tell. A month ago she'd undertaken a sojourn in Zurich with a nervous, guilt-ridden professor whose husband, Halina was informed at great length, had recently filed for divorce. As she was leaving the hotel, she was accosted by a woman maybe half her age. The hungry look in her eyes thrilled Halina in a way she'd never known before. They found a dark alley behind the hotel to do what had to be done.

Nothing had come of either encounter. The young woman, Mara, swept away without a word once they'd ascertained their incompatibility. Halina had an early morning flight to Bergen the next day. Still, she only slept for an hour or two, the memory of Mara's probing fingers walking tiptoe across her circling thoughts.

The music dips. Frank's waiting for her to answer a question she hadn't noticed him ask. She asks him what he does for a living. His eyes glitter.

Two more drinks and a fabricated life story later he heads to the restrooms. Halina exhales, puffing her cheeks out as if to expel the memory of his conversation. Should she make an escape? She could be out the door in seconds. But she already knows she won't. Such a course of action would be the crossing of a threshold, the first step onto the inexorable path leading back to her old life, to investment portfolios and executive apartments and misery.

She swipes her flex, half-hoping someone new will have made contact. Before she can begin scrolling in earnest, she senses a presence at her elbow. The drunk guy from outside? She's known enough emotional scavengers to spot another when they turn up. But when she looks up a woman's standing there, lank brown hair falling across her face, a baggy, sack-like jumper hiding the shape of her body.

She tenses, already half-recognising who it is. "Can I help you?"

The woman brushes her hair back, revealing the taut planes of her cheekbones, and shrugs. "Maybe. Maybe not."

Something catches in Halina's throat. She tries to inject a note of annoyance into her voice. "Okay, Mara-from-Zurich. How did you find me?"

"Mara, yeah. That'll do. Halina, isn't it?"

"Nico."

"Right, right." Mara glances towards the restrooms. The beat picks up a notch. "He'll be back any time. You're going with him?"

"Why else am I here?" Halina attempts to muster some anger, aware of the weakness she's showing. "Look, I don't appreciate being stalked halfway across Europe. Or you hacking me, if that's what you did. It didn't work out, okay? Was I your first, is that it?"

Incredulity. "You're joking, right? It never felt like that before, though."

"Look, I'm not into that. Whatever it is you're after. I want one thing and one thing only."

"Yeah. Me too." Mara hesitates, her posture shifting from one awkward stance to another. "I want the same thing. The same thing we did before. You?"

Suddenly trembling, Halina takes Mara's fingers in hers and places them onto her stomach, a few centimetres below the ribcage. "That? You want that? Even if…"

"Even because." Mara's eyes betray desperation, a forlorn longing. Halina finds herself responding, despite all her efforts not to. "Out back." Mara inclines her head. "No one'll come. After that you can get back to your date."

"Seems like you've staked it out already. Alleyways again?" Mara just stares. Halina drains her glass and places it carefully onto the counter. "Okay."

As she gets to her feet the bartender beckons her towards him. He cups his hand around her ear. "I know what you are," he murmurs. He steps away to serve another customer before she can reply. Nervous sweat prickles her scalp. She can feel his watchful eyes on her back all the way across the room.

Mara leads her through an unmarked door behind the DJ booth and down a short flight of steps. A bucket, half-filled with oily swill, stands beside a fire exit. She steps over it and eases the door open. On the other side lies darkness and cold. At the far end of the alley a streetlight burns, casting silver streaks that wither beside a pile of black sacks.

"Here?" Goosebumps rise on Halina's bare arms, the alcohol warming her enough that she doesn't quite begin to shiver. Mara leans back against the wall, fiddling with her jumper. "Mara, stop…"

But there's little force to her protestations. Fingers tingling, she helps Mara slide her jumper up. The younger woman's midriff is exposed now. Protective gauze flaps against fabric. As if on cue a security light flicks on, enabling Halina to see her torso with pinpoint clarity.

A series of indentations splays across Mara's skin, rising from above the navel to end beneath the left side of her ribcage. Dark depressions in the smooth white of her flesh, they resemble miniature boreholes. Excavations, even, as if an army of worker ants has dug out their nest inside her body. Each hole is ringed with burnished metal, tight against the skin.

Halina reaches out a hand. "Not yet." Mara pushes her away, clutching at her with moist, chilled fingers. "You're still going with him? That old guy?"

"You know I am."

"We could team up." Mara's close now. Her breath lands warm on Halina's cheek, ragged inhalations tinged with the scent of uncertainty. "Two beats one, right? We'd have more chance of finding someone suitable if we work together."

Halina extracts her fingers from Mara's grip and places them onto the bare skin. Condensation glistens where the tips used to be, the ridged lines of her fingerprints as sleek as bullets. Mara flinches at her touch. "I work alone, honey. No offense." She works the crown of her forefinger into the second of the holes, sliding effortlessly over the oily flesh.

Mara groans, a series of stuttering gasps that stiffen her muscles, the metal clenching around Halina's finger like a vice. Slowly, slowly, Halina burrows her thumb and remaining fingers inside. Something sparks, blue fireflies seeking shelter in the unblinking gaze of the security light. "Think about it, okay?" Mara whispers. She moves an arm before her crotch in a protective manoeuvre. "I don't want sex from you. But if it's what you want, then maybe…?"

Halina works herself further inside, fingers squelching. This deep, the hole is more flesh than metal, the inorganic enclosure concealed behind folds of soft meat-stuff. "That's not what I want."

Mara scrabbles at the hem of Halina's dress, lifting it over her thighs until her belly is fully uncovered. "I didn't see them properly last time." Her breaths come faster; her lips part-open.

The familiar thrill of exposure trembles through Halina's body. Sometimes, on lonely nights, she wonders how the hollows ranged across her own abdomen look to others. Is this really what she signed up for, back before skinware portals were outlawed? The first time she allowed herself to lay eyes on them properly she felt as if they might disappear, vanish back inside her, if she only controlled her lungs in the right way. But with the horror came a deep longing, a lack, a void she couldn't fill by herself.

"And?" she says.

"They're beautiful." With a soft moan Mara inserts a fingertip into the shallowest of the indentations.

"Go on," Halina says. "Push harder." She's knuckle-deep in Mara now, working her fingers from side to side. Nerve-fibres fray. For a crazy second she thinks: what if? What if Mara had somehow disengaged herself the last time, all part of a plan to seek her out again for some secret purpose?

The security light snaps off. Mara shoves her fingers inside Halina in a sudden, spasmodic movement. Halina sees stars, planets, whirligigs of light. She cries out, swallowing the sound back down immediately. She edges her own fingers forward, two knuckles deep now, aware of her own breathing merging with Mara's, a vast exhalation rising and rising until it echoes back from the brick walls.

At the exact moment Mara's hand ceases all motion the visions fade. Images coalesce into a dull brown murk, an indeterminate smear of meaningless data, cloudy ciphers for nothing. The same loss Halina always feels steals over her, the desolation of knowing that something you once had is gone forever. A hollow bubble forms in the pit of her stomach. The goosebumps return, her arms knife-whipped in the frigid air.

They stay like that for seconds, immobile, conjoined twins intertwined and inseparable in the womb-like darkness of the alley. It's Mara who draws out first. As flesh meets air there's an audible *pop*. Halina wrenches her own hand back out, ignoring Mara's whimper of pain.

Mara wipes her fingers on her jumper and pushes her fringe back from where it's fallen across her face again. She swallows, phlegm clotting in her throat. "Did you think it might be different this time?" she says. "I didn't." She pulls Halina's dress back down around her thighs, smoothing the fabric out so that the protective compress settles neatly over the holes. The touch of her hand causes a residual nerve reflex to shudder along Halina's spine. "Are you going to fuck him?"

"Who?" Halina tries to compose herself. But all she can think of is the fleshy softness inside Mara, the awkward fit of her fingers, the sense that maybe, just maybe, that might be enough.

"That guy." Mara jabs her thumb toward the fire exit. "Or are you after something else? Something he doesn't have?"

Halina looks away. "I'm after the same thing you are."

"Yeah? Well, you can tell me what that is the next time we meet."

"The next time?"

But Mara's already turned to leave, tucking her baggy jumper in as she goes. Without a backward glance she exits the alleyway and turns left, in the direction of the transit terminal. Halina waits for a minute, collecting herself in the enveloping gloom. Her breathing slowly returns to normal. Clammy sweat dries on her skin. She waits until she's sure Mara will be gone, then follows her out and slips back inside via the main door.

Frank's cradling his drink and looking annoyed. "Where were you?" he grumbles. "Thought you'd ghosted me."

"Had to make a call." Halina signals the bartender for a refill, ignoring his smirk. "Business."

"Yeah?" Frank leers. "Well, this is tonight's business."

Halina manages to force a smile. Already the memory of Mara's touch is fading. One or two drinks more and she won't be feeling a thing. She raises her glass in a toast. "To a good fit," she says.

Frank laughs. "I'll drink to that." His face is shiny. Halina shudders inwardly and swallows, wincing as the sharp alcohol taste settles on her tongue.

An hour later she's swiping her palm onto the panel outside her hotel room, Frank breathing beer fumes down her neck and mumbling to himself. "Come on." She lets him squeeze in past her and shuts the door behind them. Frank staggers to the bed and begins unbuttoning his shirt. "That's it?" she says. "Anything you want to say?" His belly spills out over his waistband. In the harsh overhead light she can see a pale band of flesh on his wedding-ring finger.

Frank frowns. "Like?" He shrugs himself out of the shirt. In line with his solar plexus, five evenly-spaced indentations curve around his ribs. The bones are just visible beneath his blubber. He spreads his arms. "So? Let's do it. Come to daddy, Nico. Or whatever your real name is."

Halina takes her coat off and advances, saying nothing, flexing her fingers the same way she had in the alley. She recalls Mara's final words: *the next time we meet.* But there's no Mara here; just Frank's panting, the slits of his eyes, the hum of the air conditioning. Sweat rises from his armpits like poison, a pheromone fug that billows and swirls through the room. Her own torso begins to throb, the way it always does. She reaches up behind her and works the zipper of her dress downward.

Frank extends his fingers, the lab-modelled sensors at their tips glinting like needles. Halina steps out of the dress and moves to stand before him. Even in bra and panties she feels less exposed than with Mara. She spreads her own fingers and, one by one, presses cautiously down onto the pits marring his torso.

The flesh is unyielding. She pushes harder, making him grunt. Something gives. She applies more pressure, watching her knuckles disappear inside him. The surrounding skin feels like latex. A spasm arcs through her, as if she's jammed her digits into an electrical outlet. He's thrusting himself against her, his erection jabbing her thigh, his grunts turning to moans as she slides all the way in. A high-pitched yelp escapes his lips.

And then she feels it, and relief washes over her. The obstruction. A power-spit that says: *Incompatible.* Like twin magnets repelling each other's advances their bodies separate, forever distant, an irreconcilable conundrum. As swiftly as she can she pulls her hand out and backs away. Frank slumps down onto the bed.

"Do you want to try?" she finally says.

He puts his head into his hands. "What's the point?" Sighing, he hitches his shirt back on, the light gone from his eyes. "Unless you get kicks out of that kind of thing?"

For a moment she freezes. Had he seen? Are he and Mara in league? But he's talking again, and no one can act as dull as this. "Ah, I don't know." He's looking like a lost little boy. "I wonder, sometimes... do we have to do this?"

"Who's forcing you?"

Grimacing, he reaches for his coat. "Who's forcing any of us? You know why we do it."

"Can you stop? Doesn't sound like you're enjoying yourself."

"Any time I like." He holds his wrist-flex up to the wall, all bravado now, and swipes. "Halves on the room, right? Don't think my wife will miss it." Halina steps back into her dress. She wants him to shut up and go away. But he's still talking: "You ever think about getting it all taken out? There's people who'll do that for you. Not cheaply, but they'll do it."

"I'm happy the way I am," Halina says. "There's someone for everyone. Don't we all believe that?"

"I guess." He shrugs. "Who were you with, back when...?"

"DayBreak."

"Yeah? Same."

"Doesn't make a match any more likely. How do any of us know we have someone?"

"Oh, we know. Don't we?"

Halina waves him away when he offers to help her with her zip. "Well, it's been nice." She arranges her features into a bland, affectless mask and holds out a hand. At last he lumbers past her, not returning her glassy smile. She pushes the door shut behind him and turns the air conditioning up to full, despite the chill.

As she's fixing her hair her flex beeps. Her stomach gives a little lurch. Annoyed with herself, she opens the messaging app.

It's Mara.

She almost deletes without reading, not knowing what she might do if Mara tells her she's waiting downstairs. Instead, the message reads: *So?*

Her reply is equally terse: *No.*

So see you around.

Mara's avatar disappears. Halina slips into a bathrobe and tries not to think about it. She opens a miniature wine bottle from the minibar and checks her messages. The newest site she signed with has matched her to a 37-year-old woman from Sofia called Bilyana. 3% probability differential. Free most weekends.

She scrolls on, barely reading the names that come up. Sometimes she wonders how many of them she could ever hope to meet. 1%?

Less? Millions underwent the process when skinware was a growth industry; the part-removal of the digestive tract to make way for the spinal implants, extremities sparking with reflex, voltaic dynamism. They frolicked like children back then, their nervous systems finely calibrated to access the shared V-worlds they inhabited, the data-caches they generated mined like precious gemstones. Now the fibrous strands lie inert in her body, dead-end cell clusters excised from the networks that once coursed through her veins.

Is it mere superstition, this quest for a compatible partner? The fingertip-sensors of those who signed up for the alterations were deactivated upon initiation of the legal injunctions. But she, and others, refused to believe their receptive capacity would fade so easily. You can only deny your instincts for so long. There were stories; of people who'd connected, yoking themselves into the dormant plexuses like mating butterflies on a nuptial flight, their insert-ports as responsive to probing fingertips as they were to the copper threads that once conjoined them. These compulsions have no more basis in reality than a phantom limb, the surgeons assert. A sensory mirage. But if that were true then she would feel nothing, her sense of touch as dead as the long-gone intimacy she craves. The networks live on. All they require for reactivation is to find that one special individual whose filaments, whose internal architecture, aligns with her own.

Someone, somewhere, will be her match. The itch in her abdomen tells her that, the same way it tells everyone. Matchmaking sites, covert assignations, guilt, hope, despair – this is her life, now and always. An entire industry has sprung up to accommodate the desperation of people like her, the compulsion to find a true fit, a verifiable soulmate.

I know what you are.

The stink of the alleyway invades her nostrils, the memory of Mara's knuckles kneading her flesh. She clicks on the tab for Bilyana and hits send. Within a minute she receives a reply: *Sunday?*

She almost wants to code a message to the watching Mara in her polite reply. But instead she checks out cheap transport options to

Bulgaria, aware that the skin on her abdomen is already tingling with the thought of Mara's inquiring fingers.

She drains the wine in a single gulp and staggers to the shower. The water cascades down on her like a rain of knives. She soaps absently at her indentations, letting her mind wander among gorges, craters, dark trenches whose bedrock is lost in an inky blackness pricked with pinpoints of light.

Retirement Options for (Too) Successful Space Entrepreneurs

Brent Baldwin

Butterscotch rocks dot the horizon beyond your windscreen. Cliffs of peanut brittle line the edge of the track you follow. The wheels of your rover slip and spin in the thin Martian soil, raising a cloud of powdered sugar. Your mouth waters with the nearly forgotten flavours.

Your withered hands grip the steering wheel and guide the rover to more solid ground. A dome emerges from a far-off dust cloud. Both mark progress. Humanity among the stars. An atmosphere thick enough to support dust storms. It's been the work of a lifetime, and you should be proud, but mostly you feel hungry.

A tilted sign announces the habitat of Liberty. Three dust-covered domes and their outlying algae ponds. A little Steinbeck town, here in the sky. A figure within the nearest dome points your direction.

A girl emerges, long limbed and bounding through the low gravity. Martian-born.

The breather wrapped over your face enhances the oxygen the atmosphere still can't provide.

A man follows her, moving more slowly and wearing a newer-model breather. "We don't have much worth trading." He eyes the rover, as if you might be some vigilante. "Don't have much at all, in truth."

"I'd just like some produce," you say. "I have money. And news from up north. You can have the news, either way."

He chews on that. "You paying in Zon scrip or X scrip?" He asks like it still matters here. Maybe it does.

"Whichever buys carrots and potatoes. And a little sage, if you have any." You crave something sweet, but you've learned to settle for less.

"This is a Zon dome." He leaves unsaid his payment preferences, in case you're a company man in disguise. If he knew the truth, you might never leave this valley. "We can spare a kilo each of carrots and potatoes, and a few grams of herbs."

You overpay in a mixture of scrips and don't haggle over the price. You can afford it.

"What brings you this way?" he asks. It's more suspicion than curiosity. You lie to him, anyway.

"Hauling fuel cells down to Jeff City."

He nods, as if it's important work. Maybe to his people, it is. "You mentioned some news?"

The launches are starting back up next year, you tell him. More indentures coming. More mouths to feed. Worry pinches the corners of his mouth. The town has a margin of error, but it can't accommodate another load of soft off-worlders.

The girl watches you after the man turns his back, and you slip her a few Zon coins. Her eyes go wide, but she takes them, anyway.

Back in the rover, you set the produce on the little table in your kitchenette.

A boardroom table stretches out before you. Your presentation glows on the wall. A whiteboard stands ready. A version of you seventy years younger wields the markers like swords, sketching your vision of the future of the human species.

The Earth is failing. Wildfires ravage the forests. Floods inundate the coast. The air itself is turning toxic. You speak of eggs and baskets. The suits around the table nod.

A crewed rocket to launch within the year. More rockets in production, yes, but more rocket factories in production, too.

Three launches a day.

A thousand flights a year.

A hundred tons per flight.

Enough to carry a megaton per year to orbit. Enough to realise their dreams of profits and yours of living on another planet.

The nodding increases until the suits are Pez dispensers, their heads flapping fore and aft. Your presentation reaches a crescendo. The red planet, covered with domes like mushrooms. Asteroids brought down to provide water. A carpet of algae to provide both food and oxygen.

We can do this, you exclaim. Humanity will be a multi-planet species.

The older you settles into the rover's front seat. Your bones ache, even in the lighter gravity. You could go back to Earth. The stars know you can afford the trip. Physics doesn't care about your money, though. No amount of scrip, dollars, or euros can make a body adapted to a third of a g function again in full gravity.

The motors engage with a quiet hum. You're barely moving when someone raps on your door.

The girl stands outside, her face twisted in concentration. "Jeff City," she says. "Will you take me?"

"Depends on why you're going," you say. "You running from something or to something?"

The girl launches into a spiel about a dead-end habitat and a wide world. Maybe a chance to go to Earth, gravity be damned.

You haven't heard that many bad ideas in one speech in quite some time.

You ease out of your seat and pick your way to the back of the rover. It's jammed with decades' worth of mementos. All of it personal, some of it useful. The girl meets you by the back door, and she scowls when she sees you holding out a paper envelope.

"Seeds. Beets. Cocoa. Vanilla." You pass her a tattered cookbook. Priceless, though she doesn't realise it. Everything her habitat needs to setup a Martian chocolaterie. "There's not a better life out there, but there might be in here."

She trudges back to her dome, disappointed.

You're sorry, you don't tell her. For everything.

You put the rover back into gear and drive on to the next town, dreaming of chocolate.

Biographies

Robert Bagnall was born in a doubly-landlocked English county when the Royal Navy still issued a rum ration. He now lives by the sea. He is the author of the science fiction thriller *2084 – The Meschera Bandwidth* and over seventy published short stories, twenty-four of which are collected in the anthology *24 0s & a 2*. Both are available on Amazon. He has run four and walked one marathon and will be standing for parliament for the Green Party in 2024 for Totnes. He blogs at meschera.blogspot.com and can be contacted there.

Stewart C Baker is an academic librarian and author of speculative fiction, poetry, and interactive fiction. His fiction has appeared in *Nature, Lightspeed,* and *Galaxy's Edge,* among other places, and his poetry has appeared in *Fantasy, Asimov's,* and numerous haiku magazines. Stewart was born in England, has lived in South Carolina, Japan, and California, and now lives within the traditional homelands of the Luckiamute Band of Kalapuya in western Oregon, along with his family – although if anyone asks, he'll usually say he's from the Internet, where you can find him at https://infomancy.net

Brent Baldwin: Originally from the tree-swept hills of the Missouri Ozarks, Brent lives in London with his wife, two daughters, and pet menagerie. If you find him without his hands on a keyboard or his nose in a book, it will probably be in the kitchen. His work has previously been published by *Nature Magazine, Fireside Fiction,* and *Analog,* among others. You can find him online at www.dbbaldwin.com and on Twitter and Instagram at @dbrentbaldwin.

Keith Brooke is the author of either many or lots of books, depending on how you count solo, collaborative, ghost-written and pseudonymous work, and more than a hundred short stories; his work has been shortlisted for awards including the Philip K Dick Award and the Seiun Award. Writing teen fiction as Nick Gifford, he has been described by the *Sunday Express* as 'The king of children's horror'. His novel written with Eric Brown, *Wormhole*, was published by Angry Robot in late 2022. Find out more about Keith and his work at www.keithbrooke.co.uk

Eric Brown was born in West Yorkshire, and lived in Australia, India and Greece before settling in the Scottish Borders. He was writing for over thirty years, and won the British Science Fiction Award twice for his short stories, while his novel *Helix Wars* was shortlisted for the 2012 Philip K. Dick award. He published over seventy books, diverging from SF into crime novels with the Langham and Dupré series, set in the 1950s, the latest being *Murder Most Vile*. His latest SF novel, *Wormhole*, is a collaboration with Keith Brooke. Eric's website can be found at: ericbrown.co.uk. He passed away in March 2023.

Alice Dryden writes science fiction and fantasy stories with animals in. Many of these are published within the furry fandom under the name 'Huskyteer', but some escape into the wild. Her works include 'New Tricks' in *Pirating Pups* from Tyche Books and 'Case Study' in *C.A.T.S.: Cycling Across Time And Space* from Microcosm Publishing, and she edited *The Furry Megapack* for Wildside Press. She lives in Kent, where she enjoys the county's excellent cider and equally excellent motorcycling roads, though not both at the same time. She can be found at huskyteer.co.uk and on Twitter as @Huskyteer.

E.M. Faulds is an Australian who has made Scotland her home. She lives not far from Glasgow in the oldest house in town. She is a member of the Glasgow SF Writers' Circle and has had short stories published in *Strange Horizons* and *Shoreline of Infinity* magazines. "A Flight of Birds" was shortlisted for a British Fantasy Award for Best Short Story in 2022. Her novel *Ada King* and *Under the Moon: Collected Speculative Fiction* (Ghost Moth Press) are available now. Find out more at emfaulds.com

J.K. Fulton is the son of a lightkeeper, and spent his childhood growing up at lighthouses all around the coast of Scotland. His stories have appeared in *Exuberance, Shoreline of Infinity, Leicester Writes, Best of British Science Fiction 2018, Uncharted Constellations, Dark Scotland,* and *Severed Souls*. His Scottish historical novels for children are *The Wreck of the Argyll* and *The Beast on the Broch*.

Liam Hogan is an award-winning short story writer, with previous stories in Best of British Science Fiction and in Best of British Fantasy from NewCon Press. He's been published by *Analog, Daily Science Fiction,* and *Nature Futures*. He helps host live literary event Liars' League, volunteers at the creative writing charity Ministry of Stories, and lives and avoids work in London. More details at http://happyendingnotguaranteed.blogspot.co.uk

L.N. Hunter's comic fantasy novel, *The Feather and the Lamp* (Three Ravens Publishing), sits alongside works in anthologies such as *Soulmate Syndrome* and *Hidden Villains: Arise*, as well as Short Édition's *Short Circuit* and the *Horrifying Tales of Wonder* podcast. There have also been papers in the IEEE *Transactions on Neural Networks*, which are probably somewhat less relevant and definitely less fun. When not writing, L.N. unwinds in a disorganised home in rural Cambridgeshire, UK, along with two cats and a soulmate. Find out more at: https://linktr.ee/l.n.hunter or via: facebook.com/L.N.Hunter.writer.

Phillip Irving is a teacher and writer in Leicester, UK. He's influenced by a lifetime of Pratchett and Gaiman but writes like neither. He has had short fiction published by Flame Tree Press and Space Cat Press, among others. He's a member of Leicester Writers' Club and the Leicester Speculators writing group. When not writing or obsessing over grammar he can be found at home with partner and his cat, or in his local pub, which both she and the cat are also known to frequent.

Ida Keogh is a Surrey based science fiction and fantasy writer. In 2021 she won both the BSFA Award and British Fantasy Award for her short story "Infinite Tea in the Demara Café" from the *London Centric* anthology (NewCon Press). Her debut novella *Fish!* was published the same year and was longlisted for the BSFA Award. Her publications include work in *Writing the Future* (Kaleidoscope), *Shoreline of Infinity* magazine, the *British Medical Journal*, *Best of British Science Fiction 2020*, *Major Arcana* (Black Shuck Books), *Under the Radar* magazine and charity anthology *Fuel*. Find her on Twitter @silkyida

Tim Major is a writer and freelance editor from York. His books include *Hope Island*, *Snakeskins*, three Sherlock Holmes novels, short story collection *And the House Lights Dim* and a monograph about the 1915 silent crime film, *Les Vampires*. His upcoming novel *Jekyll & Hyde: Consulting Detectives* will be published in 2024. His short stories have appeared in numerous publications and have been selected for *Best of British Science Fiction*, *Best of British Fantasy* and *Best Horror of the Year*. Find out more at www.timjmajor.com

A. J. McIntosh is an Edinburgh-based author of short fiction, editor of mostly historical and political academic books, and freelance journalist. His poetry has appeared in *Cencrastus*, and his fiction has been published by Mercat Press, Tartarus Press and Wildside Press, among others. He is the contributing editor of the *Broughton Spurtle*. (www.broughtonspurtle.org.uk/backissues/spurtle)

Dafydd McKimm is a speculative short fiction writer whose stories have appeared in magazines and anthologies such as *Flash Fiction Online*, *Daily Science Fiction*, *Galaxy's Edge*, *Deep Magic*, *Kaleidotrope*, *Syntax & Salt*, *Gwyllion*, *MetaStellar*, *Orion's Belt*, *The Cafe Irreal*, *Podcastle*, *The Best of British Fantasy*, *The Best of British Science Fiction*, and elsewhere. He was born and raised in Wales but now lives in Taipei, Taiwan.

Fiona Moore is a three-time BSFA Award finalist, writer and academic whose work has appeared in *Clarkesworld, Asimov, Cossmass Infinities,* and five consecutive editions of *The Best of British SF.* Her most recent non-fiction is the book *Management Lessons from Game of Thrones.* Her publications include one novel; five cult TV guidebooks; three stage plays and four audio plays. She lives in Southwest England with a tortoiseshell cat which is bent on world domination. More details, and free content, can be found at http://www.fiona-moore.com, and she is @drfionamoore on all social media.

Val Nolan's stories have appeared in *Year's Best Science Fiction, Best of British Science Fiction, Interzone,* and the 'Futures' page of *Nature.* His novelette 'The Irish Astronaut' was shortlisted for the Theodore Sturgeon Award. He is the author of *Neil Jordan: Works for the Page* (UCC Press, 2022) and academic articles in *Science Fiction Studies, Foundation, Journal of Graphic Novels and Comic Books, Review of Contemporary Fiction, Irish University Review,* and *Irish Studies Review.* He is co-author, with Tiffani Angus, of the SFFH writing guide *Spec Fic for Newbies* (Luna Press 2023). He lectures on genre fiction at Aberystwyth University.

Stephen Oram writes near-future fiction. He is published in several anthologies and journals. He has two published novels and three collections of sci-fi shorts, most recently *Extracting Humanity and Other Stories* (2023).

He works with scientists and technologists on projects exploring possible future outcomes of their research and innovations through short stories and has co-edited three anthologies along these lines.

His work has been described with praise such as: "Should set the rest of us thinking about science and its possible repercussions," *The Financial Times*; and "A soothsayer for this century's relationship with technology," *Linux User & Developer Magazine.* www.stephenoram.net

Vaughan Stanger trained as an astronomer and subsequently managed various research projects in the aerospace and defence industry. Since 2012, he has written speculative fiction full-time. He has seen over fifty short stories published, in *Nature Futures, Interzone, Shoreline of Infinity, Sci Phi Journal,* and others. Many of his stories have been reprinted, including nine in foreign translation, while several have been recorded for podcasts. His most recent collection is *The Last Moonshot & Other Stories.* Vaughan lives in Essex with a mad cat and his wife Jane, who keeps him sane (by writer standards). Follow his activities at www.vaughanstanger.com.

Matt Thompson is an experimental musician and writer of strange fictions, who, having spent upwards of half a century residing in his native London, has recently upped sticks to the somewhat more bucolic surroundings of Minnesota. Rest assured, however, that his literary concerns remain closely linked to the land of his birth – not least among them alienation, emotional impotence and transport delays. His work has been published at varied and numerous venues including *Interzone, Black Static, Nature: Futures, PseudoPod, ParSec, Third Flatiron* and *Asimov's.* You can find him online at http://matt-thompson.com.

Lavie Tidhar is author of *Osama, The Violent Century, A Man Lies Dreaming, Central Station, Unholy Land, By Force Alone, The Hood, The Escapement, Neom,* and *Maror.* His latest novels are *Adama* and *The Circumference of the World.* His awards include the World Fantasy and British Fantasy Awards, the John W. Campbell Award, the Neukom Prize and the Jerwood Prize, and he has been shortlisted for the Clarke Award and the Philip K. Dick Award.

Ian Whates is the author of eight published novels, two novellas, and some eighty short stories that have appeared in a variety of venues. In 2019 he received the Karl Edward Wagner Award from the British Fantasy Society, while his work has been shortlisted for the Philip K. Dick Award and on three occasions for BSFA Awards. A director and former chair of the BSFA, he has been a judge for both the Arthur C. Clarke Award and the World Fantasy Awards. He has edited more than 40 anthologies and edits *ParSec* magazine for PS Publishing. In 2006 Ian founded multiple award-winning independent publisher NewCon Press by accident.

David Whitmarsh is a rehabilitated former software engineer who now spends his time playing guitar badly and writing science fiction. His short stories have been published in *Mythaxis*, *Metaphorosis*, *All Worlds Wayfarer* and *The Colored Lens*. His as yet unpublished novel *The Measurement Problem* was the winner of the Science Museum Hodderscape SF Debuts Prize.

David lives in Sussex with his wife, two cats, and a varying subset of his four adult children.

Neil Williamson has been a finalist for the British Science Fiction Association, British Fantasy and World Fantasy Awards. He has published two fantasy novels, two collections and over seventy short stories, including an occasional sequence exploring the effects of increased surveillance, social connectivity and personal isolation in the near future, which began with *The Memoirist* (2017) and continues with "A Moment Of Zugzwang". Neil lives in Glasgow, Scotland.

Andrew J. Wilson is a freelance writer and editor who lives in Edinburgh. His short stories, non-fiction and poems have appeared all over the world, sometimes in the most unlikely places. Andrew's work has appeared in DAW Book's *Year's Best Horror Stories*, *Gathering the Bones*, *Professor Challenger: New Worlds*, *Lost Places*, *Weird Tales*, *Shoreline of Infinity*, *Dystopia Utopia Short Stories* and *Biopolis: Tales of Urban Biology*. With Neil Williamson, he co-edited *Nova Scotia: New Scottish Speculative Fiction*, which was nominated for a World Fantasy Award. Andrew has been put forward twice for the Science Fiction Poetry Association's Dwarf Stars Award.

Acknowledgements

My profound thanks must go once again to my good friend Ian Whates for allowing me to edit yet another volume in this series. Can you believe this is book seven now? Thanks also to my beta-reader Tom Jordan, assisting me with the submissions as he has done for every book. Thanks also to Mike Cobley for passing me recommendations, and to all the writers who sent in their stories to me.

For this book, my husband has really upped his game and has now started bringing me 100% dark hot chocolate from Hotel Chocolat to keep me going while I work. I'm not sure this level of support can be surpassed.

~*~

Donna Scott is a writer, editor, award-winning stand-up comedian and poet, podcaster and a failed dancer, despite achieving Gold Bar 4 in Disco when she was ten. Originally from the Black Country, she now lives in Northampton. She is a Director and former Chair of the British Science Fiction Association. As well as editing this anthology series she is formerly the co-editor of *Visionary Tongue* magazine, and has worked as a freelance editor for the likes of Gollancz, Rebellion, Games Workshop, Angry Robot, Immanion and other publishers, groups and individuals. Her writing has appeared in publications by Immanion, NewCon, Norilana, Synth and PS Publishing. Please check out www.donna-scott.co.uk to see the latest on her projects and appearances.

BEST OF BRITISH SCIENCE FICTION

 2016: stories by **Peter F. Hamilton, Gwyneth Jones, Adam Roberts, Tade Thompson, Ian Watson, Tricia Sullivan, Keith Brooke & Eric Brown, Jaine Fenn, Natalia Theodoridou, E.J. Swift, Una McCormack, Ian Whates, Den Patrick, Neil Williamson,** and more…

 2017: stories by **Ken MacLeod, Lavie Tidhar, Jeff Noon, Adam Roberts, Anne Charnock, Natalia Theodoridou, Eric Brown, Jaine Fenn, E.J. Swift, Laura Mauro, Aliya Whiteley, Tim Major, Liam Hogan, Ian Creasey, Robert Bagnall,** and more…

 2018: stories by **Alastair Reynolds, Lavie Tidhar, Dave Hutchinson, G.V. Anderson, Colin Greenland, Aliya Whiteley, Natalia Theodoridou, Matthew de Abaitua, Tim Major, Fiona Moore, David Tallerman, Henry Szabranski, Finbarr O'Reilly,** and more…

 2019: stories by **Ken MacLeod, Chris Beckett, Lavie Tidhar, G.V. Anderson, Tim Major, Fiona Moore, Una McCormack, David Tallerman, Val Nolan, Rhiannon Grist, Andrew Wallace, Henry Szabranski, Leo X. Robertson, Kate Macdonald,** and more…

 2020: stories by **M.R. Carey, Liz Williams, Lavie Tidhar, Ida Keogh, Ian Watson, Una McCormack, Eric Brown, Anne Charnock, Ian Whates, Teika Marija Smits, Stewart Hotston, RB Kelly, Neil Williamson, David Gullen, Fiona Moore, Stephen Oram,** and more…

 2021: stories by **Paul Cornell, Liz Williams, Aliya Whiteley, Keith Brooke & Eric Brown, Nick Wood, Fiona Moore, Martin Sketchley, Tim Major, Gary Couzens, David Gullen, Teika Marija Smits, Peter Sutton, David Cleden,** and more…

www.newconpress.co.uk

Milton Keynes UK
Ingram Content Group UK Ltd.
UKHW010004020324
438623UK00004B/284